I0646915

Sudhindra Nath Ghose (1899–1965)—best known as Sudhin Ghose—was born in Bardhaman in Bengal. He moved to Europe as a student in the 1920s where he first studied science and art history before completing a doctorate in literature. Though he spent his entire writing career in the West, Sudhin Ghose, like his contemporaries Mulk Raj Anand, R. K. Narayan and Raja Rao, based his work on India, drawing material from the villages and towns of Bengal. An impeccable prose stylist and a master of sprawling narratives which draw inspiration from myths, fables, legends and epics, Sudhin Ghose is among the greatest writers in Indian English literature.

Sudhin Ghose wrote journalistic pieces, a scholarly tract, and three volumes of Indian folktales apart from the work for which he is best remembered: a quartet of novels comprising *And Gazelles Leaping* (1949), *Cradle of the Clouds* (1951), *The Vermilion Boat* (1953) and *The Flame of the Forest* (1955).

CRADLE

OF THE

CLOUDS

SUDHIN N. GHOSE

SPEAKING
TIGER

SPEAKING TIGER PUBLISHING PVT. LTD
4381/4 Ansari Road, Daryaganj,
New Delhi–110002, India

Copyright © Sudhin N. Ghose 1949
First published by Michael Joseph London 1949
This edition copyright © Speaking Tiger 2017

ISBN: 978-93-86338-28-0
eISBN: 978-93-86338-27-3

10 9 8 7 6 5 4 3 2 1

The moral right of the author has been asserted.

Typeset in Adobe Jenson Pro by Jojy Philip
Printed at Thomson Press India Ltd.

PART ONE

The Red Valley

'There is little virtue in arrogance, my son.' The Punditji admonished me for my shyness as he dragged me along with him to meet the people gathered under the *peepul* tree. They were there, in the village square, to give me a warm send off, and I had no business to feel shy! An excess of modesty, according to him, was a form of arrogance. At the same time, a moderate measure of aloofness, he counselled, was necessary for preserving one's own individuality. And, above all, whatever happened, I was advised not to ignore the writings of the haughty: they were more instructive than the works of the self-effacing.

'Take Makolee Sahib for example,' the Punditji said as he took his seat in the midst of the group clustered in the shade of the two-centuries-old *peepul*. The men squatted cross-legged on the stone dais round the base of the tree. The women formed a knot on their own; they sat apart, nestling together. 'Take him as an example,' the Punditji repeated and the men nodded as though Makolee Sahib was their common acquaintance. 'Who could be more arrogant? Makolee Sahib was stiff-necked, close-fisted, and argumentative….' The catalogue of this Sahib's failings was impressive: it included his refusal to have any progeny and to learn the Sanskrit language though he did not mind mastering Greek, Latin, French, German, Italian, and various other tongues. Nevertheless, his writings deserved a close scrutiny by every Bengali living in Calcutta. 'Makolee Sahib wrote some home-truths about them: a feat no Sahib would dare to attempt in these days. They lack his courage and bluntness. They have become complacent.'

Kathak the professional story-teller and the scribe of the village took up the cue. His twice-told tales were stale. Nevertheless his rural listeners loved them: they were never tired of hearing the same story recounted twenty times. A few anecdotes of Makolee Sahib's bumptiousness were repeated amidst general applause. The listeners were delighted to learn that this strange and uncommonly gifted genius once met his match: a classmate who specialized in the science of numbers.

Once Makolee Sahib took this expert in mathematics with him to a playhouse, and the *Jung-i-Lat* Wellesley Sahib, better known as Wellington, happened to be entering the place at the same moment by another door. The aged veteran was recognized, and the house testified their respect by a loud ovation. At this Makolee Sahib's friend bowed low and murmured, 'Well, well, Makolee! This is more than I expected. I rarely visit a playhouse. How is it possible that these good people should already have discovered that I am here?'

'Makolee Sahib was so hurt,' Kathak concluded, 'that after that he never put his foot inside that theatre, nor spoke to his friend.'

I wished that the spirit of long-dead Macaulay or of the Senior Wrangler who was his friend would give me the necessary courage to face my admirers in the village square. The farewell party was for my benefit: I was expected to profit from the words of wisdom of the assembly for guidance during my forthcoming sojourn in Calcutta.

How I loathed such gatherings! Being young, I was constrained to listen in silence to the interminable colloquies of the grown-ups. Everyone talked on every possible subject and Kathak interjected from time to time his well-worn yarns.

Through the corner of my eyes I saw Neela, the Santal school-mistress, talking to my aunt Mashi-ma.

'I told him more than once,' Mashi-ma was explaining to Neela and other women, 'it is no good hiding in a corner. You can't keep people waiting. They have invited the *Bhat* from Kusum-pur. He has composed an ode in honour of my nephew....'

The way she talked made it clear that Mashi-ma was proud of me. But her eyes were red and swollen: the result of her weeping off and on for the last few days. At first she was elated: she kissed me when she heard of my success in the competitive examination and that my scholarship entitled me to finish my teachers' training course in Calcutta. But, later on, as the day of my departure approached, she broke down. 'Who asked you to win the first place?' I was reproached for my excessive zeal! 'Others too have won the *jal-pani*, the scholarship for continuing their studies. But they have not been asked to go to Calcutta. Why must it be *you* who should leave the village and the Red Valley to finish your course? Once you go to Calcutta you will stay there! And I shan't live to see your return....'

I felt thoroughly ashamed of myself. Yet what could I do? It was beyond me to foresee the result of the examination. Only a few weeks ago the greyheads of the village were expressing their grave doubts about my passing the examination at all, let alone the possibility of my winning a scholarship. 'The *jal-panis* are so few and the candidates are so many,' they said among themselves and referred to many great scholars of yore who had failed to attract the attention of the education authorities. 'Moreover,' they reached the sad conclusion, 'our youngsters are becoming duller every day. Mashi-ma's nephew is a real devil. He is mad over horses.'

'He is a *kumli*,' Kathak the story-teller confided to Ramdas the village watchman as I passed him by the other day. 'That's what he is. How can a *kumli* ever pass an examination?' The *kumli* happens to be an obnoxious caterpillar which raises painful weals on human skin and consequently a sufficiently repulsive epithet for a troublesome boy! However, I ignored Kathak's commentary.

Now every one of the villagers felt proud of my achievement. The Calcutta Radio announced the full list of successful candidates and though no one owned a radio-set in the village this news reached them like a flash of lightning, within a few minutes after it had been broadcast! The *Kusum-pur Sangbad*, weekly which came out only three times in the month printed my name and address in bold letters under the caption: *Penhari Parganas*, the districts of the Red Valley and the Blue Hills. This was the only paper which covered the events of our area, and it was not surprising that it should devote a few lines to the news of the competitive examination; local news-items were so rare just then. The villagers, however, interpreted the insertion in a different light. It was a major event, a triumphal achievement. They vied with each other to inundate me with complimentary copies of this issue of the *Kusum-pur Sangbad*. I was destined, so they reasoned, to be the occupant of an exalted post.

'What sort of a post, exactly?' 'A *daroga*,' declared Ramdas the watchman; he was more or less convinced that I was foreordained to become a police officer. According to Kathak the story-teller my sharp intelligence would lead me to the dais of a *munshijf*, a subordinate judiciary. 'All doors are open to you now,' the village elders assured me.'It's the first step that counts.' Evidently I had cleared this hurdle of paramount importance well: in due course, therefore, the world would resound with my praise. Our village in the Red Valley—the cynosure of envying eyes and the jewel of the Penhari Parganas—was destined to acquire greater celebrity on account of my future activities!

They wanted to know if I aspired to a government post. Or was I thinking of following the steps of the illustrious Punditji and his more illustrious master, Jagannath Tarka-Panchanan?

'Ah! To be like Jagannath Tarka-Panchanan!' murmured the *Bhat* who came from Kusum-pur. He was a professional reciter

of verses and claimed to be a poet as well. He was our Kathak
the story-teller's great rival. No marriage took place in the Red
Valley at which he was not present to recite poetry in honour
of the newly-wedded couples. His fees varied according to the
affluence of the parties he honoured with this presence. 'To be
like Jagannath Tarka-Panchanan,' he shook his head meditatively.
'That would be something. He lived all his days as a poor man,
subsisting on mere handfuls of rice. But what a great teacher he
was! Who knew the Law better than he? He lived for exactly two
hundred years: not a day more and not a day less. Our Punditji
ought to tell you more about him. It was on him Jagannath
Tarka-Panchanan bestowed his brass-bound blackthorn staff
named Mahendra Chandal. Tarka-Panchanan was a wise man
while Makolee Sahib was just a learned man....'

Someone cleared his throat. That was a polite hint for the
Bhat to bring his vocal reflection to an end. There were a lot
of people and every one of them was anxious to make some
comments on how people lived in Calcutta and what were the
more treacherous pit-falls in that city. A stranger sitting next to
the *chowkidar* Ramdas, the village watchman, wanted to know if
I contemplated settling down in Calcutta. He referred to me as
the young scholar.

'Does the young scholar know Calcutta at all?' he asked.

II

'If you want to prosper in Calcutta,' the stranger began without
bothering to find out whether I had ever lived there or not, 'you
must be subtle. And you must settle there before you are twenty.
Otherwise it would mean misery.'

'Or late success and bitter remorse,' added the man with
a *veena*, the stringed instrument resembling a guitar. He came
from Asansole. I knew he was fond of regaling anyone who cared
to listen with his instrumental music. He was quite good with

his *veena*. But his performances generally lasted too long and that was why he was not popular with some of the village boys who preferred the flute. They nicknamed him the *man with the drooping moustache*. 'Late success,' he groaned, 'that's the same as misery. So too is an early success.'

'One must start young,' interrupted one of the village elders of the Council of Five. I did not dare look up because I had had a row with him some time ago and called him the Goatee to his face! He wore a short, trimmed beard, and so he came to be called the Goatee by a number of our boys: Pocha the Huntsman, Bumboatee the Pirate, Sashe Raha, nicknamed the Split Cucumber, and others. He hated this appellation and it was not nice of me to enrage him. But then, he called the Santals of the Blue Hills *just savages*, and they were my friends. He also told Mashi-ma that I was a good-for-nothing because I often did hill-climbing with Para-manik the headman of the Santal village of Madhu-ban. 'It is like getting married,' he philosophized. 'One should marry young or never marry at all.'

I noticed the flicker of a smile light up the usually morose expression of the *veena*-player. He gave a nudge to his neighbour.

'That's true enough,' said the man commonly known as the *Calcuttan*. He had spent long years in the country's premier city and had a second wife much younger than himself: she was born in Calcutta and somehow did not like our village at all.

The epithet *Calcuttan* was not considered quite complimentary in our Penhari Parganas. A slight twist in pronunciation readily changed *Calcuttan* to Black Dog. And who cared for such a nickname? The Black Dog was for us a sinister omen, the messenger of the God of Death: God Yama the Green-visaged and Red-robed.

I knew all that could be said about the God of Death's Black Dog.

Its other name is Sarameya and it is known as one of the *vehicles* of the God Yama, the Judicator of the Dead. Yama the

God of Death has many names, one of which is the Restrainer, and this is the one the villagers generally use.

Sarameya is the favourite courier of Yama the Restrainer. This insatiable and monstrous hound has wide nostrils and four eyes and is as black as night. The God lets it loose among mortals to harry the languid and the spiritless and so fasten them to the abode of the dead. He has instructed it: 'Answer a fool according to his folly, and show him the pit that he shall fall into, if he take not heed.' But a dog with four eyes can be easily recognized and carefully shunned! Therefore, it has been accorded the gift of taking any shape at will. The Black Dog makes the most of this faculty: at times it accosts its victim in the guise of an abandoned child, at times as a lovely woman anxious to console a man, or as a pious fakir desirous of helping the downtrodden.

Yama's Black Dog tempts the fool to seek power by fair means or foul. Woe to him who listens to its counsel of evil. Once caught in the fangs of this deadly monster a man would rarely succeed in extricating himself: he would perish from ever-increasing, unquenchable thirst. He would continuously crave for more power, more wealth, and more renown. Nothing would give him satisfaction or satiety: his over-reaching ambition and his never-to-be-satisfied desires would destroy him and his associates.

Yama the Restrainer has no pity for a man who worships the Bitch-Goddess known as Easy Success.

'Every poison has, however, its counter-poison,' the villagers say. 'Every disease has its cure.' There are, of course, remedies against the bite of the Black Dog. A man on the point of dying from the venom of a female serpent can be saved if he is inoculated with the poison of a male snake. If bitten by a male, a female of the species would be necessary for procuring the healing counter-bite. The main difficulty, therefore, in treating a case of snake-poisoning lies in the timely identification of the sex of the noxious aggressor. And this is not easy.

Similar is the trouble with the Black Dog's bite. The victim will recover only if he tries the antidote promptly. The time factor is of paramount importance. The medicine is extremely simple: the Black Dog's prey must practise restraint. He should teach himself to renounce, at least temporarily, his heart's desire. In other words, he must, unasked, exercise self-discipline. Otherwise even the most potent *mantra* would not save him from destruction and dissolution.

~

'What exactly is a *mantra?*' someone asked: not precisely I thought, for any definite information, but to give a different trend to the general discussion.

'At Kalighat', the *Calcuttan* propounded, 'the *mantras* are said to be Sanskrit proverbs. At College Square the students think that the *mantras* are just slogans: they are generally translations from Feringhee languages. Quite a few young men in Calcutta wear button-holes and badges with foreign *mantras*. They say these will help them to solve all their difficulties. I have seen a number of them wearing the symbol of the red star....'

The *Calcuttan* was interrupted by a violent fit of coughing. It came from a man sitting behind the *veena*-player. Several voices murmured protest. It was an over-simplification according to the majority. Most of them wanted to know what the Punditji thought about it.

'If we are to believe the ancient sages,' the Punditji explained, 'the *mantras* are the formulas or the vibration sounded by the Creator as the earth was lifted out of the primal ocean. Their true significance came to be discovered by the great *rishis*, wise men, through long years of meditation and *yogic* exercises.

'The deities and the demons have ever since tried to keep these *mantras* back from mortals. For the mastery over the mysterious utterances of the Creator would make men immortal like the deities and indomitable like the demons. Thanks, however, to the prayers, sacrifices, and supplication of the *sadhus*, the hermits and saints, the super-human agencies have not been entirely successful in carrying out their wish. At least some of the *mantras* have not been irretrievably lost. The *rishis*, our spiritual masters, who are steeped in traditional wisdom and learning, are the repositories of the ancient sacred formulas.'

~

'What are these *mantras* good for?' I wondered. However, I did not dare to formulate my question. The village tradition demanded that in a gathering of grown-ups a youth should not speak unless spoken to. Nevertheless, my mind often played a strange trick, when the elders were immersed in what was supposed to be profoundly philosophical discussions, I would formulate in silence frivolous questions of my own. I knew it was not prudent to do so in the presence of the Punditji: somehow he gave one the uncanny feeling of reading other people's thoughts. How did he manage to answer my unspoken questions? Did my looks invariably betray my thoughts?

'The *mantras* are repeated in the performance of every religious rite,' the Punditji continued as he gave a reproachful glance in my direction and fondled his brass-bound blackthorn staff. 'What are they good for? They are good for many purposes. Above all, they strengthen your faith. They belong to various categories—invocatory, evocatory, deprecatory, conservatory... They are beneficent or baneful, propitious or pernicious. Through their medium great and varied objectives may be attained. For example, some formulas are for casting out evil spirits, some for inspiring love or hatred, some for curing diseases or causing them, some for procuring sudden death or averting it. Some are of a contrary nature to others, and counteract their effect: the stronger overcoming the influence of the weaker. Some are potent enough to occasion the destruction of a whole country; while there are others which gods themselves are constrained to obey.

Janardan, who was very good at repairing watches and clocks gave a start when he heard that in order to be efficacious a *mantra* must be correctly pronounced and its duplication fully grasped.

'Ah! There's the rub.' Janardan rubbed his chin and stared at me as though my thoughts disturbed him. 'The Black Dog's bite changes his voice as well as his way of living. He becomes incapable of uttering a single *mantra* properly. A victim of Sarameya, Yama's messenger, loses even the capacity of praying for his own soul. In Calcutta everyone has a drawl....'

What conclusion was I to draw from this detailed information about Yama's Black Dog and the *mantras*? Were the remarks meant for me? Or destined for anyone who desired to profit from them? If so, I must confess I derived less benefit than anyone had anticipated from what was said at the gathering. 'It is a curious way of congratulating me,' I said to myself.

III

This technique of offering their advice in an indirect way was a speciality among the villagers. 'It is called the elliptical fashion,' someone told me. Whatever it may be, it is confusing. The fault is perhaps mine: probably I am more dull-witted than other village boys. It might also have been due to the fact that my early years had been spent on Rani Nilmani's Estate near Calcutta: there the grown-ups offered the children their counsel in a different way. Anyway, I found the elliptical explanations difficult to follow.

Take Janardan for example. He was known as the Instrument-Maker in the village. But in Asansole he was more renowned for his gift of repairing watches, clocks and precision-instruments. Whenever a delicate piece of machinery had to be set right

Janardan was called for. He was said to be very good: an expert, capable of dealing with any clock-work, from a tiny watch no bigger than an eight-anna-piece to gigantic mechanical mill-stones in flour factories. He was constantly summoned here, there, and everywhere. In fact, most of his time was spent at Asansole and Rani-gunj.

Shortly after my arrival at the village it occurred to me that I might perhaps learn something of watchmaking from him. So I spent many long hours during the Puja vacation at his workshop at Asansole trying to follow how he worked. One day I felt bold enough to ask him if he would care to help me fix my watch.

'Where's the watch?' Janardan stretched out his left hand: that was a bad sign. 'Let me see it.'

I proudly handed over to him the gift I had received from Rani Vabani just before I left Calcutta for the village. It was round like a small cricket ball: lovely to look at, but not much good at keeping time. It worked erratically like a crazy mule and kept time indifferently, moving either too fast or too slow, and then stopping altogether for a couple of days and starting again on its own without any cajoling on my part.

Janardan examined my watch with an air of indifference and even of contempt. He did not utter a single word in its praise. I wondered if he noticed that the case was beautifully enamelled and that the dial showed that it was made long ago.

'You want to get it going?' he asked as he adjusted the curious blinker with which he often covered his right eye. He did not even notice how eagerly I nodded my head. He just sat down at his table turning his back to me. 'Do you see that hammer over there?' he finally muttered. 'Take the watch out of its case and smash it with the hammer.'

I was simply amazed and stared vacantly not knowing what to do.

'Smash it first, I tell you. We shall then see what can be done about that toy of yours. Where did you pick it up?'

I had not the heart to tell him what I felt about his advice. Only years later I gathered from Kumar the Potter that Janardan usually gave his first lesson to his would-be apprentices in that way: he wanted to drive diffidence out of my head and put some pride into it. That was what Kumar told me. A strange reason for advising me to smash up an eighteenth-century watch of great beauty. It did not make much sense. Nevertheless, Kumar's explanation helped me to understand that there was some method in Janardan's madness: it was well intentioned.

The same could be said about Tchutore the Carpenter.

When I told him that I wanted to be of some service to him, he simply groaned and asked me if I did not mind losing my caste! I shook my head and he stared at me incredulously for full two minutes. Then he told me to sweep the floor clean and collect the saw-shavings.

What about making me do something more interesting? Wouldn't he teach me how to make things?

The village carpenter lost his patience. 'Look here, Little Son! Do you know the difference between a hawk and a hand-saw?'

I shuffled my feet in embarrassment and mumbled something. The question was so unexpected.

'Son!' he spoke very firmly. 'Unless you are born a carpenter, you will never become one. Neither will you ever know the difference between a hawk and a hand-saw.'

I was very much upset. It was, however, a relief to hear from Tchutore that there were other things to learn than carpentry.

~

What these *other* things were neither Tchutore nor anybody else cared to explain to me.

In the village every boy followed his father's profession or calling. The misfits alone drifted to the coal-mines or to Calcutta. Whoever left the Penhari Parganas was regarded as permanently lost unless he happened to get into a government post or into the teaching profession.

Being an orphan I was badly handicapped. My aunt Mashi-ma knew too little of the outside world to give me any practical guidance as to the selection of a suitable career. She had vague notions about greatness being thrust upon all obedient and studious boys; they were the protégés of Saraswati, the benevolent Goddess of Wisdom and Learning.

I did not do too badly in my school examinations. Therefore, all that was necessary for my career in life was to pass the Matriculation and other examinations equally well. The rest would look after itself. A good degree at the University in no matter what faculty was a sure passport to success in life. The good Goddess Saraswati never let any of her protégés down!

'The sooner you finish your studies the better,' Mashi-ma counselled me. 'You are now in your teens. You may hope that a few more years of real, sound study will help you to be appointed a Judge in the High Court.' She laid particular emphasis on the word *sound*. 'You are sure to succeed if you work hard and your studies are *sound*.'

~

Whether of the Valley or of the Hills, the inhabitants of the Penhari Parganas thought very much alike. They reasoned in the same way as Mashi-ma: a boy capable of winning a scholarship and heading the list of successful candidates was bound to be pounced upon by the great! The world's eminent personalities were, they declared, on the look-out for worthy successors. And who could be more worthy than a young scholar whose name appeared in the pages of the *Kusum-pur Sangbad?* Did not Jagannath Tarka-Panchanan prolong his mortal existence to two hundred years for the sole purpose of handing over his charge and his staff to a deserving pupil—no other than our Punditji? 'Poor Tarka-Panchanan!' the villagers discussed among themselves. 'He wanted to die like Sankara in his thirties. But how could he leave this earth without bestowing his blackthorn staff, Mahendra Chandal, upon a really meritorious successor?'

'What was true of Tarka-Panchanan,' Kathak propounded, 'is true of every wise man.' Tchutore the Carpenter, Janardan the Instrument-Maker, Ramdas, and others nodded their assent: they knew that was the case all over the world! They congratulated the Story-teller for calling me a caterpillar, a *kumli*: it was an appropriate designation for a cherished child from whom it was desired to ward off the influence of the Evil Eye. Janardan confessed that he was called *Ox-dung* when he was a boy and that it did him a lot of good, while Ramdas shook his head: he had his doubts. Our *chowkidar*, the watchman, wanted to know what made wise men look for studious disciples.

'Who knows?' interrupted Tchutore.

'Who inspires the bee'—Kathak spoke like one inspired—'to search for honey from orchids growing in the innermost recesses of the most inaccessible jungles? Who teaches the mighty hawk floating among the clouds to swoop down upon its tiny prey crouching in the crevices of the earth? Who guides the delicate swan's flight across snow-capped mountains to its final resting place at the Manasa lake? The same unerring instinct urges the great to seek out talented youths.'

A young scholar, they concluded, is potentially a wise man! My angularities would disappear as I grew up. Moreover, it is good for a boy to behave like a boy. As I was deemed by the villagers to be highly gifted, all that was necessary for me to do was to wait for the arrival of the heralds of the mighty at Mashi-ma's door-step. My future was well nigh assured. I had no need to worry.

No villager was ashamed of his hereditary calling. Even the lowliest of the lowly would have been greatly humiliated had his sons abandoned the parental occupation to take to some other calling. Nevertheless, all of them had a vague but almost limitless admiration for the so-called scholar. The learned were the salt of the earth. The rest were mere hewers of wood and drawers of water; just craftsmen and labourers.

It was my good fortune, they reasoned, to be an orphan: I was not tied to any hereditary occupation. Providence destined me for the unfettered pursuit of knowledge. I was eventually going to be a wise man. What need had I of advice or guidance from any of them? Were they not the unlettered? Were they not, therefore, objects of a scholar's compassion and pity?

IV

Even the principal of the Hathkura Intermediate College was not very helpful with his precepts. If the unlettered villagers thought in their own fashion that I was destined to soar to the highest heavens, he more or less assumed that I was to float all my life with my head just under water. Certainly he was not a pessimist by nature. His constant encouragement during the time I was at his college meant much to me. It was at his suggestion that I did some voluntary teaching among the Santal children at Amritaban.

'Respect the gods of the copy-books,' he advised me when I called on him to bid good-bye. 'That's the best you and I can do. You won't find any better in these days.'

He shoved me rather unceremoniously into a three-legged arm-chair, the only seat in his library. He had the habit of doing his reading on his feet. He did his writing too in the same way. There was a special desk in the room for this purpose. Not exactly a desk but a book-shelf with a sloping top, decorated with a pen-rack holding his collection of home-made fountain pens. Tradition demanded that I should remain standing while he was on his feet. But as it was a parting visit he wanted to treat me as his honoured guest. He did not like the idea of my going to Calcutta: it was a dangerous place: it put ideas into innocent heads.

'They talk a lot of nonsense over there. And plenty of cant. Take everything you hear with a grain of salt. Keep your eyes and ears open, but your mouth shut.' He put his right forefinger cross-wise over his lips to emphasize this last point while with the fingers of his left hand he gave a tug at my unruly long curls: that was his way of showing extreme cordiality.

He then spoke at length on his favourite subject: the top-heavy system of our university education. Most of the university graduates were, according to him, worse than the unlettered: they learnt how to repeat a set of formulas by rote and aspired to be politicians. Whereas the country needed men capable of clear thinking and above all, men of character.

'I want men of character,' he repeated. 'That's the main function of education as I understand it. But where am I to get them from? You wrote to me about your ambition to become a social welfare worker. Welfare worker? My brother-in-law!' He threw up his arms in the air: his gesture of supreme despair.

'This is no time for conundrums!' he continued. 'Reform? Can we afford that luxury? Do you want to change Hinduism? Can Hinduism tolerate such sabotage? You won't cure the country's evils by social welfare work. Nor by religious reform. Build, rather, the men of to-morrow: men of character. Social reform will then look after itself. Don't be misled by shibboleths.'

He wished me success and hoped to see me back soon as a diploma holder for elementary teaching! 'Get rid of your long locks. In Calcutta cranks and communists wear their hair long. Keep out of the clutches of the revolutionaries. They bode no good for the country.'

V

'Perhaps,' I thought, 'he has seen me with Gopaldas. That was why he advised me to keep out of political controversies.' Gopaldas was the nephew of our *chowkidar* Ramdas and was considered a dangerous character. But when I came across him for the first time I noticed nothing diabolical about him. That happened ages ago: shortly after my return to the village from Rani Nilmani's Estate. Even now I recall the thrill it gave me to be greeted by the nephew of the village watchman.

'Ever been to the coalfields?' Gopaldas accosted me with a friendly smile. 'Ever been right down into the heart of the earth?'

It was nice of him not to greet me as Curly-Head or Bobtailed-Buck: those were the epithets the villagers used for me. No youngster was ever addressed by his real name. Whether a boy liked it or not a nick-name was foisted upon him by the grownups. Some of the names sounded definitely rude, for example, The Grinning Donkey, Dirty Hoggy, Filthy Porcupine. And some were distinctly bawdy. A *kumli*, a caterpillar, was nothing compared with these. I hated all the nick-names they gave me, and it was a relief that Gopaldas did not use any of them.

'You know Ramdas,' he went on, 'the *chowkidar*. I am his nephew. My uncle is the watchman of the village.'

It was not necessary, I found, to give him any details about myself. He knew more about me than I did! 'Home is where you know everybody,' they say, 'and everybody knows you.' Judged by this adage, Gopaldas was more at home in his parental birthplace than all the rest of the inhabitants put together, though he was rarely to be seen in the village, being one of those misfits who strayed out of bounds of the Penhari Parganas. He was supposed to have some sort of work somewhere in Calcutta; but no one knew for certain the precise nature of his activities. He did, however, revisit his village at irregular intervals and some of the villagers thought that his office work demanded his presence more often in the coalfields than in his headquarters at Calcutta. He was frequently seen in such places as Jharia, Rani-gunj, Asansole and Hira-pur. It was natural for him, I thought, to want me to share his interest in the mines.

I was glad to accept his invitation, especially as I was feeling lonely at that time.

~

I have often tried to assess for myself what has been the greatest trial of my boyhood days. It is not easy to find a clear answer. But the more I think it over the more I feel that it is neither heat nor hunger nor cold and penury, but the feeling of complete isolation and loneliness. To be companionless, to be left all alone with no one to play with, to be forced to rely entirely on one's own resources for recreation is, I believe, a harrowing experience for a young boy, probably the most harrowing of all his trials. Judging from my own experience I should say a solitary child must be an unfortunate being. Unless he gets playmates no amount of solicitous care on the part of those bringing him up will make him bright and happy.

I can only speak for myself: I know the glory of the rainbow was far more gorgeous when I admired it with some companion. The songsters sang more melodiously when I heard them in the company of friends. The fatigue of an exhausting journey was lessened when there was a fellow wayfarer. And the hazards of a dangerous venture disappeared if there were others interested in its successful issue. My heart yearned for companionship. I longed to share my joys and sorrows, my hopes and fears with others, preferably with someone of my own age. This sharing did not necessarily demand an exchange of words: it could be a silent communion of thoughts. It needed, nevertheless, the presence of at least a comrade or an associate. And there were none to be had for me at that time.

The older boys of the village, those of my age, did not go to the same High School as I did. Their school-going days were, in fact, over: they worked with their elders in the fields, work-shops, coal-mines, and stone quarries. Most parents considered school-going for their children a luxury and a waste of time. Of course, they did not mind sending their children to the *local path-sala* to learn how to read and write. Some thought that the attendance of the youngsters at the Middle School, some three miles away, was justifiable, as it kept them out of mischief till their thirteenth year. But the idea of encouraging the older ones to go to the High School was deemed preposterous. Moreover, this High School was so far away: the journey involved many hours of trudging on foot, necessitating departure from home at dawn and return at dusk.

'What's the use of making our boys spend most of their time in walking to and fro?' the parents asked one another. Sending a boy to High School means money. Hard cash in fees, books, writing materials, subscriptions, and what not. Is there any advantage in forcing a youngster to learn a lot of strange jargons and abracadabras?'

The grown-ups were in a way afraid of the High School. In some mysterious manner it was held responsible for a number of village tragedies. 'Take Ramoni,' they whispered. 'What has become of her? She went to High School. And now she dances on the stage like a performing monkey. She has become too refined to work with her hands.' 'And what about Devidas? He went to High School, too. Now he is ashamed of his unlettered parents.' A few more names were mentioned as the elders shook their heads. The latest casualty in this field was Gopaldas: he had sought higher schooling and then university education, and finally gone to the dogs. How he lived no one knew: some thought he worked as a *kerani*, a clerk in a Calcutta concern, while others suspected him of working with some shady organization that was interested in procuring boys and girls for indentured labour abroad!

It was generally agreed that the High School was all right for those who won scholarships or wanted to be 'smart'; but not for those who were destined to follow the steps of their fathers, in the traditional crafts of their forebears.

~

Politicians rarely bothered to visit our village: it was off their beaten track and had so few voters. It was hardly worth their while to make a detour, except when they wanted to make collections for their party funds. Even then they never lingered long. The villagers were too poor to pay cash. Our life was regulated by the traditional system of bartering. Politicians never cared to collect sacks of potatoes, bags of flour, or parcels of cucumber even when raising their so-called Relief Funds. They wanted hard cash and the villagers had none to spare. No wonder all politicians became suspect in the Red Valley.

Once some followers of Langoti Baba turned up in the village square with loud-speakers and gramophone records. They had strange headgear and they came to be named _topiwallahs_ by our people. One of the _topiwallahs_ put on a gramophone record on 'Free and Compulsory Higher Education for All' and this caused no end of bother. Their cheer-leader received no response from us.

'Something for Nothing!' The villagers shrugged their shoulders sceptically. 'We have never heard of such nonsense. Their talking machine is promising us a _free_ High School in our midst. It means they want to raise our taxes.'

'That's the long and the short of it,' the Goatee growled angrily. 'What's the use of beating about the bush? Do the _topiwallahs_ take us for fools? What's this higher education for? What good will the High School do to us?'

'Your children will have a higher standard of living,' shouted back the spokesman of the _topiwallahs_. And that created a big commotion. There was a storm of protests from all sides.

Our people declared indignantly that what was good for their fathers and grandfathers ought to be good for their children and grandchildren. Ramdas's wife produced a broomstick to give greater emphasis to her demand: 'Who gave the *topiwallahs* the right to preach subversive doctrines in the hearing of the village children?' She did not want her daughter to be changed into a Painted Lady or a gadfly. Several other women asked the *topiwallahs* what they thought of Ramoni. Did they advocate the breaking up of all family ties?

The driver of the *topiwallahs'* motor van ran the risk of being manhandled. Fortunately, the Punditji succeeded in calming the crowd. Their spokesman thanked him profusely.

'That's nothing,' said the Punditji. 'I want, however, to ask you exactly what you mean by higher education? What would be the contents of *your* brand of higher education? Who will prepare the programme and who will impart the instruction?'

The *topiwallahs* found the Punditji's long list of questions annoying. 'You don't know,' one of them mumbled as he got into the van, 'you don't know what is good for you. India demands Free and Compulsory Higher Education for all.'

'Free and Compulsory!' The Punditji tried to explain how from the logical point of view these two words in juxtaposition happened to make a contradiction in terms. Or something as the elliptical fashion of speaking. Anyway, the *vallahs* did not stop to listen to him.

'Let the whole world enjoy Free and Compulsory Higher Education,' the villagers muttered. 'But let us have our own way. We don't care for abracadabras.'

The visit of the *topiwallahs* rendered the near-by High School more unpopular than ever. I was the only village boy who attended it and therefore I was eyed with suspicion for a long time. The youngsters were told to keep away from me.

~

The village affairs were regulated by its own codes and laws: written and unwritten. The unwritten ones were by far the more important. Tradition was to be respected at all costs. And it was laid down that no young boy was to talk to an older one without a direct invitation from the latter. It was always the senior boy's prerogative to speak or not to speak to his juniors.

In these circumstances I deemed myself especially favoured when Gopaldas spoke to me of his own accord. He was several years my senior, and as he knew all about the coal-mines I was glad to have him as my guide. Moreover, I should add there was some thrill in going out with one who was said to be *bad*. What exactly was *badness*? Gopaldas was not accused of bird-nesting or throwing stones or picking fruits and flowers or making bonfires. What then led people to whisper that he was positively bad?

'We shall go to the opencast Beauri mine to-day,' he said. 'The gate-keepers there do not make much fuss. Anyone can go down the steps.'

Gopaldas was perfectly right as far as the *durwans* were concerned. They did not even bother to ask what we wanted inside. But the mine we visited proved disappointing to me.

It was anywhere but in the heart of the earth! Some two hundred steps leading down to a depth of only 150 feet brought me to the galleries where coal was being cut. It was so dark there that I could not at first see anything. I stood for a while straining my eyes into the blackness trying to make out why Gopaldas left me to shift for myself. However, I gradually got accustomed to the gloom and noticed that the main galleries were about the height of two men and were supported by solid pillars of coal, looking and feeling exactly like hard stone. In fact, the corridors resembled the passages in our rock-cut temples, and some parts were lit in the same way: by circular shafts known as light-wells. These are cut like wells but their main function is to allow some glints of light from above to reach the galleries below: they also serve the purpose of ventilation.

I gathered from Gopaldas that a few days ago two children playing above ground fell through one of the light-wells and were killed instantly. And yet there were still other children romping about totally unconcerned about this tragedy: the fault was mainly their parents'. But what could they do? Very often both the parents worked in the mines, leaving their children to look after themselves. Life for the Santal miners was hard.

Some fifteen hundred men and women worked in the mine I visited. There were a lot of children too: some helped their mothers while others were too young to do anything but lie wrapped up in their swaddlings till they were taken out at the end of the day. The women generally collected the lumps of coal their men cut out with pick-axes. The coal inside the mine looked exactly like black basalt and when hit with pick-axes and shovels gave out a metallic sound. All this was very interesting. But I had to bring my visit to an abrupt end on account of a violent altercation in a corner: it was Gopaldas quarrelling with a foreman.

Perhaps Gopaldas was in the wrong because he slunk away all of a sudden, leaving me behind without even saying good-bye. The foreman went round with an electric torch looking for tiny booklets full of pictures which Gopaldas had distributed among Santal women-miners.

~

It was late when I got back home. Fortunately, Mashi-ma was not yet back from the next village.

'Otherwise she would have given you a nice hiding,' remarked Bum-boatee the Pirate. He was much younger than I and had no business to talk to me in this way. But when no one was about he and his boon companions, Pocha the Huntsman and Sashe Raha, nicknamed the Split Cucumber, spoke to me as though I was the youngest of the lot.

'So you were with Gopaldas the Pilot Fish,' grinned Sashe Raha, nicknamed the Split Cucumber.

I did not bother to discuss anything with these three, though I reminded them of the deference they should show to their seniors in age, and status. At this Pocha the Huntsman pursed his lips and produced a sound which he thought was funny: a cross between a cat-call and the whoop of the langur-monkeys when they raid unguarded vegetable gardens. Pocha's trick did not make me laugh. I did not even smile.

'Between nineteen and twenty,' Bum-boatee the Pirate whistled and rolled his eyes. He was great at making faces. 'Between nineteen and twenty there is no great difference.'

'What are you talking about?' I asked, genuinely surprised at his ignorance of his own age. 'Don't they teach you how to count in the *path-sala*? You are not yet nine. What's this nonsense about nineteen?'

'And what about your being twenty?' all three blared at the same time.

From that day onwards these three became more impertinent than ever. They often asked me on the sly, sometimes twice in the course of the same day, when was I to celebrate my twentieth birthday and bring a bride to the household! 'He is mighty slow in growing up,' they chattered like magpies among themselves. 'At the rate he is progressing it would take him ages to be twenty. Perhaps he does not want to grow up. Maybe he doesn't want to get married.... He hopes to become like Gopaldas.'

There was something mysterious about this elusive Gopaldas. Mashi-ma advised me to keep away from him. Her injunction was superfluous: Gopaldas disappeared from the village in the same inexplicable way as he had turned up.

But how did Mashi-ma come to know about my excursion to the coal-fields with the watchman's nephew? Like most of our women she possessed a special gift: she managed to overhear anything that was said anywhere within a league of the village.

Gopaldas was accused of playing with fire and tampering with boys.

'What exactly is tampering?'

'Now don't argue!' Mashi-ma looked at me angrily. 'At your age I didn't dare talk back to my aunt.'

VI

'An eighth child bears good luck.' Everyone knows that Krishna, the eighth incarnation of the Great God, was the eighth progeny of Yadu. And Babu Hem Chandra Chahar was the eighth son of his parents: he was born on the eighth day of the dark fortnight of *Vadra* (August-September): Krishna's birthday. Though he never considered himself lucky, the villagers regarded him as their mascot. Like the *Bhat*, the expert versifier, he was to be found at every festivity. 'Hem Babu's presence assures good luck,' they said, and Babu Hem Chandra Chahar rarely failed to profit from the invitations he received; like the priest who officiated at religious ceremonies he received his *dakshina*, his sacrificial fee.

He did not really belong to our Penhari Parganas, but he taught at the Municipal School at Rani-gunj, and that was near enough for the people of the Red Valley to invite him as often as they wanted. Two hours' journey on foot was usually regarded as hailing distance.

No one called him by his name. He was universally known as the Second Master, an epithet which Babu Hem Chandra Chahar did not like very much. He aspired to be the head of his school. Owing, however, to an unfortunate quarrel with the Department of Public Instruction, his legitimate claims were overlooked by the authorities.

'He never got his promotion,' they said, 'because of his love for Krom-bell.' Who this Krom-bell was very few knew. Not even Kathak the Story-teller. This much, however, everyone gathered from the Second Master's incidental remarks: that Krom-bell was godfearing and plain-speaking: his sterling virtues led him to fight with a tyrant: in the duel Krom-bell received divine succour and the tyrant lost his head.

The story of Krom-bell's success as due to direct intervention by God did not somehow fit in with the villagers' conception of things as they should be. Had he really been a man of God he ought to have experienced defeat, calumny, persecution, and martyrdom: that was the fate reserved for most saints—except those rare ones attaining *Siddhi* or *Nirvana*. 'In *this* world Evil triumphs,' they reasoned. 'Krom-bell's phenomenal success makes him a suspect. He might have been, unknowingly perhaps, in league with the Evil One. One cannot have it both ways—here and hereafter.'

This sort of logic enraged the Second Master: he had a profound contempt for all country-folks and in particular for those of the Penhari Parganas. He did nothing to hide his horror of their illiteracy and superstitious practices. His own birthplace was Vardaman where, according to him, there were few illiterates and no superstitious citizens at all. The villagers did not mind his method of reasoning. For Vardaman they had little respect, because its main thoroughfares were lined with courtesans' houses.

'Illiteracy has nothing to do with general character,' the Punditji argued with the Second Master. 'Our villagers are perfectly right in their evaluation of your hero Krom-bell.'

'How?'

'*Thou art not entitled to the fruits of thy labour*, so says Krishna in the *Gita*,' the Punditji emphasized the word *not*. '*Not to the fruits of thy labour but only to the sacrifices thereof.*'

The Second Master shook his head. He was not interested in the *Gita* and applauded Macaulay's decision to ignore the existence of the Sanskrit language and, solely for the purpose of exasperating the Sanskritician, asked him to make his point more concrete.

'Those favoured by the demons receive earthly success,' the Punditji summarized the ancient myths. '...Whereas those blessed by the deities attain spiritual felicity and, maybe, earthly sorrow in contrast to paradisal joys.'

The Second Master gave a hollow laugh. He did not care for old wives' tales: myths and legends. Why did he then attend the superstitious rites and ceremonies? 'Not that I like these cults,' he explained. 'But if it gives pleasure to the villagers to honour me, why shouldn't I accept their homage?'

~

'If only Hem had been less imitative of Cromwell's blunt-ness,' the principal of the Hathkura Intermediate College confided to his students, 'he would not have rotted all his life as an assistant teacher at Rani-gunj. Hem has misinterpreted Cromwell, who was a statesman as well as a general. He was not great because he was blunt. On the contrary, he was great in spite of his occasional lapses into bluntness. '...Hem has got everything muddled up. Be careful how you choose your heroes and how you interpret them.'

The principal thought that his timely warning would put some of his students on their guard. But they took it in a different light. 'Evidently,' they whispered among themselves, 'the old fellow is green with envy. He is jealous about the Second Master's large following... It's so easy to give lip sympathy.'

Many of the students of the Intermediate College, all future teachers, venerated the Second Master. They came in contact with him because their practical work brought them to Rani-gunj: to the same school where the Second Master taught. There they found him waging a ceaseless war of applications and petitions single-handedly. Was that not enough to win them over to him? The Second Master was opposed to all forms of superstition! So were they. Was he not an advocate of modernization? Of transforming the whole country by building a dam; something similar to the Sukkar Barrage? So were they too....

'The Second Master calls a spade a spade.' The students were delighted to find a man bold enough to tell the truth at any price. 'What good is Sanskrit in these days? Sheer waste of time. The Second Master is right. He is for abolishing poverty. And that does not please the *baniahs* and bankers.'

'How is poverty to be abolished?' a sceptic asked.

'Why? By equal distribution of all property!' the majority replied in chorus. 'Equal wages for all.'

'That would mean after five years' grinding I should get as much as an unskilled labourer,' the sceptic persisted. But the rest moved away from him: he was renowned as a boot-licker of the old order, a follower of Langoti Baba, a potential *topiwallah*. The majority of the students did not care for the sceptic.

~

During the months of the long vacation the poorer students at the Intermediate College stayed on. It was cheaper to stay in the college hostel than to live elsewhere. Besides, it was greater fun than being at home, badgered by the elders with silly questions. And then there was the possibility of calling on the Second Master every day and profiting from his words of wisdom.

They listened to him with veneration. They were keen: they had no faith in the doctrines of Langoti Baba and still less in those of his followers, the *topiwallahs*. The members of the party in power were not sufficiently forward-looking, were too timid with reforms.

'Superstition must be scotched.' The Second Master was perfectly clear about it. 'The power of the money-lenders, bankers, and industrialists must be curbed. Bureaucratic red-tape must be abolished. We don't want a totalitarian government. Freedom of speech for all. We want a system of perpetual progress.'

They all agreed with everything he said and eyed me occasionally with suspicion. I was too young in their opinion to profit from the exhortations of the Second Master, their *guru*, their spiritual master. I had no business to be there! I too felt in the same way as they, and would gladly have stayed away from these gatherings if I had my own way. But there was Mashi-ma to be reckoned with: she had made an arrangement with the Second Master behind my back.

'Mashi-ma! Is Gopaldas really bad?' It was silly of me to put this question bluntly to her. And it was sillier still to have taken up Gopaldas's defence. Mashi-ma assumed that the *chowkidar's* nephew had cast some magic spell on me, and that I had to be weaned away from his influence: and she thought that the best person to do this exorcising was the Second Master. So she fixed private lessons during the long vacation for me from Babu Hem Chandra Chahar, the eighth child of his parents, the man who was supposed to bring good luck to all. She slaved away cooking food in different households to earn hard cash to pay for my private lessons. The Second Master was insistent on being paid cash, but when it came to giving lessons, all that he did was to ask me to join the discussions he led for the benefit of his admirers from the Hathkura Intermediate College.

'Can't we do something concrete to start our fight against superstition?' asked one of the more fretful students one day. 'It would certainly take a long while to get the dam built to water the Red Valley. Meanwhile each one of us ought to do something.'

'Certainly,' declared the Second Master. 'We must begin from the very beginning. If the country would only abandon its tenacious admiration of the past. You young people! You should start the campaign in your own households first, and then carry it further afield in your villages—and beyond.'

I gathered from the general trend of his remarks and the comments from his listeners that the Penhari Parganas were inhabited by the most lethargic and mentally dull of all peoples, and that the dwellers of the Red Valley were the worst of the whole lot: my village people were no good because they lived side by side with the Santals, the curse of the Penhari region.

'Immorality is rife among them,' the Second Master expounded. 'Their way of living is simply shocking: men, women and children live promiscuously.'

What did immorality imply? What constituted immorality? I did not dare ask the question.

VII

The only Santals I knew at that time were those living in hamlets not far from my village. They were called Dharkars, and as far as I could make out they were in no way different from others of the Red Valley. Their faces were, however, rounder and their men taller and great experts with their bamboo flutes. Moreover, they wore their hair long as I did. Occasionally they anointed their cattle with oil and vermilion as protection against gadflies, and they showed a distinct preference for buffaloes over bullocks. Most of the Dharkar men-folk worked in the Beauri coal-mine and so did some of their women. What was wrong with that?

The Santals of the Blue Hills were called Pasis. Their men were great hunters, while their women produced vegetable dyes like blue indigo, red madder, and yellow turmeric. They too were good flautists and also, clever archers.

Whether of the Valley or of the Hills, these simple folk were renowned for their handicraft: they were good weavers and in wicker-work they were unbeatable, much better than the Hindus of the village and much less fussy. They did not mind showing me how to make cane seats or produce beautiful patterns on cloth.

Did the Second Master disapprove of their toiling in the mines? Or of their carrying coal to Calcutta in their barges? Why were the Santal women accused of being more immoral than their men? Was it on account of their tiny feet and small hands? Or because of their slightly prominent cheek bones and brimming gazelle-like eyes? Or was it their costume?

The Santal women dressed somewhat quaintly. 'They wear nothing under their short *saris*,' Pocha the Huntsman confided at the top of his voice to his friends one day as I was passing by. Bum-boatee the Pirate and Sashe Raha, nicknamed the Split Cucumber, declared 'This was no news.' However, that has nothing to do with the way Santal women wore their *saris*, which were generally dyed deep blue or saffron and made of heavy home-spun material.

The *sari* was wound round the waist, producing the effect of a skirt, and carried over one breast, then passed round the neck in neat folds, and finally brought down to cover the other breast with the free end. This end was rarely tucked in, but left loose, and allowed to flap, revealing in some measure as they walked, their shapely bosoms. The back was left entirely bare, and the head usually uncovered.

Owing either to the narrow width of their *saris* or their way of draping it round their bodies, when the Santal women walked they partially exposed their beautifully moulded thighs: the effect was not very different from that made by European ladies when they wore their 'stride-out skirts' or 'split Chinese gowns,' once in great vogue at Asansole and Hazaribagh.

I do not know if it was on account of their uncovered backs, bare heads, ill-concealed breasts, or partially exposed thighs, or for the flowers they put in their hair or for some other reason. Whenever a townsman came across any of our Santal women, he invariably stopped and stared. Some even whistled as though they saw something funny.

'What are you whistling for?' I once asked a lanky fellow with rimless spectacles who was gaping at two Santal girls of about sixteen carrying enormous loads of firewood on their heads. I knew he was a townsman from his ill-breeding and awkward ways. He carried a carpet bag in one hand and in the other a rolled-up sunshade with a shining handle of either aluminium or German silver. '*Mahasoy*! What are you whistling for?' I repeated my question as I ran towards him. 'Are you whistling at our Santal girls?'

'Do you want a thrashing?' the seedy townsman glared at me and raised his sunshade: he wanted to hit me.

'Thrash me if you like,' I said as I came closer to him. 'But tell me what have you been whistling for? Certainly the Second Master, Mashi-ma, and others would be glad to know.'

He did not let me finish my sentence. Without even bothering to listen to me he made off hurriedly as though chased by a mad bull. I tried to follow him for a while repeating my question at the top of my voice, but drew no answer from him. He ran faster than I.

I had, of course, interrogated Mashi-ma, Neela, and the Second Master on this matter of whistling, and all of them confessed they did not know the reason. That was how I accosted a townsman, a grown-up to boot, all of my own accord, and made a fool of myself.

'Never associate with such men,' was all that Mashi-ma had to say when I told her about the spectacled man carrying a carpet bag and a rolled-up sunshade.

~

'At times,' Neela the Santal girl said, 'one becomes fond of someone or of something without reasoning and without knowing why.' Neela was then in charge of a tiny one-room school at Amrita-ban which is near the jungles of the Blue Hills. She made me think: I agreed with her.

If I were asked why I was thrilled by the sight of Sirius, the brightest star of the evening, known to some as the Dog of the Great Hunter, or why the music of the flutes from the palm groves filled my young heart with ecstasy, I should be at a loss to give any rational answer. In those days I knew for certain that if one year in spring some unknown curse prevented the Hibiscus flowers in my back garden from blooming, that year for me would have been a twelve-month of blight. It would have remained for ever a black patch in the almanac of my months, seasons, years, and decades. Yet what was the value of the bell-shaped scarlet blossoms of a jasper-green plant in the majestic scheme of the universe or even in the languid life of my rural community? Just nothing. Or next to nothing. All the same, what made me so fond of that particular shrub in a neglected corner of a half-abandoned walled enclosure?

I did not know the answer then. And I do not know it even now.

Reasoning played little part in my juvenile hopes and fears, faith and doubts, desires and longings. My likes and dislikes, my loves and hates were all equally irrational.

~

'The flock reveals the bird,' Gopaldas laughed at me one day when I was on my way to Rani-gunj. 'So you have become one of the Second Master's birdies! He talks and talks, and befuddles the young with chalk.'

I did not pay much attention to Gopaldas's remarks. Drawn gradually within the circle of the Second Master's admirers, I had then come to regard him as an oracle. Babu Hem Chandra Chahar's judgment on most matters I accepted as final.

Though I did not just then take Gopaldas's criticism seriously, it came to my mind spontaneously the day I heard the Second Master denouncing the Santals as savages. I felt deeply hurt. I was genuinely fond of them: I was enamoured of their broad-hipped and ample-bosomed matrons clad in blue *saris* with vermilion and saffron hems. Those wearing red oleanders and yellow poppies in their jet black hair were for me sylvan goddesses. Their movements were so graceful, their laughter so infectious, and their glances so haunting. The dreams of my wakeful hours were peopled by them. I simply adored the Santal women and all that went with them: their water jars shaped like amphoras, their heavy bangles fitted with tiny berry-like bells, their coral necklets and floral necklaces, and, in particular, their bouncing babies with big eyes filled with wonder. It was a pleasure to watch them tarried astride their mothers' backs or straddled across their fathers' shoulders.

'But they are immoral,' the Second Master affirmed. 'They are superstitious. More so than the Hindus. They worship the sun and call it Sing-Bonga. They believe in ghosts and ghouls and are under the thumb of their magic-men, their Jagmanjhis, Naryas, and Sayas. The death rate of their children is the highest in the land. They sacrifice cocks to bring down the rains. They lightly let themselves be prostituted. They are a drag upon the rest of the community. When the dam is built these women and their men will be shifted somewhere else.'

VIII

'Time is a subtle thief,' the villagers say. 'It carries the bag of oblivion on its back. It ruthlessly robs memory's garden of its rarest fruits and finest flowers.' Blame time, whoever will, but I have only myself to blame. For as the years swiftly glided past, my views on men and manners underwent many modifications and curious transformations while my memory's field remained as green as of yore.

The Dog Star remained as it had always been—by the side of the Great Hunter—the brightest of all evening stars. The scarlet bells of Hibiscus flamed in the jasper-green bushes as glowingly as before: they were prized with undiminished enthusiasm. With the years Mashi-ma became more and more dear to me. The langur-monkeys varied little in their characteristic thievishness and filthiness. The passage of years did not change them.

But what about my boyhood's heroes?

Imperceptibly most of them ceased to interest me: they no longer gripped my imagination. Some grew in their stature and then suddenly shrank. Others diminished steadily till they became no more imposing than mere mortals of the common mould. Some dwindled into risible or even despicable pigmies. A few were found to be giants with feet of clay. While some others shrivelled up into rotting totem-poles of stink-wood or into decomposing mummies—lifeless, malodorous and pestiferous.

I longed for worthier heroes to admire and to emulate.

Where was I to find them? It was uncomfortable to find out that my tin gods were paltry. But it was still more distressing to discover none of a superior grade to replace them. I felt bewildered. Was it the lot of every boy to pass through this trying experience?

~

Casual remarks unintentionally overheard in the village square on market days brought me occasional glints of hope.

'None but fools cease to grow.' I heard the Punditji upbraiding a vegetable-seller one afternoon. The man was lamenting over some bad deals made in the town. It was, I thought, strange that the Sanskritician should be consulted on questions affecting the price of potatoes, brinjals, and cucumbers: I overlooked the fact that though the Second Master and his admirers had little respect for the Punditji, to the villagers he was the oracle of wisdom and the prophet of prudence: the paragon of all virtues.

'A wise man knows everything,' our villagers contended. 'Everything that is under the sun. A sage has no need to travel. No need to look out of the window. Yet he is conversant with the ways of Heaven. He sees all without looking: he achieves all without stirring.' That being the case, the peasant was perfectly justified from his point of view in consulting the Punditji. And

I pricked up my ears to hear what the aged Sanskrit scholar had to say.

'Only a fool ceases to develop,' the Punditji repeated as he thumped his brass-bound staff on the ground: that was his way of emphasizing his arguments. 'Only dunces and half-wits are incapable of admitting their errors and cutting their losses. It is wise to institute seasonal inventories. Go and make yours.'

This set my mind working. What about making an inventory of my affairs?

Thus I came to effect a general revaluation of my heroes and rogues, and of saints and sinners. Many portraits from my album and most clippings from my scrap-book were discarded. The repudiation of the erstwhile gods and demi-gods was not altogether easy. Some were thrown aside with an exclamation of surprise or relief, some with a sigh of regret, and a few with tears. But in one instance I felt totally confused: when I came across the image of the Second Master, Babu Hem Chandra Chahar.

That I did learn something from him it would be idle to deny, and yet as I tore up the page containing his autograph I felt ashamed to admit that fact to myself: I thought it humiliating to have associated with him for so long. Yet he had for a number of years been my hero, one whose word was law to me. All the same, he was the person who first shook my 'faith in man.' He inflicted a wound to my sense of pride that time failed to heal. Had anyone else but the Second Master behaved inconsistently it would not have mattered so much to me. But he, the arch-enemy of all superstition, ought not to have taken part in a ceremony he had denounced in most vehement terms.

IX

It happened during an excessively dry summer when the monsoon rains forgot to visit my village in the Red Valley.

Most places in our district had nothing to complain about

in the weather. Nevertheless, the rains were denied us. The villagers anxiously prayed for showers. But each day the heedless sun rode high in our cloudless sky, and gradually parched up our ponds and pools with its fierce rays. It slowly evaporated the water of the larger tanks, reservoirs, *jheels*, natural and artificial lakes, transforming them into the dried mud craters of dead volcanoes. The rills, streams, and rivulets were changed into cracked, clay-lined gullies and dusty, winding trenches: senseless scars scooped, as it were, by cruel demons on the body of the exhausted earth. The mighty Damodar river shrank into a mere trickle of water scarcely perceptible in its mile-wide bed of saffron and orange sand.

It became hotter and drier. The wind blew eddies of dust across the desiccated plain, parching the skin and burning the eyes. It brought in its wake swarms of gadflies and red ants. It was simply horrible.

Fortunately, a few of our ancient, deep, stone-lined wells were not affected by the drought. They continued to yield some water. Not much: only a few pitcherfuls for each household: just enough to keep the village alive. The live-stock and the draught-animals had to be sent away for pasturing in more fortunate areas.

The price of rice, lentils, and other food rose steadily. Whispers were heard about an impending country-wide famine on account of a comet with a brush-like tail.

'A comet bodes evil,' they whispered. 'This one is the queerest ever seen in our skies.' Its peculiarities were discussed with bated breath: it appeared in the southern horizon between two and three in the dead of the night. It moved swiftly like a rocket: its trajectory was like a half-circle.

'Its brush-like tail is brighter than the body of Sirius, the Dog accompanying the Great Hunter.'

'The Dread Hunter, you mean?' Kathak the Storyteller asked. 'Kala Purusha, Lord of Time and Annihilation is the Hunter's other name.'

'Has the comet's brightness angered the Hunter?'

'Who knows?' Kathak folded the palms of his hands and bent his head. He made the sign of prayer and reverence. The others did likewise. 'No mortal should discuss the movements of heavenly bodies without due meekness and proper veneration.'

'Maybe, the comet is the charger of Kalki.'

'Kalki is the tenth *avatar* of the Great God. The tenth *avatar* will be the last one.'

'Time will stop when Kalki comes.'

'Would it then mean the end of the world?'

'Who knows?' Kathak murmured. 'Who can tell? It is written in the *Puranas*, our ancient epics, that the sun will cease to set when Kalki comes.'

'But they say,' interrupted Kolej Huzoor, 'the comet cannot be seen from Delhi.' At least that was the report given in the paper *Kusum-pur Sangbad*. If it was the end of the world, the signs of Kalki's arrival ought to be the same all over the country.

'The *Delhiwallahs!*' Ramdas the *chowkidar* had little faith in the people of Delhi. 'They simply do not know where to look for it.'

'Or perhaps they don't want to admit what's plainly visible.' Kathak recalled how the Delhi wireless kept back the news of the big fire in the Chandni Chowk for three days.

'But Kalki's wrath will hit them all the same.' Ramdas was sure of it.

'Why should Kalki come riding on a comet?' I murmured. No one bothered to answer my question.

~

A few days later the wireless messages of the AIR, All India Radio, referred to the comet, and announced its imminent disappearance or disintegration. 'It was seen for a couple of nights only,' the AIR broadcasted. The villagers, however, knew better.

The wireless messages were so confusing. No villager ever relied on the weather reports broadcast from Delhi or Calcutta. Sometimes one station contradicted the information given by the other, causing even greater confusion. During the general strike of the Transport workers these contradictory news-items created no end of embarrassment. At that time no villager owned a radio-set. Yet everyone knew all that was transmitted either from Delhi or Calcutta!

Little by little, certain new rumours began to spread in our midst and gradually gained strength: rain-clouds were being deliberately diverted to the regions of the north! Dhan-pur, only half-a-day's run from our village, received five inches of rain while we failed to obtain a single drop. Were they forcing the clouds to change their course by means of the wireless waves?

'Who knows?'

~

Then as though to mock the villagers several bits of fluffy clouds came sailing overhead one early afternoon. Everyone ran out in the open to gaze at them: men, women and children as well as their pets, dogs and donkeys. Our herds of cattle had been sent away long ago to areas where water was plentiful, otherwise these too would certainly have come out lowing their delight at the arrival of the first clouds of the season. The sky looked overcast.

Our weather-prophets professed utter confusion. Such strange packs of clouds they had never seen before: they were unable to make any forecast. Some of the younger land-labourers, on the other hand, sniffed: they were convinced that it would rain soon—and even very soon!

Bum-boatee the Pirate, Pocha the Huntsman, and Sashe Raha, nicknamed the Split Cucumber, were anxious to know the rules and regulations of betting on rainfall. They had heard from Kumar the Potter that in Bombay it was fashionable among some *baniahs*, grain merchants, and cotton brokers to gamble regularly on weather forecasts and the expected amounts of rainfall. As the grown-ups never paid much heed to the trio's importunities, I was the person to whom they turned. They crowded round me: I was not an adult in their reckoning. This was annoying. I managed, however, to get rid of them by suggesting that they should consult Kolej Huzoor, the newly arrived visitor from Vardaman. He was, in my opinion, the best qualified person to enlighten them on this matter of betting.

Kolej Huzoor was in our midst simply because his parents insisted on his spending his vacation in the country. Some distant relations of his were in our village. So he came here to stay with them and recover from the effects of a recent operation on his groin. He was a student of the Raj College: hence his appellation 'Kolej Huzoor'. He was a nice enough man, so far as the Raj College students were capable of being nice, but he managed to make himself notorious within a few days of his arrival: he went about questioning everyone, 'Don't you ever get bored?' 'I am terribly afraid of boredom,' he confessed. 'Does nothing ever happen here? How can you always listen to the tedious yarns of Kathak the Storyteller?' So I took Kolej Huzoor to our most famous building, the Golah, and showed him the *elephant steps* built within its walls of several cubits thickness. But he was not in the least impressed. 'Your Golah is like a gasometer,' he remarked and wanted to know if there were any cinemas and 'sporting houses' in the neighbourhood. 'At Vardaman,' he confided to me, 'there are lots of "sporting houses". Some of the hostesses are as good as film-stars. Life here is pretty boring.'

The arrival of the strange clouds in our sky furnished him, however, with some unexpected distraction: he gazed at them like the rest of us with rapt attention.

~

'Clouds coming over the Western Hills bode no good,' mumbled an old husbandman who rarely spoke. At this ominous warning our weather-prophets nodded their heads: they shared his view. 'They forestall dust storms,' the old man went on. 'I don't like the look of these scraggy cloudlets.'

'Scraggy?' Kolej Huzoor edged towards the aged peasant. 'Why do you call them *scraggy?*' He raised his voice for no reason in particular. One would have thought that the word *scraggy* hurt his personal pride and susceptibilities. He was thoroughly sick of our country air and the chance remark was enough to cause a break-down: it brought about an explosion. Here at long last was his opportunity of showing his mettle: his erudition. He pegged a claim for a quarrel over nothing. In this respect he was no different from other college students and townsmen constrained to spend their holidays in the country. They never missed an occasion for altercations and for insulting the village dwellers. 'Only crass ignorance,' Kolej Huzoor proclaimed, 'would lead a man to call these clouds *scraggy*. And even if they were really scraggy, there is no reason to assume they won't bring you rain.'

No one save the youngsters paid any attention to Kolej Huzoor's outburst. This annoyed him still more and he planted himself right in front of the old peasant and bawled: 'In popular language these might be termed *Cat's tail* or *Colt's tail*. But *scraggy?* Never.'

Our peasant stared at Kolej Huzoor in silence while the young expert on cinemas, films, film-stars, and sporting ladies went on rasping that he had never heard such an idiotic word as *scraggy*. 'It is most unscientific.' He would have, no doubt, gone on raving in this way had not Pocha the Huntsman made his intrusion just then. With Bum-boatee and Sashe Raha, nicknamed the Split Cucumber, Pocha was anxious to collect information on betting rules from Kolej Huzoor, therefore he broke in cleverly.

'Pardon me,' began Pocha quite politely, 'I think *Cat's tail* or *Colt's tail* would be more scientific. But what about the clouds called *Undone tresses?*'

'Mr Visitor!' the Split Cucumber asked, 'What would you say?'

Bum-boatee the Pirate did not say anything but came closer waiting for the opportunity to raise the question of betting. Or perhaps he was praying in silence: 'Narada! Narada! Broomstick! Broomstick! O Narada! Let's see a jolly fight!'

'They are all unscientific,' according to Kolej Huzoor. He did not mind the youngsters' ignorance of scientific terminology, but a farm-hand of seventy-two (or thereabouts) ought to know better than to use the term *scraggy*! He then explained that in the reading room of the Vardaman Raj Public Library there were charts showing different cloud-formations: *Cirrus, Cumulus, Stratus* and *Nimbus* as well as *Cirro-Cumulus, Cirro-Stratus…*

The ancient husbandman's eyes became round like marbles. He was simply amazed: he forgot the insulting remarks of Kolej Huzoor and followed with profound interest the exotic names of clouds. He tried to pronounce them, and wondered if the atmospheric conditions at Vardaman were entirely topsy-turvy. Vardaman must be a curious place, he reasoned. Otherwise how could its inhabitants hit upon complicated words to name their cloud-packs. Could any normal human tongue utter such words as *Cirro?*

He was too astounded to say anything. He wiped his brow with the back of his right hand and shrugged his shoulders. Was it a sign of resignation? Or humility? It was just plain admission of a fact: his ignorance. Our villagers had unbounded admiration for learning. As Kolej Huzoor frequented an institution of higher education, the Vardaman Raj College, he was bound to be erudite! And who was he, a poor unlettered peasant, to challenge a university undergraduate's nomenclature of the cloud-packs over Vardaman?

'I know what I am talking about.' Kolej Huzoor raised his voice to a higher pitch; quite unnecessarily, I thought. He was perhaps still hoping that someone would accept his challenge to a disputation over scientific terminology. No one, however, bothered to respond. As for the taciturn peasant, he was hopeless: he remained dumb as before while Kolej Huzoor went on with his catalogue of names: '*Strato-Cumulus, Cumulo-Nimbus, Alto-Cumulus, Fracto-Stratus.*'

The old man nodded his head at each Latin term pronounced with evident pride by our visitor from Vardaman. His nods, of course, did not mean much except that he acknowledged a profundity which evaded his comprehension. He remained as reluctant as ever to enter into a discussion over expressions beyond his grasp.

In this respect he was no different from the other villagers: they evaded all debate over issues outside their orbit and the limits of their comprehension. Vardaman was too far away, more than a hundred miles run. It mattered little to the peasant if Kolej Huzoor talked arrant nonsense or high philosophy or modern science which affected Vardaman only. So far as the Red Valley and the village were concerned, he knew what the clouds coming over the Western Hills spelt. 'One does not quarrel over facts.' The villagers had their own way of reasoning. 'In time everyone will know the truth. Did not Ananda say: "Eternity is long enough." Given time even a mule will be redeemed. So, what's the point of quarrelling over the obvious?'

'You may,' Kolej Huzoor went on, 'if you like, compare these clouds with the *Spade and Shovel* formation. I am deliberately using a popular term. If they really are the *Spade and Shovel*, it would mean heavy showers after twelve hours. Though, mind you, the sky will remain overcast from now until the end of the rainy season. Whereas...'

This was too much for the old man. He shrugged his shoulders again, indicating that he refused to be baited into a debate with an erudite college undergraduate. Much to the annoyance of Pocha the Huntsman and his friends, the peasant suddenly moved away without saying a word.

The youngsters had already betted in their own fashion on the outcome of 'a disputation on the nature of the cloud -formations overhead.' This was not surprising. The favourite sports of the villagers were wrestling and debating. Champions from distant places were invited from time to time to give demonstrations of their prowess. They often walked many miles to witness bouts between well-matched rivals. Popular opinion was, however, divided as to which of the two sports furnished the greater diversion. The subjects of the debates were, as a rule, abstruse, and beyond the grasp of most youngsters. For example *Why do dreams survive their dreamers? Is Faith really a Gambler's Daughter? What is Thought? Was Ravana the Demon Pious?* So quite naturally Pocha, Bum-boatee, and Sashe Raha looked forward to a disputation, albeit impromptu, over a theme within their comprehension: The nature of cloud packs: Kolej Huzoor versus a semi-mute husbandman! They were greatly disappointed at the peasant's withdrawal.

Kolej Huzoor, too, was shocked. He was disgusted, and spat noisily on the earth to show his contempt for rural obduracy. His indignation, however, did not last long. Presently the overcast sky cleared up and he was surprised.

To everybody's sorrow the clouds floated away to the north without giving any rain, leaving the land and the sky once again to the scant mercy of the implacable summer sun.

We all ran back from the open and sought shelter in the shade, while the all-conquering sun re-affirmed its unchallenged sway over our world. Its rays became more scorching than before, making it impossible to stay outside without the protection of a sunshade.

Only a black dog with bloodshot eyes remained where it had stumbled. It howled piteously as it dug its fore-paws in the dust heap by the flowering cactus bushes. It refused to move out of the burning sun though the wife of our watchman Ramdas tried her best to cajole it back into the shadows.

'That's an evil omen,' several voices murmured. Everyone felt discouraged. No one had the least urge to talk or argue or quarrel. The general disappointment was beyond words.

~

The same phenomenon in the sky was noticed at about the same time the next afternoon and on the afternoons that followed. Scraggy, fleecy, or spruce clouds gathered overhead to darken the horizon for a while, raising hope in hundreds of hearts, and then, for no apparent reason, dispersed in all directions without shedding a drop of rain. On certain afternoons clouds coming from the west and the south met together at the zenith for a few minutes: they herded together till they formed a huge mass, lingering low, almost touching the tops of the taller trees in the distant jungles; and afterwards, in obedience as it were to a pre-arranged signal, they broke up to scurry towards the north and disappeared from the horizon.

Every day it was the same, sad story. The same bitter disappointment. An overcast sky at about two o'clock—the expectation of an imminent downpour—swiftly succeeded by a newer and fiercer sun-burst. Each afternoon the fiery orb of day impatiently tore apart the passing cover of unstable clouds and pounded with doubled fury the dusty earth with fiery particles. It kept up this atrocious persecution till it was time for it to retire behind the Western Hills.

~

The villagers were perplexed. They did not know how to interpret the signs in the skies.

Why did the clouds refuse to yield the much-desired showers?

'The sable clouds are malicious demons,' the grandmothers told the young ones as they put them to bed, while the mothers mutely turned the millstones for grinding corn or worked with the spinning wheels. 'These demons are heartless. They prevent the rain-clouds from shedding their blessings on us. Sometimes these black monsters intercept the rain by gathering on their back what has already been poured out for us. They then fly away to distant lands where no man lives, to abandon their spoils. They are mean thieves. They never surrender what they have stolen unless struck with thunder and lightning.'

Late at night grandmothers and mothers gathered in the back gardens carrying lighted earthenware lamps. They prostrated themselves in the dust before the holy *tulsis*, the basil plants, and prayed in silence.

'Man is too weak,' it is said, 'to overcome the demons of darkness. He has, however, been accorded a potent weapon to combat the evil ones: the privilege to pray. Each and every prayer for heavenly succour, if reverentially uttered, becomes an arrow in the armoury of Indra, Lord of the Sky, Leader of the Celestial Host, the Rider of the Winged White Horse....'

'The celestial deity empties his quiver when he thinks it meet. His arrows never miss their mark. The lightning is the glittering of his shaft—the thunderbolt—with which the arrays of dark demons are routed and their towering battlements are breached. He scatters them to the end of the earth and showers the rain to slake the thirst of the lands and of the rivers.'

'Pour down your rain upon us, O Thunder-wielder!' the grandmothers and mothers intoned softly. 'Shower your blessings upon us, your children, O Master of the Firmament! Sound your mighty trumpet, O Matchless Warrior!'

'How are the prayers to be properly worded?' they asked one another in whispers.

'Who knows?'

Heart-shaped lamps, filled with scented vegetable oil, were left burning at the feet of the sacred basil plants in every household.

'Who will teach us how to pray?' The men looked at one another. 'Who knows the answer?'

The one unpardonable blasphemy, the villagers knew, was to complain of misfortune: for this would imply either that an event might occur otherwise than by the will of the Great God, or else that the will of the Great God was unjust. The Punditji held a different view, but then…he was so different from the rest. 'Only through sufferance,' he told them, 'vengeance passes you by! You have got what you have deserved through your *Karma*—your words, your thoughts, and your deeds.'

'How are we to pray?' asked Janardan.

'Let none sin nor try to hinder the fulfilment of the divine decrees,' Kathak murmured.

'But that is no answer,' I said to myself.

'What's sin?' I wondered. 'What's blasphemy? What have we done to deserve vengeance? What is *Karma*?' It was useless to put so many questions at the same time to Mashi-ma. So I asked her how did she pray? In those days of drought my aunt used the traditional entreaty:

'Let thine arrows go forth and make the mountains quake. Let the clouds pour forth water and the earth resound with thy praise. Let the heavens echo the voice of thy thunder and make the universe tremble and jubilate.'

During the drought the hours moved languidly. The days seemed longer than ever. Yet the weeks advanced and the calendar showed that the date of the *Kajri* dances were nigh. Men and women sighed when they thought of the *Kajri*: it coincided with the sowing of the seeds after the first showers of the monsoon. How could the paeans of praise for the god of rains be raised when the fields remained untilled and unsown?

With heavy hearts they watched the play of the capricious

clouds in the sky. The monsoon failed to break. There was no rain in those clouds.

Individual and family prayers produced no change in the general state of affairs. Collective prayers and *pujas* were proposed in hope of obtaining better results. To propitiate the god of rains, different smaller groups started a number of mysterious rites of their own.

The Second Master, who had not hitherto bothered about *pujas*, was found participating in some of the more esoteric rituals. What was he doing in those gatherings, Kolej Huzoor wanted to know from me. Had he not advised his followers to fight superstition in their own homes and villages? Was he not the man who considered these ceremonies to be the relics of a barbaric past when man was ignorant about the laws of science governing natural phenomena?

Who was I to answer for the Second Master's presence in some Santal secret rites which took place in the dead of the night? Kolej Huzoor's quests for distraction led him to slip out of the house when everyone was abed and to make some strange discoveries.

'Do you believe,' he asked the Second Master one day in my presence, 'in Indra? What does he look like, this god of rains?'

Everyone looked at me—somewhat reproachfully, I thought—for at Mashi-ma's insistence I had done some Sanskrit and the rest were ignorant of it. It was pure Chinese to them! I was expected to say something.

'In some of the Sanskrit prayers,' I said as I swallowed a lump in my throat, 'Indra is represented as a fair-haired deity. His locks are lightning-enmeshed. His charger is a white horse. He is supposed to be waging a perpetual warfare against Ahi, the demon of dearth. Some of our myths say that Krishna asked his followers not to worship Indra.'

'That will do,' interrupted the Second Master.

'But do you believe in all this?' Kolej Huzoor was insistent. 'If not, then why attend the midnight…'

The Second Master banged the table and upset a brass pot standing on it. He hated being interrogated by his disciples. And Kolej Huzoor was not even a member of his circle: only a casual visitor. Anyway, he avoided answering all questions by turning everyone's attention on me. He was trying, he said, to dissuade the elders of my village from inviting a disreputable priest from Baidyanath. 'Your village folks are a queer lot.' I was reprimanded for the short-comings of my people. 'They believe that if a fellow mumbles something in Sanskrit in the midst of the village square God will do what the villagers want.'

'Why do they need a priest from Baidyanath?' I asked. 'Especially one with a bad name!' A moment later I regretted my intervention. My mentioning the fact that there was the Punditji to perform such ceremonies brought forth an explosion: the Second Master and the Sanskrit scholar were not on very friendly terms.

'Your Punditji!' the Second Master glowered at me, 'He is neither fish nor flesh, but a queer bird with queer views of his own. He has refused to pronounce *mantras* which do not please him. And yet he believes in those old shibboleths. Anyway, he is sick. So your villagers want to get hold of a man from Baidyanath. And what a man! He is said to be buying and selling Santal girls.'

'Buying and selling?'

'Yes,' the Second Master spoke as though this was an everyday event. 'Like chattels. That's what this priest has been doing. But the fault lies with the Santal parents. They are callous. They are leaving their hamlets for the mines where ready cash is easily made. And they are selling their children on the quiet to this priest.'

At this point someone produced the latest issue of the *Kusumpur Sangbad* and said that there was something in it about the famine conditions at Sagra, just beyond the Western Hills.

Certain tracts of the country, more particularly the valleys which formed pockets in the hilly regions, had not received any rain according to this paper, while other parts were getting their

usual monsoon showers. Therefore there was no fear whatsoever
of a general famine. But the conditions at Sagra were terrible:
'Famished mothers, as they lay in the streets unable to walk, have
been seen holding up their infants, and imploring the passing
stranger to take them into slavery, so that they might at least live.
Hundreds were seen creeping into gardens, courtyards, and old
ruins, concealing themselves under shrubs, grass, mats or straw,
where they might die quietly, without having their bodies torn by
birds and beasts before the breath had left them.'

The Second Master interrupted further reading from the
newspaper. This was, of course, a very different picture of the
situation from the one he had painted. What made him so
prejudiced against the Santals? I was distressed. The newspaper
report set my mind working: 'What would *my* villagers do if they
were reduced to the same plight as the Santals at Sagra?'

~

By now quite a few people of the village were convinced that the
drought was due to some evil *mantras*, magic spells, which some
malicious people must have uttered against certain patches of the
Red Valley, the pockets of the hilly regions. Counter-spells were
therefore necessary, and in order to be efficacious these had to be
correctly pronounced.

The elders seemed to be not in the least concerned about the
reputation of the priest at Baidyanath, to whom an invitation
had been sent. They were not interested in his morals, according
to the Goatee, but rather in his knowledge of Sanskrit and his
capacity for uttering faultlessly the counter-*mantras*.

The Goatee's reasoning was simple: 'When you travel by train
do you make a point of finding out if the engine-driver washes
his hands and feet before taking his meals? Do you bother to ask
him if he is a vegetarian or a pork-eater? As a rule, no one even
troubles to find out if he knows how to drive a locomotive: it

is simply taken for granted. Why then make so much fuss over the priest's morals? He is not being asked to marry one of our daughters. All that we need of him is that he should conduct the religious rites correctly. If we have *faith*, our *faith* as well as the *rites* would save us.'

When Kolej Huzoor asked if faith was not enough, the Goatee shook his head and said 'No.'

'I'll give you a wireless set without valves.' The Goatee had a sly glint in his eyes. 'Will you please help me to tune in to Calcutta? If I give you only the valves and ask you to switch on to the Calcutta Broadcasting Corporation, the result would be the same. No response. It is the same with faith. Faith alone will not end the drought. Neither would the rites by themselves. We must have both faith and the rites.' He then gave us a lecture on the Drummer and the Drum: not each of them studied apart would give the slightest information as to the message of the drum-beat.

'*Svalpa vidya*… A little learning is a dangerous thing,' Kolej Huzoor muttered to me as we took leave of the Goatee.

~

Was there a note of suppressed delight in the Second Master's voice when he recounted the progress of the Punditji's sickness?

'He has been swallowing uncooked grated carrots,' the Second Master laughed. 'The result of overdoing his apples and of learning too much Sanskrit: he is now dying. The Punditji will depart unlamented. He won't live long. To whom will he bequeath his staff, Mahendra Chandal, I wonder. If only he had died some thirty years ago when I came over here! The Red Valley would not have been in its present sorry plight.'

Thirty years ago! That was long before I was born. How old was the Punditji? From his looks one would have thought he was in his forties. But we knew he was much older. In the Second

Master's circle they called him *the aged senile*: this, of course, was of little help in guessing his exact age. I asked Mashi-ma what happened thirty years ago in the village.

~

'Some quarrels are never patched up,' Mashi-ma told me. 'That's the curse with many a learned man in this land.'

Some thirty years ago the two pedagogues, the Second Master and the Punditji had a wrangle over gas and electricity and that led to their permanent estrangement.

The people of the Red Valley were then concerned over an offer made by a newly formed Gas and Electricity Supply Company. This Company wanted to serve our area on certain specified conditions, and the villagers gathered under the *peepul* tree to discuss whether they should accept the offer or reject it.

The Second Master though not a resident, was invited. Being born on the same day as Krishna, it was even then assumed that his presence would help the gathering to reach a lucky conclusion, and that was how the trouble started. Unasked, he gave his views: he advocated 'modernization' and the introduction of gas and electricity in every rural home.

The Punditji, as a traditionalist, was bitterly opposed to the Company's project. He thought that the beauty of the countryside would be spoilt by the wire-carrying posts, electricity-girders and gasometers.

'What about your Golah?' the Second Master interrupted him, and made fun of the round structure only a few miles away from the village. 'Does not that old Golah resemble a gasometer? Why don't you get it pulled down to make the countryside more attractive?'

The villagers shuddered. Few ever bothered to visit the Golah and still fewer thought about getting it repaired. Nevertheless, it was their joy and pride: the most memorable building in the

Penhari Parganas. How did anyone dare compare it with a filthy gasometer? The Second Master prejudiced the gathering by this tactless remark. 'Babu Hem Chandra Chahar,' they muttered, 'is the eighth child of his parents. That's all right. But now he is talking arrant nonsense. Krishna the eighth *avatar* of the Great God did the same on certain occasions to try the faith of his devotees.... It's good to have one's God-given horse-sense put to the test.'

'How would our villagers pay for the gas and the electricity consumed?' asked the Punditji. 'Hem! You are a newcomer and perhaps you don't know we can't pay cash. Will the Company accept sacks of flour or bunches of bananas in settlement of the monthly or quarterly bills?'

This made the Second Master roar. Our villagers must do the same as others did elsewhere in civilized countries; they should pay cash and conform to the standard of living in more progressive and forward-looking lands.

The word *civilization* unleashed a storm!

'Civilization?' the Punditji arched his eyebrows and took a pinch of snuff while the villagers nudged each other. Whenever the Sanskrit scholar delivered his knock-out blow in a debate he produced his snuff-box. Did the Second Master know the origin and meaning of the term *civilization*? Perhaps he didn't. Therefore, for his benefit, the Punditji told him that in the language of the Ionians, the *Yavanas*, it implied that which went with *the cities* whereas in Sanskrit, the language of gods, it meant the culture associated with the village councils, the *savas*.

The Goatee was delighted. Though he was not a member of the village Council of Five at that time, I gathered from Mashima, he beamed to hear the village council mentioned and caressed his beard: it was jet black thirty years ago.

'That's neither here nor there,' the Second Master tried to retrieve his position. 'Civilization as it is universally understood to-day means general culture.'

'And you are going to measure this general culture by the consumption of gas and electricity? What amount of gas was consumed by Buddha? How much electricity was turned to produce the *Song of Songs*? Or the *Cloud Messenger*?'

The discussion next veered to the issue whether it would be preferable to adhere to the ways of our forefathers or to follow new-fangled ideas. It was generally agreed that it would be better to live in the same way as the illustrious personalities of the past: Buddha, Kalidasa, Jaya-Deva and others of their calibre. Moreover, the Gas and Electricity Company stipulated cash payment. No villager had much cash to spare.

The Second Master had little to say when the Punditji declared that the habitual use of *powerful* artificial light would weaken the strength of the villagers' eyes and in the long run make it difficult for them to find their way in star-light.

'But rush-light or lamp-light is just as artificial as gas or electricity.' The Second Master tried his best to explain the advantages of modernization. But his tactless remark about the Golah had set the people against him. As far as they were concerned he was completely knocked out the moment the Punditji took his pinch of snuff and asked: 'Tell me, was Buddha as civilized as your smart friends who read detective novels in gas-light, and dance such steps as *black-bottom* or *camel-walk*?'

The Second Master never forgave the Punditji for making fun of his cult of modernization. The old Sanskrit scholar was now dying. The drought occupied everyone's attention. The villagers even forgot that his condition was becoming more and more critical every day.

~

The unreliable clouds continued to sail waywardly over the village as before without shedding a drop of water. As the price of the food and grain soared higher and higher, the villagers became more and more convinced that the rain was being held up by the machinations of a rascally-minded grain merchant. Who was the rascal? If they could only lay their hands on him they would teach him a lesson: the lesson of his life!

There were so many people interested in bringing disaster upon the village, and that made it difficult to fix suspicion on any person in particular. Who was the culprit who was pronouncing *mantras*, magic formulas against our village, as well as a number of others, seven localities in all? Take for example, they mused, the *baniahs*, the vendors of rice, lentils, and other articles of prime necessity. What about the money-lenders, others suggested. And the land-grabbers? Or the traffickers in women and children, the promoters of emigration to Guiana, Guinea, and God-knows-where? And their agents, middlemen and brokers? And what about the Gas and Electricity Supply Company? Some time ago a number of people had surveyed the area and talked about building a dam as high as the hills. Were *they* not interested in ruining the seven villages?

Tchutore and Janardan reached the conclusion that if by some lucky chance they could get hold of the first name of the devil who was trying to destroy us, they would be able to identify him. Ramdas the village *chowkidar* was asked by the elders to keep a sharp look-out day and night.

'It is in the interests of a rogue or of a number of rogues,' Ramdas was told, 'to drive us out of the village of our forefathers. Evidently they want to buy us up, to give the appearance of legality. Report to us if you find a stranger practising any abomination, *maran* or *uchatan* rites within a league of the village.'

'It must be a stranger,' the Goatee added. 'Not one of our people, not even those who have left us for Calcutta would dream of doing harm to this village.'

Gopaldas's uncle, Ramdas, was a decent fellow. But he was as credulous as he was slow. He was the man who first launched the fear about black magic.

In one of his rounds he came across some tiny, human-shaped cakes of wheat-flour and a small toy horse made of clay, painted white. These were found scattered about the flowering cactus bushes at the eastern entrance to the village. It was precisely the spot where a mangy dog had died a day earlier, and its carcass had been collected by Methar the Scavenger during the night. Either Methar had not seen the cakes and the clay horse or, even if he did, he simply forgot to attach any importance to them.

Ramdas's fertile imagination led him to conclude that his discovery proved the village was being put under a spell; and not only that: the man who was pronouncing the *mantras* was named Indra!

~

'Even a madman has his method,' Kolej Huzoor reproached me, 'a sleep-walker his logic.'

I was blamed by everyone in the Second Master's circle for my friendliness to Ramdas. 'Do you know,' they asked me, 'what led your pal Ramdas to conclude that an unknown grain-merchant called Indra has been administering poison in the atmosphere of the Red Valley to drive away the rain-clouds?'

I did not know the answer. But they did.

'Because the toy horse is white and the charger of the mythical god of the sky is also white! It's sheer lunacy to think that because someone has thrown away a few stale cakes and a white toy horse Heaven's ire will descend upon the village.'

My people merited chastisement, they concluded, on account of their credulousness. What prevented their taking to industry? Why had they refused the offer of the Gas and Electricity Supply Company some thirty years ago? What was the reason of their opposition to the dam which would make the Penhari Parganas independent of the monsoon rains?

The answer to all these was—sheer stupidity. What had I to say to that? What steps did I contemplate taking for the education of my people?

'Do you know Ramdas's point of view? He thinks that some *mantras* must have been pronounced while kneading those cakes. Moreover, they must have been also handled in a way which has caused offence to the gods. To throw away good things in times of dearth is a grave sin.'

I mumbled something: Ramdas was my friend, but I was not responsible for his views nor for his logic.

'The tail reveals the fox,' Kolej Huzoor smiled sarcastically. I was advised not to associate with fools who believed that the grain-merchants were interested in such a poverty-stricken area as the Red Valley. 'Who can swallow such nonsense?'

'It isn't quite as simple as that.' The Second Master quite unexpectedly came to my defence! 'Neither is it pure nonsense. Grain-merchants are capable of anything.'

This intervention of the Second Master surprised me. Only much later did it occur to me that once he had had some bother with a rice merchant in Asansole. The exact details I never knew except that the wealthy personality in question wanted to establish a 'Free School' and the Second Master was to be appointed its principal; then something went wrong and he was offered the post of an assistant teacher.

'I should not be surprised,' the Second Master went on, 'to see the merchants banding together for the sole purpose of ruining the country—provided they succeed in making some money. They are in league with the bankers and the industrialists. They are capable of doing anything and everything to promote their own interest.' Not that the merchants believed in the efficacy of magic spells and *mantras*, but, all the same, they employed fakirs, *kapaliks*, the red-robed *sadhus*, and others wearing tiger-skins to frighten the credulous.

That day I heard a number of stories about the depredations

caused by the hired thugs of rich merchants. The Second Master had seen with his own eyes some spirit-filled jars containing dead *Shankha-churas*, Russell's vipers, cobras, and other venomous snakes in the reception room of a Jain merchant. What were those dead snakes? The favourite ones of their master. Why were they preserved? The master wanted to be reminded of the good services they had rendered when alive: the trained snakes were used by that rogue to get rid of his rivals.

I never knew that snakes could be trained in the same way as dogs or *moynas* or monkeys. But there were very many things in the world about which I had little knowledge. Before meeting Para-manik the Fowler I was ignorant of the habits of many so-called wild animals and also the fact that the *baya* finches, the dully brown weaver-birds with bright yellow caps on their heads could be taught to thread bead necklaces and carry messages.

Anyway, I was amazed to hear of the many machinations of the wealthy people known to the Second Master only.

'Ask any of them,' he went on, 'if he would subscribe to my *Life of Cromwell*, the volume on which I have been working for ages?' The glare in his eyes became fierce. 'Ask them to buy a book and you will hear they have no money. They are close-fisted and mean. All the same, they are prepared to pay high fees to unscrupulous scientists. Nothing prevents them from making use of cosmic rays to blight or blast a tract.'

Cromwell was quoted: 'I have no faith in princes,' he said, and the Second Master declared that he had no faith in the Indian princes either. The merchants, bankers, and industrialists were the princes of India. He had no confidence in them. For they were, after all, capable of holding up the monsoon.

Somehow his attitude reminded me of Kolej Huzoor's anger at the word *scraggy*. What did Ramdas think of such people? 'They would be reborn as snakes for their sins.' And that was all.

I had a hang-dog expression, according to Mashi-ma, when I returned home that evening. I do not remember what I looked like, but I was most certainly depressed: about that I have a distinct recollection. I was worried because the young students in the Second Master's house had jeered at me for being friendly with Ramdas and also for my growing interest in Sanskrit literature, and, above all, because of my discovery of irrationality in the Second Master. In what way was he different from the village watchmen when it came to explaining the cause of the drought?

Even if all the grain-merchants bearing the name Indra came forward and swore that they had put the human-shaped cakes and the toy horse by the flowering cactus bushes, would that be the cause of our not getting the monsoon showers?

When I was turning over this matter in my mind, Mashi-ma showed in one of the village elders, reminding me at the same time that my birthday coincided with that of Balaram, the elder brother of Krishna and one of the *avatars* of the Great God. It was a surprise visit as far as I was concerned, but I could do nothing to avoid it.

'The village counts upon your help, Little Son,' the elder declared. I was moved to see him fold his palms in greeting me as though I were his superior. 'You and the Second Master will have to help us. Otherwise we shall perish. We need you for the Ploughing Ceremony.'

What was that?

The details would be explained to me later, I gathered. But meanwhile I was to give my word of honour that I would help the village women… and take part in the Ceremony. As the Second Master had, according to the elder, expressed his willingness to co-operate, there was no justification for my behaving differently. The Ploughing Ceremony was for undoing all magic spells cast on the village and for bringing in the monsoon. I said 'Yes' to the elder, simply to be left in peace. My mood of depression, however, worsened.

~

'Why don't the village matrons go to Dwarka or to Muttra or wherever else they will?' I muttered to myself as I unrolled my reed-mat on the flat roof-terrace of the house. I was getting ready to lie down and sleep: during the summer months when there was no rain I slept on the open terrace.

It was now dark, and the night air was refreshing. It must have rained somewhere within a few miles. The flowering tobacco plants which grew in a row of tubs on the roof-terrace were alive to this slight change of humidity in the air: their fragrance spoke of it. It was like a balm. I stripped myself bare and let every pore of my naked body imbibe the perfumed air and the night's coolness.

I lay down to sleep and closed my eyes. However, my head was too full of thoughts and my brain worked too busily to let in sleep. My reflections centred round the recent remarks made by the Second Master: he claimed to be a rationalist: rationalism was his religion. Yet he was willingly taking part in many local *pujas* and rites. Why did he show malicious pleasure in telling me about the Punditji's sickness?

Usually I brought out on to the roof-terrace, along with my mat, a few books and an earthenware lamp: it was especially made for me by Kumar the Potter to allow me to use it as a dark lantern and a reading lamp. I loved reading in bed at night-time, sprawling on my stomach, my back turned to the star-strewn sky and my legs fondling the hard cylindrical bolster *pash-balish*, which some call 'the Dutch wife'.

'Let the matrons go to the devil and get Balaram's present address,' I mumbled to myself. 'Balaram is dead as a door nail. What do the village cronies want of him? His demise took place ages ago: millions of years ago, if I were to give credence, to the Sanskrit epics and to the statements of Kathak the Storyteller.'

I went on grumbling in this way for I do not remember how long.

~

Balaram's soul, they say, left his body in the shape of a myriad-headed snake and sought refuge in the depths of the unfathomable ocean. It was a white snake, just as Indra's charger was white.

What made the Sanskrit authors furnish the minutest detail about the heroes of myths and ignore the heroes of history? Why were they so fond of legends? A myth, according to the Punditji, impels men to action regardless of the limits of apparent truth! If that be so, to what action will Balaram's story lead the villagers?

Balaram is considered to be the seventh incarnation or *avatar* of the Great God.

Immediately after his birth he had to be carried away to Gokula and hidden in a cow-shed to preserve him from the wrath of a bloodthirsty tyrant. This monster, named Kansa, was bent on massacring all newborn infants because some wise man had foolishly divulged to him that his reign was nearly at an end: 'And a little child shall lead us all.'

Though an incarnation of the Great God, what pranks and tricks did Balaram not play! His earliest exploit as a tiny boy was the destruction of a mighty demon called Dhenuka. He was picking fruit in an orchard belonging to this demon and it was not at all surprising that Dhenuka decided to give the young intruder a thrashing. Being a demon Dhenuka could take any shape at will, and chose the guise of a donkey to kick Balaram. The juvenile incarnation of the Great God, however, seized the demon-donkey by his hind legs and whirled him round till he was dead. The carcass was then thrown on to the top of a palmyra palm. Dhenuka's servitors ran to their master's rescue only to receive similar chastisement at the hands of boy Balaram. The palm-trees became all laden with dead asses.

Balaram's next heroic feat was equally unbelievable. There was a dearth of holy shrines in the dominion of the demons, and a particularly bold fiend wanted to endow it with one. He took the form of an athlete and proposed to give the divine child Balaram a lift on his shoulders, though, in fact, his intention was to kidnap the boy and carry him off to the demon-land. The ravisher's intentions were guessed and his brains beaten out.

This particular adventure of Balaram somehow appealed to Mabool the Tanner. Mabool was the friend and associate of Methar the Scavenger and was known as a pious Moslem. 'In the north country,' Mabool told me, 'a man with the name of Sayyed runs the risk of being murdered by its Moslem inhabitants—simply because there are no holy sepulchres over there. They build a shrine over the murdered Sayyed's grave and honour the murderer by burying him alive for the crime of having raised his hand against a holy man.' This seemed to me a most horrible custom and I told Mabool what I thought of it. He, however, had a curious argument to justify the crime: 'The assassin lays down his own life to secure a shrine for his people. You can't blame him. It is blessed to sacrifice oneself for a holy cause.'

Anyway, to come back to the legends of Balaram: the demon who tried to kidnap the holy child considered himself extremely fortunate when he found that the boy was stronger than he. Death at Balaram's hands, I was told, assured him paradise!

Once in a state of inebriety, Balaram expressed the wish that the river Jumna should come to him so that he could bathe at the spot where he was carousing. As his injunction was not immediately obeyed, he plunged his weapon, a ploughshare, into the river and dragged its waters wherever he went till the river besought his forgiveness.

Later on Balaram bequeathed his weapon to the sky and it became the constellation known as the Plough. He had many names and attributes: one of these was *Madhu-priya*, a winebibber.

~

My mind lingered over the word *Madhu-priya* and the chain of my thoughts was broken.

There is a beautiful formula of benediction in Sanskrit which begins with *Madhu*. *Madhu* in that context means ambrosia. In popular belief *Madhu-priya* is considered to be a drunkard or a winebibber. But with equal justice the same word might be translated into a lover of ambrosia or one fond of goodness.

'Balaram's epithet of drunkard,' I wondered, 'might be due to a misinterpretation of the term *Madhu-priya*.' Those getting drunk on palm-toddy are called asses as well as demons: this potion temporarily gives demoniacal strength and renders a man stupid like an ass.... He loaded the palm-trees with the carcasses of donkeys, dead demons. 'Was there any hidden meaning in all this?'

~

Suddenly a dog started barking furiously, and brought the stream of my speculations and half-awake mutterings to an end. A second dog joined in with greater frenzy.

What was the reason of this strange duet? In summer time our dogs were not given to barking. Heat made them languid. It was a moonless night so far. Was there a tardy red moon rising somewhere behind the palm-groves or by the Blue Hills? I never knew where to look for the moon when it rose late. The dogs were perhaps barking at the moon, I thought. Or was there a stranger coming to our village?

I got up and walked to the balustraded end of the roof to peep down below. There was nothing to be seen. Not a thing stirred. What irritated the dogs? Was there by any chance a new comet on the horizon? Like their masters, our rural domestic animals hated unexpected luminaries. I looked overhead: there were only stars. Sirius, known as the Dog of the Dread Hunter, was as usual the brightest in the firmament. However, there seemed to be something wrong with it. I rubbed my eyes: its hue appeared to be changed.

I never liked gazing at the stars. Somehow they distracted me too much with their beckonings to the farthest corners of the universe. They made me ask: 'What is man in this limitless stellar system?' The obvious answer was, according to me, just mere microscopic particles: insignificant trifles. Why then should the nebular world be affected if man ceased to exist on the globe? What did it matter to the starry host if the sun burnt up a small conglomeration of men in an insignificant corner of the earth, the inhabitants of the Red Valley? Was the Creator primarily interested in the welfare of my village and its human beings? What right had man to the Creator's bounty any more than other beings, visible and invisible? I could go on asking myself such questions for hours without finding any satisfactory answers. That was precisely why I preferred lying on my stomach every evening and burying my nose in my books, turning my back to the stars.

That night, however, my gaze was fixed unwittingly on the Dog Star and I noticed a modification in its usual tint.

What made my favourite star Sirius change its colour? Or was it just my imagination?

'What about the other stars?' I asked myself. 'The Dread Hunter and the other constellations? Lyra with the burning Vega? Arundhuti or the Pleiades? The Plough? The Mighty Weapon with which Balaram drew the waters and which was left as his legacy to the universe?'

Was I dreaming or was I awake? I felt dizzy and closed my eyes and sank on my knees.

The barking of the dogs increased. At first there was only one, and then there were just two. By now, however, all the dogs of the village were howling ferociously: they seemed to be mad with rage. Or was it with fright?

When I opened my eyes again to make sure that I was not dreaming, the cause of the incredible clamour was perfectly clear. Not only Sirius but all the stars had, one by one, altered their usual coloration: their glow too was affected with the change of their tint. 'But the dogs, are they barking at this unknown spectacle of red constellations? What would happen if a stranger strayed into the village just now?'

I covered my face with my hands and on bended knee prayed. 'Let no one,' I asked fervently, 'witness this frightening transformation of astral illumination.' I pitied the outsider who might unwittingly have strayed into our village. He was bound to be accused of casting magic spells to change the colour of the stars and of bewitching the skies to drive away the rain-clouds. The drought had changed our villagers, generally peaceful and witty, into dour and cruel beings. They were credulous at all times, but just then they were more so.

I recalled Mabool the Moslem's justification of those who murdered the Sayyeds in the north country. Only a few hours earlier the village elder told Mashi-ma: 'If any stranger is found practising abomination within a league of our village, a stout noose will be put round his neck. He will be hanged like a mad dog.' This threat was announced in a quiet tone, a tone that carried conviction: there was not the slightest doubt about it being executed on the slenderest pretext.

'Let no man be hanged within the precincts of this village, O Creator!' I prayed, stretching myself full length on my face, like the pilgrims in the temple at Deoghar, in the *shastanga* posture of devotion. 'Let no one be treated as a mad dog in *this* village. Let not *my* village be tainted with any act of cruelty.'

I repeated the same formula, I do not know how often.

My prayers, I must admit, were not in conformity with the rationalist teachings of the Second Master. 'I never pray,' he told me as well as his other admirers. 'As a rationalist, I think it stupid for any man to offer prayers to God. If God existed and if he happened to be responsible for the working of the universe, he ought to know his business. He should not change his programme just to suit the convenience of a praying dunce.

Imagine his heeding all the pleas the credulous idiots utter in their distress all over the world. I hope none of you will ever commit the idiotic blasphemy of asking for divine succour.'

In this matter, the Punditji, who was poles apart from the Second Master, held views not very dissimilar. True, he was never opposed to prayers and supplications to the Great God. On the contrary, never a day passed without his reciting religious hymns at sunrise and at sunset and at the time of meals. But the underlying principle he enunciated was much the same as the Second Master's. 'The universe is the Lord's,' the Punditji expounded. 'He needs no instructions from you or me. A prayer for a favour is indirectly an injunction. Yet I pray to gain strength. My daily *pujas*, prayers and rites are a necessity for me.'

Therefore, from either point of view my prayers did not make much sense. Nevertheless, I prayed, bearing in mind Mashi-ma's counsel: 'Whatever we ask for with meek reverence and due humility will be accorded to us when we make ourselves worthy of the blessings we seek.' 'But very often,' according to Mashi-ma, 'we find out that we have asked for the wrong things. Then it is too late.' Was there anything wrong in my making the supplication, 'Let no iniquity be committed in *my* village?'

When I rose to my feet it was early dawn. In the suffused coral light of the yet unrisen sun the stars were fading fast, and the sky was changing from turquoise into aquamarine.

X

The sultriness increased. It became hotter and closer and more oppressive. The air panted and vibrated, forgetting to blow and waft. It simply wallowed in the dusty bowl of which the village was the centre. Finally it refused to stir.

The sky scintillated fire during the day, and at nightfall it drew a pall of purple which gradually changed into sacrophagal porphyry—incrusted with ruby, garnet, and carnelian luminaries:

so different from the familiar silver stars of our peacock blue firmament. A wonderment never witnessed before. It was awe-inspiring, portentous and dreadful.

Was the end of the world at hand? Or was it only our area that was to be eradicated? No one dared ask the question and no one proffered any reply. In silence men stared at each other and gloomily read one another's thoughts. They spoke in signs. The children stopped laughing and crying. The dogs ceased to frisk and bark. The crickets in the cactus bushes no longer danced and chirped. And even the purple sun-birds, usually so gay and playful, became languid, and brooded morosely in the shade of the stilled thickets.

This ominous silence was terrifying.

~

While arranging the flowering tobacco plants on the roof of the house, I noticed a thin pencil of smoke rising from behind the palm-groves in the direction of the Golah and the Santal village of Mahisha-ban. What was it? A smoke signal! Who was giving it and why?

It was as yet too early to disturb anyone, so I decided to investigate the matter myself. Near the cactus hedges, however, I ran into Ramdas our watchman. 'You can't leave the village to-day,' he told me and was very firm about it. 'Why ever not?' I asked indignantly. 'Why can't I go to Mahisha-ban or to the Golah? Or wherever else it pleases me?' Ramdas gloomily confided that he had his instructions to detain me. I was too surprised to argue. Why should the elders issue this mysterious order?

'Because you may run away, Little Son!' Ramdas spoke in his usual rambling way, and it took me a long while to gather that the auspicious days were not very many: the calendar-makers, augurs and astrologers evidently had a grudge against the human race and that was why they put in so few propitious combinations of stars. If I did not believe him I was at liberty to get the Punditji's opinion: his cottage was near-by. He would certainly confirm this statement and assure me that the Ploughing Ceremony in honour of the god Balaram could not be undertaken on any and every night: 'Better the day, better the deed.'

That was the first intimation I received that the Ceremony was to be celebrated at the end of the day. It was a strange way of imparting the news to me. But there was no point in blaming Ramdas: he was honest and zealous. He was carrying out the duty entrusted to him.

'The Punditji has become very weak.' Ramdas had tears in his eyes. He venerated the aged scholar and regarded him as a holy man, a real *sadhu*. 'He may pass away any moment. Yet he is always up at early dawn to salute Arundhuti, the Morning Star. Why don't you call on him, Little Son?'

As there was no chance for me to verify the cause of the smoke signal I decided to do as Ramdas suggested and walked into the Punditji's cottage to pay my respects to him. There was no need to knock. He never barred his doors nor kept anything under lock and key. 'If I am destined to lose anything,' his reasoning told him, 'I shall lose it. Whether it is kept under lock and key matters little.'

~

'He is failing fast,' Ramdas told me, and I found him much worse than I expected. The poor Punditji! He looked like a skeleton. The man who in spite of his great age never seemed older than the Second Master was now like a shrivelled up mummy. His skin was dried lemon rind and his body nothing but bones. Yet he sat on his wooden divan, bolt upright in the *virasana* posture: the sitting attitude of the saints and warriors in our statuary, with both legs crossed, the right foot above the left thigh, and the left foot placed similarly above the right thigh.

The image of the meditating Buddha is always carved, I was told by Kumar the Potter, in this *virasana* pose; so too are the figures of sages and monarchs granting audience. The *virasana* attitude probably added to their dignity or aided them to concentrate their thoughts. But it is certainly not relaxing. Why did the Punditji sit in that uncomfortable posture instead of lying down and reposing? Was not sitting on the hard mattressless divan trying for a sick man?

I asked him if he was doing anything to combat his sickness. It had certainly lasted a long while and it was high time to consult a doctor.

'Sickness, my son,' he interrupted as he smiled feebly, 'sickness is due to the mind. When the mind is distressed the body becomes diseased. What remedy can a medical practitioner offer me? I know what is wrong with me.'

If that was so, I said to myself, why was he not putting his mind right? 'Take a wolf by its ears and a fox by its tail,' the Second Master advised his disciples. 'Catch a word-chopper by his words. Those who revel in Sanskrit are great in weaving phrases: fallacious arguments. Use their own arguments against them.' Here was the opportunity of proving my mettle. I shuffled my feet nervously and went ahead:

Was not the Punditji the very man who told everyone that the prime purpose of every living being was to live—to live abundantly and joyously? What put him in a hopeless frame of mind? Or did he think like the rest of the villagers that the end of the world was at hand? All on account of the drought? This drought, I was sure, could not be the first of its kind nor the last—unless the project of the great dam was carried out.

He shook his head and smiled. He hoped he would never live to see the dam finished: it would be such a calamity: the villagers would be forced to change their way of living! 'Our parents tasted sour grapes,' he said, 'and our teeth are on edge! If we swallow poison now, our children will all be stillborn. No. No dam for me nor for my people. Plant trees and reforest our dwindling jungles and the Red Valley will smile once again. Give the people back their forests and they will do without the dam.'

According to him, a sudden and radical change in our traditional way of living would bring about a disintegration of our moral and spiritual life. He would, therefore, have nothing to do with the projects of modernizing the Red Valley.

There was something pathetic about this dying man: he seemed to be more concerned with the Red Valley and its future than with his own sickness. The quiet heroism of this stoic appealed to me. He never complained.

He was the man of whom every one of my villagers was proud. No other place within a hundred miles could boast of a Brahmin so well versed in Sanskrit as our Punditji. Everyone knew it for a fact that when the principalship of the Vardaman *tol*, the institute for traditional learning, fell vacant the Trustees begged him to accept the post. But he would not have it: because he wanted to spend his last days in his native place, our village. Similar offers from Nadia, Katwa, and Kalna were declined from the same motive. For his living he conducted *puias*, religious ceremonies and rites for the villagers. Whatever he received as gifts for his *dakshina*, his fee, he gave away to others! How did he manage to subsist? Only on the fruit and vegetables which grew in his own backyard. He lived by himself; he had lost his wife and children ages ago. Only Ramdas and his wife were allowed to look after his cottage during his absence on pilgrimage to distant shrines.

Whatever the Second Master's personal feelings might have been, the villagers were justified in feeling proud of the Punditji. Not only was he a great Sanskrit scholar but he was equally good at many foreign languages. He mastered them sufficiently well to produce a Sanskrit translation of Gray's Elegy, a Bengali version of Hugo's *Les Misérables*, a Hindi commentary on philosophy, and the Diotima of that Greek whom Mabool called Al-Platoun the Broad-shouldered. Not many villages could boast of such a savant in their midst.

Yet what made them indifferent towards him now that he was very sick? It was simply scandalous the way they lost their heads on account of the drought, the comet, the strange coloration of the stars, the human-shaped cakes by the cactus bush, the toy horse. What was the meaning of their leaving him unattended in his last days?

Perhaps the inattention of the villagers, I thought, distressed him and that was why he wanted to die and refused to have any medicaments. What good would he do by dying? Then there flashed into my mind something I had heard long ago and I trembled with fear and rage.

'When a calamity occurs,' according to Mabool, 'a sacrifice has to be made to the unseen powers to avert greater disaster. The more serious the catastrophe, the more precious should be the object of sacrifice.' It was like something Padre Johan had said in one of his sermons: 'Abraham's Sacrifice'. The Yihudis too believed in making such an offer, only they selected a goat to replace a human being. Were the villagers bent on making a scapegoat of the Punditji? The apprehension made my hair stand on end. 'It is wicked,' I muttered almost audibly. 'It is ghastly.' They loved and admired the Punditji; he was the object of their greatest affection, and they wanted to sacrifice him in order to appease the gods and the demons. 'I won't let them do that,' I swore to myself. To make the oath more binding I repeated three times, 'I won't! I won't! I won't!' and touched the earth with the tip of my fingers in the same way as Buddha had asked the earth to bear him witness.

Without my knowing my eyes became filled with tears of indignation. I felt like falling at the Punditji's feet and crying: 'Don't die! Punditji! Don't die! I don't want you to die! It would be a sin. Let not the villagers commit this grave iniquity.' However, I checked myself and told him of a doctor known

to Mashi-ma: he lived in Giridih and had a car and a number
of letters after his name, V.L.V.M.S., Vernacular Licentiate in
Veterinary Medicine and Surgery, and V.L.M.S. His reputation
was so great that he was consulted not only by sick people but
also by the priests when any of the holy cows attached to the
temple in Deoghar fell ill.

The Punditji did not say much: he simply declared that he
was not pious enough to profit from such a doctor.

'All right!' I said. 'I shall consult Mashi-ma and bring someone
else. Only I can't go out of the village to-day on account of the
Ploughing Ceremony. They won't let me stir out of the village.' I
told him of the pencil of smoke I had seen from the roof of my
home.

Involuntarily a groan issued from his lips as though he was in
pain. Did I tire him with my babbling?

'No. No. My son!' he assured me. 'I am happy to have you
here. In fact, I have been waiting for you all these days without
knowing when you would come. Only, the villagers could have
spared themselves the sin of burning down a hamlet. The
Ploughing Ceremony by itself would have been enough. This
holocaust is a crime against God and man.'

To what holocaust was he referring? I did not dare to interrupt
him.

'The demons have cast a spell over my people,' he continued.
'Why have they abandoned the project of a scapegoat? That too
would have been enough. It would have been less cruel.'

All this was pure puzzle to me. Anyway, to change the subject
I told him that I was born on the same day as Balaram, and the
Second Master on Krishna's birthday: hence both of us were to
participate in the Ceremony. It was perhaps silly of me to refer to
the Second Master: for the moment his name was mentioned the
Punditji grasped his brass-bound blackthorn staff. It was lying
by his side.

'Hem Chandra need not have accepted this invitation. He

is a man of little faith. What business has he to be with the believers?'

I remained quiet.

'Do you know what Balaram did?'

This question put me at my ease. Balaram did so many things, and I wondered what particular exploits of the god the Punditji had in mind.

'The story of his success with his toy plough when he was only a boy? You ought to hear about his Ploughing Ceremony.'

~

An unusually hot summer once reduced the river Jumna to a thin thread of water, and that was the time when the tyrant Kansa decided to throw a dam across the river and divert its course to ruin the inhabitants of Brinda-ban: he wanted to subdue them but they were unwilling to accept his sway.

The dearth of water constrained the people of Brinda-ban to send their cattle away to the pastures of their friends at Dwarka, many leagues away. This news pleased Kansa.

'While the men are away with their cattle their women remain undefended,' Kansa said to himself. 'I will send my mercenaries to Brinda-ban now and in the dead of the night they will burn down the town and humiliate its proud matrons.'

The tyrant's project was partially carried out. The women of Brinda-ban had just time to run out of their burning houses snatching their sleeping babies with them. They had no opportunity to dress nor to save any of their belongings. Under the cover of darkness they sought shelter in the mango groves near the ploughing fields.

'What shall we do when the day dawns?' they sobbed. 'Who will protect us? Who will clothe us?'

'Will you help me to pull my plough?' asked a little boy. 'I want to plough the fields round about here. In the morning when

Kansa sees the furrows he will think that our men have not only been back, but have already been at work and getting ready to wreak vengeance on him.'

The boy's proposal was accepted and his surmise proved to be correct. Even Indra the god of the rain-clouds was so pleased with his pluck that he rewarded Brinda-ban with abundant showers, which broke Kansa's dam.

~

'Balaram was the little boy who guided the plough while the women pulled it and Krishna, Balaram's half-brother, played on the flute to beguile the hours of trial and travail.'

Did the Punditji take the story of Balaram and his ploughing ceremony seriously? It was useless to put the question to him; I knew the answer. 'Whoever studies Sanskrit,' the Second Master told me, 'loses his sense of proportion and diminishes his reasoning power. Mythology and history become one and the same to him.' And this was one of the many reasons for the perpetual feud between him and the Punditji.

'History,' according to the Punditji, 'is not a catalogue of the names and dates of rulers, prime ministers, generals, wars and battles. Nor is it a bare statement of facts about the varying prices of food-grains, land-taxes, salt-revenues, and excise duties. History is not mere chronology. It is the story of man's endeavours to find the Absolute, his God: the account of his aspirations and achievements. And what could be a better revelation of this than his mythology? Myths tell more than bare facts. Men would die for their favourite myths, but not for bare facts and imposing statistics.'

However, I was tempted to ask him timidly if it would do the village matrons any good if they ploughed the fields.

'Don't they want a cloud-burst?' the Punditji interrupted me impatiently.

'But will they get any by simply repeating a ceremony performed aeons ago?'

'Of course they will.' He spoke as though he was making a matter-of-fact statement! As an after-thought he added, 'Provided they manifest their faith and no evil beings produce contradictory thought-currents in their midst.'

The Punditji's assertions were clear-cut: indigo dyes blue, red madder is for scarlet, fire burns, water quenches. Only at one's own risk and peril would one challenge such a statement coming from him.

'Whatever you ask,' he affirmed, 'you will get. Provided you know how to ask for a blessing. That's why it is important to master the art of thinking correctly.'

I remained speechless.

'Now if you find anyone at the Ploughing Ceremony showing the least sign of disbelief, just use this stick.' He got hold of his blackthorn staff and dug it playfully into my stomach. 'Beat up an unbeliever mercilessly and chase the creature away from the field. Such a vile being has no business to be with the others on a holy occasion like this. Thrash with my staff anyone who dares to express the least doubt in the efficacy of the Ploughing Ceremony once it has started. Bring it back to me to-morrow and tell me all about what you have seen.'

I took leave of the Punditji, saluting him for the first time in the traditional way, as a disciple should bow to his *guru*. I joined my open palms together, bent my knees, and bowed my head till it touched the ground in front of his divan. He gave me his blessings and asked grace that I might be a second Balaram.

Of course, I was glad to take with me his brass-bound blackthorn staff: it was a historic stick with a name of its own: Mahendra Chandal. I forgot all about the Second Master's advice regarding *pranams*: 'Never bow in the traditional way: it is abject, degrading, undemocratic.'

XI

To be truthful, when I took leave of the Punditji I did not pay much attention to his remarks about beating up all the doubters with his heavy staff. I was a doubter myself and so was my then hero, the Second Master, whose rationalism appealed to me more than the mystic theories of the Sanskrit scholar.

What occupied my mind just then was the brass-bound blackthorn staff itself. I was going to have it with me for the Ploughing Ceremony: the idea thrilled me. I had coveted it for years: it was an imposing rod, taller than I, nice and smooth, pleasanter to feel than any Malacca cane or ivory baton or ebony stick or knotless bamboo. It was the only one of its kind as far as I knew: a blackthorn staff with a name of its own: Mahendra Chandal.

Many were the legends attached to it. Pocha's father affirmed that it was at least three hundred years old, while Tchutore the Carpenter asserted that it dated from the time when Buddha visited the Penhari Parganas to bless our hills and valleys and leave his footprints on a stone slab facing the Badri-nath temple on the Saffron Crag. Tchutore's reckoning made Mahendra Chandal about two thousand five hundred years old. Up till then I had not seen any small object as ancient as that and therefore I was inclined to give more credence to what Pocha's father said. 'Three hundred years,' I calculated, 'implied that the Punditji's staff was older than the Golah.'

Mukund Deo, the last independent monarch of Orissa, built a splendid *ghat*, a beautiful flight of stone steps along the banks of the sacred Ganges at Tribeni, the north-west limit of his dominions. There he set up a *tol*, a seat of Sanskrit learning, to rival the three famous *samajs* of Nadia, Shanti-pur and Gupti-para, renowned throughout the centuries for their erudite Pundits. For his *tol*, Raja Mukund Deo wanted someone whose reputation would surpass that of all other Sanskrit scholars of his age and he was told that whoever had 'Mahendra Chandal' as his staff was the man for him. For this blackthorn rod even in those far off days was famous. It was always handed over from one distinguished master to another and had never fallen into the hands of an unworthy disciple.

To come to more modern times, Pocha's father knew that Pundit Rudra-dev Vattacharji of Tribeni had received this staff as a legacy from a Manipuri Baba, and he gave it to his son when he handed over to him the charge of the *tol* of Tribeni. Rudra-dev's son was no other than Jagannath Tarka-Panchanan who, as has already been stated, taught till he was two hundred years old and handed on the staff to our Punditji. It was difficult to guess the Punditji's age from his looks. A rough reckoning could, however, be made from a number of well-ascertained dates; the Punditji met Macaulay in the house of Prince Dwarka Nath Tagore, and Taranath Tarka-Vachas-pati of Kalna was a few years junior to him. All this goes to show that the blackthorn staff, Mahendra Chandal, could undoubtedly claim a pedigree of great masters for over three hundred years.

Apart from its age, and its associations with illustrious scholars, this smooth knotless staff had other attractions. It was said to be a divining rod, extremely useful for locating *baolis*, hidden wells, and underground springs, as well as a formidable weapon for combating *Bhoots* and *Mamdo-Bhoots*, gnomes, demons, and evil spirits.

~

One may well wonder what the difference is between a *Bhoot* and a *Mamdo-Bhoot*.

'To the ignorant, they are one and the same,' Pocha's father confided to Bum-boatee the Pirate, Sashe Raha, nicknamed the Split Cucumber, myself and several others on the evening of the Diwali festivity when Pocha ran the risk of being gored to death by an enraged buffalo. 'To the ill-informed,' he continued, 'the *Bhoots*, the unfortunate gnomes, are the same as the *Mamdo-Bhoots*, the malicious devils. But there is a lot of difference between these two sets of disembodied spectres. The *Bhoots* are simple gnomes and are not very dangerous: they are the spirits of those whose desires have remained unfulfilled. They greet you in the dark and if you do not respond to their solicitations nor follow their beckonings, they leave you in peace, mumbling a nasal greeting, "All right! Till we meet again." The matter ends there. A *Bhoot's* reasoning is simple: if a man does not want anything to do with it, there is no use badgering him.

'With a *Mamdo-Bhoot*, however, it is an altogether different proposition. Those whose passions have not been satisfied are transformed into *Mamdo-Bhoots*, malevolent devils. A *Mamdo-Bhoot* will go on pestering you till it breaks down your resistance. If you ever return its greetings you will never be able to shake it off. And if you ignore its salutations you are no better off. It will quarrel with you, accusing you of ill manners! A malicious *Mamdo-Bhoot* will challenge you to wrestle with it. It knows well that no man worth his salt will ever refuse such a challenge in the Penhari Parganas. But then, who can ever wrestle with a phantom—especially when its main object is to make you fall by fair means or foul, more often by foul means than otherwise. It can't do you much harm as long as you are on your feet. But once you have been floored you are finished. It will squeeze your guts out. You may take the name of your *guru*, but you will take it in vain: he won't hear it and therefore will not come to your succour. The *Mamdo-Bhoot* will squat on your stomach and press hard till filth comes out of both your ends. Be careful, therefore, not to tumble in the dark as Pocha did this evening.

'The Diwali night is particularly propitious for ghosts and ghouls who wish to torment innocent mortals.'

Pocha's father laboured under the impression that his son's

accident was due to a *Mamdo-Bhoot*'s malice and that it took the form of a buffalo to torment him. I had not the heart to tell him that Pocha the Huntsman had thrown a packet of lighted Chinese crackers in the midst of some sleeping buffaloes and frightened them out of their wits. The herd-leader naturally charged him with all fury. Pocha's escape was almost miraculous. Our buffaloes have little liking for Chinese crackers, Bengal lights, and Roman candles—the very things the youngsters love to burn on the night of the Diwali.

To come back to the story of the staff called Mahendra Chandal, the great jurist and scholar Jagannath Tarka-Panchanan was once passing through a jungle all by himself on a Diwali night. It was imprudent of him to undertake such a journey all alone without even a hurricane lantern. The jungle in question was reputed to be infested with venomous snakes and such strange creatures as the flying-foxes, blood-sucking vampires, fire-breathing jackals, talking hyenas, man-eating tigers, and were-wolves, as well as with *Bhoots* and *Mamdo-Bhoots*.

In spite of his great scholarship—or because of it, Pocha's father was not quite sure—Jagannath Tarka-Panchanan was somewhat stiff-necked and hot-headed. Though advised to wait till dawn as no palanquin-bearers were to be had for the late night journey, he continued his wayfaring without paying much heed to his well-wishers and admirers. 'The people on the other side of the jungle urgently want my legal opinion,' he said. 'The question of the succession will have to be settled before dawn. I can't let good people down. If no palanquin-bearers are to be had nor any torch-bearers, I shall do the journey on foot. Though I am in my nineties I am not decrepit. For company, I have my faithful friend and servitor, the blackthorn staff, Mahendra Chandal. What more do I want?'

'A solitary man,' Pocha's father continued, 'rarely realizes the fulness of his strength. Though solitude is necessary for training one's own self, perpetual solitude is a corrosive. It saps one's strength and provokes gall, it renders a man sad and sadness is no good: it infects the atmosphere and affects others.

'The strength of the strong grows by measuring it against a worthy companion, or a conscientious rival, or a meritorious disciple. You can't ask your rival to keep you company. Nor can you allow your disciple to accompany you on a perilous journey. As for worthy companions, they are not to be had easily. Krishna was constrained to choose the flute as his constant comrade and Narada the great sage had to rely on his lute, and many a prophet depends on his staff.

'A diadem enhances the kingliness of a king, and a baton a marshal's authority. So too does a staff add to a prophet's dignity. Without his companion, the blackthorn staff, Jagannath Tarka-Panchanan would have been a lesser man: not in erudition or courage, but in strength.'

~

During that memorable night journey the blackthorn staff, Mahendra Chandal, proved itself worthy of its master in a strange way: it demonstrated its right to be the journey-mate of the greatest Sanskrit scholar and jurist of the age.

'It is never easy to pass through a jungle,' Pocha's father said. I felt like adding, 'You needn't tell *me* that!' but I held my peace and let him have his say, though I knew his first-hand acquaintance with dense jungles was limited. 'Even in day-time it is no pastime to cross a jungle, let alone the dangers of a night journey. It is never easy to find one's path. Too often one hits upon what seem cross-ways or bifurcations and one is never sure which way is right. The temptation to take short-cuts is as great as it is dangerous: that is the readiest means of getting lost. Moreover, one comes across many fallen branches of trees and thick bamboos lying astride the beaten track. What would one then do?'

'Just straddle the obstacles,' burst out Sashe Raha, nicknamed the Split Cucumber, and made everyone laugh.

'The moment your feet are astride the obstacle,' Pocha's father explained, 'you are liable to find out your error. And that would be too late! For the fallen branch or the low-lying bamboo will suddenly spring back and become bolt upright, flinging you into a hole fifty yards away, proving in this way that you have been trying to straddle a *Mamdo-Bhoot* in disguise!'

'I should just lift the obstacle and pass under it,' Bum-boatee the Pirate spoke as though he knew all about the strange things in a forest. 'It is silly,' he added, 'to jump in the dark.'

'Even then,' Pocha's father said, 'you are no better off. If you are quick with your jumping you may get away with it. But not if you put yourself underneath the stumbling-block. The moment you are under it you will find the obstacle's weight increase a thousandfold. The *Mamdo-Bhoot* will simply crush you and keep your body pinned to the ground till your filth is forced out of you. Here again you will make your discovery when it is too late.

'Being filthy spirits themselves, the *Mamdo-Bhoots* are always anxious to drive out all filth from others.'

When Jagannath Tarka-Panchanan traversed the jungle he found his path barred by many such stumbling-blocks, dangerous *Mamdo-Bhoots* in disguise. They, however, failed to interfere with his journey, thanks to the vigilance of the scholar's boon companion and faithful servitor, the brass-bound blackthorn staff, Mahendra Chandal. It rose from Tarka-Panchanan's hand of its own accord to hit hard and shatter dormant encumbrances.

~

A highwayman called Raghunath once got hold of this staff by stealth. But he could not keep it. Mahendra Chandal returned to its legitimate master after having dealt some fearful blows to the managers of two powerful companies which were exploiting the coal-bearing areas near Pushpa-pur about one hundred and fifty years ago: the Bangla Kutir Coal and the Equitable Koyla Company. These two trusts were, they say, in the wrong and that was why Mahendra Chandal allowed itself to be wielded by a highwayman, the lesser villain in that particular contest.

Mahendra Chandal's exploits and adventures were many. It would be untrue to say that I accepted all of them as authentic. But whether real or fictitious, they were thrilling, and made Mahendra Chandal all the more esteemed. I considered it a prize of invaluable worth.

Mashi-ma told me that even the smallest article handled by a great man or a saint retained something of the owner's personality and was capable of communicating his message to others. The Second Master pooh-poohed this theory; however, he had had a very bad night as a result of his disputation with my aunt and accepting her bet!

'Go and sleep inside the Golah one night,' Mashi-ma challenged the Second Master. 'But don't forget to come back and tell me about your dreams! The Golah retains the dust of the feet of the Jung Bahadur Shumshere Jogendra Malla Rana. It contains also the dried blood-clots of the Vargis, Pindaris, and Pathans.'

The Second Master did spend a night in the Golah, but he forgot to recount his dreams.

'I know what they were,' Mashi-ma smiled triumphantly. 'Always the same dreams have been dreamt in the Golah, ever since the day the good Jung Bahadur lured the Vargis to their destruction in that spot. It is the spirit of the place that affects the credulous as well as the incredulous.'

The Second Master neither affirmed nor denied Mashi-ma's contention after his night's experience at the Golah: so there must have been some truth in what Mashi-ma said. I knew the Golah well, but it was not possible for me to slip out at night-time to sleep there.

'The Punditji's staff is no ordinary staff.' My aunt knew more about it than she cared to tell me. 'It is called Mahendra Chandal. If ever you go to the Cradle of the Clouds carrying it with you the holy men there will greet you as a brother. Only the fortunate are allowed to touch it. It's a privilege to hold it in one's hand for an hour.'

Was I not proud to have such a staff with me? For full twenty-four hours!

XII

Ramdas the village watchman took no chances. He told me so, rather grimly. I found him waiting patiently for me just outside the Punditji's cottage. Did he really think that I would run away from the village?

'You never can tell,' he mumbled.

What made him so gloomy? Often his face wore an expression of perfect vacuity: that was a bad sign. It told of his utter defeat in domestic debates and quarrels. The Second Master made fun of our *chowkidar*, 'The more trying his ordeal at home the more expressionless is Ramdas's face. Such a face is an asset.' According to the would-be biographer of Cromwell, the *topiwallahs* would have done well to select Ramdas for a diplomatic post abroad! 'He would make a success of his job,' the Second Master chuckled. 'But his wife must be retained here. She has too much energy and brains. She won't do for the *topiwallahs*. She is a marvellous pastry-cook too.' Whoever loved sweetmeats had nothing but praise for Ramdas's wife, while they made fun of him. This was enough to make any man morose.

'What's the trouble, Ramdas?' I asked, and had to wait for some time before I got any answer, and even that was not much help. Why was the *chowkidar* so worried?

He murmured vaguely about his job and how necessary it was for him to be exceptionally careful in times of stress and strain.

About the seriousness of his occupation there was not the slightest doubt in anyone's mind. Without Ramdas's presence no sitting of the village Council of Five could be deemed official! The post of the *chowkidar* was a hereditary one. Like Methar the Scavenger, Ramdas got his job when his father retired owing to senility at the comparatively early age of seventy-two. Ramdas's father, Gurudas, was appointed our watchman when he was still a baby! Gurudas's father served as *chowkidar* for only a few years: he met premature death while pig-sticking, in other words, boar-hunting. For many generations the charge of looking after our village, namely, protecting the villagers from the attacks of brigands and wild animals, has been handed down from father to son.

It would have been tantamount to a crime if a village *chowkidar* had abandoned his parental occupation for some other calling.

~

Kumar, our village potter, though a most skilful and dexterous craftsman, was condemned by some because he was not a hereditary potter. 'He is a sinner!' they said. 'He is not a true potter'—because he was descended from a family of diamond-cutters and jewellers who once worked for the long-defunct Santal rulers of Penhari.

Centuries ago the Rajkumars of Penhari were overthrown by the Pathans. Their capital was destroyed, their temples desecrated, their subjects dispersed, and their diamond-cutters and jewellers deported or decapitated. One of these craftsmen, somehow, managed to escape and sought refuge in the Red Valley. We had no potter in our village then. So he settled down in our midst to serve us as one.

Since then the task of keeping us supplied with clay images of gods and goddesses, earthenware pots, jars, pitchers, and such articles had remained with this refugee family. For generations without any break the diamond-cutter and jeweller's descendants worked as potters and image-makers. Nevertheless, quite a few people considered Kumar to be 'an upstart potter' and told him so to his face.

Fortunately, Kumar was not a man to be ruffled easily.

'Look at the sheen of my pottery and then talk!' Kumar smiled while his detractors jibed. 'My pottery shines like the frosted-diamond vessels in the king's treasury. How many potters can produce that blue sheen? You won't find many in this land.'

That was true enough. Our earth yielded only red pots, red pitchers, red tiles, red bricks, red tumblers—red everything: in the varying shades of scarlet and vermilion. This I could see for myself from the wares sold on market days by the rival potters of the neighbouring villages. Nowhere within ten leagues did one come across any earthenware articles with the lustre of blue diamonds, save those coming out of Kumar's special kiln. His blue pottery gave out a lambent glow like fire-flies in the dark, and its iridescence in sunshine shamed the jewellery of Benares and the gems of Golconda.

How did Kumar produce his blue pottery out of our red earth?

'All due to the lump of clay my forefather brought with him.'

'How is it possible, Kumar?' I asked. 'Isn't clay the same everywhere?'

'No,' replied Kumar as he shook his head meditatively. 'Not for me.' The soil of the long overthrown capital of Penhari was more precious to him than pure gold, and the waters of its silted Shanka river were more delectable than milk and honey.

No one knew the exact location of the lost city of Penhari nor the whereabouts of the silted Shanka river. But Kumar had heard from his father and grandfather that the Shanka's banks were laden with blue groves, lit by the wings of Painted Ladies, of dainty demoiselles, and of delightful dragonflies. Blue birds nestled in the *babool* trees lining the Shanka's curves. The Shanka's bed was blue sand, strewn with blue diamonds bluer than in any land; its streams were indigo, sapphire, and ultramarine.

'The earth isn't the same everywhere,' Kumar repeated with a sigh. 'My forefather knew that well. So he took with him a clod of his native land and with its touch he tinted the first blue pot ever made in the Red Valley. He wanted to remind himself of his despoiled home on the banks of the Shanka.' The descendants of the diamond-cutter followed his technique when they made their finer pieces of pottery: they imparted a blue sheen. It was their blue and nobody else's. The secret process was known to them only. The lustre spoke of the jewelled diadems of the princes of Penhari, as it recalled the sapphire glory of Penhari's sky and the azure beauty of Penhari's river.

Every night they sprinkled under their sleeping mats handfuls of Penhari's dust, only to be collected piously in the morning for re-use at nightfall. It was said that Kumar buried his face in a lump of Penhari's sod whenever he wanted to dream of his ancestral sky. He rarely bothered, however, to talk about his dreams and visions.

'Never squander your pearls,' he advised me. 'Never cast them before swine lest they trample them under their feet. They are too precious to be scattered aimlessly. Dreams and visions are more precious than pearls and rubies.'

Kumar liked me, I believe, and therefore told me many stories about which he never breathed a word to others. 'You are an exile here like myself,' he said. 'You do not really belong to the Red Valley, otherwise you would not have shown so much fondness for the Blue Hills. We are brother-exiles and we shall have to stick together.'

It was good of him to adopt me as a younger brother and let me watch him when he worked. In this way he was like the other Santals: they were so different from Tchutore the Carpenter, Janardan the Instrument-Maker, and other Hindu craftsmen. I was happy to hear the legends and stories known only to the clan of Kumars. None of the villagers were acquainted with them. Not even Kathak the Storyteller. I made Kumar repeat more than once how the capital of the Penhari princes came to be destroyed, and what the Pathan forces did to silt up the Shanka river.

It was from Kumar too that I heard for the first time about the Cradle of the Clouds, the region beyond the Himalayas, and of the ranges nearer home, such as the Seven Sisters—the seven hills forming a closed circle to hide from view a small hillock called the Little Brother. This Little Brother was expected to grow like any healthy boy and eventually surpass in height the surrounding Seven Sisters. But there was once a quarrel among them over a Santal flute-player and they detained him in their midst. 'Choose one of us,' the Sisters asked the flautist. 'All of you look the same to me,' the annoyed Santal shepherd replied. 'And why should I choose any of you? There are lots of pretty Santal girls who admire me.' 'We love the music of your flute,' the Sisters declared. 'If you choose one of us you will not leave this place and we shall always hear your music.' 'That's no reason for a man to marry a mountain,' the impudent flautist retorted. 'I shall play on my bamboo flute when it pleases me. I don't like to be ordered about and I shall go with my flock wherever I like.' Hardly had these words escaped from his lips when the Seven Sisters joined hands to form a closed circle to bar his escape! The flute-player had his vengeance: he clapped a block of star sapphire on the crest of the Little Brother and thus stopped his further growth.

All this happened ages ago, long before the Penhari princedom was overthrown, and the Red Valley came to be incorporated with the Blue Hills to form the Penhari Parganas. Nevertheless even to-day when travellers pass by the range of the Seven Sisters at dawn, they distinctly hear notes of music coming out of the closed bowl formed by these hills. The Little Brother remains in their midst as diminutive as ever, on account of the block of star sapphire.

~

A star sapphire has many magical virtues. It is a beautiful stone and very precious: this much is known to all but the blind. Kumar, however, knew more about its properties than anyone else on the Red Valley. 'When worn in a ring,' he told me, 'it engenders an equable temperament and sound judgment. It gives joy to the wearer's heart, makes his mind alert, and bestows dignity upon him.'

In laying the foundations of our buildings this brilliant gem was, in the past, widely used. In the olden days our master-builders believed that the placing of the corner-stone of an edifice over a star sapphire guaranteed its permanence. The Penhari architects took the necessary precaution of putting caskets containing star sapphires underneath the gigantic Black Pagoda they constructed at Konark, a desert waste by the Bengal Bay. Had they not done so, this colossal structure of red laterite would soon have sunk into the sand and disappeared like a needle in a deep mountain lake, never to be retrieved.

The same star sapphire when placed on the topmost peak of a hill would prevent it from adding an inch to its height. The most petulant volcano might be readily restrained by this bewitching jewel. No wonder the Little Brother of the Seven Sisters range remains for ever stunted.

'There is no limit to human cupidity,' Kumar continued. 'And it surprises me that no one has been tempted to verify the truth of this legend about the Little Brother. The closed bowl formed by the Seven Sisters collects water every year and the level of the mountain lake is rising steadily. Maybe, the Little Brother is already under water and therefore no explorer has bothered about that block of star sapphire forming its crest.'

The story of our sapphires below the foundations of the more ancient temples tempted many rapacious hordes to invade the land and put mines under our holy edifices. That was their way of collecting precious gems! The White Huns, the Scythians, the Afghans, the Pathans, the Uzbecks, the Vargis, and others of their sort have destroyed most of our once beautiful and imposing shrines. Sometimes they found a few tiny precious stones, but more often they came across a few coins of no great value. This was a disappointment to them while to us it was a calamity. The looters in such cases razed neighbouring towns and villages to the ground to give vent to their fury.

'Who will put up such temples in these days?' Kumar lamented. 'We lack faith, and without faith no great shrine can be set up. Shall we ever see another Black Pagoda built? The Vargis blew it up with gunpowder. The great temple is in ruins. When I visited the place I could not hold back my tears. What still remains is a marvel. The statues of the Sura-Sundaris, the dancing divinities at Konark, are the very images of our Santal girls.'

~

'But, Kumar!' I asked. 'Where is the Cradle of the Clouds?' The name pleased me and I wanted to know more about this place where the wise are honoured.

Kumar shook his head. He never told me much about this Cradle of the Clouds except that the wise alone knew its whereabouts, and they were the only ones to talk about it.

He knew the land of the Lamas, for he had gone to see their image-makers at work, and there he had heard about the Cradle of the Clouds. He gathered that once a huge land-wave rose to separate different tribes of the Tibetans: some of them were sent to a country where it was dark for six months of the year and bright for the remaining six. That was the time when the Cradle of the Clouds became like a mirage: 'It is here, it is there, it is everywhere, and, at the same time, it is nowhere.'

This, of course, was not much help to a boy in locating the whereabouts of the Cradle of the Clouds! All the same, I knew Kumar was sincere and was not trying to keep anything back from me. Did I not know of his many fruitless journeys in quest of the lost capital of the Penhari princedom?' 'It must be somewhere,' he would say when I rushed to greet his homecoming. 'It must be somewhere between Nagpur and Gaur. It has been overrun by the jungles, I suspect, like the city of our cousins, Kachar in Assam. I must try again next summer. If I come within a league of it, I am sure I shall recognize it. My memory tells me vaguely what the house of my forefathers looked like.'

Every year Kumar spent several months moving about.

What made Kumar so restless? What made him undertake his long journeys—especially when he knew how much I missed him. 'A craftsman must see how other craftsmen work,' was one of his explanations. 'And then, who knows? I may come across the lost capital of our Penhari princedom.' I was not quite happy about these answers. Different people told different stories of his annual pilgrimages.

'Because he does not really belong to the Red Valley nor to the Blue Hills,' my aunt explained, 'Kumar has no mother and no aunt to arrange his marriage.' His forebears when they married had to fetch their brides from among a particular tribe of the Santals in the Maurbhanj State, and Mashi-ma thought that his peregrinations were primarily in search of a suitable bride. 'One day,' Mashi-ma hoped, 'he will come back with a nice girl and then he will settle down properly.'

I thought Mashi-ma's imagination was somewhat fertile. No wonder Pocha, Bum-boatee, and Sashe Raha made fun of my not being twenty and bringing in a bride to lighten Mashi-ma's household burden. Anyway, she was not sarcastic about Kumar's travels, whereas the Second Master certainly was.

'Kumar has a few cards up his sleeve,' the Second Master remarked one day as he shuffled a pack of playing cards for a game of *binti*, a local variation of whist. 'Only I don't know what his cards are. A man does not gad about for nothing. He is a sly fox. Certainly his journeys are to sell his images.'

Apart from being a potter, Kumar was an image-maker like

the rest of the potters in the Red Valley. Every potter had to be a sculptor as well. Otherwise from whom could the villagers get their holy idols, the clay statues and statuettes of gods and goddesses? Every holy day demanded the worship of a particular deity. The image of the divinity was modelled in clay by the local potter and then painted like a picture and finally decorated with various ornaments and floral garlands and chaplets. It was worshipped with veneration for a day and then immersed in the near-by rivers or *jheels*, pools and lakes. It was a matter of pride for each village to have a potter capable of making the most beautiful gods and goddesses. In fact, a village worth its name would lose face if it failed to produce a magnificent image of Durga for the great *puja* ceremony. The goddess Durga is the only one worshipped for three consecutive days in the Penhari Parganas.

'Losing face is worse than death,' the villagers say, and some of the Penhari villages ordered their images of Durga from such distant places as Krishna-nagar and Vardaman. They had to pay cash: this they did not mind. 'It's better to lose money than to lose face. What would the children and the neighbours think of us if we produced a shabby goddess for our *puja*? Thanks to Kumar, our village was spared the humiliation of buying images from strangers. Some of the statues he made looked so beautiful that I thought it was a pity to immerse them in water after a day's worship only. I told him what I thought about it. He did not say anything, but simply pulled at my curls: this showed that he loved his sculpture more than his pottery.

On one occasion he made me pose as his model though he generally worked without one: he was preparing something for Padre Johan—the Great Betrayal, a group of two figures. One could not make much of me in that statue because I was made to turn my head away from the Second Master, his other model, who was shown protruding his lips to kiss me. I was terribly ashamed of this statue. Fortunately, no one understood the cause of my feeling embarrassed: I was naked, while the Second Master had a long robe, painted yellow, and a peacock feather headgear.

I do not know what the Second Master thought of this polychrome group called the Great Betrayal. But, in principle, he was much opposed to Kumar's making images of gods and goddesses. 'They are objects of superstitious adoration,' he declared and advised me to have nothing to do with 'these abominations.'

Kumar also made porcelain vases: for his own pleasure, he confided to me. They were not for sale, 'You would have to murder me,' he said seriously, 'if you wanted to get one of these!' He prized them enormously. Nevertheless, the Second Master showed little enthusiasm for them. 'The game isn't worth the candle,' he told Kumar. 'The trouble of murdering you for a vase would be too much. Even if you give me a dozen such fragile knick-knacks I shall get rid of them the moment I receive them. What's the *use* of such readily breakable things?'

'What's the use of a rainbow?' Kumar muttered as he covered up his porcelain vases with a piece of black cloth. Since then he showed them to no one except me.

They were really magnificent: some were pale blue, some deep indigo, and a few ox-blood. Their sides were thin like egg-shell, smooth and semi-transparent. When filled with water and placed in the light, these vases looked as though they contained a number of fishes swimming among trembling reeds and floating nenuphars.

'Tell me, Little Brother! You who are going to be a scholar,' Kumar occasionally enjoyed teasing me, 'where do these fishes come from? The vases were empty when I poured in water.'

Their sides were incised and painted in a special way with figures that could only be seen when they were filled with liquid. A very rare art, I was told—not known to many in India. Only an old Chinese who ran an opium den for his living in Terittey Bazar at Calcutta was skilful enough to produce porcelain vessels rivalling those of Kumar.

Though such a master craftsman, Kumar did not mind being called an upstart potter. He was following an occupation, he himself declared, that was not his by birth-right. He was descended from a diamond-cutter and jeweller, and was not, therefore, a hereditary potter and image-maker. He was just an interloper—a stopgap at best. A mere upstart.

~

To come back to Ramdas, had anyone dared to call him an upstart there would have been some serious trouble. Such an insult our *chowkidar* would have brooked from no one, not even his wife. He took his calling seriously, and others did the same: Ramdas was the hereditary watchman of the village.

It might have been difficult for a stranger unaccustomed to our ways to discover the precise practical value of the services rendered by Ramdas. But this question did not worry any of us. The *chowkidar* was the official announcer of the opening of all formal meetings. It would have been impossible for the Council of Five to begin any of their sittings without Ramdas's solemn— and to some ears, lugubrious—cry: 'Theeeeeeeeeek hai! All's well!'

He managed to draw out the first word of his announcement to such a length that this feat alone, I thought, entitled him to his weekly rations: mustard oil, lentils, treacle, chick-peas and various other dues from different households. He was part of our rural rituals and traditional institutions. Nobody cared if he kept a sharp look-out for the wild animals and the descendants of those merciless hordes who mined our temples. No one bothered as to whether he made his nightly rounds or not. But it was the villagers' duty to maintain a *chowkidar*, and this obligation they fulfilled with pleasure and pride. It enhanced the prestige of our village. None grudged the expense. No one complained. Nor grumbled.

Ramdas's wife, however, had a lot to grumble about for her husband. She did not know when—in which prehistoric period or antediluvian age—the list of dues for the village watchman was drawn up and fixed for good. Soon after her marriage she learnt to her cost that what held good for the very first *chowkidar* of the village was to hold good for all his successors till Doomsday. That was our tradition. The *chowkidar* was not a *durwan*, a mere caretaker or a bum-bailiff! His was an honourable post: he was not entitled to any cash payment, but to certain articles of food and clothing.

'Only menials work for money,' and the *chowkidar*'s post was anything but menial: therefore, it behoved the villagers to look after their watchman handsomely. The list of his requirements was most carefully prepared. Chick-peas were muscle-builders, especially when soaked in water and metamorphosed into *chana*, germinating gram; beans were good for hill ponies and therefore good for every climber; treacle produced energy; mustard oil was a prime necessity for anointing professional wrestlers. And that was that. No one was entitled to introduce any modification in this catalogue of dues for Ramdas.

Our *chowkidar* was, of course, at liberty to supplement his rations with anything he cared to add. He could, if he so desired, work for hard cash in the fields or factories or stone quarries or even in the coal-mines. That was his affair and it did not concern the villagers. What did concern them was: the watchman's rations were sacred and no *chowkidar* was entitled to sell or barter them; he could give away what he received, if he wanted to, but not for money.

Ramdas's wife found her larder glutted with certain commodities which she could not possibly utilize for her small household, while she had to forgo a number of articles she needed urgently. What was she to do? She began confectioning pastries to give away to her friends in the fond hope of receiving in exchange some of the things she wanted. Her friends misunderstood her motive and loaded her with gifts of chick-peas: germinating gram was wonderful as a restorative for a hard-working watchman!

She often complained to Mashi-ma whom she called *Didi*, the elder sister, that she was at her wits' end to vary her menu and her husband was too lazy to seek any decent work. Whereas Ramdas deemed it undignified for a man of his high calling to toil for hard cash. 'Only menials work for money,' he argued.

'But what am I to do with the pots of treacle he brings home every other day?' Ramdas's wife lamented. 'One cannot live on treacle! What am I to give my daughter, Khukoo?'

Being a sympathetic listener, Mashi-ma received some of these pots of treacle and I came to lose my 'sweet tooth' earlier than other boys. I had occasional rows with Mashi-ma for her violating so blatantly the law of the land: by accepting the gifts of Ramdas's wife she was depriving our *chowkidar* of the energy-imparting ingredient of his rations, namely, treacle. But she did not take my complaints seriously, nor did Ramdas's wife. They both laughed at my face and twittered that treacle was good for growing boys! Very soon I made the discovery that Mashi-ma was no longer a *Didi*, an elder sister, but a *Didi-Mani* to Ramdas's wife: *Didi-Mani* means the Jewel of an Elder Sister.

'As for chick-peas, Didi-Mani,' our watchman's wife moaned and slapped her own cheeks noisily, 'you may knock me down with a flower! In the first year of my married life, will you believe it? I ate my share of chick-peas for a whole generation. In the next twelve-months I swallowed enough to satisfy me for ten re-births. Nowadays my inside writhes at the very sight of a single chick-pea. So I ask my husband to try some place where they might need an announcer or a crier for the village council, say, once a fortnight or once a month. But he won't work for money. "All right," I say, "work for love, and go somewhere to secure anything except treacle and chick-peas." But he won't listen to me. He has always one excuse or another for doing nothing.'

Ramdas, however, could not go on indefinitely extending his area of supervision, or jurisdiction, as he called it. Grave risks, he declared, were involved in following up his wife's frivolous suggestions. In his own opinion, he was more than a mere watchman. His occupation as interpreted by him included, among other duties, *thief-catching*. Only for convenience' sake he allowed himself to be called the village watchman. Brains or no brains, wife or no wife, he did not relish the idea of being confronted with too many thieves at the same time in different localities.

Fortunately, so far as our area was concerned, there were no professional thieves, not even casual ones. The same, however, could not be said about the near-by towns.

'There are heaps of them,' Ramdas regretted to say. 'The towns are simply teeming with them. Every second man you see in a town is a professional thief. And the other man is a casual one. In times of dearth they are likely to invade the countryside at any moment.'

~

Ramdas's technique of thief-catching was original: he had a system of his own.

Whenever a visitor came to our village he had to be warned discreetly about our *chowkidar*. Otherwise he ran the risk of losing his nerve on account of our zealous night guardian's noisy vigils, unexpected cries—weird, bloodcurdling—challenging all the thieves of the world. Ramdas shrieked shrill defiance to the long defunct, notorious lawbreakers of antiquity as well as to the unknown, lesser ones, the would-be disreputables of the coming day. He denounced loudly all bandits, brigands, burglars, cattle-lifters, cutthroats, dacoits, deserters, foot-pads, free-booters, marauders, pick-pockets, pirates, sneak-thieves and smugglers as well as the White Huns, Scythians, Afghans, Pathans, Turcomans, Vargis, Thuggees, Kalmuks, and Uzbecks. His war-whoops went forth without forewarning at any odd hour between sunset and sunrise. He adhered to no time-table nor to any fixed itinerary.

Pocha's brother-in-law, a smart dandy, better known as Swagger Cane of the Asansole Amateur Swingers came to pass a week-end in the village and made a fool of himself on account of Ramdas's watchcry: '*Kay-Ray, Kay-Ray, Ghoom! Kay-Ray, Kay-Ray, Ghoom!*' 'An absurd alarum,' according to the Second Master, 'hatched by the brainless *chowkidar* after intense cerebration and the profound cogitation of many years. It is not going to frighten a chicken, let alone a thief.' Anyway, Swagger Cane mistook the watch-cry for an alarm signal for fire or earthquake or some such catastrophe and rushed out of his bed as he was, stark naked, and ran right into the heart of the crowd in the village square.

The place was then full of people, though most of them, particularly the youngsters and the strangers from the next village, had no business to be there at that late hour.

A monocled fellow—from nowhere in particular—wearing patent leather pumps, alpaca *sherwani*, three-quarter length black coat buttoned up to the chin, and a Turkish cap at a rakish angle was there, giving that evening a demonstration of a newly launched dry-battery receiving set. Earlier in the day this stranger's request, accompanied by a few packets of *Hawa-ghari* cigarettes, had induced Ramdas to go about our village and a few neighbouring ones beating his drum and announcing that the *tamasha* or the show of the evening would be gratis and there would be no collection for any political party. As there was a full moon and the time fixed for the demonstration not so very late, a fair-sized crowd gathered in the village square to admire the monocled stranger's well-cut long coat worn with uncommon composure in midsummer's terrific heat. His remarkable contempt for our climate evoked involuntary murmurs of astonishment. Some, however, took him to be a lunatic at large on account of his tilted *tarboosh*, the round rimless cap of black Astrakhan fur, looking like an upturned flower-pot painted with tar. A few others thought the same about his mental state for different reasons: for he was trying to sell us something we did not want to buy and also because he had given away many packets of cigarettes to Ramdas whose wife never allowed him to smoke.

Many hoped that he would begin his demonstration with a general distribution of free *Hawa-ghari* cigarettes. They were, however, grossly mistaken, and became fretful without any moral justification. Anyway, the wireless demonstration was not a success. Something went wrong with the set. 'Owing to the weather,' he insinuated, rather tactlessly, and this made the more aesthetically minded section of the gathering comment adversely on the appearance of his wireless. It was a box closely resembling Methar the Scavenger's contraption for ensnaring musk-rats and pole-cats. A man with a sensitive nose complained loudly that it smelt of skunks, while the demonstrator was trying to explain the use of a long flexible rod. At times he referred to it as the 'hearall', or 'ear-all', and at other times as the 'ariel' or the 'aerial'. When he turned on a knob, his box-like instrument uttered a series of ear-piercing screeches and then a long nasal wail which was said to be modern music broadcast from Calcutta for the cultural benefit of the country.

By now the majority of the crowd were won over to the belief that the monocled man was without any doubt a run-away from an asylum. The short speech he made in a drawling tone on the usefulness of owning individual, dry-battery, all-wave, household radio sets, as well as flexible metal rods, for the purpose of securing reliable weather forecasts from the AIR stations, did nothing to alter this unfortunate impression. His wrongly-timed attempts at engaging smiles made matters worse. Most people lost patience with him when he declared that he was not there to give away free packets of *Hawa-ghari* cigarettes. Several indignant men ran to the village elders, all of whom were accustomed to go to bed with the sinking sun, no matter the time and the season. They appealed for Ramdas to be summoned immediately to the village square to detain and interrogate a dangerous madman: an absconder from the Hazaribagh Mental Hospital.

The wireless salesman, smelling danger, hurriedly packed up his things and disappeared in his back-firing two-seater torpedo without giving anyone the chance of questioning him. He vanished literally in a cloud of dust and smoke.

Instead of dispersing, the crowd lingered on and on. They formed small groups and discussed interminably among themselves many curious happenings in various mad-houses, about harmless lunatics and dangerous maniacs, and about the so-called sane townsmen who broadcast on weather for the edification of the simple rustics.

Swagger Cane burst into their midst at this juncture crying like one demented, '*Arre*! *Khoon*! *Khoon*! Help! Murder!' They naturally mistook him for the man with the tilted *tarboosh* bereft of his fine clothes. The confusion was all the greater because Swagger Cane carried in his hand Pocha's fishing rod without tackle. Why in his fright he should have grasped at a toddler's fishing rod nobody ever understood—not even his wife, Pocha's sister. Anyway, at that time the rod was thought to be the aerial of the wailing wireless. To make a long story short, the whole affair was unpleasant and complicated, and since then Swagger Cane has never spent a weekend in our village.

It was a pity that no one had bothered to inform Swagger Cane that Ramdas never ventured out after sunset without sounding his warnings to all would-be thieves. Our honest and peace-loving *chowkidar* plainly wanted them to be out of his way. He had not the least intention of making a stylish young man like Swagger Cane the laughing stock of the village.

Once in my ignorance I asked Ramdas why he carried with him a lighted hurricane lantern when he made his official rounds.

'I may be night-blind,' Ramdas smiled, 'but I am not heartless. Whether I take a lantern with me or not is of little consequence to me. But what about the poor thief? My light would mean a lot to him. It would prevent his running into our cactus hedges and killing himself outright. I don't want anybody's blood on my conscience.'

'And that big conch shell? What's that for?'

Its purpose was to put the fear of the Lord into the heart of the wicked and of such inconsiderate pilferers as might refuse to run away at Ramdas's cries of warning.

The enormous ribbed harp shell was a fine rose-coloured specimen from an antipodean coral strand! It would, I agreed, have done honour to any of our temples as a show-piece in the treasury, where holy relics were on exhibit for the benefit of the pilgrims. Even the proudest priest would have felt prouder to blow it as a horn at religious ceremonies. It was a legacy from an engine-driver on the Mogra Narrow Gauge Railway, who retired long before the introduction of 'cow-catchers'.

According to Ramdas, this shell was capable of emitting a deep and frightening blast, something akin to the choral bellowing of a hundred thousand bulls in the luscious pasture-lands of the happy vale of Kashmir. The god Krishna, when he went out to fight the titans, did not carry any weapons with him, but a huge conch shell similar to the one I had before my eyes: the pride and joy of Ramdas's accoutrements. 'Even *Sheytan*, the Evil one,' Ramdas affirmed, 'the master of all the ghouls, would run for his soul if he heard the full blast of my marine trumpet. Would you care to hear what it sounds like?'

There was no need for me to give any answer: Ramdas decided to give me 'a slight demonstration' of his shell's penetrating power.

He sat down cross-legged by the road-side and advised me solicitously to move away to some distance and cover my ears carefully. Otherwise I ran the risk of ruining my yet immature tympanic membranes, my ear-drums, for good. (Though usually taciturn Ramdas loved sonorous words, like Kathak.) He then took a deep breath to expand his chest, puffed his cheeks till his eyes could hardly be seen, and pushing his head backwards, blew slowly but deliberately into the hole of the shell, pointing it skywards and making use of both hands to hold it. I watched him expectantly, tightly pressing my hands against my ears, and wondering all the while if the shell's blast could be as deafening as the explosion in the dynamite dump. Road-builders were engaged just then in blowing up a side of the hills. A few days earlier there was an accident in their depot of high explosives due to Gopaldas's mysterious manoeuvres.

Ramdas puffed and huffed. He changed his posture and tried different techniques of blowing. Perspiration streamed down his face and his limbs. At one moment his eyes almost bulged out of their sockets. I waited and waited, and Ramdas went on blowing into his shell with all his strength.

The wretched thing, however, refused positively to give out the least squeak.

The poor *chowkidar* was on the point of collapse when after many frantic efforts, all futile, he abandoned his self-imposed task of demonstrating the magical effects of his harp shell's blare. He lay panting on the ground for a long while to recover his breath. 'It is the fault of *Khukoo's mother*,' he gasped. She was responsible for taking away his breath and undermining his strength with her bad cooking.

Khukoo's mother was no other than Ramdas's wife. He never referred to her by her name: she was just the mother of his baby daughter, Khukoo. On rare occasions when he was particularly happy with himself he would call her Khukoor-ma or simply Ma.

When he had sufficiently recovered his breath Ramdas declared that it would serve Khukoor-ma right if she fell into the hands of thieves, or, still better, into the clutches of thugs! She was a fanatic, possessed by a *Bhoot*, an evil spirit. What else was she if not a maniac? She was a grave social menace who spent her nights as well as her days in the kitchen, cooking nothing but savouries, gewgaws, knick-knacks, tit-bits and sweetmeats, but never a proper, decent meal fit for an honest man. What was still worse, she never listened to him nor allowed him to talk.

'Little Scholar!' Ramdas spoke in a dejected mood. 'When it comes to choosing a bride, never choose one who has any doubts about her birthday. Khukoor-ma has not the faintest notion whether she was born on a Saturday towards midnight or on a Sunday in the early morning. What can you do with such a woman? You don't know what amulet to put on to drive away the *Bhoot*, the evil spirit that has taken possession of her.'

Ramdas's depression grieved me. Could not Mashi-ma be of some help in solving his worries? After all, Ramdas's wife called her Didi-Mani, the Jewel of an Elder Sister.

Mashi-ma well merited this appellation of Didi-Mani from both Ramdas and his wife. At one time when Khukoo's parents had given up all hopes of seeing their daughter walk like other children, it was Mashi-ma who 'taught the soles of the child's feet to talk,' in other words or less poetic terms, she taught Khukoo to walk. The pitter-patter of the pair of tiny feet was soon followed by the patter of the child's lips. Here too, Mashi-ma rendered them a great service. Khukoo was an original girl in many ways: she learnt to walk first and then to talk whereas it was the other way round with most children of the Red Valley. However, Khukoo quickly made up for her inactive days by surpassing her father in the gifts of walking and talking. Unfortunately, in all differences between her parents, Khukoo always sided with her mother, and this discouraged Ramdas.

I tried to make Ramdas talk. This was only following up one of Padre Johan's precepts: 'Make an unhappy man talk and reduce his burden by half. Deserve his confidence first and then the burden will be lightened by itself.' Therefore, I told him rather casually that it was natural for women to stick together: Khukoo, Khukoor-ma and Mashi-ma, Men should do the same: I was not fond of treacle-tart, neither was Ramdas. This produced a remarkable change in our *chowkidar*'s attitude.

~

Ramdas scratched his head as he searched for words. He did not know, he complained, how to express himself properly. Nevertheless, he knew he was a lost man on account of Khukoo's mother. Her faith in cakes was the cause of an impending calamity: he was going to be hanged in the near future like a mad dog and he had no knowledge of the whereabouts of his truant nephew Gopaldas! To whom was he to hand over his charge? For generations his family members had served the village as *chowkidars* and now what was he to do? Had Khukoo been a boy it would have been different. He did not mind being hanged because he deserved the gallows and, therefore had no right to complain, 'But to think of the disgrace of leaving this village without a *chowkidar!*' The very thought made him shudder: it made his heart sink. 'Think of the disgrace, Little Scholar! To lose one's life, that's nothing. But to lose face! If only I knew Gopaldas would take up my task, I should die a happy man.'

'Are you crazy, Ramdas?' I asked impatiently. 'Why should anyone think of hanging you?'

Ramdas shook his head: the charge against him was extremely grave. He did not know whether he would ever live to see such a day: he had failed in his duties. He had not been watchful enough. A crime of the first magnitude had been committed almost under his nose and he had failed to prevent its occurrence. So, he thoroughly merited the gibbet.

'What's the crime? I haven't heard anything about it.'

Ramdas broke down. An abomination committed by his wife made him liable to capital punishment. A woman could not be hanged, according to him, but her husband could volunteer to replace her: that was the tradition. The human-shaped cakes by the flowering cactus bushes were deposited there by no other person than his thoughtless wife. 'Not with any evil intention,' Ramdas groaned, and struck his forehead with the palm of his hand. 'But will the village elders accept such a plea? An abomination is an abomination and must be expiated by punishment.'

I felt like laughing, but restrained myself. So all those fine conjectures about the tail-less toy horse and the cakes came to this: Ramdas's wife took pity on a dying black dog and wanted to feed it, and Khukoo thought that her toy horse would enliven the sick mongrel's last moments.

'The Punditji advises me to remain silent,' Ramdas whispered, 'till the rains begin. He says as soon as the Ploughing Ceremony is over we shall get rains. What should I do?'

'Just follow the Punditji's advice.' I looked at his face and forgot all about my laughter. He was woe-begone and remorse-stricken. I felt like shouting to the four heavens: 'I will do my best at the Ploughing Ceremony and will bring down the monsoon and thus save the Punditji and my good friend Ramdas, and others too.' But somehow the words refused to come out of my mouth. Anyway, I tried to persuade Ramdas to remain quiet for at least another twelve hours. 'What's the hurry, Ramdas? Can't you wait for a few more hours before you divulge the secret of the cakes? Will it help the village very much to have a hanging on the same day as the Ploughing Ceremony?'

Ramdas was still hesitant.

So I produced my trump card: I knew Gopaldas's whereabouts, but I wouldn't give him the details unless he remained quiet till next morning. This had a magic effect; it helped him to make up his mind. He decided to do as the Punditji had advised him, and in return made me swear that I would stay indoors all day and not run away from the village before the Ceremony.

He accompanied me to the very threshold of my home, and congratulated me on having obtained Mahendra Chandal on loan from the Punditji.

XIII

It was too hot to shut myself up in a room, so I decided to install myself on the *stoep*, the canopied and balustraded verandah from where I could watch the village square. There was, of course, nothing much to see there at that hour. The sky was swathed in shining silver and the earth was draped in burning brass. There was a dazzle even in the shadows. Except for a few bullock carts without their drivers the square looked entirely deserted. I wished something dramatic would happen just to furnish me with some excitement.

A moment later I realized how stupid it was for me to formulate such a thought. 'You must be worthy of the Punditji's staff,' Mashi-ma advised me. 'So long as it is with you it is absolutely necessary for you to commit no sin in words, thoughts, and deeds.' It was, therefore, a grave error on my part to ask for something extraordinary to happen. 'Mahendra Chandal is like a *kalpa-taru*, a wishing rod. If you hold it in your hand and ask for something you will find your wish fulfilled. But, mind you, not many people know how to wish well.'

What a terrible responsibility, I thought, to have such a staff in one's hand. I carefully put it away from me. I tried to make it stand upright. That was difficult. So I placed it almost at a right angle against the wall by my side. I gave a sigh of relief. I was now at liberty to think out my thoughts and to wish for anything without violating Mashi-ma's injunctions. It was not quite easy for me to do much clear thinking just then. My musings centred round my visit to the Punditji and Ramdas's worries. What a different man from the Second Master was our Punditji! What prevented my calling on him more often? He welcomed questions, whereas the Second Master got annoyed if one asked anything that did not please him.

'Of course,' the Punditji told me, 'there are questions and questions. Some people ask questions simply because they want to hear their own voices. Others ask questions to annoy the speaker. For such people I have my Mahendra Chandal. I hit them hard and don't bother to answer them. There are still others who put questions for the purpose of repeating by rote a string of trite shibboleths and foolish slogans, their own favourite *mantras*. They are ignorant people and I pity them. But the moment *you* started your arguments and questions I knew my sickness was over. What could be a greater remedy for my disease than an alert rival, an awakened mind, and an enquiring youth?'

The Punditji treated me as though I were his equal! He did not try to snub me like the Second Master.

But what made the Sanskrit scholar believe in old traditions? He was a learned man, there was no doubt about it. Otherwise how could he translate Gray's Elegy or Hugo's *Les Misérables*? Nevertheless, it was difficult to justify his excessive fondness for ridiculous local rites and customs. 'If no convincing argument can be adduced for abolishing a custom,' the Punditji generally contended, 'tradition alone is reason enough for maintaining it.' 'Most problems,' according to him, 'are complex for those endowed with insight. There are no cure-alls. Propounders of panaceas suggesting the destruction of time-honoured religions and cultural patterns are dangerous lunatics. With what will you replace ancient tradition? I am a traditionalist because I believe in the power of the Mind. Try to understand its tremendous significance. Then the rest will be easy. You will have the gift of tongues the day you understand the import of your mental power. That day you will also grasp the meaning of holiness. Holiness and wisdom are the same.'

All this was confusing. Yet, I thought I ought to have called on the Punditji long before he fell so dangerously ill. If Ramdas's wife could take serious risks in order to be charitable to a dying dog, I should have done something to show my appreciation of a scholar's trials. It was my duty to bring some comfort to a man who was well acquainted not only with Sanskrit writers but also with such authors as Gray, Macaulay and Victor Hugo. (Plato did not then figure in my list of celebrities.)

So far as I could make out, the Punditji was a traditionalist because he believed a community's mind mattered more than its material prosperity. He was afraid more wealth and greater comfort would transform the people of the Penhari Parganas into godless atheists. He was consistent from his own point of view. I could neither prove nor disprove his thesis about the power of Mind. He was convinced that the Ploughing Ceremony would give us rain. 'If you have faith,' he propounded, 'the angels of the Lord will work miracles for you. Whatever you ask you will get. Know only how to ask well...only those blessings worth having. How many people know how to wish well? Is anyone justified in asking for miracles?'

'But what is faith?' I asked myself and found no answer to my question. So my thoughts ran on and on. My aimless musings only came to an end when I noticed a group of Santal women rushing into the village square. They bore on their heads huge amphora-shaped jars for carrying water.

What did they want?

A good many reflections passed through my mind before I found an answer to the query.

PART TWO

The Blue Hills

I

The Chinese boy Tu Fan, one of my class-mates at Svenska-Bibi's kindergarten, told me something about his father which comes to my mind whenever I witness a party or a gathering in honour of anyone.

Though once a professional writer, Tu Fan's father was reduced to earning his living as a rickshaw coolie. The publishers were not willing to handle his essays on such scholarly subjects as *The Hexagrams of Wen Wang, Duke of Chou; Moral Values in Hung Lou Meng or Red Chamber Dream Analysed; Confucian Analects as modified in Meng Tse's Precepts*, etc. The firms were more interested in the Chinese political puzzles of the day. 'If you can't write on politics,' they told him, 'why don't you try your hand at Chinese detective stories? Our readers like thrillers and mysteries. Chinese ghost stories may find a market, too. What about the adventures of a Sing-Song Girl from Shanghai?'

'Our rice bowl was empty,' Tu Fan confided to me, 'when father sold his rickshaw and hired the Madrassi Highlanders' Band and went out to welcome the incoming ships at the Outram Ghat. The bare-footed and red-turbaned Madrassis with Scottish kilts over their *dhoties* piped their loudest as the passengers landed, and father waited with a banner at the exit. It was the banner that did the trick. It carried the inscription: "Welcome! The Music is for You! Please remember the Music-

Master!" No passenger failed to drop his coin in the collecting box. Except the essayists. Father says they are born sceptics and you can judge them by their looks.'

I solemnly promised Tu Fan that I would never aspire to be an essayist, because I did not know what it was to be a sceptic: I lacked in my own estimate the essential qualification.

II

This shortcoming of mine could easily have been read in my face the day I came to the village and witnessed a Santal dance in a corner of the square: I was convinced that the dance was given in my honour.

It happened years ago. Yet I remember every detail of that performance. I have only to press down my eyelids whenever I want to see it again in my mind's eye: that rustic cotillion danced by some twenty Santal youths, joyous young men and smiling maidens of the neighbouring Blue Hills.

The musicians with their fifes, flutes, and drums formed a wide circle, while the men dancers, loaded with garlands of red oleanders, stood with outstretched arms, barely touching each other's fingers to form a closed ring, at the centre of which stood the women, clustered together, arms interlaced, closely packed—a compact mass of bright hues: their *saris* were colourful, and so were the wreaths of flowers round their necks and the chaplets of jasmine, *champaks*, and hibiscus entwined in their jet black hair. They carried shining armlets, bracelets, bangles, and other ornaments on their bare arms, and round their ankles were stringed rows of tiny, globular bells, no bigger than the berries of *neem*.

A number of Santal boys and girls of about my own age formed a separate knot on the stone dais at the foot of the *peepul* tree. There was a look of expectation and delight in their wide, almond-shaped, black eyes. They were anxious to start clapping their hands to keep time with the music and steps. By their side sat their leader, a bigger girl called Neela. She wiped a square yard of the dais next to her for me with her *sari*, a gesture of welcome.

A seat might have been cleaned a thousand times and polished like a mirror, nevertheless, for the honoured guest it has to be wiped again just before he sits down. That is the custom.

The *Bhat*, the professional reciter, was then repeating something from the *Maha Bharata* about a handsome warrior and I wished he would stop. There was a personal allusion to me in his recital: he was referring to a pleasant youth who was mistaken for a woman! I wore my hair long, parted in the middle, and my wavy curls reached my shoulders. In that group, however, I had no reason to be ashamed of my locks. The Santal boys wore their hair long like the girls, so too did the men. All the same, I felt that the *Bhat* had no business to be so long-winded nor to keep the dancers waiting.

It was the Santal women who gave the musicians their signal to start: their leader stamped the ground with her bare feet and the bells of her anklets tinkled. She stood on tiptoes and brought her heels down with a thud. Her immediate neighbours did the same and the rest took up the cue. They then moved a step forward, clapping their hands and bowing to the outer ring of the men dancers.

The men responded with bows and began moving in a circle, keeping their arms outstretched as before, and occasionally bringing them together to clap or to make the gesture of the *anjali* greeting. They moved clockwise while the women stepped in an anti-clockwise fashion, their arms at times clutching their girl-partners and at other times, placed akimbo.

The moving circles of the dancers approached each other and the men raised their hands to let the women slip through and form the outer circle. Shortly afterwards the women started whirling like tops, and this was the signal for the men to make symbolic gestures with their hands inviting the women to abandon their gentle female partners and join the men to form couples. This invitation was at first refused indignantly with symbolic movements of bodies and arms. The men persisted, however, and by and by some concession was made. The women, instead of whirling like tops with their arms on their waists, slowed down; then they stretched out and withdrew their arms, rhythmically, as though they were caged birds circling inside their narrow prisons, and inadvertently hitting, from time to time, against the iron bars. Their finger-tips fluttered: the wounded wing-tips of exhausted birds. The delicate agitations of their arms and hands intimated their willingness to be taken out of their narrow bounds by whoever cared to come to their succour: the tired winnowers of the air were anxious to be released. The men then grasped the women by their fingers and steadied them. Different couples were formed, and a new whirling movement commenced, each man serving as a pivot for his partner. They moved like steel springs uncoiling. The music grew quicker and the dancers stepped faster and faster, while the rhythm, with faultless precision and delightful delicacy, flowed unbroken from limb to limb. It was surprising that the wheeling couples did not collide with each other. The musicians struck a different note and the dancing couples changed partners to form various patterns of twirling figures: a swirling whirlpool of variegated colour.

Finally when the music ended abruptly the dancers were back to where they stood at the beginning of their cotillion: the same postures and the same groupings as at the very start. It is a part of our art of dancing and singing to rise to an intensity of disciplined abandon and then to finish suddenly—without a tremor or a quiver. No one showed the least sign of fatigue: no bead of perspiration on any brow. However, the lithe bodies revealed their ecstasy of delight: though immobile, the rhythm of the dance was still visible in them.

The compact group of women for a while continued the melody of the jingling bells of their anklets, but that too ceased when they bowed with folded palms: the parting *pranam*. The men responded in the same way. The spectators bowed too. The dance was over. There was no applause as in the towns when stage-shows are given. In the village the close of the performance saw only *pranams* and benedictions: it was like the end of a prayer.

No verbal description can do justice to the spectacle I saw: the grace of the dancers, the beauty of their superb physique, the moving masses of colour, the rhythmic music, the sound of foot-falls—now slow, now fast—the delightful gestures, the perfume of the sandalwood oil with which the dancers had anointed themselves, the fragrance of the flowers, the contagious spirit of bird-like freedom. How shall I transcribe these in words? I was stirred to the very depths of my heart. I was mute with wonder.

'They are from the Blue Hills,' Neela whispered to me. 'Did you like the dance?'

Of course I did. I simply nodded: I did not know how to express my thankfulness. Also I felt shy because the perfume of Neela's breath pleased me. It reminded me of some rare and fragrant orchids which grew only in the innermost recesses of the jungles. For a while I remained tongue-tied. But when Neela asked me which of the dancers pleased me most, my tongue was loosened: every one of them pleased me. 'When I grow up,' I declared boldly, 'I shall marry all the dancers of the Blue Hills. I love them all.'

'The whole lot!' Neela smiled. 'There would be too many cooks in your kitchen.'

'Mashi-ma's kitchen is big enough to hold twenty women,' I was happy to inform her. 'If they want to dance instead of cooking, they may do so in the inner courtyard.'

~

'When I grow up,' I told Mashi-ma before going to bed, 'I shall marry Neela and all the other Santal girls.' It was imprudent to divulge my secret on the night of my arrival at the village.

'Aren't you quick?' This was all that my aunt said. But in the morning she passed on my cherished thoughts to Ramdas and instructed him to keep the Santal children away from me. Thus was I deprived of their company and particularly Neela's for many months, till I started escapades of my own during the long vacations: climbing the Blue Hills, making bonfires near the Golah, exploring the jungles, visiting Deoghar, Jamtara, and other places. These were far more interesting than my outings with Gopaldas.

Neela was an asset in exploring the unknown nooks of the Santal country. I came to be very fond of her. Years later it was Neela's presence at Madhu-ban which tempted me to accept readily the temporary post of a student-monitor in her experimental school in the Blue Hills.

~

This village of Madhu-ban had other attractions too. It would always be associated with my first juvenile quest for a glimpse of the Cradle of the Clouds, the seat of All Wisdom.

Some of the local Santal boys were one day going out in search of the nest of the golden eagles. 'The planes of the *Delhiwallahs* are fast,' they said, 'but *our* eagles are faster.' They were proud of the fact that some of these eagles had brought down an open plane for training pilots. They were justified in their sentiment, I replied, and this permitted me to re-establish contact with some of the boys I had lost sight of since the day of my arrival in the Penhari Parganas.

I heard from them about the *moucharaby* of the Penhari princes, built at an even greater height than the level at which rain-clouds generally linger. 'If that be so,' my young mind reasoned,

'I shall perhaps get a distant view of the Cradle of the Clouds from the *moucharaby*.' However, I discovered that it was not high enough. But, all the same, my journey was certainly worthwhile. Though the Cradle of the Clouds remained undiscovered I found very many other things in the Blue Hills to compensate for my disappointment.

How often did I not visit and revisit Amrita-ban, Madhu-ban, the Saffron Crag and the *moucharaby* in the company of the Santal children of the Blue Hills?

III

Perhaps I ought to mention here for those who do not know that this *moucharaby* is a small covered balcony with latticed windows and an open verandah, built against the high cliffs overhanging the village of Madhu-ban. Its real name is the Nest of the Hawks.

A Moslem nawab once called on the princes of Penhari who then ruled over the Red Valley and the Blue Hills, and complained to them that he was tired of life. Could they suggest any antidote against boredom?

This nawab, an expert in breeding prize mules and hybrids, loved watching cock-fights and the mating of animals. Late in life he became interested in aquatic creatures and made the sad discovery that the male and the female fish never went to bed together. This upset him. His plan for breeding bigger and better fish went by the board! He felt sorry for the fish on account of the fun they missed and finally became sorry for himself as his various baits failed to procure him a spectacle of piscatory blandishments. What was he to do? Could the Penhari princes suggest any worthwhile distraction?

'Have you ever watched the mating of the clouds?' the Santal princes asked him. 'Cloud-gazing is the best remedy for every disappointment.' They brought him to the *moucharaby* above Madhu-ban in the Blue Hills and invited him to admire the vast panorama beneath him and the immense bowl of the horizon overhead.

'This *moucharaby*,' they said, 'this gallery of latticed stone-work is known as our Nest of the Hawks. From here we watch the clouds. Our honoured guest is welcome to do likewise and forget his grief. The clouds furnish us with the most moving of all spectacles.'

~

Thanks to our clouds there are days known to us as the *Wedding diurnals*: when the marriage takes place of the white woolpacks with the blue of the horizon. The shadows cast by the nuptial veils of the espousing clouds then link the azure-and-green of the mountain ridges with the red-and-russet of the valleys below and fuse them into one. That is the time we deem most auspicious for forging the first links of lasting friendships. Fortunate are the pairs that clasp hands and embrace each other during the propitious moments, and invite the clouds in the heavens to bear witness and carry the declaration of their abiding amity to the ends of the earth.

The marriage of the white and the blue does not, however, take place often. The *Jackals' Weddings* are much more frequent.

Clouds are capricious in our firmament: they have their own inscrutable ways. Some move across our sky in fleets or flocks. Some in scattered groups or strange formations. And some by themselves, all alone—the solitary ones. At times they move fast: hastening phalanxes of caparisoned elephants or hurrying ships in convoy with swollen sails or flying flocks of herons bound for the north. At other times they linger long like wallowing buffaloes or pasturing cattle or grazing sheep.

However, be they in huddled crowds or in lone isolation, the clouds of our clime are always delightful. On certain days for no reason in particular, they are especially wayward and frolicsome. A solitary cloud no bigger than a man's hand will then spread itself out and grow great before the watcher's gaze. And another with its shadow stretching over leagues will fold itself up, finally rolling its gigantic form into an insignificant ball of fleece-wool. One will sail away leaving no trail in its wake and another will shed familiar or fantastic forms from its body and suspend them in mid-air to tell the tale of its course. Yet another will construct a castellated floating island in the firmament and dissolve its captivating creation as soon as it is completed, in a thin, vaporous haze. Some play hide-and-seek with the sun for a while and then race across the horizon to outstrip the wind. And not a few clothe themselves for their journey with dazzling splendour to disconcert the worshippers of the day-star.

On *Wedding diurnals* the white woolpacks of the mid-day may be displaced towards sunset by the black thunderheads. They fashion with the sun-beams aerial pyramids of such stupendous proportions that the eye cannot gauge their amplitude. The beholder is struck speechless by their awful majesty. The clouds veil the solar disc, allowing only a few streams of its radiance to reach the earth. The escaping rays form a ramp whereon vows of eternal harmony mount up to the very gate of heaven—at the apex of the impalpable and immeasurable pyramid of light.

~

The dispirited nawab was cured of his melancholia by the magnificent pageants given by our changeful clouds, and this peculiar diversion of the Penhari princes, cloud-gazing, spread rapidly from the region of the Blue Hills to other parts of the country. Anyone was welcome to enjoy it, be he prince or pauper.

Maharajahs, Rajahs, Ameers, Omrahs, Lords, and Lordlings vied with one another in setting up *moucharabies* with sloping Bengal roofs and balustraded balconies. Those in the plains put up tall towers with projecting galleries and those in the hills sought their loftiest crags and built pavilions. Even the rulers of rainless tracts thought it shameful not to possess high alcoves for sky-gazing. Clouds or no clouds, they refused to be outdone by their peers in more fortunate areas.

The Aravalli Range, known to the people of the Penhari Parganas as the *Curse of God* because of its eternal dearth of rain, came to be dotted with galleries. In the heart of the rainless Thar desert lies Jaisalmir, over which shadows are cast only once in seventeen years by the passing clouds of locusts. Nevertheless, its ruler, Maharawal, took as much interest in the construction of his frail latticed *moucharaby* for cloud-gazing as in that of his formidable and cyclopean fortress.

Artists were summoned to rainless Rajputana to portray Rajput warriors sitting quietly in exquisite *moucharabies* with their sloping Bengal roofs—sloping to let the rain-water run down—and admiring non-existent cloud-formations. The painters had not the heart to disappoint their princely patrons: they drew woolpacks, mare's tails, thunderheads, or pouring rain-clouds as their sitters desired.

In Bikanir, clouds are as rare as in Jaisalmir, and water is to be found at a depth of 200 feet: its wells are lined with camel bones. Yet Bikanir had not only its cloud-watching alcove but also an unrivalled collection of brilliant miniatures depicting cloudbursts in the Penhari Parganas: these were shown to distinguished guests when they sat down to sky-gazing and sipped cold sherbet, refreshing fruit drinks, prepared in the Penhari fashion. The most treasured illumination in the Bikanir collection was the *Song of Songs* by Jaya-Deva, Penhari's master-poet.

Eight hundred years ago Jaya-Deva penned the opening verses of his masterpiece *Gita Govinda* while he was watching the thunder clouds from that very spot where often I took my seat in the *moucharaby* of the Penhari princes. On clear days his own native village Kenduli could be seen in the distant east.

I deemed myself extremely fortunate to sit, albeit temporarily, in a *moucharaby* with these historic associations. I owed my good fortune to the Santal children, and in particular to Neela, who guided my steps to that long-abandoned and almost-forgotten balcony of sublime vistas. Years later, when I taught for a few months as student-monitor at Amrita-ban, I took up my living quarters in this gallery. Here again, my sojourn was made possible by the Santal children and Neela: I worked as Neela's assistant.

~

A mile's walk on the surface of the earth is but a short distance. In the plains a wayfarer will rarely find a change in the horizon when he has covered the slight stretch of a mile. But let the same man watch the earth from a high hill and judge for himself what an immense transformation the altitude of a mile brings about in his field of vision. The familiar landscape undergoes a magic metamorphosis: it becomes an enchanted fairy-land where distant vistas are thrown open. The air is rarer, and the sky clearer. One feels oneself nearer to heaven than to earth.

The *moucharaby*, the Nest of the Hawks, must have been much more than a mile high from the plains. It overlooked the Red Valley. While there were ranges higher than the Blue Hills in the west and north-west, there was nothing to obstruct the view towards the east, the south, or most of the north. How was this gallery of cloud-gazing built? The construction must have demanded considerable ingenuity on the part of the architects. It seemed, when seen from below, to be suspended in the sky, only slightly touching the almost perpendicular rock which rose like a gigantic bastion from Madhu-ban.

The general view from Madhu-ban itself was sufficiently imposing. Its height was certainly much higher than the level to which low clouds descend. Such clouds in the hills did not, however, interest me much: they were like mists and layers of fog, even though from the Red Valley they appeared to have the consistency of tight packs of huge cotton bales. From the *moucharaby* the same mist banks looked like a solid mass of opaque sea.

But low clouds rarely interfered with the general vista from the *moucharaby*. Others, better qualified than I, told me the mountain scenery from this gallery of cloud-gazing was one of the most imposing in the world. I gathered from the villagers that even the Jung Bahadur from Nepal held the same opinion. Who could be a better judge of mountain scenery than the Jung Bahadur? He knew not only the mountains and valleys of his own country, Nepal, but also those of Kashmir, Tibet, Assam, Northern Burma, Siam and Sinkiang.

IV

From what I heard about the Jung Bahadur, I became a great admirer of his: I had a great respect for his views and opinions. So much so that I made quite a few attempts to emulate him— not in his military feats and generalship, but in horsemanship. One such attempt caused me much bother, but I need not refer to that incident here.

The Jung Bahadur Shumshere Jogendra Malla Rana of Katamundu might be forgotten in the land of his birth. But his memory will be always cherished by the inhabitants of the Penhari Parganas, by Hindus as well as by Santals. It was he who saved our forebears from total extermination at the hands of the Vargis, the Maratha marauders, and their Moslem associates, the Pindaris and the Pathans.

When the Imperial government of Delhi became corrupt under effete rulers, the empire of the Grand Mogul fell to pieces and the country was given over to anarchy and general disorder: the law of man was ousted by the law of the jungle. Various armed bands roamed over the land, looting and pillaging: the most destructive among them were the Vargis. And the people of the Penhari Parganas had a hard time.

The inhabitants of the Red Valley and the Blue Hills were mostly unarmed cultivators, while the Vargis were armed to the teeth, moving in hordes as big as twenty thousand strong, carrying with them heavy and light artillery. They were said to be excellent horsemen and astonishingly clever at mining buildings, and razing towns and villages to the ground. What they could not take away with them they generally burnt down. They made their descent upon West Bengal each year after the harvest festivity, and claimed one-fourth of the total produce of the land as their due. Of course, they were never satisfied with a fourth: they took all that they could carry with them and the rest they simply committed to the flames. The Penhari people managed to save their skins by hiding in the jungles which in those days covered the major part of the Parganas.

In that era of anarchy the Jung Bahadur Shumshere Jogendra Malla Rana came to our area to pay a return visit to the princes of Penhari: they had called on his forebears several centuries ago when Nepal was being attacked by the Chinese. He declared that circumstances beyond their control had prevented all members of his family from undertaking any long journey in the interval; as far as he was concerned, most of his time up till then had been spent in fighting the Marathas, Pathans, Jats, and others. Fortunately they had now been driven out of Nepal and her friendly territories, so he was anxious to fulfil a long-standing obligation. 'How far off is the capital of the Penhari princes?' he asked. 'The city of Penhari on the banks of the Shanka river.'

'The Penhari princes! The city of Penhari by the Shanka river!' the oldest of the elders covered his face to hide his tears. It was considered bad manners to sob before a visitor.

'*Arre! Hai! Hai!*' the villagers wailed. They forgot the correct etiquette and struck their foreheads with the palms of their hands. 'Alas!' they said, 'We wish the Penhari princes were here to welcome you and to beat back the Vargis and the Pindaris. The princes were killed by the Moslems some four hundred years ago. All that remains of them is the glory of their name.'

'And the *moucharaby* called the Nest of the Hawks,' added the Santal headman of Madhu-ban. He had been summoned in haste to attend the gathering under the *peepul* tree. He was fleet-footed, as was Ramdas's great-great-great-grandfather who fetched him to meet the Jung Bahadur.

'How could the Moslems defeat the Penhari princes? They were lions in battle.' The Jung Bahadur asked why no messengers had been sent to Katamundu when the Penhari princedom was attacked; the princes ought to have informed their allies in the Himalayan regions.

~

After all, Nepal was once in a bad plight too and her rulers did not then hesitate to send heralds all over India requesting the Hindu princes to come to Nepal's succour.

Some Chinese cartographers had by mistake painted a number of countries yellow implying thereby that these were either parts of China or her tributaries. Nepal happened to be one of these, and the Son of Heaven sent an army to summon the Nepalese ruler to the capital of the Celestial Empire for a friendly discussion over his failure to send regular tributes to the Chinese treasury. Everyone in Nepal understood the implication of the invitation and the Nepalese heralds hurried to India to request immediate succour.

The Rajput princes were then engaged in cutting each other's throats to settle an abstruse point of precedence, and they were, therefore, unable to divert their attention to Nepal. The monarch of Orissa was under a vow of absolute pacifism. 'He that takes the sword shall perish by the sword,' he told the Nepalese heralds. 'God is love. Show love to God and love your enemies. All men are brothers.' The king of Gaur was to be found nowhere. A score of Moslem horsemen were approaching his capital, and in order to spare unnecessary bloodshed he decided to become a naked fakir and vacate his throne. 'Blessed are the peacemakers,' the king of Gaur chanted as he divested himself of his royal robes. The rulers in the south of India declared they were pure Aryans and were not concerned with the *mlecchas*: the people whose skin was not blue-black were bound to be *mlecchas*; the Nepalese were *mlecchas*, so were the Chinese.

The messengers were returning home crest-fallen and disgusted with the Hindu princes of India when they came across a number of herdsmen grazing buffaloes on the banks of a blue mountain stream. Some of them wore chaplets and diadems of blue diamonds. All had rosary beads round their necks and bamboo flutes in their hands. They were tall like giants, of splendid physique and smiling demeanour; clean shaven, but their smooth hair, parted in the middle, was long, reaching their shoulders.

In the near-by trees were flocks of the god Shiva's favourite birds, the rollers: cobalt blue all over except for their ash-brown and green necks. A tiny fledgling of a blue-tit hopped across the path, and the Nepalese heralds stood still. Who stirs when Shiva's servitor, the bird *nilakanta* signals 'Stay?'

'*Sita Ram*,' greeted the leader of the buffalo-men.

'*Ram Ram*,' the foremost messenger responded to the benedictory welcome, while the others repeated, '*Sita Ram*.'

'My good men! Why do you look so dejected? Are you all tired? Or has any injustice been done to you? No man has any right to be downcast in our Penhari Parganas.'

'Whom have I the honour of addressing?' asked the principal herald, marvelling at the princely bearing of the buffalo-drivers, who were wearing diamond diadems. His tale was soon told.

'I am Adi Malla, the chief of the Penharis, and the bearer of the *kabach* of master-wrestlers. I will come with you even now and help you to drive out the unjust invaders.'

And that was what he did. Adi Malla went to Nepal on the back of his favourite mount, the giant buffalo called Nil-Pahar, Blue Rock.

~

'That was precisely five hundred and fifty-five years ago,' according to the Jung Bahadur Shumshere Jogendra Malla Rana, Field Marshal of Nepal. 'The enemy was routed thanks to Adi Malla's help. Before leaving Katamundu for the Penhari Parganas, the prince worshipped at the shrine of Ananta-Narayana whose stone image floats in the midst of our holy pool. At the feet of the god he left some blue poppies and blue sea-shells.'

'Did he not also offer a blue vessel encrusted with blue diamonds?' interrupted the village potter, the great-great-great-grandfather of Kumar.

'Indeed he did. You may see it even to-day in the treasury of the god Ananta-Narayana. It is a vase of exquisite beauty, of superb craftsmanship.'

The potter's eyes became wet and his voice choked as he recounted the glories of the vanished capital city of the Penhari Parganas, and of the blue-watered Shanka river.

'Yes! Yes!' the Jung Bahadur checked the potter's lyrical outburst. 'I know all these details. But how did Adi Malla's descendants suffer defeat at the hands of the Moslems? Were they unworthy of their high rank and responsibility? Did they give up tending giant buffaloes?'

'They were destroyed because of their excessive love of wrestling,' the village Kathak explained. 'They sadly neglected the noble art of oratory, and despised spiced dishes which provoke thirst and promote eloquence.'

~

Adi Malla's heirs inherited all the virtues of their illustrious forebear, but they suffered from one shortcoming, and that was the cause of their undoing. They were actuated by the desire of convincing their own selves that they were the best wrestlers in the whole of Hindustan. That they were superior to the master-wrestlers of Bengal, Bihar, Orissa, and Nagpur was known to themselves as well as to others beyond these lands: but what about those in Delhi and Agra?

They sent heralds to distant cities, carrying seven diamond-encrusted pectorals: replicas of Adi Malla's *kabach*. Any master-wrestler defeating any of the seven Penhari princes in a fair match was entitled to receive a *kabach*.

These beautiful blue diamond ornaments came to the notice of the Begum of the Pathan Badshah of Delhi and she urged her husband to launch an expedition against the Penhari Parganas.

'Wherefore?' the Badshah was surprised, 'To wage war against a tract of god-forsaken land which maintains a few herds of buffaloes and a handful of Santals and other savages! It isn't worth the trouble. The Penhari region is poor. There isn't much to loot there.'

'You are a fool,' burst out the Begum. 'You are getting old and doting. You are a bigger fool than the Grand Eunuch who is your Vizier. Do poor people send out heralds with blue diamond pectorals? Have you seen any of the *kabaches* the Penhari princes are offering to master-wrestlers? Can't you guess they have diamond-mines richer than those of Golconda? My Circassian slaves tell me that the Kaiser-i-Roum's women prefer Penhari diamonds to those of Golconda. The slaves in Istamboul are better informed than the Badshah of Delhi. What sort of a husband have I got?'

The Grand Vizier was summoned and asked to give his opinion about a campaign against the Penhari Parganas. He declared that there were no diamond-mines anywhere in West Bengal. Centuries ago the Kohinoor as well as a few odd bits of blue diamond were occasionally unearthed near Sambalpur and Jumelpur, and were sent by boat to Rome. That was long, long ago, before the time of the Prophet. And Tamluk was then a sea-port. How these diamonds reached Constantinople he had no knowledge. 'There is, however, a mountain stream called the Shanka,' he added, 'and diamond dust is found mixed with the Shanka's sand. This I have heard from the Santals themselves. They are very truthful—these fools. In fact, the only *kaffirs* who will not in any circumstances tell an untruth.'

'Who asks you to sing the praise of the Santals?' the Begum stamped her slippered foot on the polished marble floor, and the Grand Vizier trembled. He knew what her outbursts of temper meant: he was her step-father. 'Do you want me to believe in cock-and-bull stories about powdered diamonds? Only very highly skilled craftsmen are capable of utilizing diamond-dust! You are a doctored donkey. Jallad! Where are you?'

The Grand Vizier tried to say something, but he was dragged away by Jallad, the hangman and torturer attached to the imperial harem of the Pathan Badshah.

His successor, Assad-Ullah Khan, knew what was expected of him. He had only one question to ask of his imperial mistress, who, by the way, was his first cousin and lover: 'Suppose all that has been said about the Penhari Parganas turns out to be true. What shall I do then to recover the cost of the proposed expedition?'

'Bah!' the Begum put out her tongue. That was her way of showing her contempt for masculine logic. 'Who cares for the cost? I want blue diamond jewellery. The Penhari princes have no right to craftsmen who can make such beautiful, encrusted diamond pectorals. Bring those fellows here. They must work for me; for no one else.'

Assad-Ullah Khan's spies came to the Penhari Parganas to survey the lie of the land. They brought with them bags of gold to offer to the jewellers, diamond-setters, and diamond-cutters of the capital city of Penhari.

'Gold!' the poor craftsmen of Penhari said in surprise. 'What shall we do with so much gold? We are not goldsmiths.'

'Plenty of gold awaits you in Delhi,' the Pathan spies told them, and explained their Begum's desire to have clever jewellers attached to the imperial harem. 'You will have plenty of gold and a good time if you come with us.'

'But we have just as much gold as we need. What should we do with more? And we *are* having a good time. Right here in Penhari. We love our work. We love our bamboo huts, the music of our bamboo flutes, the beauty of our cerulean hills, the grandeur of our scarlet plains, the grace of our women. What more do we want? We should be unhappy in marble palaces. We won't leave the Penhari Parganas to work elsewhere. We don't want your gold. Leave us in peace.'

The spies went back and reported all that they had seen and heard, and they added, incidentally, that the Penhari princes were mad about wrestling. There was a new decree demanding the presence of the commanders of the Penhari forces in the wrestling arenas whenever their rulers were engaged in gymnastics.

'That's good news,' Assad-Ullah Khan assured his mistress. He would do his best to kidnap the Penhari jewellers and diamond-setters. 'And if they succeed in escaping?'

'Raze Penhari's capital to the ground,' the Begum commanded. 'Let all whom you catch be flayed alive. Wait. As there are no diamond-mines in the Penhari Parganas, silt up the Shanka river or divert its course. Let no one ever be able to discover the whereabouts of the Penhari city nor as much as the existence of the Shanka river. Let the jungle over-run the destroyed seat of the Santal buffalo-drivers.'

Assad-Ullah Khan accompanied by his brother, Jonad Khan, seven stalwart thugs disguised as amateur wrestlers, and a retinue of armed torch-bearers came to the city of Penhari towards midnight. He went straight to the residence of the Penhari princes and challenged them to wrestle with his seven hired assassins. These so-called wrestlers wore gauntlets over their _tiger's claws_: glove-like contrivances, fixed with sharp tentacles of hardened steel, capable of piercing any coat of mail or rhinoceros skin. A clever mechanism allowed the steel hooks of the _tiger's claws_ to be folded up like the blades of knives or pushed open, according to the wearer's requirements, to rip any man or beast into shreds of flesh.

The Penhari princes were surprised to receive an invitation to wrestle at midnight. When they found the seven so-called wrestlers of Assad-Ullah Khan wearing gauntlets their surprise became greater.

'We are Moslems and our ways are different,' Assad-Ullah Khan explained. 'You write from the left to the right whereas we write from the right to the left. You pray facing the east while we pray facing the west. You wash your feet first before washing your head but we wash our head first and lastly our feet. Your men are smooth while your women are hairy and our women are smooth, but not our men. You wrestle in day-time while we wrestle at night. And our wrestlers keep their gauntlets on.'

The seven Penhari princes accepted Assad-Ullah's challenge.

And the rest of the tragic tale may easily be guessed. The entrails of the Santal rulers were ripped open by the _tiger's claws_ at Assad-Ullah Khan's and Jonad Khan's pre-arranged signal. The leaderless Santal guards did not know what to do. Their commanders were massacred at the same time as their princes. A holocaust was made of the city of Penhari and its inhabitants. A thousand-year-old principality vanished in the course of a night—to satisfy the whim of a Begum who wanted Penhari's craftsmen to work for her alone.

~

I do not know if the Jung Bahadur accepted this particular version of the fall of the Penhari princedom. But for my part, I am ready to believe it. Our love of wrestling is a mania and if I were to give any credence to Ramdas's statements: all women are whimsical and very fond of jewellery.

One of Mashi-ma's household helps was sent away simply because she showed too much enthusiasm for wrestling. As a rule, our women do not practise this art, not at least before men. But this girl was somewhat original in her ways. I was challenged by her to a match. 'All right,' I told her. 'But you are so much older and bigger. It won't be a fair game.' 'I am not so very old,' she retorted, somewhat hurt, 'just fifteen. Only a few years older than you. Anyway, I can teach you a few good tricks. Be ready for me as soon as Mashi-ma goes to bed.' 'It's always good to learn something new,' I said to myself. 'Especially as I am not an expert wrestler.' In the evening, however, she had hardly undressed and oiled her body when in peeped Mashi-ma quite unexpectedly. And that was the end of our wrestling match. It ended even before it had begun! Mashi-ma gave a cry of horror and dragged my challenger away without listening to me or giving the girl time to collect her clothes; she managed, however, to slip on her heavy bangles before she was hauled away. Naturally, I never learnt from her the tricks she had promised to teach me—most effective head-locks and toeholds in ground-wrestling.

When I think how this poor girl's love for wrestling cost her a comfortable place in a reasonably good house, I am not in the least surprised to hear that a similar sentiment cost the Penhari princes their lives. The *Bhat*, the versifier, told me that the Santal rulers ought not to have accepted Assad-Ullah Khan's challenge at midnight. But that would have been contrary to our tradition. A challenge to a wrestling match or to a contest in oratory can never be refused by any decent man in the Penhari Parganas.

~

To come back to the Jung Bahadur, he listened patiently to all
that the villagers had to say. He then assured them that he had
beaten the Vargis and their associates in ten different places. He
had even taken some of their Brahmins prisoners and installed
them as *pujaris* in the temple of Pasupati-nath at Katamundu:
that was the best way of making them harmless. Anyway, he
was ready for a fresh tussle with the Vargis and would fight
them again: the most he could do to repay in part the debt that
his family and his country owed to Adi Malla, the scion of the
Penharis. 'With your help,' he repeated, 'I shall beat them again.
Those treacherous Vargis, they need another lesson.'

'Jai! *Jung Bahadur-er Jai!*' the villagers cheered. They were
no longer downcast. A dispirited man, they say, is as good as
defeated! Our men were no longer dispirited or despondent:
they had in their midst the Jung Bahadur Shumshere Jogendra
Malla Rana, the Field Marshal of Nepal, and that was enough.
He would teach them, they thought, how to make heavy
artillery. Their own three-yard-long ram-loading fowling pieces
were no match for the quick firing guns and cannon of the
Vargis. '*Jai! Jung Bahadur-er Jai!*' they shouted deliriously. The
village elders were taken aback, however, when they gathered
that the Jung Bahadur was not very keen on guns nor on having
pitched battles with the Vargis: all that he wanted was a few
kukris, the long bent-bladed Gurkha knives, and a nice solid
fortress, a real Golah.

'We will make you as many *kukris* as you want,' said the
village elders, and the blacksmith, a great-great-great grand uncle
of Janardan, nodded his head. He was ready to work night and
day, he declared. As for the Golah, alas! they did not know what
to do. The Red Valley was not Nepal, nor was it Kamrup or the
Cradle of the Clouds! They had no magicians in their village.
In fact, there was not a single one in the whole of the Penhari
Parganas. How could they produce a fortress? 'We have never
owned a fortress.' The chief elder was ready to swear over the

head of his grandson. 'Not even a tiny miserable Golah. How can we offer you a nice solid one?'

'With your help,' the Jung Bahadur smiled, 'a suitable Golah will be built between now and the next autumn when the Vargis reappear. I must, however, examine the lie of the land.' Half of the Golah, he explained, was to be below ground with secret passages leading up to the Damodar river. This portion was to be a hiding place for the inhabitants and their domestic animals and also the store for food and grain. The other half, the portion above ground, should be so constructed as to give the unwary the impression of a slender pleasure house.

The next day the work on our Golah began. For ten months relays of men, women and children worked day and night under the directions of the Jung Bahadur. It was finished in time to entertain the first batch of the Vargi scouts.

~

Though the Vargis rode in their thousands to the attack, they never ventured far afield without reports from their spies, scouts and advance guards. These latter always moved a few days ahead of the main Vargi forces. Members of the advance guard generally carried white pennants attached to their lances and bayonets and pretended to be emissaries of peace.

'This year the Vargis won't harm you,' was their usual greeting. 'The Vargis are pious Hindus. They don't touch beef. All that they want is to make the country free and everyone happy. That, of course, takes money. They don't want much. Just one fourth of your produce. One fourth of all that you have made during the last twelve months. That's very little. The price of freedom.'

The Jung Bahadur acted as the spokesman of the Penhari Parganas. He was polite to those rascally liars and gave them a ceremonious reception on the first floor of the newly finished Golah. He advised the members of the advance guard to return to their masters conveying his best regards and the assurance that the inhabitants of the Red Valley and the Blue Hills valued nothing more highly than peace, freedom, and happiness.

The Vargi spies, scouts and advance guards were greatly elated. They licked their lips and gibbered among themselves, as they came out of the Golah, that the Jung Bahadur was a fool: it was idiotic of him to have entertained them with dancing and music; that was the surest way of inviting the Vargis to be more rapacious and ruthless. They were, however, much impressed by the diversions given in their honour. Some of them admired the buxom Santal girls dressed in short *saris* revealing their thighs and momentarily, their breasts. The Pindaris accompanying the Vargi advance guards found more attractive the frail, ivory-skinned Hindu maidens because they wore gossamer-like veils which barely hid their bodies' charms. They all discussed among themselves the relative merits and demerits of the different sets of dancers, and reached the conclusion that Assad-Ullah Khan and his companions were simpletons to assume that the Penhari damsels were not as smooth as the Begums of Delhi and Agra. The thought of dishonouring the young dancers who had entertained them made their mouths water: their programme of liberating the land included defiling helpless maidens. The prettier a girl the graver the risk of her being ravished by the freedom-loving Vargis and their associates, the Pindaris and the Pathans.

They also debated the nature of the punishment that they could mete out to the Jung Bahadur when they returned to the Golah with the main army. It would be nice, some suggested, to have his inside filled with gunpowder and then blow him up. But that would be a quick death, according to others, and therefore, they would love to have him impaled with a lance and then violate the dancing girls before his eyes. The Jung Bahadur and the men of the Penhari Parganas in their opinion merited the direst punishment for having secreted their women so long.

'The poor women!' they reasoned, 'They have been deprived of the embraces of the liberators of their land. Anyhow, we shall help them to make up for lost time.'

The advance guards did not, however, know the Jung Bahadur well, and so their speculations were wrong.

'*Dakupar darja dedeo!*' was the pass-word the Jung Bahadur taught the villagers. 'Deal with the Devil devilishly! D-D-D! The three D's! My motto.' The origin of this motto went back to the remote past. The Devil once tried to enter the temple of Pasupatinath at Katamundu in the guise of a pilgrim: His objective was to defile the holy shrine. But before he could put a foot inside the sacred temple the very stones cried out: '*Dakupar darja dedeo!* Shut the brigand out! Throw the hypocrite out!'

'Had the Devil been a penitent,' the Jung Bahadur told the villagers, 'it would have been permitted to him to worship like any other pilgrim. But the unrepentant rascal has no right to step on the stones of a holy edifice. Devilry is the only weapon for undoing the Devil. To a *Bhoot*, I am a *Mamdo-Bhoot*! To a demon I'll behave like a super-demon! Remember the pass-word, the three D's: *Dakupar darja dedeo!*'

The Jung Bahadur proved to be as good as his word: the Vargis and their friends were outmanoeuvred by his ruse and the Penhari Parganas were saved from a general massacre at the hands of the liberators. The tricks he employed, the artifices he practised, the techniques he devised for luring the leaders of the marauders to the upper storey of the Golah when they returned in greater strength, and for allowing some of them to escape to carry the news of their disaster to their brethren, how he transmitted his messages by rockets and flares at night and by mirror-flash during the day—these and other incidents of his courageous leadership in our struggles against twenty thousand armed horsemen would demand more than a volume.

However, I have said enough to indicate why I admired the Jung Bahadur Shumshere Jogendra Malla Rana and wanted to emulate, and if possible, of course, surpass some of his feats of horsemanship.

Before leaving the Penhari Parganas, the Jung Bahadur visited the *moucharaby*, the Nest of the Hawks. He climbed the steep crags on the back of his horse. And I wanted to do the same. My attempt was not wholly successful: I had a minor mishap owing to my too great confidence in Sashe Raha's discretion. Sashe Raha, nicknamed the Split Cucumber, gave me away when I tried out my pony, Red Belly, at the Golah. The Santal children never let me down, but Sashe did: that was a great shame. It led to my losing Red Belly, a most lovable and sure-footed mountain pony.

V

Outwardly the Golah looked decidedly gloomy. Its walls were blackened and moss-covered: it bore all the marks of long neglect. When I brought Kolej Huzoor to inspect it, he simply sniggered: 'It's exactly like the gasometer near the railway marshalling yard at Vardaman.'

I told him about the whispering gallery. But it did not interest him: he refused to come inside to try it out. The same was the attitude of Swagger Cane. 'It is like a petrol tank,' he remarked. 'In Asansole there are scores of masonry pill-boxes just like your Golah. What's the use of seeing its inside?'

The history of the building failed to arouse the least flicker of enthusiasm in either of them. Nor were they impressed by the fact that it was constructed by voluntary labour and finished in just ten months.

'In Russia bigger buildings are put up in ten weeks,' commented Gopaldas. Being a son of the Penhari Parganas he ought to have shown some liking for it! But I was mistaken: he went a step further than the others and declared that he would not mind blowing it up. 'All old monuments ought to be dynamited. The past weighs us down. What's interesting about this depressing rotunda?' It hurt me to hear that Gopaldas was as ignorant as the other two about the underground passages leading up to the Damodar river. 'What can you do with this Golah?' he asked. 'Can you eat it?'

'It can store as much as 300,000 tons of grain,' I replied proudly. 'The underground vault is for 150,000 tons. And the same amount can be kept in the upper storey.'

'That's just nothing.' Kolej Huzoor gave a dry laugh. 'There are much bigger cold storage plants in Calcutta. The Golah is certainly not one of the Seven Wonders, I can assure you.'

His cue was taken up by Swagger Cane who gave a nice little lecture on the Great Pyramid of Egypt. I learnt it was about 480 feet high and its base covered an area of about 13 acres; it contained about 2,500,000 blocks of stone, each weighing on the average 2½ tons.

Gopaldas made a neat speech on the Great Lenin Monument also, which was to surpass in its grandeur all the Golahs and all the Pyramids put together. He gave some imposing figures about the weight of ferro-concrete already used and to be used further for building this monument. 'What's the weight of your Golah?' he finally asked and I did not answer, though I felt like blurting out that the Golah was finished in a few months whereas it took ages to finish the Pyramid and perhaps decades to lay the foundation of the Lenin monument. But I did not say anything: it was no use wasting words on such people.

I must, nevertheless, admit that outwardly the Golah was not an impressive structure. As only half of it was above ground, the portion which my visitors saw was no more than 110 feet high, though its real height was about 220—without counting the foundation. This circular fortress measured barely 450 feet around its outer circumference: not an imposing figure compared with the dimensions of the Great Pyramid whose each side was said to be about 755 feet at the base. About 12 feet was the thickness of its walls—or should it be called wall?—for it was one continuous structure of uniform breadth forming a complete circle. The diameter of the inside was precisely 110 feet, which again was not really stupendous compared with the Great Wall of China.

The interest of the Golah did not, however, lie in its dimensions, but in its historic association with the life of the Penhari Parganas.

~

The vault or lower storey of the Golah was generally dark. But for a few light-wells similar to those in the Beauri coal-mine and in our *baolis*, it would have been pitch black there. 'Darkness draws disgusting denizens,' according to the villagers, and they were perfectly right: this I can say from what I saw inside the vault with my own eyes.

As it had not been used since the days of the Jung Bahadur and the extermination of the Vargis, it came to be transformed into the hiding place of all sorts of strange creatures that hated light: they managed to worm their way through the underground passages and the airing shafts. Once I had a narrow escape while I was exploring one of the subterranean corridors and had the fright of my life: the disgusting beasts that prefer darkness to light nearly caught me! My misadventure in the vault of the Golah came about in this way.

'I am sure,' Gopaldas taunted me one day, 'your aunt holds your hand every night till you fall asleep. You are simply afraid of the dark. That's why you do not want to revisit the mines with me.'

Gopaldas absolutely refused to believe that I had given my word of honour to her that I would not go down any of the mines without her permission. Of late there had been a few explosions due to mine-damp and not a few miners buried alive. As Mashima was subject to whims, I had to satisfy her whim, and gave my promise somewhat thoughtlessly.

'But a man's word is his word,' I told Gopaldas. 'I can't break my promise.'

Gopaldas gave a wry smile and told me that the explosions were *not* due to mine-damp: they were caused by time bombs. I listened with my mouth open with amazement. The miners, he said, had to be shaken free from their attitude of apathy and the political party to which he belonged were forced to take drastic measures. 'Of course, a few people will be killed,' he added. 'But what can you do? The Party has to think of the future. Unless there is a general upheaval among the miners we can't hope for new recruits. So we want to create a feeling of insecurity in the mines. The time bombs were placed there by the Red Falcons. You come with me and I will show you how it is done.'

I reminded him once again about my promise to Mashi-ma.

'Tell me another!' Gopaldas laughed sarcastically. 'You are simply afraid of the dark like all girls of your age. If not, just go down one of the underground passages of the Golah and come out by the main staircase of the vault. I will wait for you there.'

'All right.' I accepted his challenge and he told me to bring one of the underground creatures with me to prove that I was afraid of nothing. I wanted to run home and fetch a coil of rope.

'No, no,' he shouted, 'go as you are. It would take you an hour to reach your home, while the Golah is only at ten minutes' distance. And if anyone sees you with your rope you will be asked questions. I don't want you to spill the beans. Go down a passage as you are. You have your bamboo flute with you. What more do you want?'

The journey through the dark tunnel was not trying, but the vault itself I found pretty nauseating, especially as I trod inadvertently on a bundle of wriggling snakes: those were *raj-saps*, the two-headed reptiles.

For those who have no knowledge of crawling creatures it should be pointed out that a *raj-sap* is not exactly double-headed like a Siamese twin. It is, however, called *two-headed* because its tail-end is supposed to carry fangs, a retractile, forked tongue, and rudimentary eyes exactly in the same way as its real head. The *raj-saps* may or may not be very venomous: I have no definite information on the matter. Different people have told me different stories about these snakes. Some have assured me that they are totally blind as a result of their aspiring at one time to be more deadly than other serpents! The *raj-sap* prayed to the god Shiva for two heads and two pairs of eyes, and the god in a fit of absent-mindedness granted the boon. The goddess Uma, Shiva's consort, realized immediately the folly of his act. Being the spirit of Charity she thought of other creatures and cursed the two-headed reptile. 'You will not be able to use any of your four eyes,' she said. Had she not deprived the *raj-sap* of its sight, this wretched snake, they say, would have become the most formidable of all living beings.

Whether deadly or not, my own experience with these two-headed reptiles in the obscurity of the vault was most uncanny; it sent shivers down my spine and gave me an uncomfortable feeling in the pit of my stomach. The fault was entirely mine: I ought not to have trodden on a living bundle of serpents, mistaking the tangled mass for an abandoned coil of rope. Just then my mind was bent on making a nice, strong lasso to capture a good specimen of a carnivorous monitor, probably the ugliest creature in the world, and drag it out of the vault: a token of my visit to the underground tunnel and a present for Gopaldas who falsely accused me of being afraid of the dark.

I had never seen a monitor before. My ignorance about their characteristics led to my discomfiture. Instead of catching a monitor, I was nearly caught by one of them and devoured alive.

It is extremely misleading to give wrong names to savage creatures. It is a gross error to call a monitor a *giant lizard*. This beast is more akin to an alligator than to a harmless lizard. It is capable of sitting up like a toad and turning its head like a monkey. It has sharp teeth like a crocodile and possesses the gift of sprinting like a baboon. It measures several feet in length, and it can stretch its stumpy tail by darting it out like a lizard's tongue to hit its victim insensible. Furthermore, it is carnivorous. Not in the least afraid of man. In fact it relishes human flesh. Why such a beast should be commonly known as a *giant lizard* is a mystery to me.

Anyway, my ignorance nearly cost me my life. All that I could do when I discovered that instead of being the hunter I was the hunted and that it was beyond me to wrestle with beasts twice my size, was to withdraw backwards, facing my aggressors and swinging my bamboo flute as though it was a sword-stick. A three-foot bamboo flute was not much of a weapon. Yet it was better than nothing. It helped me to keep up my courage. While retreating I noticed through the corner of my eyes a coiled mass on the floor and I immediately made my calculations: 'I shall throw the bamboo flute into the open jaw of the foremost monitor, and at the same time I shall pick up the rope using my foot and make a lasso and then I shall see.'

Imagine, therefore, my horror when I found out that my only means of saving myself was nothing but a mass of living snakes. By now my flute was gone. And I felt helpless like an upturned turtle. What was I to do? If only I had been dressed in a *dhotie* like other boys I would have ripped it and tried to make a lasso of it. But that was out of the question: I was in shorts. My frustration changed me into a coward. In that musty atmosphere of an almost eternally sealed vault where no sunlight ever entered I longed for the light of day and the breath of the fresh air. 'If I were to die,' I said to myself, 'let me die in the sun.' A moment later I realized the meaninglessness of my wish. Would the flesh-eating monitors listen to my plea? Was I not their enemy? Was I not the boy who wanted to strangle one of them for a trophy? What claim had I to their clemency? 'A careless man,' they say, 'merits no mercy,' and I was more than careless: thoughtless— vain, arrogant, and foolhardy.

And suddenly a shriek, a shrill shriek of great distress pierced my ears. It was startling. It was still more startling when I discovered that it was my own cry of despair! Several times in my life the meaning of fear had been revealed to me. But never before had I experienced one of so nauseating a character. The monitors were indescribably repellent. As they closed round me, a sickening terror crept over me. Hitherto I had not thought of shouting for succour, knowing full well that the Golah was miles away from all human habitations. But now when totally foiled, utterly defeated, when the nearest monitor's breathings almost paralysed my body, my tongue involuntarily uttered a rending scream of horror. Had I waited a moment longer my lips would have been sealed for good and I would have been devoured without emitting the least sound: the coma of extreme dread would have frozen me into a living corpse.

At that time I did not know that the underground vault of the Golah possessed the same property of giving back echoes in increasing intensity as the whispering gallery on the floor above. My cry of agony soon raised a storm of sounds such as I had never heard before: it was like the booming and clanging of a thousand giant temple bells and mammoth gongs within a closed cell. The air vibrated. The walls trembled and quivered. The ceiling shook. The floor heaved. The whole building rattled. It seemed as though the tremendous clamour was going to shatter the structure, and as a preliminary it was being rolled like a light skiff in a heavy squall. The deafened denizens of the dark vault were dazed, and this made my escape possible.

'Blessed be thou, Sound!' I murmured to myself the brief prayer which Mashi-ma repeated every evening as she sounded her hand bell and lighted the lamp at the foot of the holy basil plant in her garden. 'Blessed be thou, Sound! The first daughter of Creation. Praised be thou whose voice vibrated in the darkness and brought forth light. Blessed be thou, Sound!'

The terrific noise was more than deafening. It was like excessive brightness, which is as blinding as total darkness. This was a noise that could be felt but not heard or heard only in vague snatches. It was beyond the range of human hearing—like the low-pitched tones from Padre Johan's organ. One noticed the vibrations more than the sound. It was launched by my scream and magnified a thousand-fold by the circular walls and the concave ceiling: the echoes became doubled by the counter-echoes: the vibrations redoubled by the reverberations. Something akin to the ripples and counter-ripples produced in a shallow pool by a single stone dropped in its midst. The booming lasted for several minutes and temporarily paralysed all the crepuscular creatures. Like myself, they were taken by surprise. But unlike myself, they took it, I surmise, for an unpropitious warning of an impending cataclysm and they lay low. They did not know what to do or where to escape. They were creatures of darkness and did not dare come out into the light. In their fright they lay still in death-like trance and ignored my precipitate retreat over their prostrate bodies. None of the monitors stirred even when my trembling feet trod upon them. Only a solitary vampire bat made a bold attempt to fly. Probably it knew its way out through one of the light-wells. It was, however, immediately struck down by the unseen waves of sound. Invisible blows drove it back each time it tried frantically to flutter. It was battered against the walls and pounded and pulped to death.

Indeed it was a weird experience. The fate of the frightened bat was a warning to me: it reminded me that a blast of air can lift an elephant up like a feather or blow a fortress down like a house of cards. I crawled across the floor on all fours. I called myself a fool when I found myself befouled and defiled by the frightened creatures, the sinister twilight assassins: the vampire bats, the two-headed *raj-saps*, the flesh-eating monitors, and their companions.

It was silly of me to have sought adventure in the underground obscurity simply to prove that I was not timorous as a girl, afraid of the dark and frightened of the tunnels. Perhaps the blame lay to some extent on the soil of the Penhari Parganas: those born on it are liable to be queer. The Penhari princes gave their lives to prove that they were ready at all times to accept the challenge of any wrestler.

~

Though the basement of the Golah was steeped in perpetual obscurity, its ground floor was flooded with light. This floor was known as the Reception Hall because the Jung Bahadur had entertained the Vargis and their friends here. Although it did not receive much direct sunlight it was bathed during the day in ivory luminosity, thanks to numerous sky-lights and those peculiar contrivances called *day-lanterns* which furnish indirect lighting, so necessary in a country where direct sunlight means terrific heat.

This Reception Hall deserved comparison in its proportions with the levee halls of the most renowned palaces of India. The floor was of polished alabaster inlaid with attractive mosaics of stylized *sankhas*, marine conch shells, the heraldic sign of the Penhari princes surrounded by seven concentric heart-shaped, irregular oval patterns: four red ones alternating with three blue ones. The seven oval patterns represented the seven Parganas of the Penhari princedom; four lying in the Red Valley, and the remaining three covering the hills and jungles of the Blue Hills: all these were at one time under the protection of Adi Malla and his six co-regents. The mosaics created an optical illusion: the impression of vastness. A circular alabaster floor of 110 feet in diameter would be regarded as spacious enough anywhere, but inlaid ornamental patterns made it look infinitely more spacious, unbelievably immense.

The feeling of vastness was considerably enhanced by the sheen of the shining circular wall, plastered and polished with the finest *chunam*, made of powdered shell lime and pure white sand. It reflected light like a concave mirror. As a matter of fact, the inside wall resembled the interior of an enormous ivory-tinted porcelain cylinder of oily smoothness. The slightly domed ceiling was equally polished and shining. It reflected, even as it magnified, the patterns on the floor.

A stranger entering the hall for the first time was bound to be bewildered. If he happened to be unaccompanied by a guide he ran the risk of wandering about for a long time and knocking many times against the *chunam* wall before hitting upon a door for exit. Even then he would not have been able to come out of the Golah: because the heavy iron doors were covered with huge mirrors and did not open in the ordinary way. They had to be lifted up from the bottom like the sash-windows of a railway coach. In the days of the Jung Bahadur they were opened and closed by a system of pulleys operated from the very roof of the Golah.

One may well imagine the dilemma of the Vargis, Pindaris and Pathans when they were lured into this hall and left to their own devices for getting out while the Jung Bahadur made his exit by means of a rope ladder dropped from the roof through one of the day-lanterns: the one just above the central spot which is marked by a mosaic of a blue poppy.

The brigand chieftains were, no doubt, still more confused by the wonderful echo, for which the Golah was deservedly famous. The echo here was of a much more effective and pleasanter kind than in the vault below: this was probably due to the smoothness of the wall and the arrangement of the sky-lights and the day-lanterns, more variedly disposed than the light-wells of the vault below. A hand-clap given at the exact centre of the floor, where it bears the mosaic of the blue poppy, would after about a minute produce a series of resonances lasting for some length of time. At first the echoes gave the impression of a score of hands clapping mild applause, and then the intensity of the sound would change: the mild applause of a few pairs of hands would be slowly transformed into the thunderous sound of a thousand lusty cheers. Immediately afterwards a brief silence would ensue and this would in its turn be followed by a soft report of many muffled feet lightly touching the floor and finally by a deafening twang and clanging of innumerable hob-nailed and spurred boots on stone pavements—as though a marching army of steel-clad and iron-shod men were trying to batter down the roof of the Golah.

By opening or closing some of the sky-lights and day-lanterns the echo-effects could be varied. What a pity I never got the opportunity of demonstrating this peculiarity to Swagger Cane, Kolej Huzoor and Gopaldas: it would have been such fun to notice their reaction to my whisper 'Dakupar darja dedeo,' the password pronounced by the Jung Bahadur to lower the heavy iron-doors for shutting the Vargis in and to drop the rope-ladder for his exit through a sky-light. I wonder if they would then have persisted in sneering at our Golah.

Motorists on their way to Hazaribagh or Bhagalpur occasionally stopped at the Golah on account of its whispering gallery, which they declared to be 'unique'. The faintest murmur at any point of the round hall could be most distinctly heard at the opposite point. This feature was in my opinion nothing extraordinary. Mabool the Moslem held the same view. The mausoleum of Sultan Adil Shah, better known as the *Gol Gumbaz* of Bijapur, is just as good. So, too, is the tomb of Shere Shah at Sasseram, and therefore I need not describe a trait common to many buildings and known to most people interested in domed structures.

The hidden *elephant steps* in the walls do, however, merit a few words.

The Vargis claimed that they were the finest horsemen in the country. Those who want to justify the depredations of these cruel human locusts often dwell lovingly on the Vargis' gifts of managing their mounts, as though it exonerated the brigands from all humane duties and responsibilities. According to the people of the Penhari Parganas, the Jung Bahadur, in spite of his advanced age, was a better horseman than the most intrepid Vargi riders. In fact, he invited the Vargis to ride up the hundred and fifty elephant steps leading from the ground to the platform of the Reception Hall. He showed them how this could easily be done. Nevertheless, they refused to follow his lead. They were afraid of breaking their necks, those brave Vargis who did not mind massacring unarmed men, women, and children.

'The Jung Bahadur gave them not one, but many demonstrations of climbing up the elephant steps on horseback,' Kumar told me. 'He rode up and down the different staircases built inside the walls without even touching the reins of his horse. The Vargis declared that they had no circus horses with them and so they could not follow the Jung Bahadur's example!'

So many people outside the Penhari Parganas talked so often about the marvellous qualities of the Vargis and of their horses that at one time I had almost come to accept what was dinned into my ears. But after my arrival at the village I began having my doubts. Cruel people, the Punditji told me, are generally crude bluffers. As the Vargis were cruel, I wondered whether they were bluffers too. Though I laid no claims to good horsemanship I wanted to test out the elephant steps in the Golah with my pony, Red Belly. Once with several Santal boys as my witnesses I rode up the steps and came down without any difficulty: this showed that the Vargis were, after all, mere bluffers as far as their alleged crack riding was concerned. Red Belly was a fine mountain pony and I rode on its back without using any saddle or reins. I had little difficulty in repeating what the Jung Bahadur did. The stone steps had herring-bone grooves which allowed safe-footing for my Red Belly.

VI

I suffered a most serious loss as a consequence of my riding exploit at the Golah. The mishap took place when I was away from the village and could do nothing to prevent its occurrence. In fact I came to know about it only after it had taken place: it was then too late to do anything about it. Its memory, however, still hurts me.

Sashe Raha was terribly fond of chewing sticks of sugar cane. If anyone wanted to send him on any errand all that was necessary was to promise him sugar cane. For a bit of sugar cane he was capable of anything! He never cared for the Santal boys of his own age. But if he found any of them sucking a piece of sugar cane he would follow them about for hours for the privilege of picking up the chewed stem. That was how he happened to be in the midst of the Santal boys who acted as my witnesses when I rode up the steps of the Golah on the back of Red Belly.

One day, in order to worm himself into Mashi-ma's favour during my absence as a student-monitor at Amrita-ban, he told her that it was imprudent of me to use a horse for climbing steps! He wanted to impress my poor aunt that he was much more reasonable than I. At the same time he forgot to tell her that he was afraid of horses and that the herring-bone grooves, neatly cut on the stone steps of the Golah to allow rainwater to run away, afforded safe footing for men and beasts.

I am almost sure Sashe Raha gave Mashi-ma a garbled version of my ride. For Ramdas's wife told me later that for quite a while my aunt was almost distracted with wild dreams and strange nightmares about horses and my being thrown down deep precipices and ravines, and that was why she sold Red Belly without even consulting me! Later on, I was deprived of the privilege of owning even a bicycle. Mashi-ma's capacity of wasting worry over events that took place ages ago was simply unbelievable. In this respect she was no different from other women of the Red

Valley: Ramdas was perfectly right when he said, 'Our women are more full of whims and crazy ideas than others.'

The loss of Red Belly was a blow to me. I did not mind so much the written promise Mashi-ma extracted from me never to revisit the Golah without her permission.

A curious coincidence might be noted in this connection, particularly as it confirmed one of the contentions of our Punditji: 'We must not only think well, but also know how to dream well. Nightmares cause calamities.'

~

At the very time when Mashi-ma was indulging in strange phantasies and in interviewing my wraith astride a phantom horse, I did manage to get a bad bump falling off the back of a nag. Luckily I did not have Sashe Raha as a witness of the accident. The Santal boys and Neela were extremely discreet. They never told anyone that I wanted to imitate the memorable exploit of the Jung Bahadur when he climbed the steep cliffs above Madhuban on horseback to visit the *moucharaby* of the Penhari princes.

For this climb I had to depend on a borrowed nag, a one-eyed shy creature not too difficult to manage, but she took fright at the last moment on the very threshold of the *moucharaby*: she wanted to jump to her death through the open end of the gallery. Though I succeeded in restraining her I received a pretty bad knock and had to lie stretched on my back for several weeks.

I did not regard this matter as serious, but it was most humiliating. I had failed where the grey-haired Jung Bahadur had succeeded. He had met with no mishap, but I had. I was ashamed still more of myself when I found that I could not get on my feet and had temporarily lost my power of speech. I saw Neela kneeling over me and sobbing.

'Why did you want to kill yourself?' Neela's voice was choked with tears. The fall stunned me, but I soon recovered my senses:

I saw everything and heard everything, but my tongue refused to move and my feet and limbs were inert. 'Tell me,' Neela sobbed, 'why do you want to die? Accidents happen only when we are confused. When we are bewildered. Or tired of living. What makes you sick of life?'

'Perhaps someone has been worrying too much over him,' remarked the Santal boy who took over the charge of the frightened nag. 'Let him lie here quietly. I'll fetch a few blankets from Madhu-ban.'

My pain did not worry me. If my eyes were then filled with tears it was due to the fullness of my heart. I felt a strange yearning whose import I did not know. Neela was bending over me and through the deranged folds of her *vasanti* yellow *sari* her pointed nipples stared at me as her breasts heaved with her quick breathing: they looked like our lotus-buds which are rose-tipped.

When the body is tortured and the mind is racked should I not have thought of the cessation of my pain? Yet why was it otherwise then? What was uppermost in my mind at that moment? I wanted to be in Neela's arms. 'If you were to die,' my inner self whispered to me, 'would you not like to die in her arms? Clasped to her bosom? Her breasts are lovely?'

Neela sobbed in silence. Her eyes rested with a curious puzzled look on me. I lay on the floor of the *moucharaby* immobile like one totally paralysed, and vaguely guessed that she was removing my soiled clothes and wrapping up my undressed body in the blankets brought from Madhu-ban.

Lying on my back as helpless as a nursling I watched the heavens. The azure sky with constantly changing clouds seemed vaster than it had ever been: it appeared immeasurably immense.

VII

The Santals are renowned for their hospitality and those of the Blue Hills were more hospitable than others. Even if I had been a stranger they would have given me every succour, but the fact that the accident took place when I was teaching their children how to read and write made them more than generous. They did everything possible to make my convalescence pleasant. Para-Manik, the headman of the village often called on me, and of course Neela, and others too. They were discreet and the news of my accident was kept back from my village.

Madhu-ban could be reached by various routes from my village. The narrowest tract cut out in the days of the Jung Bahadur was the shortest as well as the steepest. I rarely made use of it for climbing the Blue Hills. My preference was for the meandering disused path which was once the route of pilgrims to the shrine of Badri-nath, on the saddle of the Saffron Crag beyond the Blue Hills.

The temple of Badri-nath is in ruins to-day and no pilgrim goes there chanting the holy formula '*Jai! Badrinath-er Jai! Jai! Nara-Narayan-er Jai!*' No one now wends his way to lay flowers on the foot-prints of Buddha, on the platform near the dilapidated Jaga-Mandir: the Enlightened One stood there once to bless the hills and the valleys of the Penhari Parganas. We know the words of benediction he pronounced: 'May truth be your quest though suffering be your portion.'

I preferred the pilgrims' path for many reasons: its historic associations were not the least of these. For at least two thousand years, right up to the middle of the eighteenth century, when with the collapse of the Mogul Empire the shrines on the Saffron Crag came to be desecrated, an annual pilgrimage to the temple of Badri-nath and to the foot-prints of Buddha by the Jaga-Mandir was deemed essential for every pious inhabitant of the Penhari Parganas. When Jaya-Deva, our master-poet, went to the crest of the Saffron Crag he used this track. What was good for him was certainly good for me.

Though this path demands at times that one should traverse stretches of hard volcanic rocks, it has been worn fairly smooth by the bare feet of innumerable pilgrims of many centuries.

Apart from its smoothness it offers the climber the exhilarating experience of observing the gradual changes in the flora and fauna with the varying altitudes.

Up to a certain height, maybe two thousand feet or thereabouts, the trees, plants, and shrubs of the Blue Hills are more or less the same as in the Red Valley below. One notices a marked change, however, as soon as the ridge beyond the village of Amrita-ban is crossed. The path then traverses a thick forest of flowering *sal* trees and giant bamboos. Though the ground seems to be nothing but broken and powdered slates, it permits the growth of a luxuriant vegetation: the clumps of the bamboos here are much thicker than those on the plain, and the timber of the *sal* trees is said to be harder than anywhere else: as strong as the teak wood, on account of the soil. At a greater height the *isvara* or ixora trees, the mountain ebony, the oaks, maples and walnuts become conspicuous, while wild plantains, tree ferns, and tree rhododendrons make their sudden appearance in strange profusion, forming oases of their own. The height at which scarlet and aubergine magnolias are found is remarkable for its lack of undergrowth, and also for the presence of the creeping bougainvillias with *avira*, purple flowers and the misleading, treacherous-looking *maloo* climbers.

Higher up, as one approaches Madhu-ban, the vegetation is less rich. The oaks, the maples, and the chestnuts become gnarled and widely dispersed. The trees are stumpier and fewer as one climbs still higher. And they disappear altogether when one reaches the perpendicular ridge which forms the spine of the Blue Hills, stretching for many miles from the north to the south.

Of the different varieties of vegetation, the one which fascinated me most is to be found in the region where the trees are of an average height of about two hundred feet. The trunks of these tall trees are generally branchless to their very apex, but there they throw out sudden profusions of foliated arms to form a solid and continuous canopy of leaves cutting off the sky from the ground below: this leafy canopy is the cause of a perpetual gloom even in day-time. This jungle gloaming was frightening. Its uncanny effect was heightened by the rope-like lianas of the creepers and climbers, and also by the fantastic roots of wild fig trees growing on the branches of the two-hundred-foot-tall trees. These parasitic fig trees drop their weird radicles and tendrils to the earth from a great height. I noticed a variety of orchids with beautiful purple flowers, and rhododendrons with gorgeous magenta and scarlet blooms, all growing in the same way as these jungle figs—the *sun-worshippers*.

Is life really the resultant of contradictory forces? What truth is in this belief of my people?

The more I examined these strange plants with their bewitchingly attractive flowers the more was I mystified. How did they come to lead a parasitic existence? How did they learn the art of absorbing their nourishment by subsisting on other trees? What made the epiphytes and saprophytes repay the generosity of their hosts by gradually smothering them to death and utilizing their lifeless trunks for their own benefit? What tempted them to seek this curious course of living?

'Fascination,' according to the Punditji, 'is a form of attraction that has nothing to do with love. To revel in loveless attraction is the same as playing with fire.' Perhaps he was right. The green-canopied, gloomy regions of the forest attracted and repelled me at the same time. They tempted my curiosity without ever satisfying it. I know I never liked the eternally dimmed-out areas very much, yet I wandered about there. What was the reason? Was it the hope of coming across those occasional circular knolls and depressions, open to the sky, free from all trees and climbers: rings of grassy plots—bright, sunny and cheerful? In my mind's eye I saw these round open spaces peopled at nightfall with mythical beings, the *kin-naras* and the *kin-naris*, the male and female centaurs who are choristers to the gods, according to our poets. The wind plays strange melodies *only* in these places, and it is not surprising that in ancient days people thought that the horse-headed and human-limbed *kin-naras* and *kin-naris* danced in these open circles while the human-headed horses played musical instruments. These choristers to the deities are said to be benevolent to lost travellers, and at the behest of the sylvan goddess Aranyani chase away the malicious demons who delight in misleading the unwary.

To pass through the different regions of the forests following the pilgrims' track was an experience in itself. It was like exploring the dark caverns underneath the earth and then re-emerging into the world of light as a man re-born. Was it for this reason that the pilgrims deliberately chose the narrow, winding path to reach their goal? Did they bear in mind the same counsel as is given to us to-day? 'Unless a man be re-born he shall not see God.' Did the men of yore think in the same way as I? Did the journey through the dark glades, the forbidden gloamings, the delightful knolls, and the sun-lit ridges evoke in them the same sensations as in me? Did they too feel a sense of relief and of triumph when they attained their objective on the treeless heights, and looked down on the tree-top canopy of the jungles below? When the pilgrimage was over did they get a glimpse of the Cradle of the Clouds?

~

Seen from the heights near Madhu-ban the canopy of tree-tops presented the aspect of a solid sea of emerald green—a world of its own—sheltering creatures that never came down to the solid earth of their own will nor sought the sky. They seemed to be eminently suited for their mode of existence: tree-top dwelling. They were endowed with the gift of gliding or planing through the air.

As far as I could judge, the forest belt on the slopes of the Blue Hills maintained three distinctly different types of fauna: one flourishing on the firm ground, another preferring the tree-trunks, and finally those thriving on tree-tops. These last were the jungle dwellers which interested me most and to whom I have just referred. There was a projecting ledge of rock near Madhuban from which I made my observations. How I wished I had a pair of good binoculars to watch the birds, butterflies, insects and animals of this leafy sea.

The unaided eye—without any spy-glasses—did not permit any close inspection. I never saw anything remotely resembling the Seven-footed Flying Serpents about which I heard such a lot from the Santal children. This strange snake is supposed to look like a shoot of the long gourd, the *laudogah*, and to possess the power of paralysing its victim by the lick of its forked green tongue, while its bite has a contrary effect from that of its lick! Its bitten prey would dance on till overtaken by death from sheer exhaustion caused by the venom-induced, uninterrupted caperings. Only those born with kingly virtues are immune from the attacks of this nefarious flying reptile. Therefore, in the olden days a number of these snakes were kept in a special pit in the residence of the Penhari princes. Before receiving his diadem every prince had to go through a series of ordeals and trials to prove his courage and qualities of leadership. One of the trials was to go down into the snake-pit. If he came out safe and sound he was hailed as a true prince. Otherwise it was assumed that the aspirant for the diadem was a mere changeling, placed in the nursery of the princes when he was a baby.

It might well be that the Seven-footed Flying Serpent does not exist and never existed at all, not even in the days of Adi Malla. As a mythological reptile it furnished and will continue to furnish interesting themes of discussion among our children, and particularly among the Santal youngsters of the Blue Hills.

Only the fearless were deemed worthy of occupying one of the seven princely thrones of Penhari. Since we hold it to be an axiomatic truth that a truly fearless man, and he alone, will never be overcome by a reptile however vile, there is nothing absurd about the story of the snake-pit in the home of the Penhari princes. Has not the god Shiva a venomous cobra round his neck? Is not Krishna represented as dancing on the outstretched hood of the serpent Ananta? And Padre Johan's Redeemer, is he not shown triumphing over a snake? Even so, the wise and the brave are expected to have the power to subdue the Seven-footed Flying reptile.

'In a way it is a good thing,' I said to myself, 'that I have not come across the Flying Serpent. Not being wise or brave its bite might have caused me to start a St Vitus's dance. There are other creatures to see and admire. Some of them are not even known by their name to most people.' That was true enough, but I did not know their names either.

Take, for example, the flying frog with its enormously expanded feet acting like sails when this animal leaps from tree to tree; the flying squirrel which does not really fly, but gives that impression when, in a single jump, it clears the enormous round gaps, some thirty feet in diameter, in the otherwise solid roof of foliage; the tailless gibbon with extraordinarily long and remarkably agile arms, who is expert at catching birds on the wing and at producing strange sounds from its throat as though from a windbag; the eternally shivering and terribly shy slow loris, an ungainly creature with saucer-like eyes and emaciated limbs, afraid of the light.

All this, however, is somewhat of a digression. What concerned me most as I watched so many sorts of creatures in the jungle was to find out in which way men were related to them. 'Man is a lump kneaded of all the beasts,' the Punditji told me once. 'If you understand the ways of animals you will be able to see through man. Take the creatures that shun the light: they are generally unpleasant and unsightly. Ugliness shuns brightness. It hates clarity. The children of the Light can never be unsightly: they are god-like. Be one of them.' Padre Johan too made some such remarks in one of his sermons in the corrugated iron chapel at Jamtara. '*Sheytan*, the Supreme Evil,' he preached, 'prefers perpetual darkness. So do his followers, the foul beasts of malediction. Rankness, debasement and corruption flourish only in obscurity, where there is no light. The worshippers of the heaven's glory are clothed in splendour.'

How extraordinarily apt these comments were I came to realize only after having spent some time in the jungles and forests. The repulsive creatures, I noticed, hated the light of day while the most lovable rejoiced in sunshine.

There were the large butterflies that danced gaily over the green carpet of the tree-tops: of such marvellous coloration that it was sheer joy to see them flutter about. They were simply gorgeous: their equals in beauty to be found nowhere. The Painted Ladies and the Red Admirals were pale compared with them.

And the insects that hovered over the trees. Were they not more attractively tinted than those avoiding the sun? Their breast-plates gleamed like mailed coats of gold.

What about the charming *hariyals*, our plump and rotund wood-pigeons? Were they not real beauties too? With the top of the head grey and the rest of the plumage green and yellowish green, and lilac on the shoulders of the wings? They worship the sun and made me think that they flew about aimlessly solely to show the dazzling glory of their plumage to greatest advantage in the golden sunlight.

The tree-top dwelling dwarf bear must not be omitted from my brief list. It loved basking in the sun no matter the time of the day or of the year. I found it most engaging in its ways, very charming and extremely covetable. In contrast to the ever-rocketing butterflies, the perpetually flitting insects, and the eternally fluttering *hariyals*, this four-footed round bellied sun-worshipper preferred a life of immobility, and like our wise men avoided all unnecessary movements. Similar to the proverbial sloth in its quiescence, it clung by its paws to the topmost branches of the trees and manifested supreme indifference to the ways of other creatures. It was happy in the sun and did not care how its neighbours, friends or foes, lived and behaved.

I do not know how the tree-dwelling dwarf bear came to be named *ramdas* by the Santals of the Blue Hills. In the Red Valley this attractive-looking but slow-gaited and fat-bellied animal was rare: there they called it simply the *lazy one* or *bhalloo*.

'Name a child after a good man,' they say, 'and the child will then aspire to be good. Give him a funny name and he will behave funnily all his days.' Perhaps Adi Malla lived and died like a hero because his name meant the First Wrestler and Sashe Raha conducted himself ridiculously on account of his nickname: the Split Cucumber. Anyway, whoever named our village watchman Ramdas committed a grave error and incurred a serious responsibility. Before naming him one ought to have thought twice: the slowest and the most credulous of all creatures is called *ramdas* in a wide tract of the country. Was that not reason enough to avoid naming a watchman's son, one destined to be a watchman also, Ramdas?

Khukoor-ma, I thought, was entitled to reprimand the priest who presided over her husband's naming ceremony: he should be held responsible for the monotony of her diet! For not so very long ago the jungle came up within a mile of our village, and the tree-dwelling dwarf bears were then common in the Red Valley as well as in the green belt of the Blue Hills. 'They were in fact,' Para-manik of Madhu-ban assured me, 'as numerous as the common bee-eaters. Of course, the priest must have known that the lazy bear is called *ramdas* by the Santals. With the disappearance of the jungles the bears have disappeared. But the green bee-eaters have stayed on because of the telegraph poles: these are as good as trees for tiny birds, but not for the fat lazy bears. Both the bears and the bee-eaters adore the sight of beehives. The bee-eater has attractive wings: it swoops down in a curious flight to catch its prey.'

'How does a dwarf bear attack its victims?' I was anxious to shift the conversation from the birds to the bears. By profession the headman of the village of Madhu-ban was both a bird-catcher and an animal-tamer, though he was commonly known as the Fowler. He was, in my reckoning, the ideal man for my purpose: I wanted to own a fat-bellied bear cub.

Each week on market day Para-manik the Fowler went to Deoghar carrying a bamboo pole, and a number of wicker-work bird-cages crammed to capacity hung from each end of the pole. His catch was sold to pious pilgrims: they purchased the birds only to set them free as an act of piety. They counted upon Para-manik's co-operation. Without his help how were they to acquire merit? Distributing largess to the poor was not enough: they wanted to release the caged denizens of the air. Some circus-managers too depended on Para-manik's furnishing them with tiger cubs: they, however, were never set at liberty, but taught to do tricks to entertain townsmen. Our Fowler was exceptionally clever in training wild animal cubs. The more fleet and the more dangerous an animal was, the greater was his enthusiasm over catching it. So I asked him, 'Does a tree-dwelling bear never hurry? How does it catch its prey?'

'He that hath faith need never hasten,' Para-manik replied gravely. 'Why should a *ramdas* ever hurry? Does not its name indicate that it is a servitor to the god Rama? A being that has faith ought not to hurry except at God's bidding.'

'Well,' I went on hopefully, 'in that case it ought to be easy to trap a baby bear. I should love to tame one and train it.'

Para-manik expressed profound surprise at my request. 'The dwarf bears,' he declared, 'the tree-dwelling servitors to the god Rama are born trained. They are not like the savage *lal bhalloos*, the red bears. They are born tame and they remain tame to the day of their death.' What was the point of my trying to tame such an animal still further? Were they not slow enough in their ways? Did I think of making them still slower? The poor things! They lived on honeycombs, berries, figs and nuts. They never caused any trouble in the rice-fields. Whom did they ever harm? They crossed nobody's path. Had I not enough work in taming the wild human cubs in the Experimental School? What need had I of a baby *ramdas*? School-going was contrary to the nature of jungle animals. 'Moreover,' he concluded his long reprimand, 'a single bear-cub would die of loneliness.'

'Then why don't you get me a pair? I should love to have two.'

'That would break the mother-bear's heart. To lose a baby is bad enough. But to lose two at the same time! That would be worse still. Which mother would ever relish such a tragedy?'

It was no use arguing the point further. I could not possibly keep a whole bear family in the little room allocated to me. And at the same time it was not easy for me to give up hope of keeping a *ramdas* as a pet. My pony Red Belly was gone owing to Sashe Raha's indiscretions: it was difficult for me to be reconciled to the idea that I was without an animal of my own to nuzzle and snuggle.

I consulted Neela and she proved to be worse than useless. First she extracted a promise from me not to visit the deeper regions of the forest any more. Secondly, I was not to do anything that would hurt the feelings of the Santals, as it would make them suspicious of her Experimental School. Finally she gave me a lecture on my behaving like a child. 'You are old enough to do without pets,' she twittered. 'When are you going to be a man? Now stop moping over a nonexistent companion. These dwarf-bears are simply full of fleas....'

Neela tried to impress upon me the dangers of wandering in the jungle. 'Once outside the beaten track,' she said, 'you will lose your way for good.' Only experts well acquainted with the forest-lore and the lie of the land ventured into the areas where the dwarf-bears lived. And even they never went alone or without lighted torches. The lianas of the *maloo* climbers and the roots of the epiphyte fig trees afforded convenient camouflage for treacherous pythons: those tree-trunk-dwelling twilight monsters capable of swooping down like a lightning flash and hitting their prey insensible. The striped tigers and black panthers were not too friendly either, and there were many varieties of savage apes as vicious and as ferocious as hungry wolves, and endowed with greater cunning. 'You have given me your oath,' she repeated triumphantly. 'Keep your promise and be a good boy.' She slapped my bottom and ran away into the school house.

Neela was in many ways as subject to whims as Mashi-ma. Perhaps she was in league with my aunt: she even threatened to hang herself if I ever broke my promise or did anything rash without first consulting her. This only shows that a girl, as she grows up, ceases to be a boy's comrade. She was only a few years older than I was. Yet she behaved as though she were my grandmother. Anyway, my reflections on Neela's whimsicality did not help me to secure a bear-cub.

So I decided to tackle Para-manik once again. This time I made an indirect approach. If he could trap tiger-cubs, what was wrong with ensnaring a baby bear? If he did not find it wrong to capture leopards, wild apes, and every sort of bird it ought not to be wicked to get hold of a less savage animal. Did his usual quarry consist of motherless creatures only? Why should it be iniquitous for him to secure a baby *ramdas?*

'Because it would bring bad luck,' Para-manik murmured. 'Not only to me but to the whole village.'

~

'Bad luck!' A couple of years ago I would have laughed at such an argument. But by now I was sufficiently experienced to know that some of the so-called superstitious beliefs of rustic folk were based on the experience of many centuries. Their intuition was a more trustworthy guide than the curiosity of town-dwellers. I remembered well the havoc wrought in our potato crops by a tiny insect looking like a lady-bird: it was let loose in our midst by a commercial traveller from Calcutta. He brought it in a match-box and showed it to some villagers before beginning his patter on the excellence of the goods he had to sell.

'Kill that insect straight away,' cried a Santal! 'It is no lady-bird. In God's name kill it. It's the devil's own vehicle. Can't you see it has straight strokes? It would bring bad luck.'

The smart salesman from Calcutta chortled. Later he expatiated in Calcutta on the superstitious beliefs of the rustic folks of the Penhari Parganas. 'They believe,' he wrote in an illustrated article in the *Sandya-Pradeep*, 'that certain attractive insects bring bad luck.'

The insect this commercial traveller released in our midst was the Colorado beetle! How our people wish that the man from Calcutta had listened to the warning of the Santal. The Colorado beetle has brought us much misery. Our potato growers know it better than others.

Who was I, therefore, to reject off-hand Para-manik's remark about bad luck? Only I wanted to know what sort of bad luck would overwhelm the village of Madhu-ban if he got me a dwarf bear.

'What bother, Para-manik, will you have if you trap a cub for me?' I asked.

~

'Our main trouble lies in our being a bit slow,' Para-manik began. 'We are a bit slower than others. We, Santals of the Blue Hills, are *jungli*, men of the jungles and the forests. We listen twice to a question before we proffer an answer, and even when the mouth is full of words, and the words are on the tip of the tongue, we think hard lest we fail to say the right thing. All the same, we are not always able to give the apt answer. This is due to our being slow. If we touch a dwarf bear we shall become still slower. That won't do us any good. We have had enough trouble with Baiju's excessive fondness for these lazy creatures.'

Para-manik like most Santals was modest. Just as the villagers in the Red Valley, the Santals of the Blue Hills venerated scholarship. The scholars were the salt of the earth and they were nothing! The Punditji often expressed his concern at this attitude. 'Bogus scholars,' he said, 'are not likely to be found out by our over-modest villagers.' "Their excessive modesty," according to Padre Johan, "is a sin against the Holy Ghost." Para-manik might have had his misgivings about his vocabulary. But I knew he was more gifted than many college students at telling a story or at making a point clear. Here was my chance to hear a fable or legend.

'Who was Baiju?' I asked. 'What was his trouble with the dwarf bears? When did he live?'

'Baiju lived some time ago,' replied Para-manik. 'In fact, towards the dawn of creation. It must have been right in the beginning, I reckon. For in those days the gods spoke to men.'

Once the leaders of the different races of men were invited by the gods to their seat, the Cradle of the Clouds, somewhere near the Himalayas. Baiju was designated by the Santals to undertake this journey as their spokesmen. He was a fine man, fearless and honest, and good with his flute. His people had, however, overlooked the fact that he was very friendly with the tree-dwelling dwarf bears, the lazy *ramdases*. On account of this Baiju arrived late at the Cradle of the Clouds: he had tarried too long on the way, playing with the bears and drinking the honey-mead they offered. However, he reached the seat of the gods in time to see the gathering of the spokesmen of different races dispersing.

'Hey, Baiju!' The men laughed at him. 'Did you expect the gods to wait for you? See what they have given to us. Scrolls in which everything is written down. We are to meet in a year's time. Don't be late then.'

'Late!' Baiju the fleetest of men was crestfallen. 'Late? But not too late to worship.'

This spontaneous expression of reverence pleased the god known as the Preserver: the central deity of the Triad—the Creator, the Preserver, and the Destroyer—and he gave Baiju his benediction and a copy of the scroll.

Baiju ran back home and recounted his story to his people. 'I thanked only the Preserver,' he confessed. 'He is the one who gave me the scroll.'

'That's all right, Baiju,' the Santals assured him. 'The Preserver is the only God we know. Have we not named our river Damodar after him? But where is the scroll?'

'The scroll?' Baiju scratched his head. It contained the secret of reading and writing, and at the behest of the dwarf bears he had thrown it away! 'Your people are huntsmen and cultivators,' the bears told him. 'What business have such people to become readers and scribblers like the *baniahs*, the shop-keepers, bankers, and lawyers.' So Baiju had thrown away the scroll before climbing the slopes of the Blue Hills.

'That's quite all right, Baiju,' the Santals said. They did not mind his throwing away the scroll. 'Let the peoples of the valley profit from it and do more book-keeping. We shall remain as we are and earn our bread with the sweat of our brow. But, Baiju, next year you must not be late.'

Unfortunately, they forgot to advise him to keep away from the playful lazy bears, and Baiju stopped for a while with the tree-climbers on his way to the Cradle of the Clouds. The bears offered him their honey-mead to drink as was their custom in those days. Baiju declined this tempting draught: 'Last year I was late,' he said, 'on account of drinking too much mead.' 'In that case,' the bears insisted, 'drink some *mohua* juice. It's less heavy.' Baiju thought this invitation over and found no reason for declining it. The good man quaffed deeply, and as might be guessed, was late as before. When he reached his destination he found the men dispersing, carrying with them heavily loaded baskets and hampers.

'Aren't you all crazy?' Baiju laughed at the very thought that some people should carry cart-loads of scrolls with them. 'What made you bring your hampers with you?'

'To carry away the gifts of gold and silver,' they replied. 'Didn't you examine the scroll the gods gave away last year? Everything is written down in it.'

So Baiju returned to his people carrying with him only such amount of precious metals as he could take in the folded palms of his hands. And that was not much. While others waxed rich with the gifts of the gods, the Santals of the Blue Hills remained as poor as before on account of the entertainment given to their spokesman by the *ramdases*. These sluggards cannot bear the sight of a man hurrying! They try every possible antic to detain him.

Anyway, on the third and last occasion when the gods met men, Baiju arrived earlier than the others, bearing with him the hugest of hampers at the suggestion of the dwarf bears.

'How much can you carry on your back?' asked the Destroyer, the third one of the Triad. He was giving away the gifts on that occasion.

'As much as the rest of the men put together,' replied Baiju proudly and got what he demanded, while the other spokesmen did their best to take as little as possible. On his way back Baiju dropped quite a few of the Destroyer's gifts while traversing the jungles at the foot of the Blue Hills. He was heavily laden and this could not be helped. However, he did succeed in bringing his people a big hamperful of the Destroyer's benefaction.

And what were these gifts? Just curses and scourges, mere wormwood and gall. Misfortune is the boon the Destroyer metes out to man. While others escaped with as few maledictions as possible the Santals of the Blue Hills received more than their fair share on account of Baiju's friendliness with the dwarf bears.

'Baiju was a splendid man.' Para-manik had nothing but praise for him. 'But he was undone by the slothful rascals, the tree-dwelling *ramdases*. We are slow. We shall become slower if we bring a dwarf bear into this village.'

When confronted with such an argument what was I to do? A man must be feelingless like a clod, Neela told me, if he fails to be moved by this sort of logic. 'Para-manik is endowed with a natural sagacity,' she continued, 'which helps him to divine evil and feel attraction for the good.'

Had I any right to doubt this judgment? If Para-manik lacked wisdom he would have perished long ago in the depths of the jungle where he sought his quarry every day. I do not know why the story of the Colorado beetle came into my mind once again.

~

Gopaldas called on me. I was then alone. He wanted to know if I would care to join the Red Falcons. I let him do the talking. It was not often I got the chance of listening to his arguments: he wanted to make people hate the existing state of affairs. He was tired of slow progress, the low standard of living, the huge differences in the earnings of different classes in society, and above all with the apathy of the masses....

Where did I fit in with his scheme of affairs?

'Don't you want to do something for your people?' he asked. 'Your people are my people too. Don't you like to see a system in which there would be no more slaves and no more masters? If you do, it is then your duty to join the Red Falcons. The Party will look after your education. You will be furnished with the necessary documents and papers. Correctives to what the bourgeois institutions have taught you.'

Gopaldas's visit was cut short: the time of Neela's return was approaching, and he did not like Neela.

'This Neela is a fool.' Gopaldas's parting outburst was directed against such Santals as were not keen in manifesting their resentment against the existing social order. 'Neela was born inside a mine during a mine-explosion. Instead of aspiring to be leader of the Santal miners she is toying with the idea of opening kindergartens everywhere. A crazy woman of eighteen in charge of a school, with a monitor like you who still stinks of mother's milk! A strange bourgeois set-up. The so-called educated and half-educated Santals are as bad as the die-hard reactionaries. Look at Padre Johan. Is he any better than other bourgeois reactionaries though he is a Santal? He was born in a buffalo-shed at the foot of the Blue Hills. He thinks religion is of greater import than the standard of living.'

VIII

In 1864 when the news of the attack on Denmark by the combined forces of the major Teutonic Powers reached the Penhari Parganas via Asansole, a Santal of our village decided on the spot to drive his herd of buffaloes to Calcutta and take a boat for Copenhagen: he wanted to fight for his true king. The war did not last long: Denmark capitulated by the time our Santal reached Calcutta. His milch buffaloes possessed many virtues but like most of our creatures were a bit slow. Their master shed bitter tears as he handed them over to a Danish missionary and explained to him the cause of his inability to give timely service to his king. A message of loyalty and regrets was telegraphed to his Danish Majesty and an acknowledgement was duly received.

The Santal returned home with this royal reply nicely tucked inside his turban but without his milch buffaloes. The villagers laughed at him, and he smiled back. He did not care what they thought of him: he had tried to fulfil his duty and that was that. He owed his loyalty, he declared, to two great dynasties: the princes of Penhari and the kings of Denmark. Unfortunately, the former had been eliminated centuries ago by the ill-begotten and vile Assad-Ullah Khan and therefore the latter alone remained for him to venerate.

How did he come to consider himself a subject of the Danish King?

'Let the pleaders plead,' the villagers said, 'and the *vakils* wrangle! We know our law.'

'So do I,' the Santal smiled as was his wont. 'You can't sell a man like chattel. Was I not born at Baleshwar?'

'That's true.' They stopped laughing. 'That's very true indeed. We forgot all about that.' They apologized for their defective memory. The Santal was born at the ancient port of Baleshwar before it was taken over by John Company is 1846. In fact, there were once *two* towns of the same name: one belonging to the *Ollondeutsches*, the Hollanders, and the other, the finer one, belonging to the king of Denmark who ruled over the *Deenemars*. It was in the town of the *Deenemars* our Santal was born. 'To be more precise near Raja Shyam Ananada's Free Dispensary,' said someone, 'in the outhouse facing the obelisk on a triangular base. Our Santal is a Dane all right. And he belongs to us too. His father was born at Amrita-ban.'

But what had he done with his milch buffaloes? Did he sell them for a good price in Calcutta?

'No,' replied the Santal. 'I have handed them over to the Danish padre, who misses the cattle he left behind in Holstein. It isn't easy to get decent milk in Calcutta. There's money in selling buffalo-milk. From the profits my grandson will be educated at Fredericks-nagar. In the college of the *Deenemars*.'

Fredericks-nagar had disappeared from the map with the deed of transfer of the Danish territories in India! But the villagers did not guffaw. To them Fredericks-nagar was Fredericks-nagar: they did not care for the new name John Company gave it. So far as names went, Serampore or Shri-ram-pur, the new name of Fredericks-nagar, was not bad. But a town founded by the Danes ought to carry its Danish name till Doomsday. 'If we run after novelties,' they argued, 'we shall have to run all our lives. There's no end to new things. Let the children do their running as much as they want: they will sober down when they grow up. We don't care for new names.'

~

Time passed. John Company vanished into thin air like a wraith. Old kingdoms disappeared to make a new empire, and it fell into fragments. The frontiers of Bengal were drawn and redrawn a dozen times. Baleshwar became Belasore and then Baleshwar again, and finally it was removed from the map of Bengal. In the course of years the inhabitants of Shri-ram-pur came to forget the very name of their town's founder. Nowadays not one in ten thousand knows that it was once called Fredericksnagar. Nevertheless, the college established by the *Deenemars* remains: the oldest institution of its kind in the whole of Asia: a foundation for the study of Protestant theology.

Our Santal's grandson graduated from this institution, the Serampore College, and became a padre: the Reverend Johan Baptaijak Mahisha, D.D., Ph.D. To the villagers in the Penhari Parganas he was simply 'Padre Johan.'

~

'It was foolish of the king of Denmark to sell his Indian territories for ten lacs of rupees,' Dada-moshoy, the oldest villager reminisced. His listeners nodded their assent. 'He was ill advised to part with Baleshwar and Fredericks-nagar for a million pieces of silver. Had he not done so Padre Johan would have been one of his subjects. And the Danes would have been proud to have such a man as their fellow citizen.'

'The king of Denmark's loss has been our gain,' the Goatee remarked. The others shared his view: there were not many in Denmark as gifted and as straightforward as Padre Johan. He was worth a million rupees!

They praised the sagacity and wisdom of Padre Johan's grandfather. It was good of him to make the necessary provision for his yet unborn grandson's education. The Danish missionary was lauded for the interest he took in milch buffaloes and in bringing up a child of the Penhari Parganas in the right way—to be God-fearing and honest. They wondered what the college at Fredericks-nagar looked like.

'Padre Johan is a fine man,' the villagers agreed. 'In spite of the scar on his forehead, he remains good-looking. But for that scar of a cross no one would think he is a *khristan*. He is as good as our Punditji.'

'He does not drink.' This shortcoming was somewhat incomprehensible to the Santals. 'But, mind you, Padre Johan is a good man for all that.'

~

'Bear the cross,' Padre Johan proclaimed, 'and the cross will bear you.' He practised what he preached, and incised a Cross in the middle of his forehead one day after an impassioned sermon on the meaning of the Cross of Christ. This troubled the Metropolitan: he wished he had never ordained Johan a priest.

If the followers of Vishnu could openly proclaim their faith by daubing their distinctive signs on their noses, and if the worshippers of the god Shiva were not ashamed of tattooing Shiva's crescent or trident on their foreheads, why could not Padre Johan do likewise to prove his faith in the Cross of Christ? He hated the sight of labarum, the cross of Constantine, because it was associated with the name of an unworthy Kaiser-i-Roum, and expressed his views in strong terms in the weekly *Redemption*, a periodical for the propagation of the True Faith. He even proposed that the sign of labarum should be removed from all ecclesiastical vestments and ornamentations. Someone wrote a letter in the *Eucharist* condemning Padre Johan's intransigence, and this correspondent saw to his great discomfiture that our Santal preacher was better informed than most people on matters of early Christian history. In ecclesiastical questions Padre Johan did not rely on Macaulay or Ranke: he quoted only the contemporaries or near contemporaries of the Kaiser-i-Roums, the Roman Emperors; Constantine the Great he renamed Constantine the Cad.

The Metropolitan gave a sigh of relief when Padre Johan left the Church of India of his own accord to preach the *Su-Samashar*, the Good News, in his own way in the Penhari Parganas. 'Now he owes his allegiance to none but God,' said Padre Johan's admirers. 'So much the better for him,' whispered the private secretary to the Metropolitan. 'There will be some peace in the palace.' 'He is a crank,' sniggered his detractors. 'Who bothers about Eusebius, Josephus, Procopius…and hocuspocus in these days? Fancy wasting time over Hebrew, Syriac, Greek, and what not! Isn't the translation of the Bible good enough for preaching Christianity to the illiterate Santals? He will be sick in no time of his new life in the backwoods. Definitely, he is crazy. He preaches against industrialization.'

Padre Johan was not only against industrialization but also against baptismal water and sacraments. Baptism for him meant spiritual rebirth and this did not demand any immersion in water.

Some members of the Society of Friends came from Bolepur to listen to the first sermon Johan preached in his corrugated iron chapel near Jamtara: they were somewhat taken aback when they discovered that though the Padre's views were iconoclastic he was an icon-worshipper by nature. Moreover, his admiration for Quaker heroes and martyrs was lukewarm. He was no pacifist. 'My brother prayeth,' this strange pastor predicated, 'to brass and stone in heathenwise. But in my brother's cry, I hear my own unanswered agonies…' He closed the service with an unorthodox song: '*Alo! Amar alo!* Light! My light!'

'The real duty of man,' Padre Johan discoursed, 'the only true duty of every thoughtful human being, is not to extend his power or to multiply his material wealth beyond his needs, but to enrich and enjoy his imperishable possession: his soul.'

'What are you?' some asked.

'I am an unworthy sinner,' Padre Johan declared. 'But I am conscious of the machinations of *Sheytan*, the Evil One. It is my duty to warn my brethren of the snares of Satan. Satan revisits the earth to mislead the unwary. He comes in the stolen garments of the angels and preaches peace where there is no peace. He asks man to seek prosperity where prosperity means spiritual bankruptcy. Satan wants to drive out one set of injustices for another of a viler sort. Satan is crafty.'

~

What were they to make of such a Christian?

'He is fearless and incorruptible like Adi Malla,' said the villagers.

'And as stiff-necked as Adi Malla's buffalo, Nil-Pahar,' whispered the Second Master to himself. 'He is a great nuisance.' Very soon he changed his views about Padre Johan: the Santal preacher ceased to be a great nuisance and turned out to be a grave menace! A real threat! A creature capable of robbing him of his disciples and undermining their faith in Eternal Progress. What was to be done to stem the tide? Padre Johan possessed higher degrees than Babu Hem Chandra Chahar: moreover, he had travelled in Europe and America and knew a dozen foreign languages.

Previously the Second Master could without difficulty poohpooh the Punditji as one ignorant of foreign lands, hence a believer in traditionalism. Kumar's views could be discounted as those of a mere craftsman devoid of all higher education. 'Out goes a donkey and back it comes as a donkey.' But how was he to explain away the Santal preacher's profound contempt for things modern—and particularly for a higher standard of living? The Second Master was most unhappy. He was even more perturbed than the Metropolitan.

'The scar on Padre Johan's head is the mark of a fall.' He imparted this information to his disciples in the hope that they would spread it far and wide. 'Johan used to graze his grandfather's milch buffaloes in the *maidan* of Manohar Dass in Calcutta. One day he fell off the back of a buffalo and had concussion of the brain. As a result of this accident strange things happened. His capacity to memorize increased incredibly. But he lost his common sense. He became queer. That's why he eternally preaches the same sermon: 'Don't change your ways!' Fancy a man with so many degrees moving about with that old fogey, the Punditji, and that gad-about Kumar. Those three! They are thick as thieves! A Brahmin flanked by two Santals! A fine trio! Three crack-pots!'

Padre Johan's prestige in the Penhari Parganas increased beyond all bounds the year he gave away the prizes, *kabache*s, pectorals, and other gifts at the *mela* at Pushpa-pur. The way he came forward to fill an unexpected last-minute breach was commended by everyone. Even the Metropolitan was so delighted that they forwarded a cheque to cover part of our Padre's unforeseen expenses, to say nothing of the honour the Catholicos of Malabar conferred upon him by attending the opening ceremony of the *mela*.

Padre Johan's *mela* came to be held in this way:

Owing to some trouble between the Income Tax Office and the Trustees of the Rani Surabala's Endowment, the general invitation to the master-potters and image-makers of West Bengal to the annual fair at Pushpa-pur was not issued that year in the usual way. It caused no end of confusion and disappointment among the young as well as the old. For the people of the Penhari Parganas it was almost a presage of disaster.

Since the ending of the Vargi raids on Bengal, the rural inhabitants of the districts of Burdwan, Bankura, Birbhoom, Manbhoom, Singbhoom, Midnapore and Hazaribagh as well as of the Orissa States looked forward to this *mela* as a yearly event of great importance. Not so much for its funfairs, *jatras*, merry-go-rounds, wrestling matches, and other attractions as for its competitive exhibition of religious images.

For those who do not know anything about our popular exhibitions, let me make it plain that the Pushpa-pur exposition was not like those held so frequently in the towns. At the display of the images there one could neither buy nor sell any of the exhibits: the painted clay statues were just for show. One paid nothing to see them. The exhibitors were professional potters and image-makers like Kumar: they came from all parts of West Bengal.

The origin of the Pushpa-pur *mela* goes back to the days of Rani Surabala whose foster-mother was a potter by caste. She lived at about the same time when our Golah was built for the discomfiture of the Vargis. In fulfilment of a religious vow, the Rani invited all the renowned master-potters and image-makers to her Durga *puja* to celebrate the end of the Vargi raids on Bengal.

Her guests were accommodated in the large quadrangle next to her newly constructed temple of Sarva-Mangala, Goddess of Every Bliss, and were requested to model a religious statue in clay, in our traditional way, within seven days: representing the birth of Krishna, the divine child. No hard-and-fast rule was laid down as to the way the subject was to be treated: the legends connected with Krishna's birth varied in different parts of the country. Each image-maker was, therefore, at liberty to give his personal interpretation or local variation to the time-honoured story.

The guests were delighted. The competition gave them the opportunity of comparing their technique and skill, and also of finding out who was the most gifted among them. And that was precisely what the Rani had in mind when she sent out her invitation: she wanted to honour the best image-maker of the land.

To attract a large number of people to examine the entries, the Rani organized a general fair at the same time in her garden-retreat near the quadrangle. There were puppet-shows, wrestling matches, *jatras*, performances by strolling players, and various other distractions—all free of charge.

She made an endowment which permitted this fair to be held annually, and made it possible for her Trustees to award purses and a gold *kabacha*, a finely wrought pectoral, to the most deserving image-makers. The *kabacha* was destined for the craftsman whose image was judged to be the best by a show of hands among the competitors themselves.

The prize money was nothing, but the prize pectoral was everything! This was the view of the master-potters and image-makers, and this too was the feeling of the villages and towns they came from. Finally the whole of West Bengal came to the same conclusion. The wearer of a Rani Surabala *kabach* was assured a warm welcome wherever he went. He was acclaimed a hero. In some villages they even blew conch shells in his honour.

Small wonder that the annual *mela* at Pushpa-pur came to be recognized as a national institution. Our *panjikas*, calendars, nautical almanacs and astrological forecasts of coming events recorded its dates in the same way as the Car Festivity of Juggernaut or *Janmastami*, the birthday of Krishna.

In these circumstances one may well guess how disconcerted we were when we heard that owing to some new laws about religious endowments and charitable institutions, the Rani Surabala's Endowment was expected to pay an Entertainment Tax or some such impost. And the Trustees declared that the available funds did not permit them to pay the new tax and entertain the master-potters and image-makers at the same time. 'As for new laws, there is no end to them,' mumbled the Goatee and cursed the *topiwallahs,* the *Delhiwallahs,* the long-dead Assad-Ullah Khan and his brother Jonad Khan. The majority of the villagers took the news that there was to be no *mela* far more seriously: they did not curse anyone. They regarded it as a forewarning, the writing on the wall, the announcement of the end of an era and the beginning of a new one: the age of peace following the elimination of the Vargis was over!

At this juncture Padre Johan came forward with a scheme all of his own that heartened everyone. He announced that the great quadrangle near the Sarva-Mangala temple had been rented by him for ten days and that his colporteurs had been despatched to invite the master-potters and image-makers; everything was to be the same as before, only the visitors would be requested to make some voluntary contribution to cover the expenses. This enhanced his prestige enormously, as did his advertisements in the daily papers asking diploma-holders of government art schools to take part in the competition in the traditional way.

The only departure from tradition was the introduction of a secondary competition: one on a Christian subject: the Betrayal by Judas.

The choice of this Christian subject made a number of papers produce caustic editorials on the vagaries of the Income Tax Office. Though these articles had nothing to do with the *mela,* they did give it a wider publicity, especially as the diploma-holders of the government art schools heard for the first time of how the prize *kabacha* was won: that the competitors decided among themselves whose work was the best.

~

We were greatly elated when we heard that the *kabacha*-winning Christian statue was by our Kumar. I went to Pushpa-pur to see the *mela* and naturally saw Kumar's exhibit.

It was not, I must admit, much of a statue. It was more like a painting in relief. 'A painted clay bas relief,' according to the *Kusum-pur Sangbad*, 'done in the style called *cavo-relievo* by European artists—slightly raised relief on a flat surface with the outlines of the figures deeply incised. Everyone who saw it stood before it for a while as though hypnotized. Though modelled and painted in our traditional rural style, this exhibit has something peculiar about it: its stylization. The figures look exaggeratedly tall and distorted.'

In fairness to the *Kusum-pur Sangbad* it should be said that later on when the news of Kumar's success came to be known it printed a second article of a far more eulogistic character. It is not necessary for me to say that Kumar's Betrayal was an elaboration or rather stylization of the group he prepared some time ago with the Second Master and myself as his models. Judas was shown approaching the Redeemer with stealthy steps and protruding lips. The betrayer was dressed in deep yellow; he had a peacock feather headgear, a fat Shan bag slung across his shoulders; one hand held a bamboo flute while his other tried to outrage the Redeemer, a frail figure of tender years, who was shrinking from the betrayer's touch, abashed and humiliated. The betrayer Judas looked like a caricatured Krishna, the knave of some of our *jatras*—not the usual Krishna, but Kala-Yavana the blackguard in Krishna's castaway clothes, out to seduce the innocent, and to mislead the unwary.

I cannot blame the *Kusum-pur Sangbad* for its failure to report adequately on the impression this painted bas-relief created on most spectators. For me, it was most disturbing: it raised too many thoughts in my mind at one and the same time. It set every beholder's mind working in the same way as mine, I thought, because I heard quite a few people who knew nothing about the way Padre Johan's Redeemer was betrayed murmur among themselves: 'This is betrayal indeed! That yellow-robed rascal with the bulging bag pretends to be Krishna and wants to

rob Krista of his blue loin cloth. Why does he want to insult and
injure the Divine Youth?'

~

'Because of his love of lucre Judas betrayed his Master,' Padre
Johan in one of his sermons at the *mela* discoursed on this
subject. 'He got thirty pieces of silver... And some are willing to
do the same for even less. They hate that which is holy. They
are prepared to see religious temple dances on theatrical stages.
They condone sordidness. A free cinema ticket is enough these
days. The high priests of the temple of Mammon need not
now produce a purse of thirty rupees, but a cinema-pass valid
for thirty days. Culture means nothing to such people. Honour
means still less. They think pleasure-hunting is the goal of life.'

A journalist called Bottliwalla Dadachanchi, a former student
of the Jamesethji Jeejibhoy Art School, found this sermon very
funny. His sense of humour was different from ours and as he was
a clever caricaturist he drew a droll picture of Padre Johan and
forwarded it along with a photograph of Kumar's Judas betraying
the Redeemer to a periodical called *Ras-bati*, meaning 'Roman
Candle', which was *the* paper of all cinema-goers in Calcutta.
Naturally, the *Ras-bati* produced a 'leader' ridiculing Padre
Johan and Kumar's exhibit, a photo of which was reproduced to
enlighten the cinema-goers and film-producers on the low taste
of the country yokels of the Penhari Parganas.

By a curious coincidence Langoti Baba, a well-known
political figure of the day, was chuckling over this particular issue
of the *Ras-bati* when he came to be stabbed to death by one of
his near relatives. A number of journalists immediately seized
upon this incident as a confirmation of Padre Johan's prediction.
Kumar's Betrayal was reproduced in scores of papers: some went
to the length of retouching the group in such a way as to make
the Redeemer look like the bearded Langoti Baba and Judas's

bamboo—the pseudo-Krishna's flute—was replaced by a drawn dagger, and a season ticket to a cinema was shown peeping out of the murderer's breast-coat pocket. However that may be, Kumar the Potter became known all over India within a few days on account of the indiscretion of a stranger called Bottliwalla Dadachanchi—by profession a journalist. Kumar was hailed by people who knew nothing about our village potters and image-makers as the greatest *sculptor* of the land. He was flooded with telegrams and messages from different agencies, would-be touts, writers of begging-letters, and even wealthy people—all anxious to load him with favours.

IX

'The idiots!' Kumar grumbled loudly in my presence, 'The misbegotten! They came out of the wrong side of the blanket when they were born. Can't the leader of the *topiwallahs* leave me in peace? I am the same man I was a few days ago. An upstart potter. Now I have become a *sculptor!*'

'But, Kumar! You do make images. Are they not the same as the statues?' I never knew the difference between religious images in polychrome clay and non-religious statues in bronze or in marble. So it was news to me to hear that Kumar did not like making human figures in alabaster: this medium was not hard enough for his taste; but his new patrons, particularly the Jain merchants and the Parsi brokers, manifested a great weakness for it—alabaster or white marble.

'Those business magnates,' Kumar mumbled, 'I'll make them pay through the nose. I'll charge fantastically high prices.'

'Pay through their *noses!*' Sashe Raha, nicknamed the Split Cucumber, murmured to himself and rushed out of Kumar's workshop to get his sling and mud pellets ready.

He had the time of his life bespattering every car with mud that stopped in front of Kumar's workshop. In one or two cases he did succeed in hitting people with mud balls. His mischief came to an abrupt end, however, when a fat man with triple chin bawled 'What a village! Not even a *chowkidar* to deal with hedgehogs!'

That casual remark was enough to induce Ramdas to abandon his bed. He kept up his accustomed thief-catching activities during the night and by day he now kept an eye on Sashe Raha.

'Brother Ramdas! You ought to sleep some time,' Kumar suggested to our watchman. 'Once a week at least.' I suspect Kumar was somewhat disappointed at the end of Sashe Raha's mud slinging. He was not particularly fond of his new patrons— the business magnates and politicians.

'Sleep?' Ramdas expressed his surprise at such an absurd proposal. 'A *chowkidar's* duties come before his pleasure. The Punditji rarely sleeps. And I can do without much sleep myself. It isn't essential for living, is it?'

Why didn't Kumar like the wealthy people who wanted him to sculpt them?

'Because they look so exhausted,' he confessed. 'Weariness is written all over them. They are uninteresting. Their expressions have been moulded by hate, envy, fear, toil, cupidity and frustration. I can't bear them…. Slight twists round the corners of their lips betray them. I don't like uninteresting faces. The Punditji advises me to gather roses before they fade, but I find it hard to follow his advice. Making hay is not in my line.'

What about the pretty ladies who often accompanied these ugly and uninteresting people?

'Oh! The *nieces* of the well-to-do? They are pretty all right. Pretty and empty! They are even worse—because they are devoid of personality. I would rather spend my days portraying she-monkeys than waste an hour on any *niece* of a successful broker. Prettiness is not loveliness. It festers; loveliness lives for ever.'

I listened to Kumar attentively and wondered why he intoned the word 'niece' in such a peculiar way. The truly great, according to Kumar, were so much engrossed in their own thoughts and activities that they had little time to spare for my adopted elder brother. And the truly lovely were often so modest that they irritated him.

Kumar removed a piece of wet cloth which covered a clay statue on which he was working. When finished, he told me, it would not be painted like our usual religious images, but just baked in the kiln like a brick or a pot: that would change it into terra-cotta.

'What do you think of this Saraswati, Goddess of Learning?' he asked and waited expectantly to hear my answer. He stood aside to let me have a good look at his image.

I gave an involuntary gasp. It was Neela, modelled slightly larger than life-size: she was totally nude but for the traditional ornaments and the musical instrument *veena*, usually attributed to our Goddess of Learning and Wisdom. A strange feeling made me quiver and a lump rose in my throat. I did not want to look at the statue. It would be dirty of me, I thought, to spy into the secrets of Neela's body. I felt thirsty, my knees wobbled, and I sat down on a low stool wishing all the while that Kumar would not insist on my giving him an answer. I avoided the dilemma of giving him a direct reply and hinted that perhaps it would have been better to give the statue some clothing.

'Since when have you become a foul monkey?' Kumar burst out and gave me a look I shall never forget. 'Have you lost your sight? You want me to give her a *langoti* and change my goddess into a whore? Into a Bathing Beauty of Dadar or Palm Beach?' He gritted his teeth and kicked at an empty bucket to send it hurtling right out of his work-shed into the middle of the court-yard; it startled a family of playful chaffinches.

I wondered why he became so sullen all of a sudden and also tried to make out what made it impossible for me to scan that statue. Our gods and goddesses are generally represented nude. The divinities and the semi-divinities in our temples may or may not wear any garments. Had I not myself seen hundreds of such images without ever bothering about their nakedness? Yet I was ashamed to gaze on that statue of Saraswati—and felt more at my ease when it was covered up again with a wetted piece of cloth.

'Who put nonsense into your head?' Kumar raved on. 'The body's beauty is the glory of God. It's the manifestation of divine bounty to man. Only ferocious baboons and filthy apes fail to appreciate it. Who's the dirty pig that has been trying to soil your mind? Well, I shall have to look after you.'

He spoke in this vein for some time and told me that the sooner I got over my adolescent hay fever the better it would be for me. 'I shall have a talk with Neela,' he said finally. 'I am off for Delhi to-morrow. Some of the big noises want me to do their portraits. I shall try my best to induce them to stop that project of the dam. The Punditji is right. I must make hay while the sun shines. They think I am a great *sculptor*! Let them think what they like. All that I want of them is to prevent the Red Valley being flooded. That dirty dam. Anyway, I shall have a talk with Neela about you before I leave for Delhi.'

X

'Maybe,' I said to myself as I lay stretched on the floor of the *moucharaby*. 'Maybe, Kumar is responsible for my coming to Amrita-ban as a student-monitor to help Neela. Perhaps he had a talk with Mashi-ma to convince her that my staying away from her for a couple of months would not be a calamity. It was good of him to think of me. And also of the Red Valley. What would become of the jungles if they came to be submerged? Perhaps changed into peat or loam, or coal. What would become of the lizards? Changed into crocodiles.'

I was happy as a lizard in the sun: in fact I was watching their antics on the walls of the *moucharaby*. Their movements fascinated me. How did the bigger lizards manage to cling to vertical and overhanging surfaces? Some of them were as frolicsome as our clouds. While the clouds were not always plentiful, the lizards were. One with a stubby tail was my favourite. I came to know its pranks well: it, generally winked at me and flicked its tail before dashing at an insect.

The lizards interested me more than Gopaldas or his friend Comrade Dynamiter. Evidently this new-comer, Comrade Dynamiter, was no stranger to the Penhari Parganas: I must have seen him somewhere. He was taciturn while Gopaldas was extremely loquacious. At long last something was going to happen, and he was regaling himself in anticipation! The Red Valley, according to Gopaldas, would soon wake up! Was I prepared to give him my word of honour? If I was, then I was entitled to know that a first-class crook must have constructed the underground passages leading out of the Golah: a crook who was interested in coal. That was enough to make me lose all interest in lizards for the time being.

'...The underground passages were cut out of coal seams,' Gopaldas beamed. 'No wonder the whole job was finished in ten months.'

'So what?' I asked somewhat sharply. 'Instead of using charcoal or wood the Jung Bahadur made use of coal in making bricks. What's wrong with that? Isn't it easier to cut underground passages through seams of coal than through solid rock? He killed two birds with one stone. What's wrong with it?'

'Curly-head!' Gopaldas chortled, 'You are naive. That's the one trouble with you.'

'Have you filled in the form they sent you?' asked Comrade Dynamiter, and this question prevented my tackling Gopaldas about my alleged sin of naïvete. Who was this Comrade Dynamiter? Where did I see him last? Why was he given such a strange pseudonym? He wore an impressive moustache and a short beard, but his head was clean shaven. He was stocky: athletically built. His ears were like cauliflowers. The pupils of his eyes moved in a peculiar way: they flicked like the tail of my friendly lizard; but somehow their peculiar movement enhanced the feeling of aversion I felt for him. Why did he—a follower of Lenin and very much his hero's image—produce from his pocket a copy of the *Gita* and make me swear on it? Was not my word of honour enough? 'Have you filled in the forms they sent you at your Experimental School at Amrita-ban?' Comrade Dynamiter repeated and looked at me with his beady eyes.

'What forms?' I asked. 'There have been so many recently!' There had been at that time a sudden flood of forms from all sides: the District Boards, the offices of the Sub-Registrars, the Police Stations, the local Food Offices, the Provincial Home Affairs Department, the Central Publicity Office, etc. All asking for more or less the same information. The schoolboys, teachers, postmen, and others were requested to fill in details on behalf of those who could not read or write. Neela was overwhelmed with forms, tabulation sheets, and registers, and I felt extremely guilty about my accident which prevented me from being of much service to her. The Experimental School was just then the main repository for completed forms: statistical data concerning the inhabitants of the Blue Hills, their occupation, their domestic animals, their property. 'They want to raise our taxes,' the Santals of Madhu-ban complained to Neela. 'Do they want to tax our goats? Why do they want to know how many sheep we have?'

'The Government want to make an estimate of our available resources,' Neela repeated a hundred times every day to the distracted villagers. I too came to share Neela's opinion about these forms, and repeated without thinking, 'You mean the forms for estimating the district's resources?'

'Didn't I tell you that Curly-head is naive?' Gopaldas turned his head towards Comrade Dynamiter. The pupils of the Comrade's eyes flicked once again.

Why were they so mysterious? Did they advocate a boycott of all statistical data?

'No. Nothing of the sort,' replied Comrade Dynamiter. 'But if you knew the real reason of the Government's sudden zeal for statistics about the Penhari Parganas,' he argued, 'you would perhaps show a little less zeal in returning the forms!' Did I know anything about the scheme for the Power House and the Desdichado dam? Did I know that they were working on the completion of the dam night and day? 'Exactly in the same way,' Comrade Dynamiter continued, 'as the Golah was built in the time of the Jung Bahadur. The project is still far from completion. Yet when it is finished it will mean the end of the Penhari Parganas, of the Red Valley and of the Blue Hills. The entire population will have to be evacuated. That's why the statistics are being collected.'

'But Desdichado no longer rules the country.' I could not make out why the project of a man no longer in power was still being pursued by the government of the day.

'Curly-head! Don't argue,' snapped Gopaldas. 'Listen to Comrade Dynamiter and think of your future.'

'Yes, yes, of your future,' Comrade Dynamiter spoke as though this was the primary object of his making the difficult climb to the *moucharaby*. 'Your future as well as the country's.' Momentous issues were at stake; the present regime would vanish in the same way as the former monarchs of Delhi, the Pathans, the Moguls, and other rulers of yester-year. The march of history was inevitable: events were moving fast: the tempo was accelerated in geometrical progression. Reformist measures— palliatives, sedatives, soporifics—would not save the new regime. Though they might delay the on-coming of the new era. 'So it is necessary,' he concluded, 'to create temporary disorders and even to augment the trials of the masses.'

'The Party is destined to come into power,' Gopaldas took up the cue. 'Much sooner than the bourgeoisie suspects. Pink Socialism will not stem the tide. Look at China. Those rendering services to the Party would be given key-posts. Their present sacrifices will be taken into account. What will you be doing in five or ten years? Sucking your thumb and chewing a piece of parchment bearing the seal of the University of Calcutta? Now think over what the Comrade has told you, and make up your mind. There is no hurry. But you gain nothing by delaying. The Desdichado dam must be stopped.'

What had I to do with all that? Did they want me to collect signatures and thumb-prints from inhabitants who were opposed to their own transfer from the Penhari Parganas?

'Don't be a fool,' Gopaldas barked. 'If you were not sick and lying on your back, I would have gladly kicked sense into you! You are interested in the welfare of the people, aren't you? If so, remember the advice of Lenin: "To establish Communism it is necessary to use any ruse, cunning, unlawful method, evasion, and concealment of truth." We want to shake the Santals from their apathy.'

How was that to be done? I felt uncomfortable about Comrade Dynamiter's glinting eyes which scrutinized my face in a strange way. Why was he interested in me? What induced him to call on me?

'Do you know that some of the secret passages of the Golah go right underneath the builders' quarters near the dam? They could be filled with high explosive and blown up.'

What could I do to help my visitors' scheme?

'Now don't pretend to be more naive than you are,' Gopaldas reprimanded me. 'Comrade Dynamiter needs a few reliable hands. Just local lads. Their presence in the neighbourhood of the Golah will not cause any suspicion. We want courageous boys. Not ninnies and cuckoos who are afraid of the dark. They will work with Comrade Dynamiter. He knows everything. He had his training in Greece and in China.'

Someone blew a shrill whistle from below. Comrade Dynamiter leaned out of the balcony and raised his right hand. His gesture reminded me of the pictures of Subhas Bose, the Netaji, taking the salute of uniformed schoolchildren.

The visit came to an abrupt end. Neither Gopaldas nor Comrade Dynamiter bowed nor uttered a word of parting salutation. What made me think just then of the shark which is always accompanied by the pilot fish?

My eyes moved from the wall where the lazy lizards basked to the cloudless vault of the sky. There was a solitary golden eagle, poised in the blue, disdainful of the world of men and beasts.

~

Para-manik called on me. He tested my progress in a curious way: by tickling the soles of my feet with a feather. I did enjoy his trying out this feather test on me. He always had interesting things to tell me. Once he brought a couple of his trained *baya* finches with him: I was asked to name any tree or plant within a league of the *moucharaby* and the birds would fetch a leaf of that tree for me.

However, Para-manik interested me more than his birds. The day Comrade Dynamiter paid his third surprise visit to me and overwhelmed me with his homilies, my heart was heavy and I was more than grateful for Para-manik's call. When something irritated me I found it was always helpful to discuss the cause of my discomposure with someone. And who could be a better person for this purpose than Para-manik?

Comrade Dynamiter had made some disparaging remarks about Kumar. Not about his pottery or his images. That would not have hurt me so much. But about his life in general. The Second Master condemned Kumar simply because he was a Santal. 'He is immoral like the rest of them,' was his usual stock phrase. Comrade Dynamiter's insinuations were more serious. 'Your friend Kumar,' he sniggered, 'he is like a dog that goes about sniffing everywhere. He sniffs at every woman's skirt. He is a lecherous baboon. Fancy having such a man for your adopted brother?'

I could not possibly put my question about Kumar to Para-manik in a blunt fashion. So I asked him if he knew why dogs went out sniffing everywhere.

'They sniff,' he said, 'to find out if any of their own sort are about. They bark for the same reason. They want others of their particular pack to respond to their call. It is the same with man. Neela will tell you how in one place where she worked there were lots of children and when one of them cried the others joined in.'

This made me think. Para-manik probably saw something in my face which tempted him, after a pause, to go on:

'Many a man is like a lost dog. He is on the look-out for a kindred soul. He goes here and he goes there and he comes back to where he started from. And more often than not he fails to find the one person he has been looking for. So all that he can do is to show his love for the things he loved in his childhood. Happy the man who had a joyous childhood, resentment will pass him by like water from a duck's back.'

I told him that I was learning something new.

'No, Little Scholar! This is nothing new. We know we are all exiles from a distant land, the land which is the foot-stool of the throne of the gods.'

To what was he referring? To the Cradle of the Clouds? To the Himalayas? Did the Santals ever live there? 'It is a curious fact,' I thought to myself, 'that many of the hills carry the same names as the Himalayan peaks.' The towering Nanda Devi, Goddess of Blessings and Bliss; the no less mighty Nanda Kot; the holy Trisul, named after the trident of the god Shiva, whose three pinnacles cluster together; the Punch-Chulli, the five-peaked, suggesting in shape the little mud-ovens with five crests to keep the cooking pots in place; the Gangotri from which the sacred river Ganges flows; the sanctified Badrinath; the Kailas, the mountain of Precious Snow; the Kinchinjunga, the Golden Girdled on whose brow dwells majestic serenity....

'Ask a man,' Para-manik went on, 'to build a house. He will

build one which recalls his childhood home—provided he has found love in that home.'

Were the people of Madhu-ban seafaring at any time? Why did they build homes which gave the impression of up-turned barges—resting on wooden piles? Or did they perhaps ply the Damodar river in the same way as the bargees who carried coal to Calcutta?

'No,' Para-manik promptly replied, 'the reason is quite different. There was once a great flood: the flood was there because man sinned. He forgot that the path to holiness and the way to happiness were one and the same. So the flood came to separate people. It will come again to drown the region of Hihiri Pipiri, the Land of Butterflies, then Chae Champa, the Country of Flowering Trees....'

'But Para-manik,' I interrupted, 'what sins are you committing to deserve the flood again?'

'A stork caught with cranes cannot escape chastisement,' Para-manik affirmed with conviction.

Once, a husbandman fixed a net in his field to catch the cranes that fed on his new-sown corn. When he came to examine his net he found a stork among the cranes entangled in his snare. 'Spare me,' implored the stork, 'I am no crane. You may well see I am a stork, a friend of man. I bring him good luck. I am known as the praying bird and am loved for my piety. I look after my parents and children dutifully.' 'All this may be true enough,' muttered the husbandman as he unsheathed his knife, 'but you have been caught in the company of the birds that destroy my crop, and their fate shall be yours.' The stork paid for the company he kept!

'We have kept evil company.' Para-manik shook his head. 'The company of those who do not know that happiness is holiness and holiness is happiness.'

But this time, he assured me, his people would not be caught napping: their houses were built like boats, and when the land

and the hills were flooded they would still stay where they were: they would drop their sheet-anchors.

I forgot all about my original question concerning Kumar. I also forgot to thank him for the loving care with which he tended me for several weeks. I was now allowed to get up occasionally and try out my strength. My powers to coordinate movements gradually came back to me. There were no bad after-effects from my accident: I vaguely wished, however, for the same sort of miracle which, according to the Second Master, accompanied Padre Johan's fall from the back of a buffalo: 'His capacity of memorizing increased prodigiously. Previously he could not remember his multiplication-tables. But the fall which caused a scar on his forehead made a new man of him.'

~

'A judge may die but his judgment abides,' the villagers say. 'A man may perish, but his thoughts abide and work for good or for evil.' I watched the ceiling of the *moucharaby*. It was pierced with trellis patterns inlaid with mosaics of green *hariyals*, our wood-pigeons, and blue parrots. The sound of the rippling laughter of the Santal girls reached my ears: it came from far off. At great heights the silence is all pervading and the slightest murmur travels a long way. There was a golden plover crying somewhere. What a contrast it was from the sounds in the towns!

But all these were destined to disappear if the wretched Desdichado dam came to be built: the Red Valley would be a huge lake and the Blue Hills would disappear like the Little Brother in the range of the Seven Sisters.

The man who launched the project of the dam was dead and gone. Yet his plan was being carried out. The Sukkar Barrage transformed a desert tract into a fertile field. 'May those who built it be blessed,' I said to myself. 'But why should the Penhari Parganas be drowned to produce more hydro-electric power?'

Could nothing be done to save my hills and valleys?

'Only a miracle,' according to Neela, 'could change their policy. The *Delhiwallahs* think that the money already invested would be a dead loss if they did not finish the dam. The Power House would eventually repay every *pice*, every copper coin invested in the project. But Kumar believes that some of them are afraid that the completion of the dam will cost more than the sum they voted. In that case the project will be dropped like a hot brick. Just as the Calcutta Corporation stopped their experiments in building a new type of motor car after wasting thousands of rupees.'

This information was somewhat cheering. I did not know if I was at liberty to impart the information I received about Comrade Dynamiter's activities in the underground passages of the Golah. He was very busy, according to Gopaldas, with different varieties of poison gases and their effects on the twilight creatures of the vault. Some half a dozen Red Falcons, the teenage members of the Party, were working under his direction. They were waiting for me; I would be a real asset.

What was to be done? The Second Master and his disciples were for the dam. The Punditji was opposed to it; so were Kumar, Padre Johan, and the rest of the inhabitants. Comrade Dynamiter shared in this matter the view of the majority, though from different motives. He was for active action. Should I not help Comrade Dynamiter? High explosives might cause enough damage to the mountain-high dam to make the builders think twice. The Calcutta Corporation did, after all, give up the experiments with a new type of motor car....

There was only one snag. My promise to Mashi-ma: I was not to revisit the Golah without her formal permission. I gritted my teeth. Had Sashe Raha been anywhere near the *moucharaby*, I would have given him the thrashing of his life. It was his indiscretion that made me lose my pony, Red Belly, and then I had had to give a written promise to Mashi-ma about the Golah.

I was turning over these things in my mind and fuming with

rage. Part of my anger might have been due to a message I received from Kumar; I could never explain to myself the workings of my mind. What made me so angry to read and re-read Kumar's letter?

Instead of asking him bluntly what made him run about all over the world, I wrote to him for a pair of binoculars and dropped a polite hint about Comrade Dynamiter's remarks. And I also wanted to know what he thought about the situation of the country as a whole.

~

'An adolescent with an open mind and an ultramarine outlook may become an oceanographer,' Kumar wrote in his letter. 'But one with no outlook and a spy-glass is likely to turn into a pornographer.'

That was what he wrote about my request for a pair of binoculars to examine the life of the tree-top dwellers! To add insult to injury he sent me along with his letter a bundle of illustrated periodicals filled with pictures of bathing beauties, and a laconic comment: 'Get rid of your adolescent hay fever. Did you talk to Neela? By the way, the *Delhiwallahs* have banned the pictures of Pin-up girls.'

But not a word about Comrade Dynamiter's insinuations.

What did Kumar take me for? A ninny? A child afraid of the dark? Fearful of facing a fire? Or a firing squad? Evidently the fate of the Penhari Parganas and the country in general did not interest him much. Otherwise how could he write such nonsense?

'The most important thing in life is not to know whither the universe is drifting,' according to Kumar. 'But whither *you* are going. The world is the Lord's and he knows his business. And you should know yours. The *Gita* asks you to do your duty and leave the rest to the Lord. Ask for no reward and expect none. Your recompense lies in fulfilling your duty well.'

What was my duty? My real duty? 'Work,' said Comrade

Dynamiter. 'Work ceaselessly for the coming order, the classless society of to-morrow.' This doctrine would have made Kumar guffaw! 'Work for work's sake? No, thank you,' was Kumar's usual taunt to the Second Master. 'Any ass can work itself to death. For thirty-five years I have resisted the temptation to do a day's work. My work is fun; my work is not toil. It's just making the most of such gifts as I possess. I consider leisure to be the end of life, not work….' What was I to make of such a frivolous explanation? The Punditji talked about Wisdom. And Padre Johan about the Kingdom of God. The Second Master of Success. The villagers of being worthy of one's own forefathers. With the exception of Comrade Dynamiter, they all thought that a well-lived life ought to be a life full of laughter.

'A loveless man never laughs,' that was Neela's belief. 'Neither does he smile.' She advised me to keep away from humourless people. I knew she was my well-wisher and was very fond of me. She made me wonder if there was anything wrong with Comrade Dynamiter: he never laughed, nor did he smile. His disciple Gopaldas's laughter had a hollow ring; his smiles were sarcastic: caustic. 'A man who never laughs!' Kumar would have nothing to do with such a man. 'Something must be wrong with his liver and his religion.'

I was utterly confused. Comrade Dynamiter had no religion and as far as I could make out he suffered from no liver-disease. Yet he was generally very grim. Why was he like that? 'When a man has a duty to accomplish,' Gopaldas asserted, 'he must be strong enough to endure it without flinching, without smiling, and without whimpering. It is frivolous to laugh.'

Anyway, Kumar's letter made me feel miserable.

XI

Comrade Ramoni's visit to the *moucharaby* made a world of difference to me. She was the very spirit of mirth and gaiety.

So I drew the conclusion that it was not always necessary to be glum in order to belong to the Red Falcons. She was not only a faithful member of the Party, but a leading figure: the chief recruiting officer of the area. 'Thanks to her,' Gopaldas told me, 'the membership among the university students in Calcutta has been increasing by leaps and bounds. She dances on the stage. The college boys rave over her. They call her the *Pretty Smasher*. That's what she is: a real smasher.'

Pretty she certainly was, and she knew the art of embellishing nature's gifts to greater advantage than most women. And here she scored over her rivals in the Penhari Parganas: she painted even her toe-nails, to say nothing of dyeing the soles of her feet and the palms of her hands with *henna*. Most of our women, of course, used the scarlet *alta*, but cerise-red and orange *henna* was more original: it toned better with the shade of her golden skin. Her nails were long, carefully manicured and varnished; her eyebrows tastefully plucked and pencilled to enhance, one would say, the archness of her sly smiles.

How the professional dancers dressed in Calcutta I had not the slightest idea, but Comrade Ramoni's costume was very much like that of the *Pahari* women: her lower garment was a many-pleated skirt coming almost to her ankles, and her upper one was a *chaddar*, a stole going over her shoulders and covering the back of her head, the general effect being similar to the draped figure of the Virgin Mother in Padre Johan's chapel. She, however, used extraordinarily fine muslin with beautiful gold or silver brocaded hems for her costume: they were almost transparent like dew or gossamer. One could see through her *chaddar*. Her short, backless bodice which barely covered her bosom was of the same cobweb-like material. I wondered how her *kanchuli*, her short bodice, remained in position. A searching look revealed that she applied some paint to her nipples even as she touched up her cheeks, to give her honey-coloured complexion a slightly darker shade.

It was only on her second visit I noticed that some

extraordinarily fine strings of the tiniest crystal beads passed across her back and her neck to hold the two pieces of her bodice together. These bead-strings perfectly matched her earrings, bracelets, and necklaces resembling rosary chaplets. She wore no anklets nor armlets like our village women, and her jewellery was far simpler than any I had ever seen. I should mention here that whatever might have been the adverse comments on the transparency of Comrade Ramoni's costumes, this much everyone must have admitted: that she knew the art of dressing attractively and of revealing her body's grace to her best advantage. The moment I saw her my thoughts went back to the image of the goddess Rati, Amor, in Kumar's workshop and to the discussion I had with him on the undraped glory of Saraswati, Goddess of Wisdom.

Ramoni was an expert at playing hide-and-seek with her diaphanous veil. Whenever she laughed—and this she did every few minutes, as she was ever-sparkling and nimble-witted—she would draw the brocaded hem of her *chaddar* over her coral lips as though she was too shy to reveal her beautiful teeth. At times she pulled it in a way which brought the hem immediately below her eyes: her black, lustrous eyes then looked bigger and brighter. She was infinitely playful and always rippling with smiles. Did she know that her smiles and her laughter made her look prettier? Did she realize that her gestures were adornments to her loveliness?

No wonder, I thought, the privilege of working under such a delightful person induced many boys to join her section of the Red Falcons. She must have been a great asset to the Party.

On her first visit Ramoni was accompanied by Gopaldas and Comrade Dynamiter. I was then still bed-ridden and did not, or rather could not, see her from my bed as she came into the room. Her perfumed *henna*-dyed fingers covered my eyes as she whispered, 'Guess who is here?' Of course, I could not make any guess: I had never seen her before nor heard her voice.

'I bet you have heard of me. I am Ramoni. I was born under Gemini.'

I professed complete ignorance about her and her stars. A moment later, however, I gasped: I was ashamed of my hidden talent of telling a blatant untruth without any forethought! Memory played me a strange trick and made me forget momentarily that she was *the* one about whom our women talked most.

Hardly a day passed in my village without my overhearing some whispered remarks about Ramoni. These comments were mostly disparaging. In some mysterious way Ramdas our *chowkidar* was held responsible by his wife for Ramoni's alleged failings—her taking to dancing on the stage, her singing before microphones, and committing similar breaches of traditional rural etiquette. 'What would happen,' Ramdas's wife constantly worried, 'if Ramoni cast her evil eye on Khukoo? She went on to higher education in the same year as Gopaldas, that good-for-nothing nephew.' 'She is a dolled-up she-monkey,' Mabool's wife was ashamed of mentioning her name. 'She reads English and paints her behind. She is a disgrace to our village.' They were not the only women to criticize her way of living in Calcutta. Others referred to her as a *petni*, a horrid succuba, a vampire, anyman's niece, and what not. Methar's wife once slapped Kolej Huzoor and sent him home reeling from her blow simply because he had casually remarked that Ramoni was the best crooner in the land. Peshkar, Ramoni's father, disowned her publicly in a special expiation ceremony in which his head was shaven and the whole village fed at his expense. Men, however, never referred to her—with the exception of Kumar. But then, Kumar was so very different from the others! 'Let her sow her wild oats judiciously,' he remarked to me. 'She is a pretty creature who knows how to tame the bulls. Anyway, she is pretty and that is virtue enough….'

'Pretty is not the word for her,' I said to myself as Ramoni took her seat by my side. 'She is a beauty. How can anyone have the heart to say nasty things about her. How could Kumar say that she should be tending cattle? She looks so frail.'

'I am breathless,' Comrade Ramoni panted, though she looked as fresh as a dew-drenched lily of the dawn. She must have rested somewhere before stepping inside the *moucharaby* otherwise she would not have looked so fragrant and so cool. Anyway, she declared she was out of breath and as my *charpoy* bed was the only piece of furniture there she sat down on it: my being there did not apparently matter much to her.

'Isn't this place high?' she asked peevishly. 'I am footsore. My feet must be bleeding.'

While Comrade Dynamiter and Gopaldas talked about the progress in clearing up the underground passages of the Golah and also about the importance of convincing the Santals that the Party was interested in their welfare, Ramoni quietly removed her sandals and sat cross-legged in the *virasana* posture by my side as though my bed was a divan meant for her only.

'Had a fall from a horse?' she whispered ignoring the conversation of the other two. 'That's nothing. You will be all right soon. I once had a fall from an elephant and broke a thigh-bone.' She pulled at my bed sheets and slid her hands slyly underneath the bedspread to squeeze my bare stomach. She then guided under the cover of the sheet my hand to the spot where she had a scar on her thigh. And this made me feel breathless and terribly confused.

All this happened while the other two were having a serious discussion about my future and how my joining the Red Falcons would be of help to me as well as to the country and to the world. I was simply amazed how Ramoni managed to interject apt remarks into the general conversation from time to time without the least embarrassment. Her lips ignored what her fingers were doing: just then she was playing the drum on my stomach.

'She has the magic fingers of a fairy,' I thought, 'and the intelligence of an angel.'

'He is a bit pot-bellied,' she remarked about me. 'Otherwise he is all right. He will join the Red Falcons as soon as he recovers. Won't you? My young Jung Bahadur?'

I blushed. *Pot-bellied* in the Penhari Parganas means lazy-bones! Did Ramoni seriously think I was generally lazy? Or was she referring to my stomach? How could I ask her what she had in mind? Nor could I contradict her. I recalled the maxim of my grandfather who used to say that everything was permissible to a pretty woman and that whatever she might do to man should be regarded as a grace and a favour.

'Violets of Parma!' she murmured and daubed my nose with her face-powder as she got up to leave the *moucharaby.* 'My young Jung Bahadur! Let your niece help you to clear your thoughts. Nothing is as good as the perfume of the violets of Parma.' She poured out a few drops from a scent bottle and rubbed my forehead with this exquisite and exotic perfume. I felt faint and held my breath; the fragrance of violets almost overpowered me.

'Are you good at remembering names?' she asked as she arranged her hand-bag, which looked very much like the bag in which Mashi-ma kept her rosary beads.

'Parma,' I repeated mechanically. 'Violets of Parma.'

'No, my Jung Bahadur!' she arched her eye-brows in playful surprise while her lips smiled. 'Your adopted niece is called Ramoni. She was born under Gemini.' Before leaving me she caressed my chin and then kissed the tips of her own fingers.

She certainly looked like Padre Johan's image of the Madonna brought to life.

~

The memory of Ramoni will for me always be associated with the fragrance of the violets of Parma. Violets are scarce in the Penhari Parganas. They are to be found only in certain rare sheltered nooks and at great heights. We call them *dhoomals,* the 'smoke-coloured'. How did she come to acquire a taste for these exclusive flowers?

'My face powder smells of violets,' Ramoni said, 'my hair lotion smells of violets. My scent is violets. But mind you, I prefer only the lovely violets that bloom near Parma. I make the Comrades from abroad get them for me.'

I asked Para-manik if he knew of any place near-by where violets grew. If so, would he kindly care to collect a few for me? I thought of offering them to Ramoni as a pleasant surprise.

'*Dhoomals*! Violets!' Para-manik shook his head: they were not meant for men! Only *yoginis* and *dakinis* cared for *dhoomals*. The wise-women, the *yoginis*, the female fakirs endowed with the gift of levitation owned the right to collect them in the land beyond the Himalayas: they were like the semi-divinities, almost goddesses, who rarely visited human abodes; the odour of their bodies was like the perfume of the *dhoomals*. 'They move through air like angels.'

'And the *dakinis*? The sorceresses?'

'They too emit the fragrance of violets. But they drink human blood.'

'How am I to know one from the other?'

'Very difficult,' according to Para-manik, 'to distinguish the two.' But there was, fortunately, one touchstone for separating them: the rosary beads. The *yoginis* wore rosary beads of holy plants and the sorceresses preferred necklaces of the bones of their victims. The wise women conferred blessings upon mortals, whereas the sorceresses enfeebled them by destroying their manliness and their sense of loyalty. It was, therefore, most imprudent to keep double-petalled violets by one's bedside at night. 'Particularly for a young boy sleeping all by himself in a place far removed from human habitation.'

Para-manik was adamant. It was like inducing him to secure a dwarf-bear for me!

'If you were married or betrothed,' he finally declared, 'it would have been different. For a young unmarried boy violets are no good. Just place them by your bed-side and you will certainly attract a passing *yogini* or a *dakini* at night-time. They move about through the air invisibly. And when they become visible they are found to be naked without any clothes like the dryads of the hills.'

~

On her next visit Ramoni slipped her hand under my bedclothes as though it was a pre-arranged plan that she should tickle me while the others talked about the grave problems of the day. Her touch thrilled me to the very marrow and made me hold my breath. So much so that I could hardly follow the general discussion intelligently. It was a queer sensation: to touch her body or to be touched by her. On the third occasion it was still worse. I felt almost choked.

'One is uneasy,' they say, 'about what one cannot understand.' And I wanted to know why Ramoni's touch made me breathless.

I told Neela about it and she flared up unexpectedly. I had never seen her lose her temper like this. It was almost comical that she should abuse Ramoni in the same way as the rest of the village women.

'Ramoni is a slut,' she raved. 'She is a witch. The next time she touches you she will get it from me. She must be pretty hot to gad about draped in thin air and painted like a holy cow.'

I ought not to have told Neela anything about Ramoni. But it was impossible to keep back the fragrance of the violets. One afternoon, following a visit from Ramoni, Neela came into the *moucharaby* and began sniffing the air even before greeting me. She declared that I must have dirtied my bedclothes and that they should be burnt straight off. The atmosphere was foul with the disgusting stench of a civet cat in heat. My looks were queer! I was trying to hide something from her. It was high time for me to abandon the *moucharaby* for the village.

She was in such a bad mood that it was impossible for me to raise the question of my future with her. Though she was the only person at that time who could have helped me with her advice.

~

'Don't squeeze the lemon too hard,' Kumar remarked, 'or it will turn bitter.'

I listened to him in silence just as patiently as he had heard my story: Neela's getting angry with me on account of Ramoni. I told him everything or almost everything, keeping back the news about the Golah and the underground activities over there.

'I am sorry to have dragged you away from your work.' I was apologetic. But what could I do? Neela thought it was high time for me to go back to the village. I was more of a burden than a help to her. I needed someone to accompany me. Just in case my legs felt a bit wobbly. After all, the journey from the *moucharaby* to the village was not an easy one even for a man with solid legs.

Kumar, however, was more interested to know precisely what sort of adventure I had had with Ramoni.

'Adventure! How could I have any adventure with her? I was not even allowed to sit up for a long while. She played the drum on my stomach and this has made Neela angry.'

'You have been squeezing the lemon too hard.' That was the mysterious comment of Kumar. He advised me to spend one more night in the *moucharaby*. 'We shall walk down together to-morrow morning. One more night here won't hurt you or Neela. I shall run down to Madhu-ban and have a talk with her.'

~

Sombre thoughts raced through my mind; though there was no particular reason for me to be sad. But it was like this with me once in a while: everything seemed to be topsy-turvy and everything went wrong. That evening I forgot to light the special lamp which was my signal to Neela and to Para-manik at Madhuban. 'If anything is amiss,' they told me, 'if you need anything, just blow out the lamp. And someone will come for you.'

'What does it matter,' I said to myself as I lay in the dark, 'if the lamp remains unlit to-night? From to-morrow there will be nobody here save the lizards. Anyway, I told Neela that there would be no further need for her to worry about me.'

As evening darkened into night vague snatches of music reached me. I strained my ears. Was it Kumar who was playing on his bamboo flute? What was the tune? I sat up in bed, and though it was dark but for some pale patches of moonlight near the balustrade of the balcony, I closed my eyes to listen better. It gave me a thrill to recall the tune. 'It is the song Ramoni sang,' I said audibly to myself. 'The very same tune. Her voice is sweet.' How sweet? Sweeter than the fragrance of the violets, the amethyst-coloured, double-petalled *dhoomals*. It was clear. Clearer than the running waters of the mountain rill or the crystal rosary beads she wore as her necklace. More penetrating than the *kokila*'s call.

A kokila called from a *henna*-spray:

> *Lira! liree! Lira! liree!*
> Hasten, maidens, hasten away
> To gather the leaves of the henna tree.
> Send your pitchers afloat on the tide,
> Gather the leaves ere the dawn be old,
> Grind them in mortars of amber and gold,
> The fresh green leaves of the henna tree.

> A kokila called from a henna-spray:
> *Lira! liree! Lira! liree!*
> Hasten, maidens, hasten away
> To gather the leaves of the *henna* tree.
> The *tilka*'s for the brow of a bride,

And betel-nut's red for lips that are sweet;
But, for lily-like fingers and feet,
The red, the red of the *henna* tree.

How fitting was this song for her: 'In praise of *Henna*.' Ramoni was like the *kokila*, the cuckoo that sings in our bushes night and day, all the year round.

The faint strains of music became more distinct. Was the flautist approaching the *moucharaby*? He did not seem to be far away. Or was it the wind? Was it now wafting a different way? Or perhaps it was my fancy that made me think that the music was louder. The silence of the night always brought distant sounds close to my ear. The splash of water in a near-by fountain, which could hardly be perceived during the day, now resounded like a rushing spring. I opened my eyes and saw the moonlight patches mingled together to form a bright circle. A sound of footfalls, faint like the rustling of the dead leaves in the wind, made me turn my head. The melody of music became clearer and at the same time the jingle of anklet bells filled the place.

'Who is there?' I whispered. There was no reply. Who could it be?

The fragrance of violets, more concentrated than any ever used by Ramoni, made me hold my breath. Who was there? Could it be Ramoni? How did she dare come to the *moucharaby* at that hour? At Neela's request, Para-manik the headman had decided that no one was to pass through his village to climb to the *moucharaby* without Neela's formal permission: I was still convalescing, and therefore must not be disturbed by any unauthorized visits.

It was confusing. What would happen to Ramoni if she were detected? Neela had sworn that she would be branded if she was ever found in my company anywhere within the Blue Hills. I felt like shouting, 'Ramoni! Run away before they catch you. Neela will brand you with red hot iron! Run! Otherwise Para-manik will set his dogs on you. He has trained *baya* birds which twitter messages to him. His finches will give you away.' I felt like crying. But no sound escaped from my lips.

Perhaps it was not Ramoni! I had heard that the dancers on the stage did not care for the anklet bells of the peasant girls. Then was it Neela? What was the purpose of her coming in so stealthily? Was she under the impression that I had already vacated the *moucharaby*? There was no lighted lamp, the pre-arranged signal, to indicate my presence. Then it was Kumar whom Neela wanted to entertain with her dance! But Kumar was not in. He was out in the open air somewhere near Madhu-ban. What was I to do?

My heart ceased to beat and my tongue remained glued to the roof of my mouth as I saw a veiled form standing immobile in the circular patch of the moonbeams streaming through the wide arch of the *moucharaby*. Her wrap was diaphanous. She wore a diadem of blue diamonds. Round her neck were garlands of purple flowers. Her arms as well as ankles were loaded with jewellery which flashed in the moonlight. She stood on tip-toe and her arms were posed as though she held an amphora on her jewelled crown. It was the familiar attitude of the divine shepherdess Radha: the posture of waiting: biding for the signal of the flute. She looked like a self-luminous deity, attending an audience of the immortals, awaiting their formal invitation to begin her dance.

Her anklet bells jingled and at the same moment the unseen flautist began the tune of Jaya-Deva's *Lalita Lavanga Lata*. The dancer's body became taut: she was eager to begin her steps. The rather monotonous melody of the verses—famous for their onomatopoetic effect—was only a signal to the dancer to get ready. The anklet bells ceased to ring. But they jingled again as soon as the music for the steps started.

The dancer swayed: graceful as a green blade of gladiolus, trembling in the fragrant first breath of dawn. She looked like a shining shrine in the centre of a sacred bourn. Her ethereal veil wove a haze of mystery: as she moved it slid from her shoulders and fell to her feet revealing her as a divinity draped in glory. She was like a sylvan goddess in the midst of a silvery pool.

The flute-player piped and the dancer danced. The moonlight kissed her limbs and played hide-and-seek with her. My heart throbbed with delight: it kept time with her steps. I felt like a timid fawn too amazed to stir: fearful lest the least movement should break the magic spell and make the goddess fade. Oh! She looked so lovely and so lovable. I wished she would go on dancing till the end of time: my homage of adoration would have been hers for all eternity. Was it in honour of one like her our poets sang?—'The eye never tires; the soul ever rejoices; the heart never cloys. Oh! marvellous spectacle, akin to the vision of Paradise...'

Was I dreaming? Was I weaving visions out of my fevered fancy? Was she only one of the painted and jewelled statues of Kumar brought to life for a brief hour? The moonbeams receded. The circle of light narrowed, grew dim and gradually vanished. The moonlight faded to starlight, and the charm was broken. The melody of the tinkling bells ceased to sound. The lilting refrain of the flute came to an end. All became silent and dark. The vision melted away.

Did my fancy play me a cruel trick?

But even if she were a phantom why did I turn my head away when she approached me to caress my chin with her fragrant fingers? Why did I struggle to evade the proffered embrace of her dainty arms? Why did I refuse to be pressed to her heaving bosom? Why did I fight desperately to avoid all contact with her lithe limbs of sculptural beauty? What made me ignore all the gestures of the love-lorn shepherdess Radha? Why did I bury my face in the pillow heedless of her silent tears that bathed my body? What strange folly finally goaded me to cry for succour and call her a witch! 'You are a slut,' I shouted, 'a *dakini*, a sorceress, though you are as nude as a *yogini*. And as fragrant. You want to enfeeble me. You want to drain me of my strength! I know you are a witch!'

Was all this just a creation of my imaginings?

I rose from my bed long before dawn. I searched for my favourite lizard with its stumpy tail to bid good-bye. It took me a long while to find it, and I was disappointed to notice that it did not want to be disturbed. It failed to wag its stubby tail nor did it wink at me. It refused to recognize me.

As I stepped out of the *moucharaby* my feet trod on a crushed wreath of *dhoomals*, violets of *avira* purple, the rarest of all flowers in the land. Who dropped the garland there so carelessly? Or was it placed there to remind me that my vision was not a mere dream? I picked it up to treasure it in the folds of my garment.

Where was Neela? Was I to bid her good-bye or not?

XII

The heat from the valley rose in ripples as I laboured down the slopes. The plain looked like a brazen cauldron cracked with fissures of blue: the silver threads of shrunken rivers. 'When the sun god is angry,' the Santals say, 'he burns up the silver threads and changes the Red Valley into a bowl of glittering copper, and men and beasts die of thirst. The valley is waterless because the jungles have been destroyed.'

Though Babu Hem Chandra Chahar did not accept this view, I knew there were many who thought the same as the Santals. Whatever came from the Santals was detested by the Second Master! What was the reason? What made him constantly accuse them of gross immorality? Why did he continuously harp on the same theme: 'Their women are notoriously pretty'? What did he imply by the term *notorious*? Was prettiness a sin?

'Because the grapes are sour,' Kumar furnished his usual half-serious and half-comic explanation. 'He is sore because his desires are unfulfilled. He can't have them. So he must detest them! Can't you see what's wrong with him?

> The wrinkles on my face are all untold
> My hair is grey and thin;
> My limbs are sadly feeble grown, and old:
> But love is young, and sin.

'All embittered men are like him.'

If I were to believe Kumar, Comrade Dynamiter's desire for revolutionizing the country, transforming the whole to a single unit, was also based on unsatisfied love! He had no home when he was very young and therefore he would like to deny the privilege of a home, a nest of love and affection, to others. He would love to force communal hostels on all! Could that also be the reason why Gopaldas sought to destroy his own people? After all Ramdas did bother a lot about his nephew. 'Yes! And no! He was not brought up by Ramdas. His father xwanted him to get out of the rut of village life and forced too much discipline and too much genteel upbringing on him. It's the worst possible equipment for life. A university degree by itself does not guarantee you a decent job. So what is Gopaldas to do? He must hate the ways of his own people, and seek a newer variety of disciplinary existence.'

What about progress then? Anything for the betterment of the people was then liable to be called revolutionary? 'A question wrongly put,' according to the Punditji, 'can never be rightly answered.'

'All right,' I said to myself, 'I shall have to think again. I shall have to formulate my question differently.' I recalled the Punditji's disputation with the Second Master over the term *progress*. The aged Sanskrit scholar scorned that word. 'Progress?' He generally asked, 'What's progress? In the so-called progressive countries, print is getting bigger as ideas are getting smaller. And to judge by the more popular periodicals the majority of the progressive

Westerners have reverted to the picture-books of their infancy. Can you call that progress? The state of a man's mind is the true measure of his progress. The degree of serenity is the measuring rod. Is the state of mind of a man in an industrialized country necessarily better than that of a man in the Penhari Parganas? Progress is the same as holiness. It is not based on the consumption of ice-cream cones, nor on a nation's capacity of producing guns, and dancing to the music of "Waggle your behinds" and admiring surrealism. Progress lies in the appreciation of Beauty. What is Beauty?... Is it to be measured by the speed of planes? Can you measure the speed of thought? Your thoughts...' The Punditji loved thumping the ground with his brass-bound blackthorn staff, Mahendra Chandal, to emphasize his points. 'Can you measure the speed of thought?'

~

I found I too was thumping the floor of the *stoep* with the Punditji's staff, Mahendra Chandal. I was making a din and people were staring at me from the village square. I gave a start and looked guiltily about me. The arrival of the Santal women at the square had set my mind working: it had been set back on events of long ago as well as of recent date! Meanwhile the Santal women were speaking to the village elders under the *peepul* tree....

PART THREE

Balaram's Plough

I

What did the Santal women of Mahisha-ban want?

They begged for water: they needed as much as the village could spare. There was a fire and they wanted our men to put it out. One of their cottages was ablaze. Unless something was done to extinguish it, the rising wind would spread the conflagration: there was a risk of their entire hamlet being burnt down and nothing would remain of Mahisha-ban.

'How did it start?' asked one of the elders.

They did not know. They could not make out how it started so early in the morning. It could not have been due to the sun. The empty shed near the spring-fed pool where the buffaloes wallowed might have attracted the attention of a stranger. They were not sure if it was a case of arson or of negligence. The pool was now nearly dry: all its water was used up. Couldn't we give them some succour immediately?

The cottages of the Santals at Mahisha-ban were different from our houses. They were like piles of firewood in summer: built of bamboos and wooden piles, covered with straw thatches; the sides were wicker-work pleated with coconut leaves. They were neat and clean. But as liable to catch fire as match-wood. It needed no great imagination to guess the plight of these women. Their men-folk were away and so they needed our help badly: we were their nearest neighbours. Timely succour, they pleaded, would save their hamlet. Otherwise it would be too late.

The appeal of the Santal women was heard in stony silence. Kolej Huzoor stared at a Santal girl of Mahisha-ban, opened his cigarette case and closed it immediately. Probably he thought of offering her a cigarette and then suddenly realized that *it was simply not done* in a gathering attended by the village elders. He quietly put back his case and looked around sheepishly. The august elders looked at each other and said nothing.

'Please do something immediately,' one of the Santal matrons sobbed. They had done their best to cope with the fire by smothering it; with bill-hooks and scythes they had cut down the fleshy cactus-plants which grew by the roadside and tried to stem the spread of the fire temporarily. Some were even then working at Mahisha-ban to put it out in this way. If the village could not spare any water at least some men could be sent with them for pulling down the huts next to the burning shed.

'Though they lack water,' Kolej Huzoor remarked, 'they don't lack pluck.' Others thought the same though they did not utter a word. It was not good manners to make any comment of this sort before the elders had given theirs. It was evident that the village council was not too eager to give help to the women of Mahisha-ban. The elder sitting next to our Goatee coughed and cleared his throat noisily: he complained of the dengue fever which revisited him annually since the turn of the century. Another elder declared that this ailment was more debilitating than malaria. The Goatee sympathized with the victim of the dengue fever and suggested his trying out *Makaradhwaja*, the cure-all sublimate of mercury and gold, with the juice of betel leaves, and added some further counsel as to the best time for commencing this treatment. It evidently had something to do with *Makara*, the tropic of Capricorn, and the phases of the moon.

None of our village women were there: they were conducting their special *pujas*, their religious rites and ceremonies in connection with the Ploughing Ceremony of the evening.

The Santal women waited and waited, while the elders talked

about different varieties of fever-cure. In Calcutta, someone affirmed, the people had great faith in a patent-medicine called 'Dengue-Czarina': it was sold by the pint. All of a sudden the Goatee sighed noisily, 'The conflagration at Mahisha-ban is a great tragedy!' But where were the elders to find enough water to put out a big fire?

'It is a small fire as yet,' said the oldest of the Santal matrons. 'What about your *baoli* and the stone-lined wells?'

The mere mention of the word *baoli* made the elders start. They stared at one another with panic-stricken eyes. It took them a few minutes to regain their usual composure. They then fixed their gaze sternly on Ramdas the watchman. No one was supposed to know of the existence of the *baoli* save the august members of the Council of Five and our *chowkidar*.

The village *baoli* had existed long before the Golah was built. It was the secret hiding-place of the elders in times of trouble. Whenever there was any danger of an imminent invasion members of the Council were expected to seek refuge in its underground chambers, carrying with them the village archives— the *dalils*, *firmans*, palm-leaf documents, letters-patent, maps, seals, parchments, papers, and papyrus-sheets and the idol of the local deity. So even if the village was razed to the ground, the elders on re-emerging from the bowels of the earth could start reconstruction on the basis of the old plans, after the storm had blown over. Though in their life-time neither the Goatee nor his colleagues had experienced any direct threat from the White Huns, Scythians, Tartars, Uzbecks, or the Chinese, it was generally agreed among themselves that none but they and their *chowkidar* should have any knowledge of the village *baoli*! The secret of its existence was to be transmitted to their successors, the next village Council and Ramdas's inheritor.

~

A *baoli* is, in fact, nothing but an underground house with a well, generally furnished with one or more staircases leading right down to the level of the water. Its original purpose was to accommodate its owner and his family and retinue with a cool residence for the summer months. Its well was for supplying water and for general refrigeration. However, in troubled times the *baolis* proved to be safe hiding-places: thus the system of camouflage came to be introduced for concealing the airing shafts and the light-wells; secret underground passages, hidden approaches and steps were added, and their entrances ingeniously disguised.

Our people are skilful with decoys, and some of the *baolis* I know are so cleverly hidden that a stranger might be standing right on the top of one without even suspecting its existence. This fact, according to Gopaldas, was nothing remarkable. 'In Russia,' he told me, 'there are thousands of such *baolis*. They call them underground shelters. They are far more scientifically built than the best of our own. Some of them can accommodate as many as a hundred thousand people—the whole population of the Penhari Parganas. A number of Russian underground shelters are being used even now. There are people working and living in them night and day.'

Whatever might be the truth of Gopaldas's assertion, this much I ought to say, that none of our *baolis* are inhabited to-day, at least not by human beings. Though I know of a few in which numerous baboons have installed themselves and made themselves at home. There is, however, one near Dalton-gunj which shelters a grey-haired man called Sampheriya and his three wives: he can make shining silver rupees out of lead. If I ever need any money, he has told me, I should call on him and get a sackful of rupees on condition that I take away his third wife who is young and quarrelsome.

All this, however, is by the way, and to point out that the changed circumstances have brought about many changes in the use of our *baolis*. Most of these are in ruins nowadays. The walls of one near Pushpa-pur collapsed only last year, and now it is as good as non-existent. I found a coin in one of its alcoves bearing the inscription: *Maha-Rajah-Adhirajah Sri-Harsha.* 'It was minted some thirteen hundred years ago,' Neela told me. 'In the days of Rajah Harsha.'

Our village *baoli* did not, of course, date from the time of Harsha. However, it was sufficiently dilapidated to indicate that it was much, much older than the Golah. In theory, at least, as has just been said, it was supposed to be such a marvellously constructed and camouflaged arcanum that its existence and whereabouts ought not to have been known to anyone save the elders and Ramdas. In reality, it was an open secret to every observant eye. Nevertheless, its access was denied to the inquisitive by padlocked wooden hatches: only the Goatee and his colleagues and our watchman possessed the keys.

To come back to the scene in the village square, the Goatee made signs to Ramdas.

Our *chowkidar* had the unfortunate gift of misinterpreting gestures and motives. He assumed that the Goatee wanted him to fetch his wife. Poor Ramdas! I felt sorry for him. In spite of the promise he gave me he began babbling incoherently about the human-shaped cakes by the flowering cactus bush, the dead dog, the tail-less toy horse of his daughter, Khukoo, and then suddenly he burst into tears. He was ready to cage a lion, but to face his wife! That was an impossibility. Someone kicked his shins and several voices advised him at the same time not to make a fool of himself: no one was in the least interested in his stale story about the white clay horse. The elders were more concerned with something else. How did the Santal women of Mahisha-ban come to know about our *baoli* and the deep, stone-lined wells?

'There's no reason why they should not.' Ramdas replied with alacrity. He was his usual self again: prepared to twist a red bear's tail or to catch a mad bull by its horns. 'They ought to know everything. The Santal stone-cutters and masons helped in the construction of our *baoli* and the wells.' Naturally, they were aware of their whereabouts. Not only that! By an ancient agreement they were entitled to draw water from our wells. 'But not from the *baoli*,' Ramdas added.

I felt like shouting 'Well said, Ramdas,' but thought it was better to remain quiet and watch from my *stoep* the outcome of my friend the *chowkidar*'s intervention.

'Another condition was imposed,' Ramdas continued, ignoring the admonitory head-shakes of the elders. 'The Santals may take out as much water as they need provided they do it after sunset. This was the agreement reached in the days of Rajah Chattar Singha. During the day the water belongs to us, but during the night it belongs to everyone.'

The Goatee did not say anything but gave a nasty look and coughed. He and the others felt disgusted at Ramdas's incapacity to understand their signs. Now, however, it was too late: the cat was out of the bag. The Santal women once again pleaded for a quick decision. If they were accorded immediate help they would relinquish their claim to the well-water for one whole year, they declared.

'A woman's word, they say, is but a bundle of water!' the Goatee answered solemnly. 'An agreement of this kind cannot be reached with women. It is a serious matter… We are prepared to discuss it with your headmen. Can't you send your Jagmanjhi for a preliminary talk?'

'But the men are away for the day. They are in the mines.'

'For the time being then we shall wait,' replied the Goatee and the other elders nodded their assent. 'I am afraid we can do nothing just now.'

The Santal women wept in silence and I shed tears of anger.

What could I do to help them?

'It is better that one should be saved than two lost,' the Goatee philosophized. 'There isn't enough water to put out the fire over there. If we give away our water we shall perish. Thus Mahisha-ban and this village, two places, would be destroyed at one and the same time. By the way, the elephant cacti growing by the roadside do not belong to Mahisha-ban. We cannot allow wanton destruction of our property.'

The Santal women departed as they had come—with empty pitchers.

I banged my head against the balustrade of the verandah. It was my fault, I felt, that they had had to go away without any water. What made me ask for some dramatic scene? Why did I want something spectacular to happen in the village square?

II

I climbed the flat terrace of the roof and anxiously scanned the horizon. The morning's thin pencil of smoke was no longer a mystery. I wished I had not noticed that sinister sign in the sky nor heard anything about its origin. I understood now the significance of the Punditji's remark: 'The villagers should have spared themselves the sin of a holocaust. They ought not to have imitated Kansa who put fire to Brinda-ban. The Ploughing Ceremony by itself would have been more than enough.'

The rising smoke was now transformed into a twisting column of grey fog. Gradually like a monster water-spout it formed a link between the waterless earth and the cloudless sky. How could a small place like Mahisha-ban produce so much smoke? It was frightening to gaze in the direction of the palm-groves which hid this Santal hamlet. The wind was blowing away from our village. So no sound reached my ears, but more than once the house shook and the windows rattled as though there were a series of earth tremors. Was the fire spreading from Mahisha-ban to other places?

A light breeze set in, to change gradually into a strong wind. It gave fantastic forms to the gigantic sable column which by and by obscured the horizon.

There was not a fleck of cloud in the sky. But the setting sun painted it in varying shades of mauve, lavender, and purple, and the billows of smoke looked like heavy cloud-banks. The effect was unbelievably magnificent. A sinister crime had been committed: a deliberate and premeditated act of incendiarism had been perpetrated. Yet why did the skies seem to rejoice? I watched the hills, the ridges, the forests, the grey rocks, and the striated valleys: they billowed away as far as the eye could see. On any other day such a spectacle would have delighted my heart: I would have deemed myself blessed for the privilege of watching such an exquisite end to the day.

But just then my heart was heavy: I wished I had never been born and that there was no need of a Ploughing Ceremony to quench the thirst of the Red Valley.

III

'What's this madness?' I shouted at Mashi-ma when she came to tell me more about the Ploughing Ceremony. 'Couldn't you have stopped this fire? Couldn't you tell them that you won't let me play the role of Balaram unless…'

Mashi-ma's tears stopped my angry shrieks. I heard for the first time that our house would have suffered the same fate as the Santal hamlet of Mahisha-ban had she tried to interfere in any way with the villagers' decision. Those who were ready to make a scapegoat of the Punditji would have dealt with me in the same fashion. That being the case there was no point in my making a fuss so late in the day.

The arrangements were well-nigh ready: I was to be *the* Balaram during one whole night: from sunset to sunrise. The women of the seven villages struck by the drought were to be at my disposal to serve as draught-animals.

'Whatever for?' I interrupted impatiently.

'To pull your plough,' she replied quietly. 'They will enact the scene which brought down the rains at Brinda-ban centuries ago and broke the dam of Kansa at Muttra.'

'What good will that do? Can such a silly ceremony change the condition of the atmosphere?'

'Your piety and their faith can bring about a miracle,' Mashi-ma said. She was as convinced as the Punditji that the Ploughing Ceremony would be enough to make the monsoon break over the Red Valley: 'Provided you, my child, put in your goodwill. The Second Master will play the role of Krishna. He will play on the flute while you guide the plough.'

'Can you explain why it should rain? You seem to assume that as soon as I succeed in tilling a small corner of our fields it will rain.'

'Who can explain a miracle? You who are a scholar, can you explain why one grain becomes a seedling and then a plant while another grain dies and gives nothing? No man can explain the ultimate *why* of the simplest physical phenomenon. If we are worthy we shall receive the blessings of a miracle.'

Our discussion was interrupted by the entry of Kumar: he wanted to know precisely where some of the pitchers brought for the rites preceding the Ploughing Ceremony were to be placed in the courtyard of the house.

Mashi-ma ran downstairs to consult the leading lady of the Ceremony, one called Anjalir-ma, which meant she was the mother of a girl called Anjali. *Anjali* implies *prayer with folded palms*: the Great Salutation, the greeting of homage, deference and admiration.

I wondered if Kumar knew of the tragedy at Mahisha-ban. Did he witness the disgraceful spectacle in the village square? How the Goatee and the others refused to give any help to the Santal women.

'You are wasting your spleen, Little Brother,' Kumar chuckled. 'That's the trouble with you.'

How could he afford to laugh?

'Why not? Don't waste worry over Mahisha-ban. The Santal girls are tough, though they may look plump and easy-going. They tackled the fire all right. The smoke you saw was from the Golah.' So far not much news had been gathered. It was thought that owing to coal-damp or some other cause a series of explosions were taking place round about that area. 'And a part of the Golah has collapsed.'

I babbled something and stared at him.

'No time for discussion now. The courtyard is full of women, who will pull your plough. Don't forget to take the Punditji's stick with you. Good luck. So long.'

It took me a few minutes to comprehend the full import of what Kumar said. The Golah was gone! At least, a considerable portion of it was badly damaged. I was stunned as though struck by a sledge-hammer.

IV

'Whence first came the sense of shame and the feeling of guilt no one knows.' Mashi-ma talked as she arranged me for the Ceremony: she drew on my forehead with sandal paste the symbols shown on the images of the god Balaram; a chaplet of white jessamine was put on my head; I was also given a garland of scarlet hibiscus flowers round my neck and a girdle of red and white oleanders. She helped me to put on a short *dhotie* of red *cheli*, vermilion silk; the only garment I was to keep on during the anointing ceremony by the village matrons who were waiting for me in the courtyard. I was happy to notice that Mashi-ma was no longer crying. 'Whence come our sense of shame and the feeling of guilt who can tell,' she repeated. 'These sentiments vary with men and women.'

'What are you talking about?' I interrupted her. I do not know why I thought just then about Pocha the Huntsman's jibes at me. 'He is mighty slow in growing up,' he often said within my hearing. So did his friends, Bum-Boatee the Pirate and Sashe Raha, nicknamed the Split Cucumber. 'He is so slow in growing that Mashi-ma will have to wait for a century to see him big enough to get married.' Was Mashi-ma by any chance thinking of getting me married before the Ploughing Ceremony? The red *cheli* was generally worn by brides and bridegrooms.

In the circle of the Second Master strange stories were told about babies being married off to each other by their parents or grandparents: the little ones were taken out of their cradles and swaddled in red *chelis* and carried around a sacrificial fire while their sponsors repeated a sacred rite. 'Nowadays, however,' the Second Master assured his listeners, 'no girl can legally be given away in marriage before she is sixteen.' He did not, to the best of my memory, say anything about the minimum age of marriage for the bridegroom. I wondered if a boy who was less than sixteen could be married off without his consent?

What was that red *cheli* for? I was told that later on I should be given a blue *langoti*. Was that the custom? 'Perhaps just before marriage the bridegroom is expected to appear in red,' I thought. 'And after the marriage ceremony he changes into blue.'

Who would be my bride? Now that the Golah was gone I did not care—so long as my bride was not older than Mashi-ma. 'Someone older than she would create a problem. She might want to order Mashi-ma about!' Would it by any chance be Ramoni? That was hardly possible. Because the village shrews would certainly prevent her coming to Mashi-ma's courtyard. 'I should love to become Ramoni's groom,' I said to myself. 'Perhaps she would then give her stage dances in the courtyard.'

'If a woman's love for a man is genuine,' Mashi-ma went on without bothering what was passing on in my mind, 'she would do anything for him. She would eat mud, if necessary. She would go through fire to save him.' A woman's love, according to her, was unique, and no man should harshly judge a woman in love. 'No male is ever capable of experiencing that intensity of emotion which characterizes a woman's rapturous attachment. A woman genuinely in love is more happy to give than to receive. The measure of a woman's love is the degree of sacrifice she makes for the sake of her beloved.'

Why was Mashi-ma making those rambling remarks? She spoke as though she was thinking aloud. All that could be summed up from what she said was: the god Shiva worshipped for an age to win his consort, Parvati.

'Not many men,' she continued, 'are fortunate enough to secure intense love from anyone. A woman's love is obtained not by courtship nor by gold nor by prayers. Either it is offered spontaneously or not offered at all! If, through good fortune, thanks to his birth star, a man comes to be loved profoundly by a woman, he would become a better man: the gift of love would enable him to pass through flood and fire uninjured: it would give him the courage of a lion, the gentleness of a lamb, the wisdom of a serpent, and the strength of a titan.'

I listened to her in silence.

'Woe to him,' Mashi-ma finally declared, 'who fails to appreciate this great boon of love, of deep affection, of self-sacrificing devotion. Yama, Lord of the Nether-world, shall have no pity on him if he ever abuses such a great favour. Nor will the Great Dispenser of Justice show any mercy to a man who mocks a woman in love.'

~

All sins committed by word, thought, or deed, are noted down, according to Mashi-ma, in the great register, *Agra-Sandhani*, which is kept in the palace of the god Yama, Lord of the Nether-world and the Dispenser of Eternal Justice. Chitra-Gupta the Recorder of Yama's court writes down not only our major sins, but our minor failings as well: the guilt of silence, the villainy of indifference, the crime of indecorum, the error of judgment, the demerit of clouded vision, the offence of lethargy, the obliquity of gracelessness, the infamy of despondency, and, in fact, of everything that contributes towards unhappiness in general.

'We are the children of joy, conceived in joy, and joyousness is our portion. We have no right to be unhappy nor to make anyone unhappy. Only a faithless man is a joyless man, and he merits chastisement. We have no right to sadden the tiniest singing bird nor to silence the smallest humming bee.'

Every moment of a mortal's existence is permanently recorded and carefully checked by Chitra-Gupta. When the final balance-sheets of a man's good and evil actions are drawn and all accounts settled, it is generally found that the accumulated weight of his minor errors far surpasses that of his major sins.

As men and women are not endowed with the same capacities and capabilities, and as their characteristics are not identical, their virtues and vices are judged, rewarded or punished differently in the court room of Yama. The vilest of all sins for a man is mental lethargy, which is the same as incorrect thinking and failure to use his judgment. For a woman, it is immodesty, shamelessness and depravity.

A woman's sense of shame and the restraining influence of the feeling of guilt are her twin protectors in this world as well as in the Nether-world. What would then happen to one who has loved profoundly and for the sake of her love has been constrained to abandon her twin protectors? What would she do when she comes unveiled into the court room of Yama? All that she can take with her is the lamp of love whose flame is fed with affection.

When such a woman is before the judgment throne, Chitra-Gupta the Recorder opens the register, *Agra-Sandhani*, and gets ready to read out the list of her transgressions; he finds the scroll inordinately long: the inventory is an imposing one. Yama's principal custodians, Kala-Purusha and Maha-Chanda, Death and Dissolution, peer over the shoulders of Chitra-Gupta. They are amazed: her record is black. 'She is guilty,' they whisper. 'She is naked and unashamed. Why does she not extinguish her lamp and make herself less conspicuous?' 'She is a shameless creature,' murmur among themselves the female attendants in the court, Hema-mala, Susila, Vijaya, and others. 'The cloak of a woman is her virtue,' sigh the rod-bearers and mace-carriers. 'She is without any covering. She has indulged in orgies. She is a depraved creature. She has not a shred to hide her shame.'

'Let us hear what this brazen woman says in her defence,' mutters Yami the sister of Yama.

The woman with the lamp of love in her hand begs the recorder not to read out the charges against her: she accepts all that has been written down against her in the register, *Agra-Sandhani*.

'Woman!' demands Chitra-Gupta, renowned for his severity. 'What have you to say in your defence? What led you to perpetrate the blackest of all transgressions a woman is capable of committing? What led you to behave immodestly? Were you not aware that other sins might be expiated more readily than immodesty? Why did you behave shamelessly?'

'Because of my love,' murmurs the woman on bended knees while she holds forth the lamp whose flame is fed with affection.

'Love!' Chitra-Gupta is taken by surprise. So are the others: the female attendants, the custodians, the rod-bearers, the mace-carriers, and the rest of the company. 'Love is a divine virtue. Who dares take that word lightly before the throne of Yama, the Dispenser of Eternal Justice?'

'Is she not blaspheming in taking the word *love* light-heartedly?' asks Yami, sister to the dread god Yama. 'Woman! Do you know the implication of the word *love*? Have you a witness? Does your lover admit that he was loved by you? Where is he? Why is he not by your side to proclaim he was loved by you and redeemed by your love?'

Yami is sly. She knows too well that not a man in a million would openly declare how much he owes to the woman who loved him passionately. Even Krishna, the *avatar* of the Great

God, abandoned Radha when he left for Dwarka, and ceased to trouble himself about the fate of the disconsolate, love-lorn shepherdess who had given up everything for his sake.

'Where is your lover?' Yami repeats her question. 'Where is your witness?' And her attendants try to blow out the lamp which the woman has in her hands.

If the woman knows how to protect the flame of her lamp even when others try to extinguish it, she will bring it close to her heart and shield it against every offending breath. She will then find Chhaya Mata, the deity of the Shadows, descending from on high and standing by her side.

'I know her.' Chhaya will plead for her, 'I can vouch for her. I know her sorrows and trials.'

Chhaya, the divinity of charity, knows everything. She is the companion of the all-seeing sun, the god of Light. But for her loving mediation, the fiery orb of day would burn up the earth and reduce it to cinders. Daily she quenches his ardour and courts him to withdraw from the horizon at the end of every twelfth hour. It is she who unfolds her sable mantle to yield the shielding shade and when the sun-god has been laid to rest she spreads her atramental veils to cover the tired terrestrials. She caresses fervid brows with her cool fingers and blesses the restless with sleep. She shelters lovers in fond embrace: she knows the price of love; her sanctuary is the refuge of the love-lorn, and lovers have her benediction.

'I know this frail daughter of the earth,' the goddess Chhaya declares. 'I know her well. For she always sought my lap to lie on. I know her tears and her ecstasies. I know with what anguish she waited for the sun to set and prayed me to accompany her to her trysts lest she be called immodest. You need witnesses. Her scars are her witnesses.'

'Her scars are her witnesses,' the echoes repeat. The judgment hall of Yama rings with the angelic voices of these invisible nymphs, 'Her scars are her witnesses.'

'Woman!' Yama, Lord of the Nether-world gives his verdict, 'Woman! Let the memory of your love be your reward. Be it your acquittal as well. Go in peace and be judged elsewhere. Let none molest her. Nor call her immodest.'

Chitra-Gupta the Recorder expunges from his register all charges entered against her. He writes across the page in letters of vermilion: 'She was not immodest. She was in love and she sought the cover of darkness which the goddess Chhaya spread for her. In the company of the goddess she went to her trysts. Her scars are her witnesses. Let none dare condemn her. She will be judged and rewarded in heaven.' His eyes linger over the pages of the register. He reads to himself one of her love-songs, her favourite ditty:

> If you call me, I will come
> Swifter, O my love,
> Than a trembling forest deer
> Or a panting dove,
> Swifter than a snake that flies
> To the charmer's thrall—
> If you call me, I will come
> Fearless of what befall.
>
> If you call me, I will come
> Swifter than desire,
> Swifter than the lightning's feet
> Shod with plumes of fire.
> Life's dark tides may roll between,
> Or death's deep chasm divide—
> If you call me, I will come
> Fearless of what betide.

Unnoticed by others, Chitra-Gupta dries his eyes and closes his *Agra-Sandhani.*

V

Why did Mashi-ma tell me the story of Chitra-Gupta's great register? Was it to impress me that there was a woman downstairs in the courtyard who wanted fervently to get married to me? Was I expected to show a proper appreciation of her love? Who was going to be my bride? Was it Neela by any chance? I do not know why the thought of Ramdas's wife came to my mind just then. Was I destined to be treated all my life like Ramdas?

'No, nothing of the sort,' Mashi-ma assured me. 'Only to tell you,' she went on as she led me downstairs, 'that you must not be severe on the women who will take part in the Ploughing Ceremony. Let your tongue never condemn them. They will be doing everything to prove the love they bear for their land.'

'The earth is not the same earth everywhere,' I told Mashi-ma. 'That's what I heard from Kumar.'

'Kumar is right,' murmured Mashi-ma as she handed me over to Anjalir-ma, who was in charge of the ceremonies. She came from Raghunath-pur.

'He is right,' Anjalir-ma repeated, 'the earth isn't the same everywhere. The earth of Penhari is *our* earth. To us it is more precious than gold. Its very dust is holy.' She bent down and kissed my forehead as Mashi-ma disappeared in the general throng.

I was bewildered to see the courtyard crammed with women. I never knew there were so many of them in the Red Valley. All of them were decked in their jewellery as though they were going to a wedding feast.

Our women loved wearing their ornaments and whenever special ceremonies took place they loaded themselves with as many as their necks, arms and ankles could bear. Those who had no gold and silver necklaces, bangles, bracelets, and anklets would make them from flowers or with sea-shells and coral and crystal beads. The Second Master who did not really belong to the Penhari Parganas often bitterly complained about his wife's incessant demands for necklaces, ear-rings and toe-rings. 'Tell our women,' he murmured once a month when he received his salary which he had to hand over to his wife, according to our tradition, 'tell them there is a wedding feast in the sky! They will immediately start bedecking themselves with savage instruments of torture, their jewellery, and look for ladders. Those with nothing expensive to put on will strip the forests and gardens bare to make floral ornaments. Let none of my students ever fall into the clutches of the women of this backward area. Better be half hanged than ill married.' I did not share the Second Master's contempt for our women's weakness for attractive adornments.

The place was cluttered up with a large number of water-jars and pitchers filled to the brim. And the Goatee had had the heart to tell the Santal women of Mahisha-ban a few hours earlier that there was no water available for putting out their fire! It was just good luck that the elephant cactus cuttings prevented a major calamity. What was all that amount of water for?

'To wet the earth you will be ploughing,' Anjalir-ma replied, though my question was put to no one in particular. 'Also to wash your feet,' she added. 'The jars are filled with lustral water.'

What could I say or do? I blushed involuntarily: my ears tingled. I looked around me and felt terribly shy all of a sudden. I was the only boy in that crowd: there were only women. Mashi-ma was regarded as a nobody in her own home! Anjalir-ma was in charge of the whole ceremony and she was telling everyone what they should do. She was a complete stranger to me and I felt extremely uncomfortable when she made me sit in the cross-legged *virasana* posture on a small *charpoy*, a low divan, painted with turmeric and decorated with symbolic designs similar to those Mashi-ma had painted on my forehead, cheeks, and arms.

A small plough lay by my side. It was not much of a plough. It looked like a miniature anchor belonging to the boatmen on the river Damodar. I was asked to hold it in my right hand while Anjalir-ma conducted the *baran* service: the ceremonious welcome and enthronement. Others immediately raised the paean, '*Jai! Balaram! Jai!* Hail! Balaram! Hail!'

I was thus robbed of my birth-name in this unexpected fashion. Not one of the women there bothered to ask me what I thought of this method of despoiling a human being of his own appellation. It was, of course, absolutely useless to protest. The din they made would have drowned the noise of a mine-explosion! The hand-bells, the trumpeting conch shells, and the ululation of the ladies might have been heard from Asansole and Rani-gunj! I was no good at shouting. Moreover, with whom was I to argue? Mashi-ma was nowhere to be seen. She must have been squeezed out of her own home. I felt too shy to tell anything to Anjalir-ma, especially as she looked very pretty.

Anyway, there was one consolation: I was not married off to any of the women present.

'They are all married women,' someone said. 'Only wives are present in the courtyard. The widows are on the roof, and the maids are in the village square.'

'What a blessing,' I said to myself when I overheard this important piece of information. I was feeling uncomfortable. Therefore, to cheer myself up I mused, 'Suppose Anjalir-ma had pronounced marriage rites instead of the formulas for *baran*! What should I have done then? If I were made the husband of the woman who sold fried nuts in front of the railway station at Asansole: the one who suffered from elephantiasis?' This nut-seller had extremely swollen legs like an elephant's. I was sorry for her and whenever I got a chance I dropped a coin on her tray without taking any of her small packets. But it was one thing to feel sorry for her and another to be her bridegroom. Suppose she playfully placed her legs on my stomach! If Ramoni could rub the soles of her feet on my thighs when I was lying sick on the floor of the *moucharaby*, the nut-seller was entitled to do the same with her bridegroom. What would I have done then? 'After all,'

I concluded, 'it is better to look at the bright side of events. This was Ramdas's point of view. And it is quite helpful in a situation like mine.'

The noise the ladies were making suddenly stopped when Anjalir-ma knelt down before my *charpoy* and made the mark of *tilka* with red sandal paste in the middle of my brow. She used her small finger. I had a good look at her though I knew it was bad manners. Just before leaving me Kumar had told me that Anjalir-ma was a Master of Arts while I was nothing and the Second Master was a mere Bachelor of Arts. I wanted to find out if one could judge from her looks that she was a learned woman. Moreover, she was said to be more widely travelled than Padre Johan. Her family had business houses in such distant places as Amsterdam, London, Panama, and Poona. She visited all these places from time to time.

'He who travels a lot,' according to the villagers, 'learns to know a lot. You may judge him from his looks.' Being a bad judge of *men*, I noticed no difference in Kumar's looks before and after his travels. In this matter Padre Johan was also unchangeable. From his appearance no one would have suspected that he had ever been to America or to Copenhagen where he bought a few porcelain vases for Kumar. He was just like any other man in the Penhari Parganas, but for the healed scar of a cross on his forehead, and his mutton-chop whiskers which made him look like the poet Michael Madhusudan Dutt. 'Do *women* look very different when they are widely travelled?' I asked myself and tried to compare Anjalir-ma's expression with my aunt's.

I noticed she was taller than Mashi-ma, Neela, and Ramoni. But not of the height of Ramdas's wife. She wore a transparent blue *sari* with a red brocaded hem; not half as transparent as Ramoni's *chaddar*. She carried on her arms heavy bangles and bracelets studded with rubies, emeralds, and *neelas*, blue crystals. As she came from a family of diamond merchants I wondered why she did not have any diamond jewellery. It occurred to me later: 'Pastry-cooks don't eat pastry.' Therefore she was right in not showing any preference for diamonds. In the Penhari Parganas the most prized stones were the *neelas*, star-sapphires, rubies, and emeralds: even these, however, were far less gorgeous than the flowers in our forests.

Anjalir-ma's heavy bangles frightened me. They were my eyesore. Whenever a lady wearing such ornaments tried to put her arms round me when I was a child, I knew I was going to be scratched and mangled. Ever since, I have loathed approaching any woman loaded with such dangerous jewellery. I was told that these heavy bangles were first introduced in the era of the Vargis. A woman decked with such ornaments enjoyed a certain degree of immunity: a blow from her arm would break open any skull however hard. So I made no protest when Anjalir-ma installed herself near me. She sat on my left and put her right arm round my waist as though she wanted to protect me from being snatched away. I held my breath and remained still: I was sure the least incautious movement on my part would have led to fearful gashes from her bracelets. Sitting still like a stone image of Buddha in the *virasana* posture was most trying.

More and more married women from distant villages poured in. They all wanted to have a look at Balaram. 'Our Balaram,' they called me. This I thought was going a bit far. After taking away my birth-name they were trying to make me belong to some other village. Anjalir-ma was busy directing the newcomers where they should place their offerings: huge trays and platters containing all sorts of fruits, vegetables, and heaped rice and lentils: all meant for 'their' Balaram! There was enough food to bury me alive. And that at a time of dearth.

I was astonished to find in that crowd the very women of Mahisha-ban to whom the Goatee had refused water only a short time ago, and they too had brought with them pitchers filled to the brim with sparkling water! They were now laughing and joking. Some of them described their dilemma in the morning when they first noticed the fire. 'God be praised! It is the Golah which eventually received his wrath. The very ground leading out of the Golah has been blasted.' They spoke as though the loss of the ancient landmark meant nothing to them. I could not contain myself and asked Anjalir-ma why the Santal women could not utilize the water they brought with them to put out the fire?

'How could they?' Anjalir-ma clicked her tongue as our women do when they hear anything shocking. 'The lustral water destined for Balaram must not be used for any other purpose. The Santals are not atheists. They need the rains just as much as we. It is only natural that they should behave in the same way as the rest of us.'

'Are their sorrows less than ours?' asked Ramdas's wife: without bothering to find out the precise nature of my question to Anjalir-ma.

'You like honey-skinned girls only,' asked another woman slyly, as she squeezed my cheeks. 'The Santals are too dark for your taste!' It was silly of her to make such remarks, but I did not protest. I remembered my grandfather's precept about women: whatever they do to men should be accepted with grace and courtesy.

'You don't care for plump matrons,' commented another. She was thin like the handle of a broomstick. 'Then I can't please him,' broke in a big girl. 'That's sad.' She did not look sixteen! She wore fine brocaded pyjamas and a light veil. I guessed she was neither a Hindu nor a Christian. Though she was too bold for my taste I noticed she was pretty; her eyes were lovely: big like those of our spotted deer, and she had made them bigger with *kajal*, the paint of collyrium. I gathered she was a relation of Mabool the Moslem, and was called Surma.

Fortunately, I was spared from answering all these foolish questions, because just then the sound of a hundred conch shells from the roof announced the setting of the sun: its last rays no longer touched any part of the Red Valley. All present in the courtyard immediately responded to the clamour from the roof by blowing their conch shells. I noticed Ramdas's wife blowing away at her husband's huge harp shell as easily as though it were a toy trumpet: its blast, in reality, was no more deafening than that of any other shell.

'What would Ramdas be doing without his favourite harp shell?' I asked myself. It then struck me that neither he nor any other men of the village were to be allowed to come out of their homes before sunrise. The conch shells were being blown to give them warning. Only women were to take part in the Ploughing Ceremony. Thieves, if any dared to visit our village that night, ran the risk of being shot to death by the Santal women archers: they knew how to shoot and they were acting as sentries all over the village and the tilling fields.

'No *man* save you, Balaram, will be with us,' Anjalir-ma said as she squeezed my cheeks. 'Some of the Santal matrons will bring Krishna to the ploughing field at about midnight. If any other *man* came across us to-night he would be struck with blindness.'

'Provided he managed to evade our archers,' added her neighbour. She then expatiated on the deadly accuracy with which the Santal women archers wielded their bows: how they aimed in the dark simply from the sound made by footfalls. 'I pity the *man* who might come over here unawares.'

'But the whole countryside has been warned…' Anjalir-ma spoke to give me some assurance. My expression must have betrayed my fear for Gopaldas and Comrade Dynamiter: they never bothered about local traditions and customs and were perfectly capable of turning up for the sole purpose of causing embarrassment. Was the explosion at the Golah accidental? So far they had never told me that the old fortress was going to be destroyed. 'Everyone in the Red Valley knows about our ceremony to-night.' Anjalir-ma went on. 'Even the boldest cut-throat would think twice before he ventured into our area….'

Somehow Anjalir-ma's words became vague and faint to me.
A strange dizziness accompanied by a feeling of fright gradually
came over me. I could hardly explain to myself what it was due
to.

The heat was terrific and the air stifling. The smoke from the
incense-burners and the oil-fed clay lamps was simply choking.
The atmosphere was charged with the fragrance of heavily
scented flowers: heaped baskets of *champaks*, tuberoses, jasmine,
musk-roses, lotuses, frangipani....

I heard vaguely that following the lead of Anjalir-ma seven
leading ladies of seven different villages were going to anoint me
with sandalwood oil, turmeric, and lots of such things and then
wash me.... My ears became hotter and hotter. My limbs all of
a sudden began twitching. My head seemed to be caught in an
invisible grinding machine. Cold beads of perspiration covered
my forehead while my eyes and ears burned. All strength ebbed
away from me. Somehow the vision of the dark vault of the
Golah floated back to my mind. I felt sick. A vague panic akin to
a premonition of an impending peril made me twist and twinge.
I wanted to jump up and run up the Blue Hills to seek refuge in
the *moucharaby*, and at the same time I found I was too weak to
make the slightest movement.

What was going to happen to me? What did the women want
of me? Why were they all dressed in their fineries as though they
were going to attend a wedding festivity? Who was I? Why was
I there? Was I dreaming? Some of the women were undressing
as though I did not exist. Were they getting ready for a bath with
all their jewellery and floral garlands? What made all the women
so bold and brazen as to ignore my presence? They treated me as
though I were an infant.

I closed my eyes to make sure that I was not imagining things.
That was better. But when I opened them again I found the
women were really divesting themselves of their draperies and
veils. Not one of them tried to shirk my gaze; on the contrary

whenever my glance was caught it received a sly wink, a perplexing acknowledgement.

Someone made a crude joke about my not being a boy but merely a girl pretending to be one. This produced a stream of remarks from all sides on the need of verifying my sex and I had no business to keep on my red *cheli*. More than one woman tickled me under the chin and asked Anjalir-ma if she had known me long enough to vouch for my sex. 'Are you ready to choose your partner?' asked the same woman who had teased me before and declared that I was not fond of plump girls. 'Poor thing! He does not know if he is a boy or a girl.' 'They say he went to a *ferringhee* woman's *path-sala* when he was a child,' Mabool's wife remarked. 'That's why no one pleases him here. He prefers women with pink skin and cat's eyes.' 'Perhaps our Balaram is neither a boy nor a girl. What shall we do then?'

The four posts of the improvised baldaquin over my *charpoy* began all of a sudden to rotate! 'Are these women *dakinis*, just sorceresses?' I asked myself and thought of Para-manik's remarks: 'The wise women and the witches look very much the same: they wear no garments. They can make a tall *sal* tree twine and twirl like a top.' Had I not once gone through a burning forest with a holy woman I would not have believed a word of his. This *yogini* was riding a *nil-gai* as though it were a tame buffalo. 'Aren't you afraid of your mount?' I asked her and told her about a forest-fire near the *baoli* of Sampheriya the Coin-maker. 'If your *nil-gai* took fright it would become pretty dangerous.' She simply smiled at my word of caution and lifted me up to sit astride her *nil-gai* and rode through the forest-fire as though it did not exist. I was then too young to be surprised at anything and therefore forgot to ask her how she managed to tame such a ferocious beast as a *nil-gai*.

'If a female fakir could ride through a forest-fire,' I reasoned with myself, 'what prevents another of her kind from making the four posts of the baldaquin spin like a top?' Hardly had I asked myself this question when my *charpoy* too began to sway like a rocking horse. I made an involuntary movement to jump up and found myself squeezing hard against Anjalir-ma. She caught me in her arms and dragged me on her lap: I had not the strength to protest even if I had wanted to. I gladly clung to her and welcomed her gesture to protect me. I was so very afraid of making myself the laughing-stock of the whole gathering: I hated being called timorous as a girl.

Nevertheless, I did feel frightened and buried my head in Anjalir-ma's bosom and sobbed like a puling child. I was terribly ashamed of myself. Someone loosened my loin-cloth of red *cheli* while Anjalir-ma pressed me against her heart. I closed my eyes and gritted my teeth as solicitous hands spread refreshing sandalwood paste over my body and dipped my lower limbs in a basin of perfumed rose water. I was no longer in the *virasana* posture of heroes, but just being washed like a silly, sick baby. Anjalir-ma drew me closer to her and kissed my eyes. I felt more ashamed than ever and for the first time in my life I wished I were a girl: that would have spared me the humiliation of going through the anointing ceremony and making a fool of myself.

Why did I sob? What made me so upset? Even when physical pain had filled my eyes with tears I had always kept them back; rarely had I disgraced myself by weeping before others. Once I was within an inch of being beaten to death by a gang of *badmashes*, but even then my diabolical pride prevented my shedding tears before them. How often had I not been bullied and kicked about by bigger boys—still they never succeeded in making me whimper. If I had tears to shed I preferred shedding them when I was all alone. But now I was weeping like a helpless baby. Through the corners of my tightly closed eyes a flood of tears welled forth and filled my mouth with the bitter taste of brine.

Anjalir-ma covered me with kisses, assuring me, all the while, that the anointing ceremony would be over soon and that no one would hurt me: in fact many a man would be proud to receive the homage of so many women at the same time. She finally drew her gossamer-like blue veil over my head and covered my face.

It was wise of her to shield me in this way. Once my visage was screened from the gaze of the women in the courtyard I felt greatly relieved. Gradually the feeling of shame born perhaps out of my helplessness disappeared. Leaning on or rather hugging at Anjalir-ma's bosom, I thought of the *yogini* who took me for a ride on a *nil-gai* through a forest-fire. How terrifying a spreading blaze in a forest can be is known only to those who have seen it. Even to watch it from a safe distance is frightening. But I do recall that as I clung to the holy woman my fear disappeared as though by magic. Huge trunks of burning trees fell on all sides but the *nil-gai* trudged on at an even pace as though those flaming obstacles did not matter. The heat did not affect it nor the riders astride its back. The touch of the *yogini* chased away all fear from me. In the same way the feel of Anjalir-ma's body slowly gave me back my self-assurance and confidence. Though the attacks of panic came back from time to time, my spasms became shorter and fewer and finally they disappeared altogether.

I experienced then a curious feeling of elation, something like the thrill of overcoming a difficult obstacle—like climbing a steep crag or swimming across a swift stream or mastering a reluctant mount. My trial in the hands of the village matrons was not, I discovered, so very trying. Anyway, it was over. I ought not to have been upset, I chided my own self, over a ridiculous rite: the anointing ceremony.

Nevertheless, I clung on to Anjalir-ma though there was no further need for my doing so: her bosom was cool, restful and pleasant. I heard her heart-beats and felt the heavings of her breasts. It was delightful to be one with her: it was like being changed into a suckling babe in mother's arms. It may seem unbelievable, nevertheless it is true, I did enjoy listening to her whispered words of comfort and encouragement. Her kisses and caresses thrilled every inch of me. I felt transformed into a different being—no longer terribly shy nor ashamed of my masculinity.

Only a brief while ago I was positively annoyed with Anjalir-ma for her heavy bangles, and now I found her all the prettier for those ornaments: they were not dangerous in the least; these were, I discovered, so well polished and cleverly encrusted that they would not scratch even a newborn baby. It was exhilarating to be folded in her arms and to be assured from time to time, 'Don't be alarmed, my little Balaram!' She was no longer a stranger to me, but transformed into one dearer than even Mashi-ma. What brought about this mysterious change in such a short lapse of time? What made the close contact with her body an inexplicable joy? I wished to prolong it as long as possible.

But what made me weep? Was it not the same I who cried a few minutes earlier? Did I then shed tears because I was afraid of being hurt? No, that was not the case. My feelings at that time so far as I could make out were mixed. Maybe, I was overpowered with contradictory emotions: joy mingled with fear, relief and regret, desire and shame, pleasure and mortification, triumph and humiliation. In brief, attraction and repulsion. The very novelty of this curious experience—the conflict of diverse sensations—made me pant and groan.

No one had ever kissed me on the lips before nor fondled my limbs with such loving tenderness. No one had before then offered me her bosom to repose on nor breathed in my ears such words of endearment as Anjalir-ma. 'The ecstasy of intense joy,' according to the Punditji, 'is manifested in the same way as the ecstasy of intense sorrow. They are the obverse and the reverse of the same coin.' Maybe, I cried because I experienced excessive happiness.

In cold print Anjalir-ma's words would be meaningless. Lovers' assurances, I have been told, when overheard unintentionally sound extremely silly: they are meaningful only to the person addressed. So too were Anjalir-ma's remarks to me; they were whispered for me only and they meant so much to me while I lay pressing my lips against her bare bosom and drank delight from the fragrance of her body. 'You are *my* child,' she murmured and I wished it were so. How I longed at that moment to be changed into a babe in her womb. I completely forgot that the thing I generally detested most was to be like a helpless child. I was then oblivious of the oft-repeated injunction of the Punditji: 'Woe to him,' he said, 'who would love to be like a child! Childhood is not a state of grace. Innocence is like helplessness. It is not a blessing, but a curse.'

Anyway, when I felt emboldened enough to open my eyes I noticed that the transparent blue veil was still over my face: I could see everything without being seen. The first thing I noticed was that I had been divested of my red *cheli*. In its stead there was round my loins a girdle of dark blue flowers—*aparajitas*, indigo blue *dhoomals*, purple violets—and blue poppies strung in wreaths formed my bracelets and armlets. A branch of a palm, which was to be my banner was on my left while the plough, my weapon, on my right hand side, was entwined with deep blue flowers like myself.

What a world of difference a veil before one's eyes makes! 'To observe without being observed,' they say, 'is a privilege of the divinities: they see us all though we do not see them.' Screened by Anjalir-ma's veil over my face I felt almost like a god. I followed the proceedings without blushing. I was no longer ashamed though I wore nothing. Neither was I shy because I was different from the rest: the only boy in the midst of women. I did not consider myself a boy any more: I felt I was a man: I was their protector: my strong arm would defend them from all prying intruders. I felt proud to be distinct from the others in the courtyard.

VI

What was the general scene like?

In the enclosed courtyard and the passage leading to the garden there were scores of lighted earthenware lamps, all fed with sandalwood oil. Each of the jars containing lustral water had a green coconut as its covering lid. My anchor-shaped plough was encircled by a row of small lamps fed with clarified butter. The canopy over my head was intact: its four supporting posts were *not* twisted nor were they twirling; they were just entwined with garlands of white jasmines, yellow *champaks*, red oleanders, and green laurel leaves. There were also festoons of scarlet ixora flowers and purple jacarandas suspended from the baldaquin.

In front of me were neatly arranged platters of silver, brass, bell-metal, and earthenware as well as carefully cut plantain leaves, on which fruit and flowers were piled in curious patterns: rice, bananas, figs, pineapples, and stalks of sugar-cane as well as heaps of flowers in wreaths.

On a small silver tray carrying a lighted silver lamp lay a conical heap of vermilion powder mixed with sandalwood oil. This paste was used for imprinting a neat little circle in the middle of the forehead of everyone present. The implication of this symbolical gesture was known to me; vermilion being the brightest of all colours women anointing themselves with the consecrated paste were asking for the brightest of all lights to illumine them.

I recalled that men were fond of such symbols too. The delegation that called on the District Officer some time ago to request him to discontinue work on the Desdichado dam, carried lighted torches with them in broad daylight to emphasize the darkness of the situation. All the members of the delegation had the imprint of the *tilka*, the vermilion paste, on their brow. The District Officer was a newcomer to our area and thought we were crazy to hold a torch-light procession at mid-day. But the men knew what they were doing. 'That fellow was a well-mannered goat!' Kumar spoke gravely on the District Officer's reluctance to remonstrate with the Central Government authorities. 'He wanted to know what sort of *caste-mark* all of us had on our brows. I told him that we all belong to the same caste as his brother-in-law! Since when has the paint of vermilion been transformed into a *caste-mark?*'

I thought if the District Officer was a *well-mannered goat* for misunderstanding the meaning of lighted torches and red *tilka*, I merited to be classified as an *ill-mannered kid* for my ignorance of many of the symbolical gestures and rites performed by the matrons of the village. I was not sure if my interpretations of some of the ceremonies were correct. Different people I knew often gave different meanings to one and the same rite: hence my confusion.

Take, for example, the coconut: a coconut carried seven times round my *charpoy* represented to me the seven circles of the world, and the breaking of the coconut shell and collection of its milk symbolized the destruction of evil and the acquisition of benefit from an apparently inscrutable and tough problem or malediction. It would, nevertheless, be wrong to say that my interpretation was the one which the participants had in mind.

When seven vases of water were carried round in the same manner and poured away, the rites symbolized, as far as I could make out, the banishing of drought and bringing of rainy abundance. Handfuls of rice cast over my shoulders implied— food enough and to spare for scattering abroad.

All the while the women chanted sacred formulas, the meaning of which evaded me as entirely as did that of their many minor gestures and acts. I was not the only one in the company, however, to be mystified by the curious orisons and oblations. Quite a few certainly found them extremely abstruse: this could be judged from their looks.

Someone asked Surma, the Moslem woman who came with Mabool's wife, if her husband did not object to her taking part in the Ploughing Ceremony. What did the husbands of the other Moslem women think?

'How can they possibly oppose our presence?' Mabool's wife replied indignantly on behalf of Surma. 'A good husband should listen to his wife and obey her. Moreover, the drought affects the husbands as much as their wives and children.' Though she worshipped Allah and his Prophet, thank God, she was no atheist like Ramoni! She and her relations were no different from the rest of the Penhari inhabitants. Only once in thirty-six years when the Muharram *fast* and the Hindu Holi *festivity* fell on the same day did she feel like quarrelling with her Hindu neighbours. But when it came to the Ploughing Ceremony they were all one.

'The sun has scorched us as much as the others,' Surma added quietly.

'Once the Prophet was heard to say,' went on Mabool's wife, ignoring Surma's intervention, 'the time will come when my followers will be divided into seventy-three sects, and all of them will assuredly go to hell save one….' That being the case, she concluded, nobody knew which one of the seventy-three sects was predestined for paradise! 'The day when the sky is folded up and the avenging angel's trumpet is sounded, then only shall we know the truth. Meanwhile, what good would it do to us to be separated from the rest?'

'It is the same with us Christians,' remarked her neighbour. 'We are all one in our sorrows and our joys. It is only in the matter of eating and drinking that we are somewhat different. Our religion demands that we eat geese or ducks or turkeys once a year on *Barrho Din*, the Great Day, when our Redeemer was born. Otherwise we generally abstain from animal food.' I recognized this woman: she was born at Jamtara. Her husband was one of Padre Johan's colporteurs and carried his invitation to the master-potters and image-makers in Krishna-nagar for the exhibition in which Kumar obtained the master-craftsman's pectoral. She had a cross incised on her forehead like Padre Johan.

'If only our Balaram would bring down the rains,' she continued, 'my husband would get a silver cross for him to wear with his *madoolee*, the charm round his neck. He has also promised a large bronze lamp for Mashima-Didi's holy basil plant.'

~

The chanting of the hymns, the procession of those who washed and anointed my feet, and the general tittle-tattle came to an end when the barber's wife came down from the roof-terrace to announce that very soon a particular combination of stars would take place. This news brought forth fresh shouts of '*Jai*! *Balaram*! *Jai*! Victory to Balaram!'

Anjalir-ma then tied a deep blue silk scarf round my loins and more garlands of blue flowers were put round my neck. She made me climb her back as though I was a Santal baby! They were now ready to leave the house for the fields for the final part of the Ploughing Ceremony.

The appearance of the auspicious stars, or their combination, was soon heralded by the blowing of conch shells. The procession started with Anjalir-ma carrying me on her back: flanked by the youngest married woman carrying my banner of victory, a palm-branch, and the oldest one bearing the plough, my weapon of triumph.

We were on the threshold of the house when Ramdas's wife whispered in my ear, 'What would you like to take with you, Little Balaram? What would please you most?' Her question surprised me. 'Please be quick,' she said impatiently. 'There is no time to lose. What would you like to take with you as a souvenir? If you fail to bring down the rains this house will be burnt down...'

'Mahendra Chandal,' I mumbled automatically, barely realizing the gravity of what I heard. 'The staff belongs to the Punditji...'

Ramdas's wife just managed to push the staff into Anjalir-ma's hand when a surging throng surrounded us: they wanted to kiss my feet. The widows and the unmarried women had had to wait up till now to see what 'their' Balaram looked like! Anjalir-ma used the staff Mahendra Chandal to fend a way for herself and her companions. 'Otherwise we shall never reach the fields before sunrise,' she said.

The village square was almost as crowded as the courtyard: there were hundreds of women. All of them either widows or unmarried girls. There was a group of women torch-bearers: half of them formed my guard of honour and their leader blew a conch-shell to announce that there should be no further jostling to kiss my feet. Everyone then became orderly.

I was next shifted to the back of the oldest woman in the crowd while all the rest raised the cry of ululation. 'Ulu! Ulu! Ulu!' they chanted. In my village the brides and bridegrooms were always welcomed in this way. I learnt much later that the matrons in Rome did the same in the days of Rome's supremacy, and they abandoned ululation when Rome became Christian and lost her importance by trying to practise a religion which was not in keeping with the Roman character and temperament.

The oldest woman on to whose back I was finally shifted was bent with age, and I felt it a great shame to burden her with my weight. When I told her that I was ready to walk she burst into tears. 'That would bring bad luck!' she said. Tradition demanded that she should carry me to the fields and she was only too happy to have this privilege. 'My little Balaram!' she sobbed. 'Little Son! You weigh much less than the sacks of coal I carry every day on my back. I am a coal-heaver.'

This made me very unhappy: I did not know what to do. I had nothing to wipe her eyes with. So I wriggled up on her back and kissed her on her eyes. This made her cry all the more; but she said those were tears of happiness; which did not, of course, make much sense. Anyway, she became more talkative and told me how on account of the drought her sons-in-law did not know what to do with their buffaloes: they were thinking of going to Calcutta for casual work, leaving their wives behind.

It was heart-breaking to see the older women imploring me to bring down the rains. The younger ones did not say anything but simply wept with folded palms as they ran by my side shouting 'Jai! Balaram! Jai!' I felt like crying myself, but checked my tears.

'Please do something.' Everyone made the same request; otherwise their parents, husbands, children and grandchildren would be forced to leave the Penhari Parganas. If it did not rain the only outlet for them would be the coal-mines or Calcutta—and both of these were hell. There was not enough work in the mines and in Calcutta people were lining the streets begging for handfuls of rice, the unemployment there was still worse. 'We love this land. We don't want to leave it. But when hunger pinches our *men*, they do not mind going elsewhere to find work. Give us rain…then they will work in the fields. We shall all be happy. Do not delay to bring down the rains.'

~

But who was I to bring down the rains?

Had it been in my power to work a miracle should I have waited for so long? Did I not shed tears in secret when I saw the village cattle led away to unknown grazing fields far from the Red Valley? Did I not sob in silence at night time when the drought slowly dried up my Hibiscus bushes? Was it not my desire to see the Red Valley flourish that made me move in the circle of the Second Master? Was it not the same passion which made me contemplate working with Dynamiter, a man whom I did not like? Was I not the boy who prayed nightly in the *moucharaby*? 'Lord! Take me if you will, but let not the Penhari Parganas be drowned or scorched!' Was not the sorrow of my people my sorrow? Was I a stranger in their midst? Was I not a child of the red soil as much as they? Was I not tortured as any of them at the thought that the prolonged drought might ruin the villagers?

Yet why did they repeat ceaselessly: 'Balaram! Make us your bond slaves, if you will! Kill us, if you prefer. But please bring down the rains. Plough the fields and it will rain…. We are dying.'

VII

'Life is a sweet and joyful thing,' it is generally said. 'Life is sweet to everyone. Who would wish to die? All that a man has he will give for his life. It is the most treasured of all possessions.'

If it were not so, a logician may argue, there is no reason for anyone to persevere in a course of perpetually painful existence: a man might as well hang himself and terminate his onerous life. When living is pain, dying ought to be pleasure.

This form of reasoning may carry weight all over the world, but not in my Penhari Parganas. Life for others may be sweet. I do not deny it. But for my people life is harsh. Life in my village is cheap. Life is cruel. Senseless. It is not a treasured possession, but a terrible heritage: a galling legacy involving tremendous responsibilities. Yet my people live. They tenaciously hold on to life.

'Why do they live then?' a dialectician may well ask. 'Why do they not hang themselves and rid themselves of their crushing burden?'

The answer is simple enough: though it might be beyond the grasp of logicians, pleasure-hunters and worshippers of the Bitch-Goddess, Material Success. My people live because they know the meaning of Love, the love that craves for little reward, but receives without asking immense spiritual recompense. It is love that sustains them and helps them to bear with dignity and fortitude their ordeals and trials.

Would you like to know what my people love?

They love their scarlet earth and their cerulean hills with an intensity rarely known elsewhere. They are wedded to the soil where they are born. They are rooted to their native ground. They also love the memory of those who lived and laboured in the land before them: the memory of their forebears helps them to pass through travails unbearable, nay, inconceivable to others.

For their trying existence there is also a great consolation: the terrifying beauty of their landscape. The contemplation of this grandeur they consider to be more than an exorbitant compensation for their diurnal hardships. 'It is a blessing,' they whisper. 'Even the deities would deem it desirable.'

At day-time as they toil they view in mute wonder the glory of their granitine plains, glittering in the sun like glowing garnets and opened pomegranates.

At twilight they watch and marvel at the splendour of their serene, cerulean hills surpassing in beauty turquoise, sapphire, and ultramarine.

At night-time they listen enthralled to the miraculous tales of their ever-resplendent stars. Their constellated sky burns and blazes with flares and bonfires nurtured by empyrean fire.

There they are: the stars of my firmament.

The pivot of all planets, Dhruva the Worshipper, is astride the tail of the Porpoise. In other skies Dhruva is called the Pole Star. The Necklace is composed of twenty-seven beads, each one representing one of the many daughters of King Daksha whose head was like a ram's. Sati, his twenty-eighth daughter, left the heavens to hallow the earth with her body: her limbs lie scattered in fifty-one sanctuaries known to every pious pilgrim of the land; but the fifty-second and the holiest part of her lies hidden in the most secret and the most sacred spot of the terrestrial globe: only the wise know its whereabouts in the unexplored country called the Cradle of the Clouds. The Seven Sages, each of whom though born on earth attained divine sapience and immortality, and were hence transposed into the stellar sphere. Kala Purusha the Dread

Hunter carrying Time in the folded palms of his hands. The fiery Agastya or the Ocean Drinker: he was conceived, they say, when his begetter beheld the dance of Urvashi, Beauty Incarnate. As he was born in a water jar Agastya's early name was Fish of Great Lustre. He is the regent of the brightest of all fixed stars, namely, Canopus. He humbled the proud Vindhya Mountain for aspiring to reach the sky. It was he who commanded the haughtiest of all heights, the most ancient of all ranges, to lie low. 'Tarry,' he ordained as Vindhya bowed down to salute him. 'Tarry till I come back,' and the mountain awaits the sage's return even to-day and dares not interfere with the course of the sun.

There they are: the stars with their flaming lessons for the sky-gazers of my sorrow-stricken land. They come nightly without fail to console the bronze men of dour mien; the men who murmur as they watch the celestial messengers:

> Thy beauty flashes like a sword
> Serene and keen and merciless;
> But great as is thy cruelty,
> Even greater is thy loveliness.

'Do your people never leave their terrible land?' Kolej Huzoor asked Kumar shortly after his arrival in our midst. 'Do you never think of migrating somewhere?'

'One must explore in order to discover,' Kumar smiled. 'Our men go here, our men go there. But they come back in our midst to die. They mingle their dust with the ashes of their forefathers.'

'Have you never travelled? Seen better places to live in? This valley is godforsaken!'

'Travelling is not the same as forsaking the land.' Kumar was a great traveller: this was not known to Kolej Huzoor at that time. Our potter and image-maker knew the lands beyond the Great Ocean, the coral strands where the Southern Cross shines at night, and scores of places richer and pleasanter than our

Penhari Parganas. 'Yet,' he affirmed, 'I will never abandon this glittering plain of granite. Nor forsake its cerulean hills.'

'Your home,' the Punditji explained to Ramdas and Peshkar, 'your real home is where you wish to die: to spend the last moments of your mortal existence.' Ramdas's perennial worry was about truant Gopaldas's reluctance to become his successor: what would happen to the hereditary post of the village watchman after Ramdas's demise? He wanted to know if Gopaldas ever worried about the affairs of the village.

'Of course he does,' the Punditji was convinced that the *chowkidar*'s nephew was as much concerned about the Penhari Parganas as any of its inhabitants.

'What do you think of my graceless daughter?' Peshkar refused to mention his daughter Ramoni by name after the expiation ceremony which was performed on his own initiative. 'What about her?'

'Ramoni too thinks of this place. In her thoughts she lives here. Right in our midst. But let the young ones take their time. What about Padre Johan? Did he not spend long years in the *Land of the Markins*, in America? And that is further away than Calcutta. Yet Johan is in our midst and lives like any of us. What about the others? Do they not go on long pilgrimages and then come back here?'

'No one born under such a sky as ours,' the men all agreed, 'can find peace under any other canopy. Which panoply will give him greater security than Penhari's dust, the sacred soil of our forefathers?'

'What about your poverty?' Kolej Huzoor insisted. 'Are you not ashamed of your low standard of living?'

'Poverty!' Padre Johan's voice trembled with emotion. 'Did the Redeemer lead a life of ease and luxury? He is rich enough who wants nothing. We despise cheap treasures.'

~

But if our men loved the land intensely our women loved it with greater tenacity and still fiercer devotion. The women loved the Penhari Parganas, their children and their men more than their own bodies and souls.

'What is considered miraculous in one land,' the Punditji once remarked incidentally in a disquisition on Taste, 'is not necessarily miraculous in another. Take, for example, walking on fire. Which one of you will be surprised if a fakir or a *yogini* walks through a blazing bonfire or practises levitation? But in other countries, the so-called more civilized countries of our Second Master, there are people who think this to be miraculous! Take another example, the case of a woman called Alcestis. In the land of the Yavanas her memory is honoured because she readily accepted death to give her husband a longer span of mortal existence. Is that such an extraordinary story for our women? Is not every woman in this place an Alcestis?'

The Punditji's assertion was just. I have had the opportunity of verifying its truth.

~

Yama, Lord of the Nether-World is, according to Mashi-ma, green-visaged, red-robed and merciless. He strikes hard at unexpected moments: hence *men* are afraid of him. But if this god approaches the meanest *woman* in the village and declares that his messengers will visit her household and that she must prepare a victim for them, he will hear immediately the bold reply: 'Lord of the Nether-World! The victim for your messengers is ready. She stands even now before you. Take her and let others tarry. She is a willing prey for your Black Dogs. She loves others more than her life.'

Rahu, I have heard, is known as the Dragon of Disaster. He is called the Headless One also, because he is brutal and callous. No *man* can face him without trembling. But if this fiend accosts a *mother*, a *wife* or a *daughter* of the Penhari Parganas and asks her for a sacrifice, a human victim: one who would be tortured, outraged, flayed alive, slowly smothered in the smoke of moist straw, and finally left uncremated on a heap of filth—otherwise he would inflict a new blight on the land—then he would receive a similar response.

'Before you touch a single blade of Penhari's grass,' the *woman* would say without any hesitation, unabashed and unafraid, 'take me. The sacrifice is ready for you. Destroy me, if you will, but leave the land of my people in peace. I love this tract of crimson valley and its people, its beasts, its birds, its trees, its grass, its dust, its stones, its rocks, its hills, its rivers—its everything, more than my body and my life. Take me and leave others unmolested. Let nothing be added to the trials of this land.'

'Our Parganas,' the women whisper among themselves, 'received the Enlightened One's blessings. Others sought happiness. Our forefathers sought something greater, nobler. So Buddha, the ninth *avatar* of the Great God, said: "Let Truth be your quest though suffering be your portion." It takes more than one life to discover the true truth so it does not really matter if we suffer now. Kasyapa, the sagest of all sages, whose regard burns up oceans, blessed us too. "There is no ordination without ordeal," he declared. We do not mind our trifling trials. If we grumble it is only to give vent to our minor worries. We know how to make light of our sorrows with Radha's songs.'

Is it at all surprising that such women should put aside their modesty to bring down the rains?

They were convinced that the Ploughing Ceremony would procure them abundant showers, provided none of the participants doubted its efficacy. And I wondered what entries were made by Chitra-Gupta the Recorder of the Nether-World in his great register against the mothers, wives, and daughters of my village and of six others on that occasion when I acted the role of Balaram.

Who knows the answer?

This much, however, I do know: no woman anywhere could do more to prove her love for her land.

Dying is not enough to prove one's faith. There are greater sacrifices than death.

VIII

On that night if by pouring out my heart's life-blood I could have spared my village women their afflictions, I should gladly have done so and died a hundred deaths to alleviate their anguish and their agony. I should have deemed my sacrifice eminently worthwhile, nay, highly desirable for that objective.

It was imperative that it must rain. Otherwise, I was told, not one of the participants in the Ploughing Ceremony could return home. The tradition demanded that they should return triumphant or never return at all.

The failure of the miracle would be attributed, I knew, to their lack of faith: some element of disbelief lurking in them.

What could I do?

My thoughts were confused. Had I known the terrible implication of the women's proposing the Ploughing Ceremony I would certainly have run away from home. I was not concerned with myself. I was more than worried about the village women. If I had run away in time it would have been impossible for the villagers to find a substitute: I happened to be the only one in the Penhari Parganas to have the same birthday as the god Balaram. Why had I not heard about the details of the Ceremony before? It was too late to do anything about that now.

My young mind could not make out what ought to have been done in the past to prevent the drought, 'It takes a life-time,' according to the Punditji, 'and very often more than a life-time to plant a forest. And it takes a few days to destroy it. It is the same with the new-fangled destructive doctrines. Like forest fires, materialistic theories can destroy our civilization for good.' Yet, I asked myself, apart from Comrade Dynamiter and his followers, why had no one else ever bothered to tell the villagers what should be done? The *topiwallahs* were interested in collecting money for their political funds: they were not much good. The Desdichado dam if completed would certainly produce more electricity for the country as a whole. But it would drown the Red Valley. What good would that do us? We were told that the entire population would be settled elsewhere. 'But if you take a fish out of water,' the Punditji made it clear, 'and drop it in a bowl of cream, will it survive? Our civilization is our way of thinking and living. Change our ways and our civilization would perish.' 'What's the worth of the Punditji's conception of civilization?' was the counterargument of Comrade Dynamiter. 'Watch China! Watch Tibet! Watch Nepal! Watch Burma! There is only one way out—the Red Path.'

What was I to do? Many thoughts raced through my mind as the night advanced. Some of my musings had little to do with the reality of the moment.

IX

The earth was baked into hard lumps by months of unbroken drought. Its fissures and cracks were like slits and rifts in the layers of hard lava. The water poured out from a hundred pitchers made little difference: it left no trace of moisture on the soil.

My toy plough—what else was it?—slid across the red glebe without making the faintest scratch. My teeth were clenched. My eyes were wet with tears of resentment. I was angry with myself: bitterly disappointed at not being strong enough to make furrows on the field. I did not blame the women: though they apologized every time the relays were changed. They were doing their best.

The sight was gruesome. Nevertheless, they did not complain. The flint-like earth gashed their bare knees, hands and feet. For they were on all fours to pull the plough: they were all bleeding profusely. The fault, I knew, was entirely my own. I had never handled a plough before. I was clumsy. My hands lacked strength. Though tiny in size the plough felt so heavy and so unwieldy. I did not know how to press down the ploughshare. Its shape was different from those our ploughmen used. But I did what I could to guide it. Each time a fresh relay of women came to pull the plough I redoubled my efforts to make it work.

The torches went out one by one. Sheer exhaustion silenced the clamour of many voices. Paeans of praise to the gods ceased to issue from parched lips. Every tongue was dry, and every visage wet with tears. Everyone save myself bathed in blood from horrible cuts. There was weeping among those near to me and wailing among those at a distance. The relays of women were changed many times. By now most of them were on the point of collapse.

The night was far advanced and my heart stopped beating when I noticed a flush of blue light in the horizon. Was it the pale mother of dawn? Or was it the late moon? With the approach of day the Ploughing Ceremony was to end. Where would these women go? Where would they find shelter? Where would they find clothes? Who would tend to their wounds and minister to their needs? I looked up and saw neither the Dog Star nor the Plough in the sky. I held my breath. A red meteor bright as a Bengal light sped across the horizon: a sinister warning. What did that ominous sign imply?

A raucous laugh from a distance made me start. It was Babu Hem Chandra Chahar. He was laughing in an unseemly fashion. I could easily recognize him though he was still at a stone's throw from me. He was wearing a flowing yellow robe: the only one with clothes on in that throng. I was stunned at his behaviour. But my greater amazement was at finding him dressed like the relief-statue of the Betrayer exhibited by Kumar at the Pushpa-pur *mela*. His costume was evidently hired from a *jatra* company. What made him come in borrowed clothes and a peacock-feather headgear? It was ridiculous. It pained me to find him tottering in the same way as a clown in a *jatra* show. Was he bent on making fun of the Ceremony? Was that the reason why he had hired Kala-Yavana's costume from a company of strolling players?

He shouted at me that he was no longer prepared to play the role of an underling! He also muttered something about 'shepherding the younger women into brothels as there would be no rain and it would be such a pity if they ran into the jungles at sunrise.' There they would be outraged by savage baboons and eaten up by the wild beasts.

'Evidently he is drunk,' I said to myself. I bit my lips and pressed hard on the ploughshare: I pretended not to hear him. His task was to play on the flute in the distance. What tempted him to join those who were pulling the plough? Why was he drunk? Was he not ashamed of appearing in a clown's costume? Was he behaving like a buffoon because he was drunken?

~

The rites of the Ploughing Ceremony included among other things drinking of a beverage called *soma-rasa*: a mixture of honey-mead, fermented milk, palm juice, date toddy, and three other potions: seven in all. In olden days *soma-rasa*, I understand, meant something else. But to our matrons it was just a mixture of seven intoxicating drinks, matured under the influence of the moon, *Soma* in Sanskrit.

I recalled Anjalir-ma dipping her fingers in an earthenware jar of *soma-rasa* and then passing her hand over my lips. 'That will do for our little Balaram,' she told the woman next to her. 'My grandmother was at Patna and also at Moonghyr in the year of the Great Hunger. She took part in at least a dozen Ploughing Ceremonies. She knew the tradition well. I heard from her that a drop of *soma-rasa* would do for a boy under sixteen.' 'That ought to do for anyone,' commented an elderly matron. 'Unless he wants to get drunk. *Soma-rasa* is a heady drink.'

Probably no one had warned the Second Master about the overpowering potency of *soma-rasa*. This was not surprising. The Santal matrons were in charge of his anointing ceremony, and they were immune to all drinks. In fact, they thrived on rice beer and fermented *mohua* juice. They would be the last people to dissuade anyone from quaffing a heady potion.

I was sorry for the Second Master. My regrets were mixed with disgust.

~

From my childhood onwards I was taught that a decent person should always behave with decorum as befitted the company he kept, and the situation in which he found himself. Drunk or sober, I was told, no man must ever manifest vulgarity. Every child in our village knew that nothing condoned a man's lack of chivalry in a crowd of women.

On the night of *Shiva-ratri* our children are allowed to sit up till midnight and are given a drink called *siddhi* or realization: the greenish intoxicating concoction from hemp. I remember my grandmother's warning: on one such occasion when I was a mere toddler she gave me a small glass of *siddhi*. 'I want to see how you behave when you are drunk,' she said. 'If you cease to behave as the person you generally are, I shall give you a thrashing. Drunk or sober, you must know how to behave. Be gay in gay company. Sing with the singers and dance with the dancers. But among mourners you must manifest sympathy.' 'Only an evil man,' according to Mashi-ma, 'acts contrary to his outward nature when he is drunk. Under the influence of drink he reveals his hidden desires and passions—his lower self.' 'I won't have a grandchild,' my grandmother looked at me and at Mashi-ma as she spoke, 'I won't have a grandchild behaving like an evil man. Nor do I want him to associate with one.'

Perhaps my grandmother was wrong in judging too harshly people who lost control over themselves under the influence of liquor. Nevertheless, I thought there was no justification for the Second Master in sowing despair among those already downcast and sobbing. There was still less excuse for his abusing those who tried to prevent him from interfering with my ploughing.

Tradition demanded that he should play on the flute in the distance, beyond the limits of the ploughing field, while I tilled the soil. It was not the fault of the women if the rites prescribed certain limitations on him. He was told about the details when he accepted the invitation to act as Krishna in the Ploughing Ceremony. What complaints had he to make in these circumstances? Did he come to the Ploughing Ceremony for fun? Why was he muttering all the while that Balaram had 'the pick of the lot', while he had only 'hags and harridans' about him?

A pair of night herons flew past: one of these fluttered so low that its wings almost flapped the Second Master's face. This brought about an incredible change in his behaviour: for a few minutes he conducted himself as a reasonable man and played on his flute. And that was the time when I succeeded in making a few scratches on the ground.

Unfortunately, his good mood did not last long. He began grumbling and growling again, and stopped dead in front of the women pulling the plough. He had had enough of flute-playing, he declared.

'Let me administer,' he suddenly burst out in English, evidently for my dubious benefit, 'let me administer a few sound kicks to your cows. Their bare buttocks are tempting. Throw away that silly plough and let me get about the business. The superstitious cows will have to seek refuge in brothels. The Puritans did not mind whipping their women. It's a cursed Penhari custom to worship cows and mollycoddle women. Credulous cretins...'

I was petrified to hear such words coming from his lips. Did he not know that Anjalir-ma was by my side? Moreover, she was not the only woman in that concourse who understood English.

'It won't rain,' he went on in Bengali. 'These cows won't be admitted to their homes any more. What's the use of wasting any further time? Learn from me how to plough a cow.'

I never knew that I was capable of being short-tempered. Involuntary tremors shook my hands. Sudden anger bereft me of my speech. I tried to say something in English. But all that my tongue uttered was 'Mahendra Chandal!' Even that was pronounced almost inaudibly: I doubt even if Anjalir-ma gathered what I wanted, though she was by my side.

'The old fogey, the Punditji, must have had parleys with you,' he sniggered. 'You swallowed his palavers about the Ploughing Ceremony.' I wished he would speak in English: that would have spared most of the women his jibes and insults. It was simply awful: the disgusting terms he used to ridicule the Ceremony and to humiliate the participants, 'Has not the venerable boot-licker of the past told you?' the Second Master hiccoughed as he swayed like a juggler's bamboo, 'The women are classified in Sanskrit according to certain…ahem…qualities. Attributes, I mean, anatomical and psychological. They are of four categories. The *padminis*, the *hastinis* or the elephantines…'

'Where is Mahendra Chandal?' I shouted. My tongue was loosened as I let the plough go from my hand.'Where's Mahendra Chandal?'

'Don't bellow, you doctored bull-calf!' He looked up to see if there were any herons above his head. 'Who is this Chahendra Mandal or Mahendra Chandal you are hollering for? Is it a tame heron? I'll wring its neck. If it is a man the Santal archers will look after him. They will shoot him dead before he steps on this field.' He prodded his bamboo flute into the back part of one of the women attached to the plough. 'Her rump is fleshy. Eh? What do you say? You are just a ninny. I am the only man here.

I'll teach you how to make a furrow and how to plough a cow. Do you want to be ploughed by me? If not, leave the field at once. Clear out! Unless you want a thrashing...'

Anjalir-ma protested in a tearful voice.

'Eh? You don't like my language?' He swung his flute as though he wanted to strike her. 'You don't like my language! But I like your thighs. Well, I'll give you the first preference. You have not a stitch of clothing on your back. And you are asking me to behave decently.'

He tottered forward and tried to dig his flute into her thighs as she withdrew.

'Don't run away, my Beauty! Unless you want to show me your behind now that I know your front. Don't run away from the magic touch of Krishna's flute. It has beautiful names. Some designate it *The Call of the Infinite*. Some call it *Leave everything and follow Me*... Which do you prefer, my bejewelled Cow?'

Was the Second Master really drunk? Or was he simply pretending to be so? His obscene remarks about Anjalir-ma's body and her jewellery were most shocking. He spoke of a house of ill-fame in Vardaman which could be bought up with the price of her ornaments. He knew all the details about it: a fine establishment in the Mahajantoli quarter of Vardaman: it would lodge the younger women and the immature girls. He was willing to give his help and protection. 'But, I must try you out.' He advanced to grab at her and I stepped forward to prevent this. 'Wait, my Cow!' he cried. 'Wait a second while I thrash this young cub and doctor him into a real *khoja*.'

Anjalir-ma grasped my arm. She was trembling. More anxious to protect me than her own self, she tried to push me behind her and cover me with her body. I managed, however, to wriggle out, and was once again between her and the Second Master.

Just then someone put the Punditji's staff in my hand and I found myself crying at the top of my voice, 'At him, Mahendra Chandal! At him.'

X

I rushed forward to hit him hard on his shoulders. It was a brass-bound staff and I knew its blow on the head would have probably broken open his skull.

The very first knock sobered him. He drew back cursing me and took to his heels: he bolted across the field zigzagging. I was beside myself with rage and in my haste to catch up with him I made a bee-line forgetting there were treacherous boulders all over the place. One of these made me stumble: it was a tiny mound of earth, but as hard as rock. The staff got in between my legs and I found myself sprawling on the ground. The fall shook me very badly. It nearly broke my bones and covered my body with bruises.

By the time I managed to gather myself up, the Second Master was far from me. He was running towards the clump of bamboos at the distant end of the field, stopping occasionally to throw small stones in my direction. His outline could be seen distinctly. He looked like a flaming scarecrow or, better, an apparition on fire. Sparks streamed from his body, his yellow robe and his peacock-feather headgear.

Such a sight at any other time would have made me quaver. However, I was then too angry to pay much heed to it or to my bruises. As he was beyond my reach, I gave vent to my wrath by hitting the rock-like mound at my feet with all my might. The brass-bound staff, Mahendra Chandal, smashed it into splinters and a cascade of fiery particles burst forth from the broken bits. At the same moment the ground beneath my feet began to quake.

A rumbling din filled the air as though the mountains were writhing to their very foundations and the hills were collapsing. A number of sheldrakes hurtled through the air uttering strange screeches which only frightened sheldrakes make to announce imminent danger. One grazed my face in its flight. All of them were flying low, close to the ground. A squall of dust rose suddenly: it was like a volcanic whorl thrown out by the earth to the sky. It filled my nostrils and choked my breath, blinding my eyes and pricking my body with a myriad burning needles. It lifted me off my feet as if I were a sear leaf in the storm.

'Lie down!' I heard Anjalir-ma's call in the distance.'Lie down! Everyone lie down! Balaram! Fall flat on your face and cling to the ground. It's the *bijli agoon*, the electric storm.'

Was it St Elmo's fire? Or a preliminary to a volcanic eruption? An earthquake to push up a new hill? A tornado of dust? A swiftly-moving water-spout? I had no time to think or to reason. Anjalir-ma's voice, the warning cries of others, the shouts of the Santal women archers, the crackling noises issuing from the bushes, hedges, bamboo-clumps, and trees, and all the other sounds were drowned in a single terrific crash. The terrestrial globe seemed to be cleft asunder to its very core.

Lightning flashes tore through the earth as well as the sky while the thunder roared. My long locks stood up in bristles and poured forth sparks as the brass-bound staff vomited a stream of flame. The bamboo-clumps, the thorny *babool* bushes, the spiny branches of the cotton-bearing *wayfarer* trees, and the dried sedges and thickets emitted intermittently weird bursts of fire. Dazzling tongues of red, orange, and phosphorescent green light rose from the ground responding to those streaming from the heavens above.

All this lasted barely for a minute or so. Everything came to be blotted out later and merged into utter darkness. The valley and the hills and the sky were obliterated, and in a pall of impenetrable blackness came a terrifying cloud-burst. The heavens' sluice-gates were suddenly thrown open.

Its first shock dazed me and I do not know what happened immediately afterwards. When I regained control over my senses, I found myself rolled about the field like a log caught in rushing waters. The plain was flooded: it looked as though a high tidal wave was advancing, inundating the land and carrying everything in its sweep.

But the field was gasping with thirst and it imbibed the flood-water avidly. The cracks and the fissures gulped and gurgled and drank till they had their fill. The tide vanished simply through this process of ingurgitation.

Then came the rains. At first the showers of warm drops, large as *bulbul*'s eggs, mixed with white hail-stones, round and flattened like the tiny silvery pebbles lining the beds of mountain rills. They pelted the red glebe till it softened; the agate-hard ground was changed into sweet-smelling soil. The granitine earth was transformed into plastic clay, rich loam, and fertile marl. Next came balls of bluish fire with the rain and the hail to float like incandescent soap bubbles on the water and to dance like giant fire-flies among the hedges, the bamboos, and the trees. For a while the whole plain became alive with these fairy pellets of blue phosphorescence—till all of a sudden they burst harmlessly and were seen no more. Afterwards came the strong wind, and the boisterous clouds, and finally, when the thunder and the lightning ceased, came the soft, steady showers, the *ploughman's trust*.

It was a joy to feel the caress of the waters of heaven. It was exhilarating to dig my fingers and toes into the soft soil and feel its pulsing and seething. It was intoxicating to roll on the yielding earth, to hug at her bosom and to breathe in her aroma. The earth, my *Joya*—the mother Gaea—proved to be a *yogini*. Her touch cured me of my pains and torments, and made me forget my sorrows and disappointments. She gave me new vitality. I became mighty as a giant and lithe as a sylph.

I threatened the late moon with my brass-bound staff when it playfully peeped through the curtain of scurrying clouds. I talked to the Dog Star and thanked the Plough when the strong winds cleared a corner of the sky for a brief while. I blew kisses to the lightning flashes. I clapped my hands to beat time with the rolling thunder. I laughed like an imp when the showers started afresh. The fragrance exhaled by the drenched fields tingled my nostrils: it felt like the perfume of Anjalir-ma's bosom and filled me with an unknown voluptuousness. I danced and pranced as I sang and declaimed in the glistening, life-giving rain. I ran and leapt and pirouetted. I shouted and exulted like one possessed. I proclaimed my delight to the winds, and to the heavens. I felt like a sprite, one with the elements—the fields, the hedges, the trees, the rills, the rains, the clouds, and the stars.

~

It was indeed a night of miracles. The electric storm was followed by the cloud-burst and the rain in sheets; then came the strong winds and the hail, and finally arrived the steady showers. In between there were bursts of moonlight. I saw two rainbows: one of which was inverted—a half-circle of white, pale yellow, and faint blue bands.

Anjalir-ma carried me home in her arms. I hung to her breast like a tired child. Ramdas's wife carried the staff Mahendra Chandal for me. When I was put to bed the naphtha flares lit by the Santal women in the village square were still burning: the heavy downpours did not extinguish them! 'They are of tar and heavy oil,' Anjalir-ma explained. 'The flares are in special pitchers. If you pour water on burning oil, the fire will simply spread.'

'How do you put them out, then?'

'With earth and cactus.'

Mashi-ma just sobbed when I asked her if the Goatee would have used naphtha flares for burning our house down had there been no rain. Anjalir-ma dragged her away. 'Leave the child alone!' she said sharply to my aunt and turned me on my stomach to give a playful smack on my bottom. 'Am I no longer your Balaram?' I asked somewhat hurt at her calling me a child. 'Of course you are,' she said as she put her necklace of blue stones round my neck. 'You will always be my Balaram. But Balaram must sleep now.'

I was exhausted. My limbs were limp with fatigue. Yet my eyes were sleepless, I watched with half-closed eyes the fantastic patterns made by the flickering lights from the village square: the tar torches and the naphtha flares remained unextinguished in the pouring rain.

Suddenly it occurred to me that I should thank the Goatee for not giving the Santal women of Mahisha-ban the water they needed. The fire there was certainly lit with inextinguishable tar and naphtha. Had the women poured water to put it out it would just have spread. The Goatee did a good piece of work without knowing it. But who was to be thanked for the earth tremor which burst open the Desdichado dam and brought that pile down like a house of cards?

'Wakefulness,' I recalled the Punditji's saying, 'wakefulness is the first necessity for acquiring knowledge and wisdom.' It was a good thing, I thought, that I had not fallen asleep when Anjalir-ma brought me back home. Otherwise I should not have known anything about tar and naphtha. 'In the morning,' I wondered, 'what will the Punditji say when I bring him back his staff, Mahendra Chandal? Anyway, I shall never call on the Second Master any more.'

I fell asleep amidst the chanting of the full-throated frogs. Though my dreams of that night were occasionally interrupted by the sound of raucous laughter from afar, in my sleep I rejoiced to hear the whisper of growing grass, and to smell the scent of new leaves and the fragrance of fresh flowers: I understood the jubilation of our noble trees and the delight of our men, birds, and beasts: I heard Kalidasa in Ujjain reading from his *Cloud-Messenger*…and the choristers to the deities singing.

XI

What induced the villagers to invite the Second Master to my farewell party?

I lost sight of him from the time of the Ploughing Ceremony and there he was: sitting under the *peepul* tree with the others! He greeted me as though I were still one of his disciples and the intervening years did not count. Mashi-ma, I suspected, was mainly responsible for sending him a formal invitation.

'Before you leave a place be at peace with everyone.' That was her favourite precept. It was all right for her to talk in this way. She rarely left the village except for pilgrimages, which, of course, exonerated her from leave-taking and all other formalities. Therefore, it was easy for her to suggest that I should call on everyone who had at one time or other shown any interest in me. Not only that! I was to be particularly nice to those who had been nasty to me, and make up with the Second Master. It was awkward.

Kumar probably guessed what was passing in my mind and he tried his best to make the Second Master talk about Cromwell: the bait, however, did not work. And to make the situation more uncomfortable the *Bhat* decided to recite the draft of a poem he would be composing. This put Kumar off. Probably he knew what the *Bhat* was going to say and did all he could to discourage the official reciter of poetry.

Anyway, the *Bhat* managed to get a hearing. What he said was so characteristic of Kumar that I feel it worthwhile to record it here.

A man in a big car called with his *niece* at Kumar's workshop to talk over an important commission: his portrait bust. Our village potter and image-maker looked him up and down and declared that he found nothing interesting about the rich man and it would be difficult for him, therefore, to undertake the work.

'What about my niece? She is pretty. Couldn't you do her in Italian marble or alabaster?'

Kumar was shocked. He proposed black diorite and this shocked his visitors in their turn. The *niece* winced. The rich man frowned. They both talked about the money the commission would bring to Kumar. Our potter, however, remained obdurate.

When showing his visitors out, Kumar stopped dead in silent wonder before a dun cow peacefully chewing cud right in the middle of the road. He contemplated the bovine beauty for many minutes oblivious of his wealthy caller and his glamorous *niece*.

'We are going,' said the rich man. 'Hope you will think over my offer.'

'Good-bye,' the pretty lady called out as she waved to Kumar. 'Write me a line when you change your mind.'

Ramdas was passing by, quite by chance. Ever since Sashe Raha started his mud-slinging activity, our *chowkidar* had made a point of passing by Kumar's cottage whenever a car stopped there: unobtrusively, it must be admitted. And it was natural for those who did not know Ramdas well to assume that his presence was accidental. His obvious purpose was to examine Kumar's object of contemplation at close quarters. 'Brother Ramdas!' Kumar exclaimed, 'It has been a hard existence, this one. But next time, God willing, I might perhaps be reborn as a cow.'

'Ah! If only one could,' murmured the village *chowkidar*. 'A holy man alone can aspire to such felicity.'

~

'Well said.' The Punditji was delighted with the story. He thumped the ground with his brass-bound staff, Mahendra Chandal, to emphasize his approval. He nudged me too; this implied that I was to profit from this anecdote during my coming stay in Calcutta.

'What about putting the Calcuttan's story in verse?' Kumar spoke as though the *Bhat's* narrative did not concern him: it was simply a sketch of Ramdas's profoundly philosophical comment on reincarnation and *Karma*. That was just like him! 'The best comes last! Our *Calcuttawallah* has a splendid story. Balaram should listen to it attentively. And I am sure our distinguished poet from Kusum-pur will put it into verse.'

'That's precisely what I was going to say.' The Calcuttan was happy to get the chance of being the last to speak at the gathering. 'The story has a moral. It ought to interest the young scholar.' For a moment all eyes were fixed on me. Fortunately the Calcuttan began his cautionary tale without much ado, and I ceased to be the centre of attraction.

'Those who start early living in Calcutta's filth become immune to it. But for visitors who are not young, it is pretty dangerous, almost killing. Take the case of the old widow from Gilani who came on pilgrimage to Kalighat and decided to stay on with her son who looked after the Harish Chandra Park.'

~

Gilani is a tiny, unspoilt village in the hills. A widow coming from such a place would have done well to return to her mountain home as soon as her pilgrimage to Kalighat was over. However, she allowed the 'Evil One, *Sheytan*, to tempt her and prolonged her stay in Calcutta. It should be said in her defence that she was ignorant of the nefarious influence of Calcutta's soil. She was old and infirm and had not a tooth left in her head. The first false step she took within a couple of days of her arrival was to ask her son for a set of dentures: that would help her, she claimed, to feel less worn out!

Hardly had she got her false teeth in when she insisted on her son's buying her a few *saris*.

'In Gilani,' she said, 'it's all right for me to dress in heavy skirts and tight blouses. But here in Calcutta it is different. People stare at me on account of my hill costume! And when I think that my son looks after a famous park in Calcutta I feel ashamed of my clothes and of myself. Can't you get me a few *saris*? They say the Bengali women are pretty. But I think it is their *saris* and their make-up. I am sure if I dressed in the same way as other women here I won't be stared at.'

The dutiful son complied with his mother's request only to discover that she had further suits. The widow wanted to know if she was really decrepit and very ugly. The son swore that was not the case.

'Then,' came her immediate demand, 'I see no reason why I should not re-marry and cease to be a burden to you. Do you know of a suitable candidate whom you would like to have as your step-father?'

The son was horrified to hear that the old widow was contemplating consultations with the professional matchmakers, marriage-bureaux, the Association for Modernization of Hinduism, the Committee for Encouraging Re-marriage of Hindu Widows as well as such militant bodies as the *Jat-Pat-Torak-Sangha*, the Association for the Abolition of Caste Distinctions.

'Some of your neighbours think,' the widow went on, 'that I am your sister. Certainly it is not too late for me to take a second husband. Apart from my healthy complexion, my experience in housekeeping ought to make me an asset to any man.'

Anxious to spare his mother from exposing herself to ridicule, the son pretended that he knew of a suitable match, advising her at the same time not to mention her wish to any of the neighbours, as there was just then a temporary glut in the Calcutta marriage-market. She would have to wait for a while. 'Leave the matter to me and I will do the necessary,' he assured her and managed to put her off in this way. But not for long.

Finally, unable to withstand her importunities, and afraid lest she might talk to the neighbours, the son told his mother that the candidate he had in view was back in a small village, a few hours' journey from Calcutta. Would she care to see the man? The widow not only agreed but urged immediate departure.

They started on their journey next dawn. The son took with him a small bag whose contents he was careful to conceal from his mother. When they had travelled for some time the young man told his mother that they were approaching their destination and that in the near-by village he had a number of acquaintances, one of whom ought to please her: he would not mind having a step-father.

'What are you talking about, my son?' The mother was shocked. 'Have you lost your senses? Aren't you ashamed of making fun of your own mother? Whoever has heard of a decent Hindu widow getting re-married?'

The son remained silent and did not raise the matter of marriage any more during the day. But that evening when preparing his mother's bed in the *serai* he carefully placed the contents of his bag under her mat.

In the night the widow woke him up and said, 'My son, I have carefully thought over what you told me when we were approaching this village. It is true I am no longer young, but neither am I so very old. Now, my dear son, do present to me the candidate you had in mind.'

'I shall see about it to-morrow morning,' replied the son.

Next morning when the matter was mentioned to the widow she looked perplexed and confessed that she could not make out what made her behave preposterously during the night, and, in fact, during the whole period of her stay in Calcutta. 'Am I going crazy?' she asked remorse-stricken. 'What made me behave so shamelessly and ask for a second husband like a trollop?'

'That was not your fault, mother,' said the son as he pointed to his bag. 'It is the fault of Calcutta's soil. My bag is filled with it, and if its contents were spread under the bed of a *yogini* or a female fakir, she would behave like you as well.'

~

'Carry the antidote with you, therefore,' the Calcuttan advised me, 'A lump of your soil.'

'Every disease has its antidote,' the Goatee philosophized. 'Little Scholar, take with you a clod of our red earth, which is also yours. Put it carefully under your pillow every night. That would protect you against Calcutta's insalubrity.'

No further anecdotes were told. A few, however, continued to complain about Calcutta's air being thick with rank lies, wild rumours, and noxious odours. Calcutta's public conveyances were filthy and flea-infested. Public men cantankerous and crony-ridden. Calcutta worshipped Corruption and the Bitch-Goddess. Calcutta was a monstrous dragon, pitiless and all-devouring.

I was deeply distressed to hear that nothing remained of Rani Nilmani's Estate. It was handed over to a building agency in the year of the destruction of the Naba-Ratna-Mandir, the temple of Nine Jewels.

Was Calcutta totally changed within a few years' time?

'Of course,' Kumar smiled ironically, 'the old fort remains in Calcutta's heart as before.' So did the grazing fields surrounding it, the *maidan*, given to the city by Manohar Dass in the days of John Company. Heaven be praised, Manohar Dass was fond of cows and he stipulated that his *maidan* was never to be built over. Otherwise it would have suffered the same fate as Rani Nilmani's Estate. 'To the west of the *maidan*,' Kumar continued, 'lies the muddy river Hooghley. To the north of the *maidan*, they have put up slums, miles and miles of slums. To its south, there are miles and miles of docks, and to its east, miles and miles of factories, and in between there are brothels and shops, go-downs and shanties, filth-littered squares and filth-smeared dwelling houses.'

Someone coughed. Kumar, however, ignored this polite hint. He knew Calcutta and he was bent on telling all that he had to say.

'And,' he sighed mockingly, 'I have done an injustice to the premier city of the land. I have forgotten to mention its most interesting structure. A Jain temple filled with splendid alabaster statues. The structure resembled a huge *kadma*, a sugar-loaf, or rather the decorated cake they produce at the European weddings at Asansole. No other city in the world can boast of such a temple. Moreover, Calcutta sustains a larger number of cows, cranks, crooks, courtesans, communists...'

'It is time to begin the song,' someone interrupted loudly. He was sitting behind the *veena*-player. I had not seen his face up till then. His voice was familiar to me. It was Comrade Dynamiter. Behind him was Gopaldas: he gave me a knowing wink.

The proceedings under the *peepul* tree came to an end with Comrade Dynamiter's performance. In a powerful voice he sang to the accompaniment of the *veena*. His songs made all eyes wet. The first one was: '*Gram-chhara oi ranga matir patha...* the wayward red path leading out of the village beckons me far away.' He knew how to appeal to the sentiments of his listeners. But how did he steal into that gathering? He did not belong to our village.

The *veena*-player did not get the chance of singing any of his folk-songs. This must have been a bitter disappointment to him. The trouble with his songs, as I have said before, lay in their lack of novelty, and no one knew how long they would last. Take, for example, his spirited account of a legendary Lachhi, a favourite with the village girls:

> Aha! When Lachhi spills water,
> Spills water, spills water, spills water,
> There sandal grows—where Lachhi spills water.
>
> Aha! Lachhi asks the girls,
> The girls, the girls, the girls,
> Oh, what colour'd veil suits beauty's grace?
>
> Aha! The girls said truly,
> Said truly, said truly, said truly,
> A veil that's blue becomes a comely face.

What's then your fortune, Lachhi?
Your fortune, Lachhi, your fortune, Lachhi, your fortune,
Lachhi?
Ho! You boy like the moon, what then your fortune?

Who'll give you milk to drink, Lachhi?
Drink Lachhi, drink Lachhi, drink Lachhi?
Your friendship with the neatheards is sundered!
Who'll give you milk to drink?

'By the time he has finished a dozen such verses,' Pocha declared frankly, 'I feel like having a pot shot at him.'

'He does not know when to stop,' Bum-boatee grinned, while Sashe Raha nodded his assent. 'His songs are rather repetitive.'

'Like the *Bhat*'s poetry-recitals, once begun they never end.'

Ramdas was sorry for the *veena*-player who had promised to chant a popular piece for him about the arrival of spring in the holy places. I wondered whether our *chowkidar* was more sorry for the musician or for himself. For he hummed the simple tune of this song as he left the village square for his cottage. His much-loved spring song was in no way different from the one about the eternal wooer Lachhi.

Spring has come, with almond blossom,
All about Sharika Devi!
Flower-beds are walled about—
Flowers I'll offer, night and morn!

Spring has come, with almond blossom,
All about Raginya Devi!
Lotus flowers are walled about—
Milk I'll pour her, night and morn!

My own favourite chant was, I fear, unknown to the *veena*-player. It was Ramoni's choice: she once sang it to me—like a bird in ecstasy calling for its mate. Though it was just as simple as the other folk-songs it thrilled me to my innermost being.

> How shall I feed thee, Beloved?
> *On golden-red honey and fruit.*
> How shall I please thee, Beloved?
> *With the voice of the cymbal and lute.*
>
> How shall I garland thy tresses?
> *With pearls from the jessamine close.*
> How shall I perfume thy fingers?
> *With the soul of the keora and rose.*
>
> How shall I deck thee, O Dearest?
> *In hues of the peacock and dove.*
> How shall I woo thee, O Dearest?
> *With the delicate silence of love.*

XII

It was a moonless night: my last one on the roof-terrace of my village home. I was waiting for the dawn. 'My farewells have all been said,' I mused. 'The morning train from Asansole will take me to Calcutta.'

The landscape spread before me, silent and serene. Darkness enfolded my familiar Red Valley and my beloved Blue Hills in mystery and majesty. The hours advanced and the depths of the vault of heaven grew darker—it changed from indigo blue to deep amaranth. The stars flashed brighter. The constellation commonly called the Plough fascinated me. Some know it as the Seven Sages.

I watched the heavenly bodies and smiled. I was no longer the puny boy, afraid of watching the stars in their course. I was an altogether different being: a young man fond of them and proud of telling their tales. I knew them well—the brighter planets and the shining constellations. I was never tired of gazing at them and repeating the stories of their birth. They kindled my imagination. They told me of far off events unrecorded in any history book.

There was a time when the Necklace consisted of twenty-eight stars and not twenty-seven! When was that? In which history book would one find the date of Sati's descent to our earth? Once the Vindhya Range towered far higher than all mountains and the Himalayas were under the sea. Then came the sage Agastya to humble the Proud Cloud-piercer. When did that event take place? Would it be for the historian or for the geologist to answer me? Who would dare to deny the affirmation of my villagers that the Indian Peninsula is the oldest tract on the earth's crust? Who imparted this information to them? Who told them that the sun is not the brightest of the luminaries in the heavens? Where was Hihiri Pipiri, the Land of the Butterflies? And where was Chae Champa? And when was that land wave which overwhelmed the country of the Lamas and drove some of the Tibetans to the North Pole? When was it that the children of men all learnt to play one and the same counting out game?—*Eenie Meenie Minie Moe?*

When I was at High School I laughed at such questions. But on manhood's threshold, on the night that was to mark the end of a chapter of my life, I did not dare to laugh: I simply marvelled at my incompetence to give satisfactory replies to the simple queries of my unlettered villagers. I realized that my general knowledge was much less than theirs. I envied their retentive memory and pitied those who talked about 'educating' them.

'What's education?' I recalled one of Kumar's wealthy visitors blaring. 'Education is bunkum! I have had no education but have made more money than all the educationalists put together. Only a fool will go in for education and starve.'

And yet I was going to be an educationalist myself!

Even the principal of my college was not quite sure if the art of reading and writing would do the villagers any good. 'I know of no process that makes unfertile brain fertile,' he confessed. 'If you come across an educationalist making such a claim you will know him to be a politician. Steer clear of him. Literacy is not education. I would rather see my people remain unlettered than taught to read the rubbish that floods the book-reading industrialized world of to-day. From the cultural point of view they will remain better off with their own classical and popular literature of which all have oral knowledge. This much is perfectly clear, a semi-literate population can be more easily misled with cheap literature, political pamphlets, and tracts on bogus economics and falsified history than the unlettered peasants of the Penhari Parganas. A fertile brain is more capable of being poisoned than an unfertile one. Better untaught than ill-taught. It is so easy to convert a flourishing garden into a field of weeds. That's why I am afraid of our characterless politicians, crafty theoreticians, and professional patriots. They can readily change this land into a bear-garden or a cock-pit. I don't care for literacy. I want men of character, men who will not be fooled by the frauds who pretend to have the exclusive monopoly of patriotism and the panacea to all evil by raising the standard of living.'

I gazed at the horizon and wondered if the stars shone as brightly in Calcutta's smoke-laden sky.

Our air is so amazingly clear that it is the easiest thing in the world to misjudge distances entirely and not only distances of yards and furlongs, but of miles and leagues as well! How often had I not heard motorists exclaim when they caught their first sight of the Golah in ruins, 'There we are! Only a stone's throw, a hundred yards at most.' And later on, their hundred yards turned out to be more than a hundred furlongs! In the Himalayan highlands, I understand, the air is equally clear and the same optical illusion baffles strangers.

Does clarity of the atmosphere contribute towards clear thinking? Is that the reason why our sages in ancient days always advised their disciples to spend some time on hill tops and watch

the tremendous procession of stars? They were asked to meditate
on noble thoughts in a pure atmosphere:

> Mortal though I be, yea ephemeral, if but a moment
> I gaze up to the night's starry domain of heaven,
> Then no longer on earth I stand; I touch the Creator,
> And my lively spirit drinketh immortality.

In a near-by mango tree, nestled somewhere among the leaves,
a hawk-cuckoo raised its cry. Its shrill crescendo notes rose higher
and higher and yet it never attained the expected topmost one.
Why did this bird's call remind me of Comrade Dynamiter and
his parting advice to me?

'What's education, anyway?' he asked and furnished his
own answer. 'Education is propaganda. Propaganda to suit the
requirements of society. By the time you leave the university with
your piece of parchment, to-day's rulers will be nowhere. The
Party flag will be floating everywhere. Take time by the forelock
and join us now. Your admission will be comparatively easy at
present. But, later on, it will be an impossibility. There will be a
general rush to join the Party's ranks. "A profitable religion never
lacks proselytes." Bourgeois democracy is as good as dead. What's
socialism except the beginning of the Party's rule? Our people
are capturing all the key-posts in the socialist organizations. Our
day is coming. All the teachers are doing our job without being
asked. When a school-master is paid less than a rat-catcher or a
bricklayer he needs no goading from us to preach our theories.
And I have yet to see a young writer unwilling to propagate our
views. Therefore, join the Party *now*. And learn to repeat by rote
our *mantras*, our slogans. The rest will be easy.'

Ramoni talked differently, but the sum-total of her arguments
was the same.

'Education! My foot!' she exclaimed and exhibited not
only her *henna*-dyed feet but her bare legs and the half of her

thighs as well. 'Plain horse-sense. That's all I want from my Red Falcons. As for the others, I don't care what sort of education they get.... Bring me the brainiest male from the other end of the earth and see how I shall make him dance. Who cares for the Party's education programme and its catechism? I want to put a ring in the snout of the *lal bhalloo*, the red bear, and take it about with me for *my* purpose. The red bear is shaggy, cumbrous, gross. It crams itself to distension whenever it gets the chance. It makes hideous noises to manifest its gastronomic delights. It is shortsighted, but it has a good nose and it is a most formidable beast. It would be useful to me. It will help me to drive out the hyenas, the *Delhiwallahs* who act as the stooges of the Jain industrialists, the corrupt politicians who pretend to be patriots and practise nepotism...'

Ramoni was convinced that eventually Indian communism would be different from Russian communism. But it was expedient not to dwell too much on that issue. Nor on the question of co-operating with China.

'We shall take what we can secure,' she continued, 'from the *lal bhalloo* of Muscovy. I am a bear-tamer's daughter and I know what I am after. The red bear, we say, is a big liar, a treacherous beast with no code of honour. It has no sense of shame or of chivalry. But I am not afraid. I'll make the red bear dance, while you will play the flute. So you must join the Party as soon as you get to Calcutta. Don't waste any further time. You will find your name already in the list of proposed candidates. The information you gave about the underground passages of the Golah was most useful. You have been very helpful...'

The silly hawk-cuckoo's notes were now being answered by a barbet, a most pretty bird, no doubt, green all over but for its brownish head and neck. Its cry, however, was just as piercing as the grey hawk-cuckoo's: as tiresome and as persistent. Their notes never come to an end. They sing at any time, night or day, all the year round, whenever other birds are too tired or too sleepy.

Maybe, they possess the power of driving people crazy, and that is why they are commonly known as the brain-fever birds.

'The way to Jerusalem lies through Babylon,' Padre Johan declared as he gave me his blessing and made me drink a bowl of thick buffalo cream. According to him, it was my duty to spend some time in Calcutta and profit from my stay in the premier city of India. 'Quagmires suck in the unwary. But not those who have been forewarned. You have no need to be timid. He who has faith need not be afraid of anything, not even of Satan. Our trials prove our faith. The time of stress is also the time for opportunities. Macaulay profited from his sojourn in Calcutta. So should you. Remember, truth is discovered in sorrow and in exile, and there is no easy way to wisdom.'

This was all very confusing. The brain-fever birds stopped their shrill cries and a *papeeha's* song reached my ear. 'So the mangoes have ripened,' I said to myself. 'While the *papeeha* is waiting for its mate, the hawk-cuckoo and the barbet are gorging themselves.' The *papeeha* comes to the Penhari Parganas when the mangoes are ripe. In fact, its presence is the signal for the fruit-gatherers. It sings, '*Pee—kahan? Peeya kahan?* Where's love? Where is my love?' It is a sweet bird. It would rather die of hunger and thirst than eat and drink before its mate has its fill.

'The root cause of all our troubles is ignorance,' Ramdas told me as he gave me a gigantic treacle-tart wrapped up neatly in plantain leaves: it was the parting gift of the family. 'Such tarts are not to be had in Calcutta.'

The *chowkidar* was generally addicted to aphorisms. So the fable he recounted to emphasize his comment on ignorance came as a real surprise to me.

Once upon a time four men received a single coin among them. One of the four was a Persian and he declared: 'Let us spend this coin on *angur*. I am fond of *angur*.' 'Nay,' said the second man who was an Arab. 'I am for *inab*. I don't care for *angur*.' The third man who was a Turk exclaimed that he cared neither for *angur* nor for *inab*, but for *uzum*. While the fourth man, a Greek, advised them to stop their altercations and buy *istafil*.

'Would you believe it,' Ramdas concluded, 'they were all asking for the same thing: *grapes*. They were calling grapes by different names and their quarrel was due to ignorance.'

True enough! They all wanted the same thing: Comrade Dynamiter, Ramoni, Padre Johan, the Second Master, and all the others. They wanted the people to be happy and prosperous. But how could anyone bring about a conciliation among them? Where was the magic formula to bring them together?

'Wisdom,' said the Punditji, as he touched my shoulder playfully with his brass-bound blackthorn staff, 'wisdom alone can save the individual man. And unless a man is saved he has no right to talk about saving others. I am very old, and Life has revealed to me many of her secrets. Believe me, my son, one can only learn little by little. Truth is to be acquired by degrees. A man must die to one life before he can be reborn into another. Not many are willing to experience the joy of rebirth. Baulked by the fear of travail, they refuse to be reborn. Life cannot teach them much. Wisdom is to be sought for and acquired through one's own efforts. Even if I told you all that I know you would not be any wiser. You will have to seek wisdom for yourself.'

But where was wisdom to be found? That all-embracing wisdom whose possession would confer serenity and supreme bliss? That wisdom which blesses its possessor and all who come into his contact?

'The *rishis*,' I was told, 'are sages who though human excel the angels on account of their wisdom and sapience. The angels, therefore, learn from them.' Where was the dwelling-place of these sages? In the regions beyond the distant hills?

Suddenly I heard a multitude of birds praising the dawn with their songs, and my musings came to an end. The flush of early light revealed some coral-rose cloud banks. They formed a landscape of their own in the pale, tourmaline sky. They looked like snow-covered mountain ranges—so high and so remote—belonging to a region beyond the horizon, in a world other than ours. I gazed on them wistfully and thought of my first laborious climb to the *moucharaby* of the Blue Hills. I desired that my day's journey should bring me to the seat of Sapience, the Cradle of the Clouds.